I0590149

ALL YOUR MIDNIGHTS

GOLDEN FALLS BOOK 2

IZABELA KAMILA

Copyright © 2025 by Izabela Kamila

All rights reserved.

No part of this book may be reproduced in any form or by any electronic or mechanical means, including information storage and retrieval systems, without written permission from the author, except for the use of brief quotations in a book review.

This is a work of fiction. Any names, characters, places or incidents are the products of the author's imagination and used in a fictitious manner. Any resemblance to actual people, places, businesses, or events is purely coincidental and fictional.

Cover Design: Alison Warren

Editing: Nicole McCurdy, Emerald Edits

Andrea Halland, Editing by Andrea

E-Book ISBN: 979-8-9988803-2-2

Print ISBN: 979-8-9988803-3-9

For my parents.
Thank you for always believing in me. I wouldn't be able to do any of this without you.

For anyone who has ever felt like they're on the outside looking in. I hope you find a sense of belonging in Golden Falls.

CONTENTS

AUTHOR'S NOTE

Thank you for picking up *All Your Midnights*! This is a small town, rivals to lovers holiday romance with a sunshine heroine, guarded hero, meddling grandfather, forced proximity, found family, banter, and slow burn tension.

It's the second book in the Golden Falls series, a set of interconnected standalones each taking place in northern Wisconsin during a different season. You do not need to read book one in order to enjoy this one.

This book is intended for adult readers ages eighteen and up. *All Your Midnights* contains explicit, on-page sexual content and strong language.

Additional content notes include:

- Loss of a grandparent (off-page, happened in the past)
- Grief
- Mention of a funeral (brief)

- Tumultuous relationship with parents/toxic parents
- Divorced parents
- On-page anxiety attack (brief)
- Alcohol consumption

I hope you enjoy Gabe and Lily's story and your time in Golden Falls. Happy reading!

- Izabela

PLAYLIST

Listen on Spotify!

Last Christmas - Wham!
All I Want for Christmas Is You - Mariah Carey
Too Sweet - Hozier
pov - Ariana Grande
Best Day of My Life - Jesse McCartney
See Her Out (Thats Just Life) - Francis and the Lights
Butterflies - Kacey Musgraves
Would That I - Hozier
Slow Burn - Kacey Musgraves
Honey Blonde - Joe Jonas
Snow On The Beach (feat. Lana Del Ray) - Taylor Swift, Lana Del Rey
Like Real People Do - Hozier
feelslikeimfallinginlove - Coldplay
12 to 12 - sombr
New Year's Day - Taylor Swift
Adore You - Harry Styles
Hey Girl - Stephen Sanchez

You Are In Love (Taylor's Version) - Taylor Swift
I Wanna Stay - Joytrip
Sunlight - Hozier
The Sound - The 1975
It's Not Living (If It's Not With You) - The 1975
Until I Found You - Stephen Sanchez

PROLOGUE
LILY

"I don't think I'm doing this whole winter wish list thing right," I admitted to my two best friends with a grimace. We were sitting on the fluffy rug in my living room around a coffee table covered with glitter pens, sugar cookies, and three half-empty margarita glasses.

Eliza, who I'd known my whole life and was more like a sister, capped her pen and learned over. "Oh, Lil," she said with a shake of her head as her eyes scanned the paper. "This won't do. You can definitely do better. You're *obsessed* with this time of year. Channel that energy."

I'd spent more time doodling *Lily's Winter Wish List* at the top than coming up with ideas. And the ideas I had weren't great.

1. Hire help at the café
2. Decorate the cat room
3. Sign up for baking classes

What was supposed to be a fun wish list had turned work-related. Purrfect Blend Cat Café was taking up more and more of my time. I was the only employee at my café, which opened last year. I loved that I was able to combine three things I loved most—cats, coffee, and baking—into my career.

My other best friend Jules waved her hand to see the list, and Eliza passed her the paper. Jules, whose full name was Juliette, visited our small town in northern Wisconsin earlier this year. She had intended to stay in Golden Falls for the summer before moving back to Chicago, but things didn't quite go according to plan. She ended up falling in love with my older brother Wesley and now lived in town, which meant we got to keep her for good.

Jules's reaction to the list wasn't much better, but she added encouragingly, "Luckily, it's not too late! You still have plenty of space."

I let out a groan, reaching for my margarita and tipping it back, finishing it in one big gulp. "I don't know why it's so hard. I love this time of year." I gestured to my apartment, which was fully decorated for Christmas even though it was the week before Thanksgiving. Yes, I was one of *those* people.

My Christmas tree was decked out with garland, lights, and ornaments, and I had three stockings—one for me and one for each of my cats—hanging by the TV. I wanted to spend as much time as possible wrapped up in the warm and cozy holiday spirit.

"It should be easy to come up with what I want to do, but my mind is blanking. All I can think about is how busy it'll be at the café—and how I'll be drowning in orders if I don't hire help." My shoulders dropped, and I tried not to let my worries get in the way of our night. "What do you have on your lists?"

Eliza handed me hers, and I let out an amused laugh, shaking my head. "This is just a list of places you want to have sex."

She proudly took the paper back, wiggling her brows. "It's

my *naughty* winter wish list. I'm thinking I'll tuck it into my bra for a very lucky, very sexy elf to find."

Jules and I laughed while Eliza grinned. I leaned over to look at Jules's list next. Hers was a mix of naughty and nice, and I took inspiration from some of the winter and holiday activities she had, like sledding and building a gingerbread house.

"Have fun and try not to overthink it," Jules encouraged gently. "It might be a busy time of the year, but you also need to take time for yourself and enjoy the holiday season."

Eliza passed me the rest of her margarita. "Finish this, and I'm going to make another round." She stood, pointing at the list and the drink. "Progress better be made by the time I'm back—on both fronts. And turn the music up!"

Jules happily reached for her phone, which was connected to my living room speakers, and increased the volume right as "Last Christmas" by Wham! started playing.

The three of us started to belt out the lyrics, and it was easy to tell how tipsy we were by how off-key we sounded...not that we'd be any better sober.

I reached for the glass and took a big sip, which got a satisfied smile out of Eliza before she headed to the kitchen. I loved nights with my girls—whether that meant going out dancing or staying in like we were tonight.

"Oooh," Jules squealed as she looked over at Eliza's list. "Creative use of Christmas lights. I'm adding that to mine!"

I let out a mock-groan. I loved that Jules was dating my older brother, but I didn't need the mental image of them doing god knows what with Christmas lights.

"You can add it to your list, too," she said in a sing-song tone. "You never know who will come into town for the holidays."

"I think I'll stick to something more simple...maybe a kiss under the mistletoe?" Although even that was a stretch with my non-existent dating life.

"A *romantic* kiss under the mistletoe that takes your breath away," Jules amended. When I didn't reach for the pen, she looked at me pointedly. "Aren't you going to write it down?"

"Yeah, Lil, write it down!" Eliza called from the kitchen.

"Okay, okay," I conceded and added it to the list after building a gingerbread house and sledding.

A couple more margaritas and a whole bunch of sugar cookies later, we finished making our lists. Yes, parts of mine were practical and about my business, but most of it was fun and included activities I'd been itching to do.

While I baked a lot for my job, I added making a holiday recipe for fun, going to my favorite restaurant, seeing a shooting star, and finally visiting Milwaukee. Even though the city was only four hours away, I'd yet to make the drive.

My list was less...*creative* than what Eliza and Jules had, but I was happy with what I came up with. By the end, I had ten things on my wish list, a strong buzz from the tequila, and a grin on my face.

The three of us were cozy on the couch under a pile of blankets as Jules browsed for a movie to end our night with.

"I have my list in my purse, and I'm going to send it to Santa tomorrow," I joked. "Maybe he'll bring me *someone* for that kiss under the mistletoe."

How wistful my voice sounded surprised even me. I blamed it on the tequila, because I wasn't looking for love. I barely had time to sleep, let alone date.

If my friends noticed my tone, they didn't say anything.

"Maybe more tequila while he's at it," Eliza added.

"And Christmas lights, apparently," Jules chimed in, and we all burst into laughter.

1

GABRIEL

"ARE WE REALLY FUCKING DOING THIS AGAIN?" MY BOSS'S JAW clenched. His face was red, steam practically billowing out of his ears. I used to think that was an exaggeration when it happened in cartoons.

Nope, it was real.

I leaned back in my chair and took a slow sip of coffee. This wasn't the first time I'd pissed him off, and I knew damn well it wouldn't be the last.

From the minute I sent my email, I knew it was only a matter of time until he showed up at my office, zeroing in like a bull with a red flag.

I slowly set the mug on my desk and clasped my hands together before I gave him my attention. "What are you referring to?"

"You know exactly what I'm referring to," Ron Nelson snapped, stepping inside and shutting the door behind him.

"Oh, sure, come on in," I muttered. "Make yourself comfortable."

"What was that?" Each word was sharply enunciated and infused with venom.

My sarcastic comments wouldn't get me anywhere, so I quickly pivoted. If I was going to get him to agree with me—which never happened, but I had to try—I needed him in a better mood than *this*.

"It's a good proposal, and you know it," I started. Nelson Group, the real estate and development firm I worked at, was submitting a proposal to the city of Milwaukee on how to redevelop a vacant warehouse along the river. The city purchased the land years ago, and the common council was now seeking ideas for the space.

Residents had shown up at recent council meetings to speak during public comment about how they wanted something different for the space. Something that was community-focused and would bring people together.

That was exactly the type of work I'd come to Nelson Group to do—only to get turned down again and again.

I went to school for real estate and got my master's in regional and urban planning with a focus on sustainability. I joined Nelson Group four years ago right after graduation, ready to make a positive impact. The company was based in Milwaukee and had offices in nearly every major city and projects across the country.

I wanted to work on projects that made a difference in the community, namely Milwaukee, where I'd lived my whole life. I loved the city and all it had to offer—and I wanted to use development to help show that off while also ensuring everyone had access to housing, fresh food, and other basic necessities regardless of where they lived.

The years since I started working here had flown by, and I often found myself wondering if I'd wasted that time, because all I had to show for it was mounting frustration and unfulfillment. I was now twenty-eight and had barely scratched the surface of what I'd hoped to achieve. I'd never been one to give up, but the light at the end of the tunnel of getting my career to where I wanted was growing dimmer and dimmer.

"It's different from what we typically work on," I continued, ignoring Ron's displeased eyeroll. "It'll capture the common council's attention, and I think residents would be in favor of it, too."

I wanted to submit a proposal that would turn the old warehouse into a modern food hall. It would bring people together while also allowing new businesses to set up without committing to a brick-and-mortar location. There could be space for multiple restaurants to set up and tables so people could sit and eat. The warehouse was in a prime location that would attract people visiting Milwaukee, as well as those who worked downtown and needed a spot for lunch.

"No." He shook his head firmly. "It's not a good proposal, because it won't make money, Gabriel. That's the whole reason we're fucking here. It's not what we talked about, and it's not what the board of directors agreed on. I'm not looking for some *feel good* project."

"It's so much more than that. And this *would* make money if you just—"

"Damn it, Gabriel." He slapped his palm hard against my desk, the sound reverberating in my office. "You're never going to make it in this field or rise in the company if that's the attitude you have."

I wondered if he heard himself. How I wouldn't make it because I cared about people, the environment, and what the community wanted. There were days when I wondered how *he* had made it this far, even though I saw it firsthand.

Ron Nelson only saw the world through dollar signs—how much money he could make and how much money his employees could make him.

That's how he saw me.

I was good at making deals and closing them.

"You work for me." He crossed his arms over his chest, standing tall and towering over me as I stayed seated.

He loved reminding me of that. As if I could ever fucking forget how stuck I was.

"I know that," I gritted through my teeth, "but you've said I could submit one of my proposals. I thought this was *finally* my chance."

"You'll have your chance, but this isn't it. This is a good opportunity for us, and I'm not going to let you mess it up. Write another proposal—the one I and the board approved last week."

For yet *another* luxury apartment complex.

Nelson Group was known for mixed-use development featuring luxury apartments and condos in addition to commercial space. While the company didn't control the rent for businesses, it often inadvertently priced out a good portion of local businesses. It was exactly the type of concern I wanted to address, and yet, I was part of making it happen.

I thought I'd be able to fix things *from the inside*, and after working here for a few months, I'd start to make a difference on a large scale.

How fucking naive of me. It'd been four years of the same bullshit. Of constantly getting shut down. And the worst part? I couldn't leave.

"It's a mistake," I said.

"That's not your call to make." He inhaled deeply, straightening his posture and gathering a semblance of composure. "I'll entertain your ideas when things slow down, but for now, get that proposal done."

My jaw clenched, because I'd heard that excuse over and over again.

"I'll—" I bit down on my tongue to keep from saying what I

really wanted to. I'd been holding my tongue for years with him, so I had plenty of practice. "Yeah, I'll get it done."

"Good." He nodded. "You're my closer, Gabriel. Stay focused on this, and we'll secure yet another multi-million dollar deal."

"Right." I exhaled deeply. "I'll have it on your desk tomorrow morning. I'm leaving for—" I was about to tell him about my upcoming trip when his phone rang.

"Good lord. Your mother is calling," he said under his breath. "Proposal tomorrow morning." He pointed at me, his eyes—so similar to mine—flicked from me to his ringing phone. "Yes, Blaire?" He sounded so damn annoyed. I truly didn't know who he hated talking to more—me or my mother.

He turned around, leaving my office and walking down the hallway.

I knew my mother would be calling me in a few hours to complain about their conversation. It's how they worked. I had no idea why they'd gotten married, and I truly didn't understand why they decided to start a family. I *completely* understood why they'd gotten divorced, but clearly, they hadn't cut off contact from one another.

I tipped my head back, closing my eyes. I inhaled deeply for four seconds, held my breath for seven, and exhaled slowly for eight. Working for my father was not for the weak—he made that clear.

I was fucking exhausted. Exhausted with work. Exhausted with my parents. Exhausted of being a fucking disappointment.

But most of all I was frustrated that I couldn't stand up to my father once and for all.

It was hard for me to remember exactly when our relationship shifted. It hadn't always been like this...*right*?

We didn't have a typical father-son relationship when I was growing up. He didn't come to my sports games, and we didn't spend much time together. When we spent time together, it was him taking me to work. In hindsight, my father had always viewed me as a potential employee rather than his son.

I remembered a time when I *wanted* to be like him. I remembered when I wanted to work with him and follow in his footsteps. When I was younger, I was proud of my father and the company he'd built from the ground up—before I knew the lengths he'd go to for success.

But I hadn't felt proud of him in a long time.

Even worse, I couldn't remember the last time I felt proud of myself.

My father and I got along best when I first started college and told him I wanted to get into development. That didn't last long, though, because quickly into my first year of undergrad, I realized I wanted to focus on sustainability and community development. Our relationship had been deteriorating ever since, so much so that I was surprised he offered me a job at Nelson Group.

My father had said the right things when he was pitching me the job, making me feel like I'd have a say in the projects we were working on and that this would be a collaboration. I gave him the benefit of the doubt—and that was a big fucking mistake. Because now I was trapped, and that might have been his plan all along.

I had a folder of potential ideas that I'd pitched to my father, only to get shut down over and over. I wanted to prove him wrong, but more importantly, I wanted to show myself that I could do it. Maybe then it'd be easier to escape his grasp, even if that meant being on my own.

That's exactly what I intended to do with my weekend trip.

About a month ago, I'd gotten an unexpected email from my grandfather Hal, who lived in Golden Falls, a small town in northern Wisconsin. It was about a four-hour drive from Milwaukee.

My father grew up in Golden Falls but left when he turned eighteen. He never went back, not even for a visit. As a result, I'd never been there, and that brought its own anxieties.

I'd seen my grandfather here and there over the years when I was growing up, but it had been longer than I wanted to admit since the last time I saw him. As much as I wanted to be excited that my grandfather reached out, I just...didn't feel that connection. I barely knew the man, and he barely knew me. Or at least, he barely knew the adult version of me.

I vaguely remembered Hal and my grandmother Vera visiting Milwaukee when I was young, whether that was for my birthday, holidays, or my sports games. One thing I did remember clearly, though, was they always had a camera on them to take photos.

The visits eventually became less frequent and stopped when I was a teenager. I remembered instances of Hal and Vera showing up at my parents' house, and my father telling them to leave. Of them asking to see me and him saying no.

I harbored my own guilt and emotions that had been nagging me over the last couple of years. Emotions I'd tried to avoid. Until now. In a few short days, I would step foot in Golden Falls for the first time in my life.

Contrary to what my father thought, I tried not to get emotionally invested in my various projects. I tried to keep it strictly business. That's exactly what my visit to Golden Falls would be. Nothing more.

I pulled up last month's email from Hal, reading it for what felt like the millionth time.

From: Hal Nelson <halnelson@email.com>
To: Gabriel Nelson <gabriel@nelsongroup.com>, Lily Richards
<lily@purrfectblend.com>
Date: Wednesday, November 12, 2:30 p.m.
Subject: Building proposal from Hal Nelson

Dear Lily and Gabe,

As you both know, I'm nearing my mid-seventies and am seeking to pass down some of my responsibilities, namely my tasks as a property owner and landlord. I still plan to continue operating my hardware store.

I currently own the one building, which has commercial space on the first floor and apartments on the second. Lily is very familiar with this building as she rents one of the apartments and is one of the business tenants. Gabe, I encourage you to visit Lily's café when you're in town.

I'd like to speak with you both about the future of the building, because I'm unsure about next steps. I care deeply about both of you and about this town. I have a feeling this building has the potential to bring people together, and I'd like to see what ideas you may have as I prepare to sell.

I'd like to meet with you both in early December. This will only work if we meet in Golden Falls. Likely in my hardware store, although I'm open to other locations in town.

Please let me know some upcoming days and times that will work with your schedules, and I will handle the rest.

I'm looking forward to it and hope you are, too. See you both soon.

- Hal Nelson

The replies on the email thread were limited. Shortly after getting the email, I let Hal know my availability. I had no idea what this building was or why he was looping me in, but I was intrigued. For some reason, it felt like something I couldn't pass up. Lily replied with when she was available, and then Hal set up a date and time for us to meet.

Just as they'd done the past month, my fingers itched to look her up. I started to type her name into the search bar, my pinky hovering over the enter key. Right as I was about to give in, I caught sight of the time. If I didn't leave now, I was going to be late for dinner with my best friend Liam. I shook my head and shut my laptop.

I had no idea who Lily Richards was, but I'd find out soon enough.

2

GABRIEL

"Your dad's a piece of work, and that's putting it *very* mildly," my best friend Liam Haven said over the classic rock and various conversations in the background before taking another bite of his burger.

We were at Half Day Pub, our favorite spot to grab dinner and a beer after work. It was hard to believe we'd been coming here regularly for a few years now.

The dimly lit restaurant was one of the oldest spots in this part of the city, and that was evident by the worn vinyl booths and scuffed white and black tiles. A wooden bar with black stools lined the back wall, along with a row of pinball machines. It was a toss-up if you'd get to play a game or if the machine would eat your quarters. But that's what made it great. There was so much history here, and the burgers, especially after a long day, were unmatched.

I huffed in agreement, my seat creaking as I shifted forward to lean my elbows on the table. For once, I didn't bother defending my father. I'd been defending him my whole life, because I felt like I had to—he was my father, after all—but the excuses ran out years ago.

Liam set down his burger, reaching for a napkin and wiping the sides of his mouth. "The way he treats you pisses me off. You work all the fucking time, and he still hasn't let you pursue the ideas you want. The ideas you brought up in your interview. He knew that's what you wanted when he hired you. You're good at what you do, and it's a damn shame he doesn't let you pursue the projects you want."

"Well, that's the problem," I said with a dry laugh. "If I was shit at my job, he would've fired me by now."

"I don't know why you put up with him." Liam shook his head. "Well, I mean, I *do*. You don't have a choice. But still."

That was the other piece. I couldn't leave Nelson Group. At first, I didn't want to leave, because I didn't want to make my relationship with my father even worse. But in the last year, when I had seriously thought about leaving, I realized I wouldn't have a career if I did. When I signed my contract with Nelson Group, I didn't catch the five-year non-compete clause. If I had to take a break for five years to do different work, my career in development would be over.

As if he was reading my mind, Liam said, "Could always work with me." He shrugged before picking his burger back up.

Liam was currently vice president of operations for Green Haven Hotels, a large hotel and resort chain that prioritized sustainability and ecotourism. Traveling responsibly, respecting current residents, and minimizing negative impacts on the environment were some of his professional missions. Liam and his two brothers were among the leaders in the space.

I shook my head with an amused huff. "I don't think we'd get anything done if we worked together. I *still* don't understand how you're productive when you're traveling for work and have access to a pool majority of the time."

"The pools aren't as distracting as the women." Liam wiggled his brows. Women were always on Liam's mind—regardless of if there was a pool involved—and he had no shortage of options, something I knew too much about. He was my best friend, but there were some details I'd learned against my will. Still, he was also a damn good guy and friend.

"Which, speaking of women," he started, "I had another... *interesting* date this week."

I raised my brows, popping a fry in my mouth. "What happened this time?"

Liam had no shortage of outlandish stories of failed dates and women pursuing him for his wealth and status. It happened to him more and more these days. He was regularly on various lists, including most eligible billionaires and hottest men alive. He often liked to remind me of the latter.

"I met her at a work conference a few weeks ago, so I thought this could have potential for more than a date or two. I'm...well, I'm thinking it might be nice to settle down soon. But anyways, she shows up to our dinner date and pulls out this binder"—Liam leaned in—"which was actually a scrapbook of our wedding day. This is our *first* date, mind you. I knew nothing about this woman, and she knew everything about me." Liam shook his head. "I'm starting to lose hope, man."

"Fuck, that's...concerning and really upsetting." I let out a heavy sigh, hating that my best friend couldn't catch a break. "There's someone out there for you. I know it."

Our conversation was broken up when our server Fiona, a pretty brunette woman about our age, strolled up to the table. We always sat in her section when we stopped by and had gotten to know her pretty well.

She had a warm smile as she set two bottles on the table: one with ketchup and another with house-made ranch. She pushed her bangs out of her eyes. "How's the food tasting? Do either of you need anything else?" Her green eyes darted between us as she rocked back and forth on her feet. Her gaze finally settled on

Liam, and her expression softened. "I didn't think you'd come back here after your last date."

"He started telling me about it. Sounds like quite the experience," I said.

Fiona nodded with a grimace. "And will you tell him"—she was speaking to me but pointing at Liam—"to stop with the over-the-top tips. He's overpaying me and won't listen."

"Well, first," Liam interjected, "they're underpaying you here, so I'm not going to stop. And second, I always have a great time here, so I want to thank you for your excellent service."

I groaned at the same time Fiona rolled her eyes with an amused smile. My best friend really couldn't help it.

"Your charm doesn't work on me, Liam," she informed him. "But thank you. I really appreciate it."

Fiona ensured we didn't need anything else and then walked away to greet one of her new tables.

I watched the way Liam's eyes followed her, an amused smile tugging at my lips. "You like her."

He turned to me with furrowed brows. "Well, yeah. She's great."

"No, you *like* her."

A *pfft* escaped him. "Not like that. She has a boyfriend, who she's way too good for." Liam muttered the last part, but I still caught it. "Anyways, are you all set for your drive to Golden Falls? What's your plan for the meeting?"

"I think so?" My response came out more like a question, my confidence not quite there. I wrapped a hand around my water, twisting the glass and the paper coaster. "I mean, I have no idea how the meeting will go or what Hal will say. Why did he reach out to me? And why did he include someone named Lily Richards in the email?"

"There have to be some clues. Here"—he extended his palm and waved his fingers—"let me see the email again."

I reached into my pocket for my phone, pulled up the email, and showed Liam.

He skimmed the message, muttering as he read parts out loud. "One building...future of this building...ideas you both may have." Liam looked up. "Are you going to pitch him one of your recent ideas? I mean, you have to, right? That has to be what he's looking for."

I slipped the phone back into my pocket and shrugged. "Maybe? I have some ideas in mind if that's the direction the meeting goes, but I want to get a feel for Golden Falls first and see what he has to say. I don't want to pitch something and it ends up being the wrong idea." Hal knew I worked for Nelson Group, but I doubted he knew the type of work I *wanted* to be doing.

"Dude, this could be good. I don't think you need to, *but* this could be a way to get your dad's attention and do more of the work you *want* to be doing. You pitch the idea," Liam said, ticking off the point on his finger. "Get the building." Another finger. "People love it, and it becomes a success." Third finger. "Boom. Tangible proof that this type of work can be beneficial to people and profitable *and* you have evidence your dad can't dispute."

I scratched the back of my neck, leaning back in my chair as Liam's words sunk in. It might be my last chance at having a future at Nelson Group. Because if this didn't get me noticed, nothing would. While I would be fine working for someone other than my father, I knew the resources and contacts Nelson Group had. If I could turn things around and use those connections, I'd be able to make positive change on a big scale. Bigger than if I were to step away and try this on my own.

"Yeah," I said slowly, nodding. "I think you're onto something. I'll have two to three ideas ready depending on how the meeting goes and go from there. Maybe I could even try to buy the building outright."

"You have options. I have a good feeling about this."

"I'm feeling better about it," I agreed. Or at least I felt better about the business side of the visit. The rest caused a knot in my stomach that I couldn't shake.

"And if it all goes well and you're feeling extra ballsy? You can tell your dad to shove his ego and the non-compete up his ass, because you're getting a lawyer to get you out of it."

"I had the company lawyer look at it a while back. There's nothing I can do about it. My only hope right now is getting that building."

After Liam and I finished dinner, I drove to my apartment, intending to finish the proposal my father wanted, even if I didn't agree we should move forward with it. Getting an extra hour or two of work done tonight would make my life easier tomorrow and ahead of the weekend.

When I walked inside, I was greeted by my cat Beans, who brushed up against my legs. "Hey, buddy." I crouched down, petting the top of his head as he nuzzled into my hand. Beans was a twelve-year-old tuxedo cat I adopted about four years ago. With my work schedule, it didn't make sense for me to adopt a kitten who had high-energy and needed constant attention. Beans, while affectionate, enjoyed his alone time and spent the day sleeping while I was at work. I had plenty of toys, windows, and perches for him to enjoy.

Beans had a better setup than me. Apart from his various toys and furniture, there was little in my apartment that made it clear someone lived here. I had my TV, couch, bed, and enough food to get me by. At least the floor-to-ceiling windows gave me a great view of Lake Michigan.

If anything, my apartment felt more like a second office that I happened to sleep in than a home. I could add photos and other personal touches, but...it didn't seem worth my time. I could be getting work done instead.

I collapsed onto the couch, sinking into the cushions with an exhale. Beans quickly trotted over, hopping onto my lap and making himself comfortable. As I was about to reach for my laptop, my phone vibrated in my pocket. My mother was calling, as expected. I inhaled deeply before picking up the call.

"Hey, Mom."

"Can you believe your father?" My mother greeted. "He's threatening to cut me off, and I just got here!"

After my parents split when I was sixteen, my mother decided to use the money from the divorce settlement to travel. That was still what she was up to. I didn't see her often—which, honestly, was fine, since my relationship with her wasn't great either—and she was rarely in one place for longer than a couple of weeks. It was more common for me to get a call from her after she'd talked to my dad. That's all we talked about. There was no *How was your day, Gabriel?* or *What's new with you, Gabe?*

Beans stirred on my lap, a low growl rumbling in his chest at the sound of my mom's voice.

I pinched the bridge of my nose. "Oh, no. I didn't know that. He didn't mention to me that he was going to do that." I had no idea how to respond to her or what type of response she wanted. What I truly wanted was to ask her to stop involving me in these conversations because I had bigger issues than if my father was going to cut her off. One, she'd be fine. And two, she could use one of his other cards. "Uh, can you remind me where you are again?"

"Bali!" she said with an exasperated sigh. "I told you. Do you not listen to me, Gabriel?"

Listening to her wasn't the problem. It was keeping track of her various locations, and frankly, caring about her trips when she couldn't care less about anything I had to say. I'd truly tried over the years to have a relationship with her, to have real conversations, but it was never reciprocated.

"I listen to you, Mom, but I don't think you updated me on where—"

"Of course, I told you," she snapped. She paused for a moment, clearing her throat, her voice softer this time. "Will you put in a good word about me to your father? I can't stay here if he cuts me off."

Ah, so that was why she was calling. There was always something. I didn't realize it as a kid, but my relationships with both of my parents was as transactional as it got. The relationship that I saw between them was transactional, too. Unconditional love was the biggest fucking myth.

"I really don't think I should be getting involved." I dropped my hand and checked the time on my watch. It was inching closer to ten. If I wanted to work on the proposal and get some sleep ahead of the morning, I needed to wrap up our call. "Mom, I'm sorry, but I still have some work to get done tonight. Could I call you tomorrow about this?"

Her exhale was so loud I had to pull my phone away from my ear. I knew what was coming before she even said it. She'd been telling me this my whole life. I also knew the look she had on her face even though I couldn't see her.

"Gabriel, you are so selfish. You're just like your father."

Before my parents divorced, I thrived on hearing them both tell me "you're just like your father" or "you're just like your mother." I thought it was a compliment. I wanted to see the ways I was like them because they were my parents—my role models.

That phrase quickly turned from compliment to insult after the divorce. Now, the words sliced through, reopening old wounds each and every time.

I worked too late and was too focused on success? I was just like my father.

I disagreed with my father and wanted to do things differently? I was just like my mother.

There was no winning. I didn't want to be like them—and yet I'd gotten their worst qualities.

I also remembered when I *wanted* to be like my father, before I knew who he truly was. At first, I saw him as a successful business man going from small town living to creating a booming development group. I wanted to follow in his footsteps, make him proud, and eventually run Nelson Group with him. I thought that's what he wanted, too.

I realized now that he wanted a follower, not a son. But my father was the only family I saw regularly, which was another reason why I'd stuck around Nelson Group, why I kept holding out that maybe, *someday*, our relationship would be different.

A heavy feeling settled in my chest. Was I like him? I did the same type of work. Was my future, who I was going to become, already written?

I didn't want pity—I knew I was a grown-ass man who needed to make his own choices—but if I walked away from my job, that would be it. I'd be alone. And that was terrifying in its own way.

"Thanks, Mom. That's exactly what I needed to hear today." For the second time today, I bit my tongue to keep from saying more. It wouldn't do any good. "Was that all?"

I waited for a response, but all I got was the click on the other end of the line. She hung up on me.

"Great talk, Mom," I muttered dryly. I tossed my phone on my couch and leaned back, setting my hands over my face. I rubbed the heels of my palms into my tired eyes and let out a groan.

This wasn't how I imagined my life at twenty-eight. I'd taken a wrong turn, and I *needed* to find a way to get back on track.

Golden Falls looked like my best option at the moment, and I wasn't going to let anyone get in my way.

3

LILY

THE FROSTY DECEMBER CHILL SWEPT IN EVERY TIME SOMEONE opened the door to Purrfect Blend Cat Café. This time, when I looked up, I spotted Eliza and Jules entering. Instead of going for one of the round tables, they beelined toward the light oak counter where I had stools set up. If customers were feeling chatty, this was a nice spot for them to sit, since I was able to talk with them while preparing orders and making drinks.

"We came as soon as we could," Jules said, untying her scarf from around her neck and slipping off her wool coat. She looked very fashionable in an olive-green sweater and jeans. Her long, brown hair was perfectly wavy, and she had a natural blush on her cheeks from the cold air.

Eliza took off her coat and gloves. Her dark hair was down today, hitting at her collarbone. Dainty tattoos and rings adorned her fingers. She nodded in agreement with Jules. "And we're ready to help. What's the first order of business?"

I'd sent out an SOS text earlier today in our group chat, because my meeting with Hal was quickly approaching.

I wasn't surprised Hal was selling the building, because that was something we'd been talking about for months. He never said outright he would sell to me, but he had (in my opinion) hinted here and there. Hal and I were close. He was close with my entire family, actually.

I made it clear to Hal that I was *very* interested in buying the building and had been saving up for when the moment came.

Well, the moment arrived, but it wasn't what I expected.

I never expected that Gabriel Nelson would be included in the email or in Hal's plans for the building's future. I'd tried to get some extra information out of Hal, but he'd avoided answering my questions, first telling me he'd explain more once Gabriel is in town and then pretending to not hear me when I asked more questions. Yes, Hal was older, but I knew he could hear fine.

While the email Hal sent was all I'd been thinking about, I hadn't had much time to properly prepare for the meeting, which was why I needed my best friends' help.

"I thought you could help me do some research on Nelson Group?" I asked them. Everyone in town knew about Ron Nelson and his company, but I wanted more specifics beyond town gossip. "Maybe learn more about Gabriel, too? I haven't had any time to do it myself. I feel like I just finished up Thanksgiving orders and now it's time to start preparing for the holidays."

"We can do that," Eliza assured confidently. "We brought our laptops and are ready to do some sleuthing."

My best friends got comfortable on the stools and pulled out their laptops.

I used a pair of tongs to grab the last two slices of spiced gingerbread loaf. The two of them typically let me decide their order for them, which I enjoyed. I loved giving people new drinks and treats to try or giving them a recommendation based on what I knew they liked.

When customers walked into my café, they were greeted by

the welcoming aroma of coffee, cinnamon, and caramel. Three glass cases were filled with pastries—often a rotating selection of muffins, breads, coffee cake, cookies, and more. I typically set a menu for the week and offered two types of baked goods.

Hiring help was on my very, *very* long to-do list, but I was slowly making progress. My next step was reviewing a handful of applications to figure out who I wanted to interview and eventually hire.

I enjoyed making drinks, baking, and tending to the cats, but I'd love to hire someone so I could devote more of my time to baking and trying new recipes. My mom stopped in every now and then to help take orders on particularly busy days—which seemed to be happening more often lately.

Opening Purrfect Blend was a leap of faith, but it had turned out better than I could've imagined. I got a lot of my business over the summer when tourists flocked to Golden Falls, but late fall and winter were also busy with orders for Thanksgiving, Christmas, and Valentine's Day. Winter was a popular time for people to visit town for sledding, tubing, and ice skating on Lake Golden.

"It looks beautiful in here, Lily," Jules said in awe as she looked around at the decor. "I love what you did with the hanging ornaments."

Right before December started, I spent an evening decorating the café and turning it into a magical and festive holiday oasis.

Red, green, and white sparkly ornaments hung from the ceiling on clear string, looking like they were floating in the air. Balsam and eucalyptus garland was intertwined with string lights along the edge of the main counter. Each table had a mason jar centerpiece with fairy lights, mini ornaments, and Christmas florals inside.

That was in addition to my normal decor, which included

chalkboards behind the register that I updated in cursive writing to detail what drinks were available. I had paintings and drawings from local artists of cats, local views, and abstract art on the walls.

Customers could also take their drinks into the adjoining room, where four to five cats roamed, slept, and waited for cuddles. All the cats were available for adoption through the Golden Falls Animal Shelter. There were places for customers to sit, as well as toys, cat trees, and window perches to keep the cats busy.

"And this"—Jules pointed to the gingerbread loaf I set in front of her and Eliza—"looks incredible. Pretty sure I smelled it all the way from Wes's house."

"It's your house now, too," I pointed out with a smile. "And I couldn't have done the decorations without your brainstorming." I owed a lot to her for how the café looked today. Not only did we talk through holiday decor, but Jules was an interior designer who helped me revamp my café over the summer. We rearranged the tables, painted the walls, and got new furniture, giving the café a refreshed feel on a limited budget.

I knew our friendship would have survived even if she had moved back to Chicago, but I couldn't express how excited I was that she stayed in Golden Falls. Jules and my brother were perfect together, and I'd never seen him happier. He was smiling more than scowling these days.

I got to working on Eliza and Jules's drinks while they browsed on their laptops.

"So, a lot of the articles about Nelson Group are what we already know," Eliza said, tilting her head. "Lots of luxury housing, bringing in big chains to the commercial spaces, controversy over them pricing out small businesses, which they, of course, deny. Hal's son Ron is one of the country's most regarded real estate developers. They're really successful, like almost crazy to believe how much they've grown. They're incredibly profitable and worth a fuck-ton."

I shook my head in disbelief. I couldn't wrap my mind around having a *fuck-ton* of money. And if I did, I'd like to think I'd use it for good—for helping people get housing, for creating development that benefited everyone—instead of only catering to the wealthy.

Gabriel and Nelson Group could say what they wanted, but I was convinced they would take this building and turn it into something our town didn't need. They would run my business into the ground or price me out. The mere thought made my palms sweaty and my stomach nauseous.

"Let's see. What about Gabriel..." Jules trailed off. "Gabriel Nelson." She said his name slowly while typing.

I finished making two peppermint mochas—also known as Peppermint Paws on my holiday menu—and set them in front of Eliza and Jules.

I wiped my hands on a light-blue rag and draped it over the side of the sink.

Eliza and Jules had been silent during this whole time. Not a good sign.

"What—what are you finding?" I asked, leaning over the counter and trying to peer at the laptop screen.

Eliza and Jules looked at each other first and then back at me. This was only getting worse.

"He's worse than we thought, isn't he?" I asked.

"Depends on what you mean..." Jules trailed off. "He's..."

"Yeah, he's..." Eliza paused and waved me over. "Here, come see for yourself."

Curious, I rounded the counter and stepped behind them to see what they were staring at. My lips parted slightly, and my jaw dropped. I quickly realized why they were speechless.

Calling Gabriel Nelson handsome didn't do him justice.

Even in the casual photos on his social media, he looked like he just wrapped up a GQ photoshoot.

Jules clicked on his most recent photo. He had a strong jawline, high cheekbones, and slightly tousled chocolate-brown hair. He was smiling softly, and his honey-brown eyes were focused on the camera.

This didn't mean anything. So what if he looked like a model? He was getting in the way of plans I'd had for months. He was trying to take over my café—or worse, run it out of business. I didn't know that for sure...but I couldn't imagine based on Nelson Group's reputation that he'd be in favor of keeping the building as it was. All of that mattered a hell of a lot more than how he looked. He could be the hottest guy on the planet, and I wouldn't care. My business was way too important.

I closed my mouth, steeled my spine, and shook my head. "This changes nothing." I pointed to the laptop. "I'm not going to get distracted by his good looks. That's probably how he usually gets his way. I want nothing to do with him."

"That's good." Eliza paused, chewing on her bottom lip before adding, "Because he's exactly your type, Lil. Physically, at least."

I scoffed, shaking my head. "No way. I don't have a type."

That was true—I really didn't. I also didn't really have a dating life, but that was beside the point. When you grew up in a small town, and then lived in said small town, your dating options were very, *very* slim. Practically nonexistent, if I was being honest.

Most of the men in town I'd either known forever, had already gone on a date with and it didn't work out, or they disliked cats. I'd said it once, and I'd say it again, that last one was a major deal breaker. Over my dead body was I going to choose a man over two fluffy creatures who were the reason for my existence and well-being.

"I do remember you telling me over the summer that you'd like a nice, hot city guy with a cat," Jules said before lifting her mug and innocently taking a sip.

I raised my hands with an unamused laugh. "Okay, yeah, *maybe* I said that"—I definitely said that—"but the only thing Gabriel has going for him is he's from the city. Based on who he works for, he likely isn't nice, and we have no idea if he has a cat or not. Honestly, it doesn't even matter!" I crossed my arms over my chest. "He's my enemy."

Jules closed the photo and scrolled farther down. Apparently, I'd spoken too soon. She pulled up a photo that was dated from earlier this year. It was a selfie of Gabriel and a tuxedo cat with a caption highlighting how it was Beans's twelfth birthday.

Give a girl a computer and a name to do reconnaissance on and she could work wonders.

I didn't want to look at the photo—really, I didn't—but it was right in front of me. There was no way he could look that good in person, right?

"He's probably one of those people who photographs well but doesn't look the same in person," Jules offered, although I could tell even she didn't believe what she was saying.

"We can hope," I muttered.

"See, it's good we looked him up," Eliza added, "because now you won't be ogling him in front of Hal."

At the mention of Hal, I was immediately pulled out of my haze and reminded of another reason why I was going to stay far away from Gabriel. Hal's grandson had never stepped foot in Golden Falls—not even for his late grandmother's funeral—and now all of a sudden he was showing up when there was a business offer on the line. That didn't sit well with me.

"I won't be *ogling* him, and I won't be entertaining any proposals he has. I'm standing my ground. I know this town, and

I'm going to prove to myself and to Hal that I'd do a damn good job managing the building."

"And we'll have your back the whole way," Eliza assured.

"Always. You know you can count on us," Jules added.

I offered my best friends a grateful smile, hoping that I was masking my nerves well. Because a part of me—a big part, if I was being honest—was scared I was going to lose everything I'd worked so hard for.

I was holding on to hope that Gabriel wouldn't even show up for the meeting. But if he did, maybe he would only be in town for the weekend and then stay far away from Golden Falls.

After all, that's what he'd been doing his whole life.

4

GABRIEL

The drive to Golden Falls passed quickly between my phone call with Liam and a handful of work calls. Thankfully, I'd finished the proposal for my father before leaving.

Despite the dropping temperatures, we hadn't gotten any snow yet, which made for a smooth—but barren—drive. The trees had long lost their leaves, gray clouds covered the sky, and there was road construction all along the highway. I didn't know how people loved this time of year. I couldn't stand it.

I hadn't been nervous about the drive. It was everything that came afterward. I typically didn't get nervous before proposals, meetings, or presentations. I simply got them done, hence why I was my father's closer.

That was why my time in Golden Falls had to be just business. A brief weekend trip that was purely professional and would end with me sharing my proposal, getting the building, and moving on.

One slight complication was that I thought I'd be able to stay at a hotel or Airbnb during my weekend in town, but Hal had insisted I stay with him. Which was fine. I could handle that. I could stuff my emotions into an overflowing cardboard box that was bursting at the seams. I'd add another layer of tape to keep it shut.

I double-checked the address listed on the mailbox with the address in my GPS before pulling up the gravel driveway.

A pastel-yellow home with a brown roof and shutters greeted me. A stone path led from the driveway to the front steps. While there wasn't anything currently planted in front of the house, I could imagine flowers and bushes blooming there. Stones lined the garden area, including a large rock that caught my attention immediately, even from the car. *Welcome to Hal and Vera's* was carved into the stone.

My chest tightened at the sight of my grandmother's name, at realizing what I'd missed out on, and it felt like my throat was closing in. The sudden onset of emotion caught me off guard, and I tried to steady my breathing. In for four, hold for seven, out for eight.

The front door creaked open, and out came my grandfather. His jeans were tucked into his work boots and his coat was on haphazardly, like he'd quickly thrown it on when he saw my car. His thick white hair was neatly styled, and his glasses were sliding off his nose.

He looked...older than I remembered, which should've been obvious, but it was another thing that caught me off guard. I rubbed my chest and let out a sigh.

Just business.

I unbuckled my seatbelt and reached for my winter coat in the backseat before stepping out of the car, smoothing out my slacks. I rounded the car to my trunk, pulling out my duffle bag.

"Here, why don't I take this off your hands, so you can grab the rest of your things," Hal said as he reached for the bag with one hand and clapped the side of my arm with the other. He smiled warmly. "Gabe, so great to see you. I'm glad you were able to make it, and hopefully the drive wasn't too bad. I'm glad you're staying here. It'll make getting into town that much easier. It's a short drive away, or you could walk if the weather's not too cold."

If Hal sensed any awkwardness, he didn't show it. He was acting like this was normal, like I showed up every other weekend.

I also couldn't remember the last time someone in my family called me Gabe. Liam called me Gabe all the time, but at work and to my parents, I was Gabriel. It sounded more professional, according to my father.

"This"—I cleared my throat—"this is all I brought. Just the one bag. Figured I wouldn't need much. I don't mind bringing it up." I extended my hand to take my bag back, but Hal waved me off.

"Well, it'll do for now. Come on. Let's get you inside." He gestured, leading me toward the front door. "Careful coming up these steps here." He waved his hand as we walked. "They get slippery after a snowfall, and we should get a good dusting of snow by the end of the month."

"That's...good to know," I said slowly, although I didn't think it would really matter for me. I'd be gone by then.

Hal pushed open the front door, leading me into his home. Wood paneling lined the walls, making the home feel like a rustic cabin. White curtains and wood molding lined the windows. There were photos everywhere, but not in a cluttered way. It was a house that actually felt like a home. My brows furrowed when my eyes caught on a series of frames with photos from my childhood and various events throughout the years, including my high school and college graduations that I didn't realize my grandparents had been at.

"Might be your first time visiting, but you'd be surprised at how many of your photos are around here." Hal set my bag down and slipped off his coat and shoes.

I unlaced my shoes and toed them off before stepping onto the plush, beige carpet as I took in his words. I cleared my throat before speaking. "Uh, thank you for letting me stay here. I—I really appreciate it..." My words trailed off. I was unsure what I should call him. Hal? Grandpa? Something that should be simple...wasn't.

The corner of Hal's mouth lifted into an amused smile, as if he'd read my mind. "Call me whatever you want. Hal is fine. It is my name, isn't it?" Hal waited a beat, watching me curiously before walking farther into the house. "Got a bedroom for you right here, and there's a bathroom that connects to it. My room is down the hall. Then we have the kitchen." Hal waved his hand in the direction. "You're a smart guy. You'll figure it out. Plus, it's not a big house. Doubt you'll get lost."

I peeked my head into the room, which was simple but had everything I might need: bed, nightstand, lamp, dresser, and desk. "Works for me." I dropped my bag at the foot of the bed, turning back to Hal. Our meeting was tomorrow in the late afternoon, and I was itching to find out more about why he'd invited me here. What was it about this building that got him thinking to include me? "About the meeting, the building—"

"—is something you'll find out about tomorrow," Hal finished for me. "Lily's been asking about it, too, but I haven't told her anything, either. Don't you worry. It'll start to make sense when we meet at the hardware store. Take some time getting settled since you're likely tired from the drive. Make yourself at home. You'll be here for a while."

My brows furrowed. "A while?"

Hal had that amused, cryptic smile again but no response. He simply turned around. "I have a meeting in town this afternoon but wanted to be in to greet you. I'll be back in a few hours. Holler if you need anything."

I parted my lips to speak, but nothing came out. What just

happened? And what was going on? "Uh, okay, sounds good," I said under my breath. I stood dumbfounded for a moment before letting out a sigh and gently closing the door to the bedroom.

I wasn't sure what Hal meant by *you'll be here a while*, other than the obvious. But I couldn't see that being the case. There had to be more to it.

I took a few minutes to unpack, mainly taking my dress shirts out and hanging them in the closet. I wasn't kidding when I said I packed light. I had enough for a weekend trip and that was it. If I really was going to be here for longer than that, I'd have to go back to Milwaukee for more stuff and ask Liam to watch Beans for longer.

"Already off to a strange start," I muttered, sitting at the desk and pulling out my laptop. Conveniently, I spotted a yellow sticky note Hal left with what appeared to be the internet network and password.

There was one piece of this puzzle that particularly stood out to me. Lily had been asking questions, too. Did she have plans of her own for the building? That seemed likely. I still hadn't gotten a chance to look up Lily and her café, but now felt like a good time to do that. For research purposes, of course.

Once my laptop turned on and I connected to the internet, I pulled up the search engine and typed in *Lily Richards Golden Falls*. I scanned the first page of results, which included a couple of news articles from the *Golden Falls Gazette* about Lily's plans for the café and then one highlighting opening day. I clicked on the latter.

Purrfect Blend Cat Café opens in Golden Falls
Golden Falls local Lily Richards creates a cozy space for customers to enjoy coffee and pastries with cats while also boosting adoptions.

I didn't get the chance to read the article after skimming the headline, because the photo captured my full attention.

A woman with long, wavy blonde hair stood behind the counter smiling. She had striking blue eyes and full lips with freckles dusting her cheeks and nose. Her smile was pure sunshine, lighting up her whole face. I ran my hand over my freshly-shaven jaw. *This* was Lily Richards? She was...effortlessly radiant. There was a softness to her presence, yet a clear strength, too. Like she knew exactly who she was and what she wanted.

My jaw clenched, and I slammed my laptop shut, the sound bouncing off the walls. I quickly pulled my hand away as if the laptop—or the light emanating from Lily—had burned me.

It didn't matter if Lily Richards was beautiful. This was just business.

5

GABRIEL

Sleeping in an unfamiliar place coupled with the looming meeting was enough to keep me from getting a good night's sleep. By the time my alarm rang at six in the morning, I was already wide awake. I normally didn't get much sleep to begin with—around five hours on a good day—but what I got wasn't enough even for me.

Coffee. I needed coffee and fast.

I hopped in the shower and quickly got ready for the day, pulling on a pair of gray slacks with a belt and light-blue button up. I made my way into the kitchen, expecting to see Hal but instead being greeted by a note on the counter. Hal's handwriting was messy, and it looked like some of the ink had smudged, but I was still able to make the writing out.

GABE,
HELP YOURSELF TO WHATEVER IS IN THE FRIDGE AND CABINETS FOR COFFEE AND BREAKFAST. IF THERE'S SOMETHING YOU NEED, WRITE IT DOWN ON THE LIST HANGING ON THE FRIDGE. I'LL DO A GROCERY RUN TODAY

AFTER OUR MEETING I'M AT THE HARDWARE STORE. IF
YOU NEED ANYTHING. SEE YOU SOON.
— HAL

I knew he wasn't willing to talk about the meeting yesterday, but I'd hoped to catch him this morning in case he was willing to share anything—*literally anything*—ahead of the afternoon.

After a few minutes of investigating the kitchen, I found the coffee and started brewing a pot. I knew I'd need more than one cup this morning. Then I quickly made some scrambled eggs with toast.

I wanted to get into town before the meeting to walk around, get a feel of the downtown area, and see the building in person. Maybe even talk to some of the locals, if they were willing. I wanted to be as prepared as possible.

After eating, I put on my coat, shoes, and hat, grabbed my wallet, and headed downtown.

Maybe I was imagining things, but I could've sworn every person I walked past was giving me a dirty look. What about all the bullshit about how welcoming small towns were? I sure wasn't feeling it.

I didn't expect to have a red carpet rolled out for me, but I didn't anticipate getting the cold shoulder. It was likely obvious I wasn't from here, considering Golden Falls was a town of a couple thousand. But no one even asked who I was. They just... stared at me like I'd pissed on the sidewalk (obviously, I didn't) or ripped down their millions of Christmas decorations (this one I was more tempted to do).

The downtown was decked out for the holidays. Imagine a town decorated for Christmas and then multiply it by ten—maybe even twenty. The lights weren't on, since it was daytime, but they were wrapped around anything and everything. Benches, trees, light posts. The various buildings and businesses also had string lights that looked like icicles hanging along the trim.

There were ornaments and decorative presents everywhere. In the center of downtown, there was a white gazebo with *more* lights, garland wrapped around the pillars, and big red bows adorning the railing.

I was glad I was here during the early afternoon, because in the evening, downtown would become a beacon of light. I would've guessed we were at the fucking North Pole with how decorated Golden Falls was. Only thing missing was Santa himself.

I thought the weird looks and glares were all in my head, but it was pretty obvious I wasn't imagining things when I saw an older woman pull out her phone, *take a picture of me*, and scurry back inside.

What the hell?

I craned my neck to see where she had gone. A place called Lake Ridge. Maybe this was my chance to get some answers.

I pushed open the door and stepped inside. I took a moment to glance around, noticing the exposed-brick walls that were decorated with photos and newspaper clippings. There were also pool tables, dart boards, and what looked like a dance floor. The place was rather empty, which wasn't surprising given the time.

The woman who I'd spotted outside was behind an expansive wooden bar that looked to have been carefully handcrafted. She was looking down, typing away on her phone. She was wearing a black T-shirt and jeans. Her blonde hair, streaked with gray, was pulled back, showing off her candy cane earrings.

I looked for a name tag as I approached but didn't see one.

"Hey," I said cautiously. "Did you take a picture of me? Outside the bar when I was walking?" I hooked my thumb over my shoulder.

The older woman looked up, blinking in surprise. She likely hadn't heard me come in. She cleared her throat and slid her phone into her back pocket. "Who, me?" she asked with an awkward laugh. "Oh, no. I can barely use that thing in my old age." She waved dismissively. "Maybe you saw someone else."

I narrowed my eyes at the woman skeptically. I didn't believe her one bit. But she didn't change her story as we stared at each other. There were a couple of ways I could play this. I could leave and continue getting stared at, or I could try to get some information out of her. And for that, I found one of the best ways was flattery.

I pulled out one of the bar stools and sat, resting my elbows on the counter. "What old age? You don't look a day over thirty."

The corner of her lip tipped up as she shook her head, setting a coaster in front of me. "Don't think I don't know what you're doing, Gabe." She filled up a glass with ice and water and set it on the bar.

My brows furrowed, and I reared back slightly. "How—how do you know my name?" I knew things traveled fast in a small town, but I wasn't prepared for how fast.

"Because your grandfather talks about you and has pictures all over his shop. Lots of people know you around here and have been waiting for your visit. There's even a betting pool on if you were going to show up or not. I said you would, and I needed proof that you were in town." She winked as she pulled her phone out, shaking it. "Although, quite a few people had spotted you already, so I guess I didn't *need* it. It's just...you look so much like your father. I mean, you're older than he was when he left town, but the resemblance is striking."

In the span of a few minutes, my world had flipped upside down, and I felt the knot in my stomach twisting. Even when I wasn't in the same city as him, I couldn't escape the comparisons. "I guess that explains the weird looks I was getting," I muttered.

She nodded, watching me curiously. "Your father and his company have quite a reputation around here."

Great. My father managed to piss off everyone in his hometown, and I was feeling the repercussions from it.

"But I should be polite and introduce myself, unlike everyone else staring. I'm Louise. And I apologize for the photo. I can delete it if you'd like," she offered.

"You can keep the photo for your proof." I drummed my fingers across the bar top. "But I'd love to ask you some questions in return."

"Smart guy," Louise said with an amused smile. "Ask away, and I'll see what I can answer."

I spent over an hour talking with Louise, who quickly warmed up after our initial introduction. She was in her fifties, around the same age as my father, and had lived in Golden Falls for nearly her whole life.

As suspected, she knew how to use her phone just fine. She showed me photos from over the years and pulled up news articles about Purrfect Blend, Hal, and Lake Ridge, the bar we were currently in. Once I got her talking, it didn't take long to realize she was the person I should be going to for any and all Golden Falls questions.

One thing she didn't share much about, despite my questions, was the building and Lily. Her exact words were, *"You'll have to find out for yourself, but one thing I'll tell you is not to underestimate Lily and the lengths this town is willing to go for her."*

By the time our conversation wrapped up, it was time for me to head over to Hal's. I stood from the stool, reaching into my wallet and pulling out a tip to set on the bar. I'd only had water, but I appreciated her time. "It was nice to meet you, Louise. Thanks for telling me about Golden Falls. I really appreciate it." I genuinely meant it, and I hoped she recognized that.

While her smile was friendly when I first walked in, her expression was softer now, warmer. "Don't be a stranger, Gabe. I'm always happy to chat. You'll have to come back."

I nodded slowly, not sure if she meant the bar or the town. Both, maybe.

I gathered my things and slipped my coat on, about to start walking toward the door when another part of our conversation came to mind.

"A betting pool, really?" I asked, and she let out a laugh.

"Consider it your welcome to Golden Falls. It's an honor."

"Did most people think I was or wasn't going to show up?" I asked curiously.

"Oh, it's more complicated than that. Most people thought you were going to show up, but it goes beyond that. Showing up and starting a fight. Showing up and hiding out. You get the idea. Keeps it more interesting and competitive that way."

"Huh." So very strange. "What did you bet on?"

She set her palms on the bar top, leaning forward. "That you'd show up and fall in love."

I raised my brows, a scoff escaping. "Hope you didn't bet much. You're about to lose it all."

"Don't count me out just yet," she said with a wink.

6

LILY

ELIZA

So Louise met Gabriel today...

She told me as soon as I got to Lake Ridge for my shift.

ME

Ughhh so he's in town. I was hoping he wouldn't show up lol.

I'm so nervous for the meeting. I've been watching the clock all day.

ELIZA

You're going to do great, Lil. Remember how incredible, talented, and strong you are! You're prepared and ready to convince Hal.

JULES

Seconding what Eliza said. It's all going to go well, and we have your back no matter what!

ME

You two are the best, and the reason I'm sane.

Did Louise say anything about him?

ELIZA

She said she enjoyed talking to him and that he's "very handsome."

ME

Oh, great. Wonderful. Perfect.

JULES

Just don't look at him, and you'll be fine!!!

"Easier said than done," I muttered in response to Jules's last text. I set my phone on the counter and took off my apron, hanging it on the cat-shaped wall hook by the register.

As my final customers of the day finished their drinks, I wiped the counters, cleaned the machines, and fed the cats while also giving them plenty of pettings. The five cats got lots of attention today with how busy it was, but I always ensured I spent some time with them as I closed.

The meeting with Gabriel and Hal had consumed my mind today, this week, and really from the moment Hal sent me that email. I wasn't kidding when I told Eliza and Jules I'd been watching the clock all day—and my customers noticed. I confused orders, overfilled at least three cups of coffee, and nearly used salt instead of sugar in various drinks. Luckily, everyone was patient with me.

I took a deep breath, trying to calm my nerves.

I trusted Hal, and I knew he had my best interests, and the best interests of the town, in mind. But I couldn't help but wonder why he couldn't just sell me the building. Why did we need to have this meeting, and why was Gabriel in town? I tried not to take it personally and not be too hurt about it, but it was tough not to get in my head. Did Hal think I wasn't ready or that I couldn't handle it? Did he have a different vision? Did he want to keep ownership in the family?

It was the last thing that hurt the most, if true. Because Hal *was* family to me. Maybe not by blood, but he had been present in nearly every moment in my life—big and small. He was at my high school graduation and at Purrfect Blend's opening. He gave me advice after my first heartbreak and taught me how to parallel park.

I didn't want to jump to conclusions, but that didn't stop my heart from racing and my palms from getting sweaty from anticipation.

After completing my closing work, I made my way back to the main area as two of my regulars—and my final customers for the day—were heading out.

"Bye, Tom and Susan!" I called out. "I'll see you next week."

They smiled and waved in return.

I pulled on my gloves and wrapped my scarf around my neck before putting on my coat. I hiked my purse over my shoulder and locked the door behind me. Time to brave the cold.

The walk to Hal's wasn't far—a few blocks from the café—and I passed the various Christmas decorations on the walk over, which I helped put up a few days ago. Lights, ornaments, and garland could be spotted in nearly every corner of downtown. As beautiful as it looked during the day, it looked absolutely magical at night with the twinkling lights, couples walking hand in hand, and Christmas music playing faintly in the background.

As I approached Hal's, I couldn't remember if I'd grabbed my phone. I looked down to dig around in my purse, wanting to double-check. I swore this thing had an endless bottom whenever I couldn't find something.

Keys, pens, ChapStick, random scraps of paper with half-written recipes, my winter wish—

Wait. Where was my winter wish list? I'd put the pink piece of paper in my purse the night I made it with Eliza and Jules.

Had I taken it out? I'd completely forgotten about it and the various things I'd set out to do until this moment.

I let out a frustrated huff. I'd deal with that and my misplaced phone later. They were likely somewhere in the café.

I pushed both purse straps onto my shoulder and sped up my walk, finally looking up.

But it was too late.

I crashed into a broad, jacket-clad back with an *oomph*. I stumbled back, nearly losing my footing on the sidewalk. I would've fallen on my butt had it not been for how quickly the man turned around. He tightly, but carefully, reached out to grab my wrist, tugging to keep me upright. Except he overcorrected. I had to brace my palms against his chest so I wouldn't faceplant into his body.

Although, with how good he smelled—a mixture of citrus, warmth, and clean linen—maybe that wouldn't have been a bad thing.

When my gaze flicked up, I expected it to be someone I knew. Golden Falls had visitors and tourists in the winter, but it was either closer to the holidays or after a big snowfall.

Instead, I was met with a sharp jaw that could cut ice paired with warm, honey-brown eyes that could melt it. His wavy brown hair was effortlessly tousled.

His eyes scanned my face, almost like he was taking me in, too.

Time stopped, like we were frozen in a snow globe.

But then recognition dawned on both of us as the pieces quickly came together.

This was Gabriel Nelson. *Gabriel Nelson!* I couldn't be fawning over him. I *wouldn't* be.

He dropped my wrist at the same time I stepped back, more careful this time.

"You should watch where you're going." His voice was low, a warning.

"And you should really watch where you're standing. Maybe you shouldn't be in the middle of the sidewalk. It gets busy this time of day."

People were walking around us, but by the way Gabriel raised his brows, I could tell he wasn't convinced. "Huh, that's odd. It's almost like even though there's people walking around, most aren't sprinting down the sidewalk, barreling into others."

I scoffed. "I wasn't *sprinting*. You were standing in the middle of the walkway." Maybe I should've checked my surroundings before speeding up, but I didn't expect him to be standing right in the middle of everything. "How would you know what people in Golden Falls do? It's not like you've ever been here before today."

His brows raised and the corner of his mouth tipped up into a smirk. "How would you know that?"

"Because I know who you—"

"You looked me up." His smirk widened, which frustrated me even more. "And, actually, I got in yesterday. So *technically* I have been here before today."

"Well, you looked me up, too, clearly." I *swore* I saw recognition flash over his face moments ago. "Doing research on the competition?"

He leaned in, his scent enveloping me once again. "What competition?"

"Oh, you think you're—" I gritted.

"Ah, Lily. Gabe," Hal greeted—and interrupted—as he watched from the doorway of Hal's Hardware. Had he been there the whole time? I hoped not. "Don't just stand there. Come on in." He waved with a grin.

"Please, after you." Gabriel gestured for me to go first.

"Now you're being all polite," I muttered.

"It's called being professional."

I glared at him over my shoulder before stepping inside Hal's store. "Hey, Hal. Nice to see you. Are we meeting in your office?"

"We are. Let's head back, and I'll share what I'm thinking." Hal waved for us to follow as he walked to the back of the store.

Before we walked behind him, Gabriel stretched his hand out. "Nice to meet you, Lily."

How could he be acting so normal? My business—*my future*—was on the line, but he likely didn't care. I was just another person, another business owner, to him. He probably dealt with people like me all the time and didn't bat an eye at the various businesses Nelson Group drove out with their projects.

It took everything in me to not shake his hand. To not suck it up and be polite. I liked being nice and welcoming to everyone, but I wouldn't be nice to someone who didn't prioritize others, who only focused on himself.

The tight-lipped smile on my face physically pained me, as did taking a step away from his outstretched hand. "I wish I could say the same, Gabriel."

I let out a heavy sigh and turned to walk toward Hal's office, my future hanging in the balance.

7

GABRIEL

While I had a nice conversation with Louise, I'd gotten more of the cold shoulder from other residents on my walk to Hal's Hardware. I tried not to let it get to me, but that was easier said than done.

I would get it if people *knew me* and didn't like me—that was fine—but I'd just gotten here. It likely all stemmed back to my father and how I couldn't separate my reputation from his.

All that left me in a bad mood, leading to a not-so-ideal first interaction with Lily Richards. She was even more beautiful in person, with her long blonde hair, rosy cheeks, and bright-blue eyes.

The emotion on her face, in her words, and deep exhale signaled she didn't want me here. Well, Lily, join the club. Apparently, most of Golden Falls didn't want me here. It wasn't much of a deterrent, if I was being honest. I'd spent most of my life on the outside looking in. This was more of the same.

Lily keeping her distance from me was better than the alternative. Because her bright smile in the photo I saw could bring men to their knees.

Just not me.

I wasn't here for pretty blonde women with soft smiles. I was here to get my hands on that building, prove to my father what I was capable of, and get the hell out of Golden Falls.

I shook my head to get out of my thoughts and followed to where Hal was waiting for us.

Calling the room an office was...generous. It was a small room with one window, a desk, and two chairs set up across from it. Hal had a few toolboxes and supplies stacked along the wall. And...

I froze in the doorway as I saw various photos lining the walls. Like at his home, Hal had photos from over the years, including some of me. He had some photos of my father when he was younger, and, of course, photos of Vera.

I swallowed the lump in my throat, not realizing how long I'd been staring until Hal gestured to the empty chair. "Have a seat, Gabe."

I felt Lily's eyes on me, but I avoided her gaze as I sat.

Hal, who was sitting at his desk across from us, folded his hands on the surface. His eyes softened as he looked between us. "I'm so happy to have you both here and for entertaining all this. I know it's been...confusing, and I apologize for that. Admittedly, it's been confusing for me, too. You see, I'm torn on what to do with the building and its ownership."

Out of the corner of my eye, I saw Lily fiddling with her scarf, which was now on her lap, along with her coat. She anxiously plucked at a few stray threads.

"Lily, I am so proud of you and the direction you've taken your business. I'm incredibly impressed, and I need you to know that. We've talked about you taking ownership of the building, so I know this must be surprising to you. It's just that—well, I'm worried you're working too hard and not prioritizing other parts of your life. I'm worried that selling to you will saddle you with more work and prevent you from exploring what else is out there."

"Hal, you have nothing to worry about," Lily said quickly, leaning forward in her seat. Her voice was strained, and there was panic in her eyes. "I can handle this. You *know* I can."

"I know you'd be able to handle it." Hal's voice softened, and I saw his eyes getting watery. "But if this prevented you from exploring other dreams...I don't know if I'd be able to forgive myself. You've talked about hiring help at Purrfect Blend. Have you had a chance to do that yet?"

"Well, no, not yet," Lily stammered. "I've had a lot on my plate, but I'll get to it. I will! That'll make it even easier for me to take over managing the building."

"We'll get to that in a moment." Hal cleared his throat then turned to me. "Gabe, you're very smart, and I know what you're capable of. I've been following your various projects at Nelson Group, and they don't reflect what you prioritized in school: sustainability, affordable housing, or community development. I'm worried your father is preventing you from reaching your full potential. I fear he is molding you into someone he wants you to be and is holding you back."

Hal's words shouldn't have been surprising to hear. It was things I'd been thinking for months now, years even. But hearing it out loud? It was a sucker punch to the gut.

"I—I am my own person," I said, my throat dry, closing in. But it was hard even for me to believe my words. "I maybe haven't been able to turn my ideas into reality, but they're there. I...I just need more time."

Hal hummed. "I think it's more than that, Gabe. For both of you, really. I *am* planning on selling the building, and I'd like to sell it to one of you."

Lily's spine straightened as she sat up.

"But I need to see that taking over this responsibility will better your life and not add unnecessary stress."

Lily and I both parted our lips to speak, but Hal continued.

"Lily, you mentioned being busy and needing help in the café. And Gabe, you mentioned needing more time. I also think you need to slow down, think about why you got into this work in the first place. Which is why I came up with my own little plan for the two of you."

I didn't like the sparkle in Hal's eye.

Hal opened his desk drawer and reached in, pulling out a piece of pink stationary.

Lily sat up, her eyes going wide. "My list," she whispered. "How did you—"

Hal set down the paper, smoothing out the corners. "You dropped it in the shop during one of your visits. When I didn't hear you were looking for it, I assumed you didn't realize it was gone."

Lily twisted her lips to the side, not saying anything and slouching in her seat.

I craned my neck to make out the glittery words in swoopy cursive. *Lily's Winter Wish List.* Following the heading, there were items numbered one through ten.

1. Hire help at the café
2. Decorate the cat room
3. Sign up for baking classes
4. Build a gingerbread house
5. Go sledding
6. Romantic kiss under the mistletoe that takes my breath away
7. Make a holiday recipe for fun

8. Dinner at Pasta Fresca to treat myself
9. Visit Milwaukee
10. See a shooting star

Oh, no. Hal hadn't started explaining yet, but I already didn't have a good feeling about where this was going.

"When I emailed you both, I wasn't sure how this conversation would go. Then, when I stumbled upon Lily's list, it all came together," Hal started. "Life has a funny way of working out."

I let out a dry scoff. There wasn't anything *funny* about this.

"Gabe, if you want a chance at owning the building, you'll first help Lily at Purrfect Blend while she brings on a new hire. Then you'll complete the list with her. Along the way, you'll be getting to know people in town."

"What?!" we both exclaimed. Suddenly, Hal's comment from yesterday—*you'll be here a while*—made sense.

Hal continued. "Lily, I want you to enjoy the holiday season. This is your favorite time of the year, and I want to see you living your life. I'd like you to complete this list. Not only that, but I want you to have fun while doing it. Sign up for the baking classes you've talked about, go sledding, and the other ideas you have on here."

"Hal, you can't be serious." Lily shook her head vehemently. "We can't—we can't do this list together."

I rubbed my temples, my eyes zeroing in on the list, specifically number six. My jaw clenched, and I shook my head, too. "I've been in town for a day and a half and people already want me gone. There's no way I'll be able to get to know them."

"He's going to drive out my business simply by being there!"

"How much are you intending to sell the building for? Whatever you're looking for, I'll double it. Triple it, even." I was desperate, looking to cling to anything to get out of this situation. To keep this strictly business. Because if I stayed here, if I got to know people, those lines would get blurred.

"*Of course*, you're trying to throw money at the problem." Lily raised her hands, letting her palms slap against her jean-covered thighs.

I brushed off her comment, telling Hal, "I have an idea for the building already."

Her head whipped toward me, her blue eyes ice cold. "You've been in Golden Falls for two seconds. You can't possibly know what this town needs or wants. You can shove that idea up—"

"Let's get back on track here," Hal interrupted, which was a shame, really. I wanted to know where she was going to tell me to *shove* my idea. "This isn't about the money." He shook his head. "I won't be taking any offers or listening to ideas from either of you just yet. If you don't like my conditions, you can back out. I won't be offended or upset."

I turned my head toward Lily, raising an eyebrow. Was she going to back out?

Lily looked at me and scoffed. "I'm not backing out. Are you?"

"Nope," I said, popping the P. Even with Hal's conditions, and having my trip extended, this was my one viable chance to create something that would benefit a community. To get noticed by my father for the work I wanted to be doing. I wasn't going to give that up, even with a few obstacles. I couldn't go back to Nelson Group empty-handed, only to continue doing the work my father wanted me to. It was time to finally take matters into my own hands.

"How will we know when you've made a decision?" Lily asked Hal.

"Once you complete the list, I'll make up my mind and let you both know. Likely sometime early in the new year. But I have a feeling you'll know before me."

"We have to do *every* single thing on my list?" Lily asked, exasperated, at the same time I asked, "But what about my *actual* job?"

That meant I'd be in Golden Falls at least through the end of December, likely into January, too. I inhaled deeply, running my fingers through my hair. I wasn't sure how I was going to make this work, but I'd find a way. I'd work remotely, but I wasn't looking forward to breaking the news to my father that I was going to be in Golden Falls for a few weeks or more.

"I'm sure you'll figure something out," Hal said to me. "You'll likely need to make another trip to Milwaukee to grab your things. I recommend doing that before starting at Lily's café on Monday. Lily, think about how Gabe can help you and ensure you're ready for his first day."

It was Saturday afternoon, which gave me the rest of today and all of tomorrow to prepare for my first day with Lily.

"If we don't kill each other before then," Lily muttered. Her hand was wrapped tightly around the arm of the chair. "If it's too complicated with your job, it's not too late to back out. I'm sure you'll have other opportunities for your *idea*." She narrowed her eyes and faked a smile.

"It's not too complicated. Like Hal said, I'll figure something out. I'll make this work, and I have no intention of backing out. I hope you're ready to be working together."

I had a feeling this list—along with the blonde next to me— was going to be the bane of my existence.

8

LILY

Well, that went way worse than I expected.

Once we wrapped up our meeting, I couldn't leave fast enough. My coat was on halfway and I stumbled over my feet as I pushed open the door. I walked quickly to my apartment, which was above the café and another reminder of what was at stake. Not only was my business in the building that was for sale, but my apartment was, too. I climbed the stairs to the second floor and beelined to my front door.

Hot tears stung the backs of my eyes as I pulled my keys out of my coat pocket and unlocked the door through blurry vision.

How was this happening? I thought Hal and I were on the same page. I thought he *wanted* me to buy the building.

What hurt the most was that, deep down, I knew he was right. I rarely had time for myself, including my personal and professional goals. I didn't even realize until earlier today that my winter wish list was missing. Now, it was burning a hole in my pocket.

One thing I was grateful for was that I didn't add Eliza and Jules's more *creative* ideas. I would've never been able to look Hal in the eyes again.

The door closed behind me with a *thud*. I set my keys on the entry table and unwrapped my scarf, the soft wool feeling itchy and suffocating all of a sudden.

Not long after getting inside, I heard a chorus of meows and the patter of paws on the hardwood floor. My two cats, Bandit and Sylvie, trotted toward me. There was nothing like being greeted with purrs and tail hugs—and the occasional meow-scream even though dinner was more than an hour away.

I crouched down, petting both of them. My mood immediately improved, even if it was temporary. "I missed you, too," I murmured.

Even though I lived alone, there was never a dull moment with these two. I'd adopted them at the same time from the Golden Falls Animal Shelter about five years ago. They were impossible to resist, especially when my first sight was them cuddling together. They were kittens at the time who had bonded when the rest of their respective litters had already been adopted.

Bandit, a male orange tabby, was my stability and emotional support, while Sylvie, a female Calico with black fur and fiery orange and white patches, always kept things interesting. She also kept Bandit in his place, and me, for that matter. Still, they loved to cuddle with each other, and it was more often than not that the three of us would fall asleep on the couch watching TV before making it to bed.

Bandit and Sylvie followed me around the apartment as I turned on the Christmas lights and various lamps. My one-bedroom apartment was small, but I loved the way I had it set up. The front door led right to the living room, where I had my couch, Christmas tree, a television, basket of blankets, and other decorations. I had lots of photos of my family and friends around my apartment, as well as candles and knickknacks I'd gotten from various town events and festivals where people were selling goods.

The living room opened up right into the kitchen, where I spent more time baking than cooking. Usually, I had random scraps of paper with recipe notes and revisions lying around, but I'd cleaned up this week. My apartment was spotless, apart from the random socks on the floor that Bandit was known for stealing out of my hamper. His name made more sense now, didn't it?

I connected my phone to the speaker in the living area and queued up a playlist of my favorite Christmas songs. The iconic chimes of the intro to "All I Want for Christmas is You" by Mariah Carey filled the room.

Sylvie let out a loud meow, which I took as approval for my music choice. She rested her front paws on my shin, and I scooped her up in my arms, carrying her over to the couch. I collapsed onto the couch with Sylvie in my lap. Bandit trotted behind us and swiftly hopped up, squeezing his way onto the sliver of space left on my lap.

How was I going to survive working and spending time with Gabriel Nelson? *Of course*, he wanted to throw money at the problem. *Of course*, he already had an idea for the building. And *of course*, he wanted to be out of Golden Falls as soon as humanly possible.

Everything I thought about him—that he was arrogant, selfish, and money-motivated—was confirmed in our initial interaction, but…I couldn't help but wonder about what else Hal had said. About how Gabriel was passionate about sustainability, community development, and affordable housing. Those were all things that were important to me and the people in Golden Falls. Something like that *would* be beneficial to the town, but was it really what Gabriel wanted to bring here? Was his father preventing him from reaching his full potential, or did Hal have it all wrong? Gabriel was Hal's grandson, after all. Was Hal only seeing what he wanted?

And now I had to *spend time* with him against my will. At least I had the weekend to prepare and come up with an initial plan. Maybe it would be nice to have some help at the café as I figured out who to hire...as long as Gabriel actually was going to help.

I was self-taught at baking, and I'd been wanting to take classes to elevate my skills and continue experimenting with ingredients and recipes. But in order to do that, I needed to hire and train a new employee. That was going to be the first thing I checked off the list.

One thing was for sure: I wasn't backing down. He was mistaken if he thought this was going to be easy, that I was going to roll over and hand the building to him on a silver platter. No freaking way.

The fact that people in town didn't want him here was only an advantage for me. Although, it did surprise me that Louise was chatty with him. If he got on her good side, that would be a problem, since she knew the ins and outs of Golden Falls like the back of her hand.

I had my work cut out for me, and I needed to get prepared. And that preparation started with a hot bubble bath.

While I was able to relax in the bath until my skin resembled a raisin, the stress returned to my body immediately upon getting out. Not even my fuzziest Christmas socks could ward off the stress demons.

And that's why I was baking dozens of blueberry muffins at

midnight. The cats must have sensed my stress, because they'd been zooming around the apartment for the last twenty minutes.

On the bright side, my last batch of muffins was nearly done.

A knock at the door caught my attention, but I quickly relaxed when I realized it was likely Eliza coming home after her shift at Lake Ridge. She lived across the hall from me and tended to work evenings and nights at the bar with occasional mornings and afternoons leading yoga classes at her studio.

I pulled open the door and smiled when I saw her. I texted Eliza and Jules the short version of what happened during the meeting but wanted to dive into the details when I saw them next, which was at tomorrow's family dinner. Or, I guess, technically tonight's family dinner, since it was the next day. God, I really needed to get some sleep.

"Hey," she greeted, her voice gentler than usual. Her expression softened immediately. "I know you said you'll tell us all about it at dinner, but I was getting home and saw your light was still on." Eliza peeked over my shoulder, wincing slightly. "Stress baking?"

She knew the answer before asking, given the open containers of flour, sugar, cinnamon, and milk. My mixing bowls and utensils took up most of the space on the kitchen island, and any open space was covered in flour.

At least my apartment smelled warm, sweet, and inviting as a result.

I let out a breathy laugh and nodded. "I've made at least five dozen muffins." When her eyes widened, I waved my hand. "I'll sell some discounted at the café since *technically* they're from yesterday and bring some to family dinner. It's not *that* many."

"It is when it's past midnight," she huffed under her breath. "And I think that means you have one or two to spare."

"For you? Always." I gestured for her to come inside.

As soon as Eliza walked in and saw the mess up close, she ordered me to sit on one of the stools and helped me clean and get my kitchen back in order. I started to tell her what happened but quickly realized we needed Jules here to hear this, too.

The last thing I wanted to do was wake her up, but Eliza told me that Wes had worked late tonight, too, which likely meant Jules stayed up to wait for him. Before Jules, Wes worked all the damn time. He practically lived at Lake Ridge, and late nights were the norm. Since Jules, he'd limited his late nights, opting to hire more help and offload more of his responsibilities so he could spend most evenings and nights with her.

I tapped Jules's contact in my phone, and the familiar ringing filled the apartment.

"Why are you FaceTiming my girl in the middle of the night?" was the first thing my brother grumbled as he answered Jules's phone.

"I wanted to make sure you got home okay," I said to my brother with a smile.

"Liar." He rolled his eyes with an amused huff.

"Wes, don't tell me you're jealous of your sister," I heard her say in the back with a laugh. Jules came into focus on the screen, leaning her head against Wes's arm. His face softened immediately as he looked down at her.

"So, when I *accidentally* wake you up when I'm getting home from a late night, you throw a pillow at me, but when Lily randomly calls you, it's fine?"

"Exactly," Jules and I said at the same time, grins on our faces.

"Makes no sense," Wes huffed. He was about to hand the phone back to Jules, but before that, his brow furrowed and he asked, "Is everything okay, Lily?"

I smiled softly. My brother might have been a grump, but he had the biggest soft spot for those he cared about. He was always putting others first. "I had my meeting with Hal and Gabriel today about the building. It wasn't as straightforward as I had hoped."

"And? What happened?"

"That's why she's calling." Jules gently nudged his arm. "To tell us what happened."

"Well," my brother said expectantly, which caused me to laugh.

When I had first gotten the email from Hal in November, with Gabriel included on it, I had rushed over to Wes and Jules's place, so my brother was familiar with how all this started.

Jules and Wes got comfortable on the couch as they waited for me to start the story.

As I parted my lips to start talking, Eliza let out a satisfied moan, muffin crumbs clinging to the corner of her mouth.

"I was making muffins," I informed Jules and Wes. I looked over at Eliza, shaking my head with a laugh. "Do you need a moment alone, or can I start talking?"

She took another bite, waving her free hand. "Don't let me stop you. You can start talking. I'm listening." Her words were mumbled, like she was underwater, but I'd known her long enough to understand exactly what she was saying.

"Okay, *so*, here's what happened and the mess I'm in."

I told them about how the meeting went, Hal's conditions, my list, Gabriel's response. Eliza and Jules's gasps, along with Wes's mumbled swears, made my retelling rather theatrical. Had it not been me in this situation, I would've found it all entertaining, too.

"Did Hal say anything about when he'll make up his mind or how long Gabriel has to work at the café?" Jules asked.

I shrugged. "Kind of? It all depends on finishing the list. He said he'd like to make his mind up in the new year. And get this.

He said, and I quote, *'I have a feeling you'll know before me.'* How cryptic is that? I mean, it's typical Hal."

Hal had infinite wisdom and was always one step ahead, but I couldn't for the life of me figure out what his agenda was this time.

"Okay..." Eliza said. "In the new year. That could mean next month...or it could mean in a few months. Either way, you need to find a way to survive working with Gabriel. It might not be the *worst* thing, right? You can have him do the things you don't want to do. Have him help out with cleaning up for the day so you can leave work a little early. Then once you hire someone, you'll have even more free time. You can finally take time for yourself to unwind and relax."

"I know this sucks and is super frustrating, but Eliza's right," Jules added. "You were so excited to put that list together. Now, you'll have time to actually do it." Jules paused. "We're...well, we might be a little worried about you. You've been working *so* much lately."

Next it was Wes. "You need to take care of yourself. This could be a good thing, Lily."

"As long as you don't kill Gabriel," Eliza added.

I didn't bother arguing with them, because they were right. Even if this did feel like a little bit of an intervention. Although, considering I was stress baking at midnight, maybe I needed it.

"Fine," I accepted with a sigh. "I'll spend some time over the weekend thinking about what he could help me with. I am excited to sign up for the online baking classes I've been eyeing. They're just *so* expensive," I groaned. "But anyways, yeah, I think there are ways to use this situation to my advantage."

"So..." Jules said, drawing out the word. "Now that you've seen him in person...how hot was he?"

Wes groaned. "That's my cue to leave." He pressed a kiss to Jules's cheek. "The sooner you hang up, the sooner you can join me in bed, sweetheart," he murmured, but unfortunately for me, the phone still picked up his words.

A blush formed on Jules's cheeks, and I rolled my eyes. "Get a room!"

As Wes got up from the couch, he said, "What do you think I'm trying to do?"

Jules shook her head, watching him walk off before her attention was turned back to me.

"This does not leave this call," I started, letting out a heavy exhale. "He's the type of attractive that it hurts to look at. Like unfairly hot. Proof that the universe is clearly picking favorites. And his jaw line—" I cut myself off (even though I could've easily kept going) when I saw the smirks on Jules and Eliza's faces. "But it doesn't matter! Not to me, at least. I'm immune to his good looks. Plus, he's arrogant and thinks he's way too good for our small town. He wanted to throw money at the problem and get out of here. It doesn't matter how attractive he is if *that's* his personality." I paused to finally take a breath. "There are cats and baked goods involved. Nothing and no one can stand in my way."

9

GABRIEL

Turned out, I'd be in Golden Falls longer than a weekend.

Great.

I should've known it wouldn't be easy.

Hopefully, I'd talk with residents over the next few weeks, help Lily with that goddamn wish list, pitch my idea to Hal, get the building, and be done with this strange small town.

In the meantime, I was back in Milwaukee for the weekend to grab more of my belongings for my extended stay. My first stop was the office to pick up documents, folders, and notes that I didn't have stored on my work laptop. I intended for this to be a quick stop so I could get back to my apartment.

But those plans went out the window when I heard footsteps outside my door. It was a Saturday, so there was only one other person who'd be here.

I inhaled deeply, grabbing the stack of folders and sliding them in my backpack. "Dad," I greeted simply.

He stood in the doorway, his overwhelming and intimidating presence filling the whole office, suffocating me. With one look, one raised brow, he was able to make me feel small. Make me second-guess everything. *Why wasn't I more success-*

ful? Why couldn't I stand up to him? Why couldn't I just walk away?

"Gabriel," he said slowly, eyes moving to my cleaned-off desk. "I'm surprised to see you here, considering you've been slacking lately."

"I'm not sure where you're getting that from," I responded. "I turned in my work ahead of leaving for the weekend. Which, speaking of, I'm going to be working remotely for the time being. Through the end of the month, at least, but maybe a little longer than that. I'll let my clients know and make—"

My father let out a humorless laugh. "You're going to be working remotely?" he asked, disdain dripping from each word. "Consider yourself out of a fucking job, then."

I clenched my jaw, my patience thin. "There's a building. One that would be a good candidate for community development and getting the public involved on the project. I'm trying to close the deal. It's..." I paused. "It's in Golden Falls. That's where I'll be for the time being."

There wasn't any emotion on my father's face when I mentioned his hometown. He didn't raise his brow, didn't frown, nothing. He was a fucking statue, acting like the town and Hal meant nothing to him. For all I knew, they didn't.

I wrapped my fingers around the edge of my desk, my grip tightening with each passing second of silence.

"Nothing?" I challenged. "I go to your hometown, see Hal, and you can't even ask how he's doing, let alone what building I'm talking about?"

My father sneered. "You're just like your mother. Always so fucking sensitive." I'd lost count how many times I'd heard that one. "I know what building you're talking about. It's the same one I tried to buy from him years ago, but he wouldn't sell. Whatever you have going on is your problem now. Fix it—and don't come back until you do."

He didn't wait for my response before he stormed off. I heard his stomps well down the hallway. At least I got approval for working remotely as long as I needed. That was how I was choosing to interpret his words.

I loosened my grip on the desk, flexing my hand to work out the stiffness. Hal hadn't sold to my dad but was considering selling to me? I shook my head, unsure how this was all fitting together.

As much as I wanted to forget about Golden Falls, the building was my chance at putting one of my ideas in motion. Showing my father that this *could* work. In the past when I'd tried to purchase property for one of my projects, the sellers either wanted my father involved or didn't trust that Nelson Group would make what I was proposing about benefiting the community a reality given the company's reputation.

Buying the building from Hal also meant closing a deal my father couldn't. I'd be in charge and keep him out of the plans.

The various hoops I had to jump through to get the building were worth it. It was my opportunity to turn my career around and do something my father couldn't—finally proving to him that I had what it took.

I had to see this through and had no intention of backing out, even if it meant I'd be spending the next few weeks side by side with Lily Richards.

Business. It was all just business.

Conversations with my father always drained me, but this one in particular I couldn't shake, even as I left the office and made the short drive to my apartment. Every time I reminded myself I wasn't who he thought I was, his criticisms of me came flooding back. With our troubled relationship, I was constantly walking upstream, trying not to get knocked over by the rough water.

After parking my car in the garage, I grabbed my backpack and started to climb the three flights of stairs to my apartment. On the way up, I checked my phone to see if Liam had texted me back—no luck.

By the time I got to the top, I was breathless, nearly keeling over, and had a thin layer of sweat on my forehead. I wish I could say I did this regularly, but it was because the elevator was out of order.

I swiped the key fob against the door, the light turning green and beeping to let me in. When I pushed open the door, I got the answer as to why Liam hadn't answered my text. He was asleep on my couch, the television playing some house-flipping show on HGTV, and Beans was curled up on his chest.

"Don't like cats, my ass," I muttered with an amused chuckle. Liam claimed he didn't get along with Beans, that my cat was out to get him. I snapped a quick picture, fully intending on using this as proof that Liam was wrong.

I closed the door behind me, and Beans opened one eye to scope out the scene and then the other. He yawned, standing and stretching out his limbs before launching off Liam's chest.

"I'm awake!" Liam called out, sitting up and using the back of his hand to wipe the side of his mouth. He cleared his throat, looking around and spotting me. "Oh, hey, you're here. Yeah, right, I saw your text that you'd be stopping by today. We were, uh, hanging out." Liam cautiously looked over at Beans, who blinked at him before trotting over to me.

"So I saw." I shook my head with a smile. "Had to stop by to grab more clothes. Looks like I'll be gone for longer than I thought." I let out a heavy sigh and dropped my keys on the counter. "Think you could watch Beans while I'm gone? I'm not sure how long it'll be, and he doesn't do well with long car rides. Plus, it seems like you two bonded this weekend."

"I guess you could say that." Liam stood, stretching his arms above his head. "And, yeah, I'm happy to. So, not a weekend trip, huh? Do you have a better idea of how long you'll be gone?"

On my drive back to the city, I had called Liam to fill him in on how the meeting went. "Nope. Maybe through the end of the month? Slightly longer, potentially. I only really know what I told you. *Maybe* I'll find out more on Monday, if I survive working with Lily." I muttered the last part.

"Oh, yeah," Liam said with a grin, far too amused. He walked toward the kitchen, opening one of the cabinets and pulling out a half-eaten bag of chips. "You'll be working at the café and then helping her with the wish list. This'll be good. Considering the amount of death stares you said you got on your first day, this will be a chance to have the town warm up to you. You can lay the charm on them."

I raised my brow. That was more Liam's specialty than mine. "And how do you suggest I do that?"

"Flex your muscles, smile, maintain eye contact. You know, the basics." He shrugged, popping another chip into his mouth.

"I'm trying to close a business deal not *flirt* with the women of Golden Falls."

"Tomato, potato or whatever that saying is." He waved his hand. "You can walk and eat at the same time."

"Tomato, toh-mah-to. And it's walk and talk."

"Same difference, and actually, I like my version better."

I couldn't argue with him on that one. I leaned my forearms on the counter, reaching over for a handful of chips.

"I've told you this before, but it feels like a good time to offer you a reminder. You don't *need* to try to impress your father. He might be blood, but it's okay if you distance yourself from him, or even cut him off entirely. I know that's easier said than done, but you won't be alone if you do that. You'll always have me in your corner."

Liam's words were a sucker punch to the heart—in a good way but leaving me winded nonetheless. I reached up to rub my chest, brows furrowing. "I know I'll always have you in my corner." That much was true, but there was more to it. "It's intimidating to think that this all was for nothing. If I don't impress him, then why have I spent the last four years working for him? Because it sure as hell wasn't for me. This feels like...an opportunity to prove to him that I can do the work I've wanted to do. Even if I leave Nelson Group at the end of it all. I don't know if I would, but I've sure as hell thought about it. Now more than ever."

Liam listened intently, nodding. He reached over to grab a napkin and wiped his hands on it. "Well, let's get you packed up and sent off to Golden Falls. This is an opportunity to get you closer to what you want. Plus, you could use a vacation."

I huffed a laugh. "I'd prefer if that vacation was to one of your resorts instead of a small town where everyone gives me the stink eye and I have a blue-eyed blonde wishing for my death sentence, but I guess this will do."

"I'll see what strings I can pull," he teased with a wink. "Now..." he said with a wide smirk. "Tell me more about this *blue-eyed blonde* and the winter wish list you have to complete. What's on it? Anything good?"

I rolled my eyes, shaking my head and pushing myself off the counter. "Nothing more to tell, and no, nothing good. It's all the stuff I hate about this time of year." I walked toward my bedroom, focusing on what I still had to pack and not on the conversation at hand. *Certainly* not on Lily.

"Nothing more to tell?" Liam repeated, his footsteps right behind me. "What do you think, Beans?"

Beans meowed loudly.

"Yeah, buddy, I call bullshit, too."

"What, so I leave for a weekend, and all of a sudden you're best friends with my cat? Who you've claimed for *months* hated you?"

"Everyone loves a good slow burn. We just needed some bonding time."

"Apparently, you'll have plenty of bonding time in the coming weeks."

Liam stopped in the doorway, leaning against the frame. "I could use the company. Think I could bring Beans to Half Day Pub for dinner? Oh! I'll get takeout. That'll be easier."

I barked out a laugh. "I do think that'll be easier. But..." I looked over at him. "Then you wouldn't see Fiona."

Liam's face fell as realization dawned on him, which only confirmed my suspicions that there was *something* there, at least on his side. "You're right. I'll pop in for an appetizer, say hi to her, and then get my dinner to go, so I can eat with Beans."

"Sounds like you have a plan. Any dates lined up?"

Liam rolled his eyes with a groan. "Fuck no. I'm taking a break. I can't handle another bad date or a date where the woman knows everything about me because she did her research. Like, I get looking up the person you're going on a date with, but being able to recite my whole biography? Recounting details that even I'd forgotten about?" He shook his head. "That was my last straw."

"Damn." My eyes were wide as I listened to him. "Well, Beans is great company." I would know. He'd kept me company during many date-less nights. I hadn't been on a date in well over a year with how busy work had been. After the damage my parents had done on me and hearing Liam's horror stories, it was possible I'd never date again.

Not that I was having much luck when I *was* dating. I always kept things casual and surface level, despite knowing that having a long-term relationship would be more fulfilling. I liked the idea of having someone I could tell anything and everything to—and being that person for them in return—but I couldn't bring myself to open up.

Because of that, I typically sought out women who were looking for something casual. We would spend time together over a few dates and then go our separate ways without any hard feelings. It was easier that way. I didn't have to dig into how unhappy I was in my career or my complicated relationship with my parents. Or how even though I wanted a long-term relationship, I was seeking the opposite.

Liam broke me out of my thoughts. "Tell me more about Lily. What do you think being around her will be like?"

I moved around the room, grabbing a stack of shirts and then a few pairs of pants. I had no damn clue how long I'd be in Golden Falls, which made packing difficult. I had to hope for the best. That and try to survive Lily. One moment her eyes were a bright blue, and the next I swore her pupils turned into tiny daggers.

"Absolute torture."

For more than one reason.

10

LILY

THE SAVORY AROMA OF GARLIC, ONIONS AND HERBS MADE MY stomach growl as I stepped into my parents' house. It also confirmed that while I could bake, I wasn't much of a cook, because my apartment never smelled like this during dinner.

My dad was the one who cooked more often, but my mom loved helping him. As I walked through the open-concept living room—past the fifteen-foot Christmas tree and toward the kitchen—I would've been able to spot the grin on my dad's face from a mile away. I loved the way he looked at my mom, like she hung the moon.

My parents had been together since their early twenties. My dad, who grew up in Golden Falls, was the one who started Lake Ridge, the bar my older brother now owned. Dad bought an industrial building and renovated it. Once he was ready to build his staff, one of the first people he'd hired was Mom. She helped him with everything, and together, they turned Lake Ridge into a favorite spot in town. It was the place to stop by for a drink after work, spend time with friends and neighbors on the weekends, and play darts or pool.

Wes bought Lake Ridge a few years ago, allowing our dad to

step back and enjoy retirement. Wes had elevated the bar to new heights. He took the casual feel people loved about it and made it even more of a destination. He added fire pits, a custom-built wooden bar, expanded the bar and liquor selection, and included personal touches to the place, like photos of our parents from when they were running it.

I loved how much my family put into this town, and I wanted to leave my mark on Golden Falls, too. I was hoping I could do a version of that with Purrfect Blend and the building.

I stood in the doorway of the kitchen, taking another moment to appreciate how in love my parents were, even after all these years.

My dad looked up, a warm smile on his face as he saw me. "There's our Lily bear." The nickname brought a wave of nostalgia. I loved the nickname growing up but then found it childish in high school. It was only recently that I found myself not minding it too much. "You're the first one here."

My mom walked over and pulled me into a hug.

"As usual," I chimed happily to my dad. "And it smells amazing in here, Dad. Pot roast tonight?" I guessed.

"You got it. With homemade sourdough."

My mouth watered. "Well, we *could* start dinner early," I teased, causing my dad to chuckle. I peeked into the dining area and saw the table hadn't been set yet. "I'll help with setting the table. Who's showing up tonight?"

My parents liked to host dinners regularly for whoever was available that night. Whenever the weather was nice, like over the summer, my dad grilled and we'd eat outside. Every other time we ate family-style in the dining room. These were some of my favorite nights, because nearly everyone in my close circle was together. The only person missing lately had been my older sister Jade, who was in Hawaii for work as a travel nurse. We tried to FaceTime her in when her schedule matched up, but in the past couple of months, it had been less and less.

My mom tilted her head to the side, listing on her fingers who all was coming. "Wes, Jules, Cooper, Eliza." She paused. "Hal has poker, so he won't be here tonight. And I can't remember if Marnie has her knitting club or not. So, let's set the table for eight, and if Marnie isn't here, we can take that place away. Here, I'll fill the waters while you set the table." My mom grabbed the pitcher before we both walked over to the dining area.

I got my love of Christmas and decorating from both my parents but especially my mom. Most of the decorations I had in my apartment were from her, since she had saved so many over the years. This year, my mom was going with a simple white, silver, and red theme but still had decorations in nearly every corner of the house. Various snowmen, Santas, reindeer, ribbon, and garland. It was impossible to escape—and I loved it.

Mom picked up the first water glass. "How did your meeting with Hal go, by the way?"

I let out a heavy sigh, grabbing the plates and carefully setting each one. "It was...something," I said. "Hal wants to sell, but he needs time before he makes his final decision. It's between me and Gabriel, so I have a decent chance, but Hal has some *conditions* in place."

I proceeded to tell my mom about Hal's concerns about selling the building outright to me and his conditions for both me and Gabriel, including working in the café and completing my winter wish list together.

"That sounds like Hal." My mom shook her head with a gentle laugh. "He's always up to something, but he sees things others in town miss."

"I just...I don't want him to think I *can't* do it."

My mom shook her head. "I don't think it's that. He knows

how capable you are, and he has never doubted you. Not for a second. I know it might not feel like it now, but it's also a push to get you thinking about how to continue your business. You can't do it all, right? And the last thing I want is for you to get burned out. I mean, I think about your dad and me running Lake Ridge. It was *a lot* at times, and it was the two of us plus a small staff. You're running Purrfect Blend on your own. You've wanted to hire help so you can focus on other things. Hopefully, having Gabriel around will help you with that."

I nodded in agreement. "That's what Eliza and Jules were saying, too, and that's how I'm trying to see it. I'm trying to think of it as setting me up for my future plans instead of an obstacle." I sighed heavily. "I wish I didn't have to be around Gabriel to do it," I muttered.

My mom's eyes softened, and she reached over to gently squeeze my arm. "It's not easy. I completely understand that. But...see how things go. See if you can give him a chance."

Stubbornly, I shook my head, grabbing the silverware and setting the forks and knives on the table a little more forcefully than I should've. "I don't want to give him a chance, Mom. The articles about Nelson Group, all their projects, that's not what Golden Falls is about. Yes, I'll admit I don't *really* know why he wants the building, but all the signs point to him wanting it for some sort of luxury project. A project that wouldn't have space for my café or Eliza's yoga studio or the apartments. This is his first time in town. He didn't even come back for Vera's funeral." I shook my head again, frustration bubbling inside me. "That's not someone I want to give a chance to or get to know."

Something I always appreciated about my mom—both my parents, really—was how well she listened. She let me speak, voice my feelings and frustrations, and saw what I needed. And always managed to drop some sage advice...even if I didn't want it in the moment.

"Oftentimes, there's more to the story, and more than one thing can be true. Keep that in mind, Lily."

A pang of guilt twisted in my stomach, heavy and unsettling, because I knew my mom was right. Multiple things could be true, and I didn't *really* know Gabriel. I thought I did...and it was easier to dislike him when I didn't know much about him. "Right." I gulped. "I'll, yeah, I'll keep that in mind."

She finished filling the final water glass and came over to where I was standing on the other side of the table. She pulled me into another hug. "You'll figure it out, Lily. I know you will."

Christmas music played softly through the speakers my parents had in the kitchen and living room. Apart from the music, there was a comfortable silence, reminding me how much I enjoyed being around my parents, even if we weren't talking about something.

That silence didn't last for long, though, because right at six thirty, the door opened and everyone came barreling in within a few minutes. Laughter and conversation (and a little bit of bickering) filled the house. I made my way toward the front door, seeing Eliza, Cooper, and Marnie entering, with Wes and Jules not far behind them.

"Cooper, I told you I could drive Gran," Eliza huffed to her older brother while sharply pulling her coat zipper down.

"And I told you her house was on my way, which is why I picked her up," Cooper, who sounded equally annoyed, responded.

When Eliza's eyes met mine, I offered her a sympathetic smile. She dramatically rolled her eyes—silently saying *Can you believe him?*—before smiling at me in return. With how long we'd known each other, communicating without words was second nature.

"But that was after—"

"Eliza, I saved you time. This shouldn't—"

"Will you two stop it?" Marnie cut in, which had both Eliza and Cooper shutting their mouths. "Had I known this would cause this big of an issue, I would've walked the four miles and met you both here."

Marnie Hayes, Cooper and Eliza's grandma, was a force to be reckoned with. She was tiny—standing at about five feet—but her personality and colorful wardrobe more than made up for her lack of height. She was blunt, kind, and loving—a powerful and wonderful combination. Marnie had also suffered more loss than one person ever should. So had Eliza and Cooper.

Marnie's husband died a couple of years after they had their first and only child, Cooper and Eliza's dad. Marnie raised Eliza and Cooper after their parents, Daniel and Harper, died in a car accident nearly twenty years ago when Eliza was six and Cooper was fourteen.

It was around this time of year, which likely added to the heightened tensions between Eliza and Cooper.

Eliza's lips parted, and I knew my best friend wanted to get the last word, but I cut in instead. "Marnie, I didn't realize you'd be able to make it tonight. No knitting club?"

Marnie gave both Cooper and Eliza one final pointed look before turning to me, her lips spreading into a genuine smile. "There's my Lily. Don't you look gorgeous tonight." She walked over to me and pulled me into a hug. Once she'd taken off her coat, Marnie's outfit came into full view. She was wearing a long, colorful dress with whimsical, flowy sleeves. With each movement, she looked like she was floating on a cloud.

"I couldn't miss yet *another* one of these dinners. I told the ladies they can meet without me. I'll catch up on the gossip another night," Marnie said with a wink. She pulled away from the embrace and gave my arms a final squeeze. "I'm going to go see if your parents need any help in the kitchen." Her voice dropped to a playful whisper. "I'll leave the mediating duties to you."

When I turned toward Cooper and Eliza, Cooper was wrapped up in conversation with Wes and Jules. I gave my full attention to my best friend. "Are you okay? What happened?" I reached over to fix her necklace, moving the clasp to the back.

"It's going to sound stupid when I say it out loud," Eliza said with a sigh. "But earlier this week, Cooper and I coordinated that I was going to drive Gran over tonight. As I was about to leave my apartment to pick her up, he texted me saying he had stopped by her house after all and that I should come straight here. And I know who drove her over doesn't matter at the end of the day. It's just...*frustrating* that he needs to have everything in his control, even if he means well. It feels like he doesn't trust me or doesn't think I'm responsible enough." Eliza ran her hands over her face, pushing her shoulder-length black hair behind her ears. "I know this time of year is hard for him, but it's hard for all of us."

I nodded, listening intently to my best friend. My heart ached for her, and while there wasn't anything I could do to change what happened, I always wanted to be there for her. "It's hard for him, but it's hard for you, too," I said softly. "And it's not stupid at all. Your reasons for being frustrated are valid, even if you can see where he's coming from. I'm glad you're not holding it in. Maybe you two could talk about it sometime this week? He might not realize the other reasons you're feeling frustrated and what it stems from."

Eliza took a deep breath, slowly exhaling. "Yeah, I think

talking is a good idea. Get on the same page. He's annoying as shit, but I hate fighting with him," she said with a laugh.

I grinned at her, knowing exactly what she meant, since I felt the same way when Wes and I argued. Our protective older brothers, who were best friends, loved control and taking care of others. Usually, it was a good thing. But there were those moments when it was too much and overbearing.

As Eliza and I were finishing our conversation, Cooper walked over, giving her a tentative smile. "I know I messed up, and I'll work on it. We good for tonight?"

She twisted her lips to the side, giving it some thought and making him sweat a little, before nodding with a smile. "Yeah, we're good. That was faster than usual to get some sense knocked into you. Was that Wes's doing?"

"Mostly Jules," Cooper said with a chuckle.

We looked over at Wes and Jules, his arm wrapped tightly around her waist. In perfect timing, Jules looked in our direction, giving us a wink.

Eliza and I grinned in return.

I wasn't sure what I'd do without Eliza and Jules. Luckily, I didn't have to find out.

The first few minutes of dinner were always quiet as everyone took their initial bites, but by the end of the meal, the conversation and laughter were bouncing off the walls. I used the back of my hand to wipe the happy tears from my eyes.

It was easy for my stress to melt away, even if it was temporary, for my shoulders to relax, and to focus my mind on *this* moment. Not on Gabriel or the uncertainty that was waiting for me on Monday.

When the conversation and laughter died down, Marnie looked across the table at me. "Lily, are you switching up the menu this week or keeping it the same? I didn't have a chance to try the cranberry orange scones, so I'm hoping they'll be back." Her eyes sparkled with amusement.

I was happy to tell her luck was on her side. "I'll be keeping it the same, so spiced gingerbread loaf and the scones. I can set some aside for you this week. Do you know when you'll come by?"

Marnie adjusted the stack of bracelets on her wrist. "Thursday, maybe? Will your new helper be there?"

So much for not thinking about Gabriel.

"Assuming he decides to stick around after the week starts" —my lips formed a tight smile—"I think he'll be there."

Marnie hummed in response. "I'm looking forward to stopping by. I heard from Louise he's very handsome."

"The girls were saying the same thing on the phone the other day," Wes chimed in. Of all moments, *of course*, he picked this one. My brother enjoyed these dinners as much as I did, but he typically spent more time listening than talking. He'd always been more introverted, and I loved that Jules brought him out of his comfort zone while also giving him a safe place to be himself.

I shot him a look that said *really?*, and he shrugged. I rolled my eyes.

Marnie looked at me expectantly, still waiting for an answer.

"I...didn't notice if he was handsome or not. I was too busy trying to figure out how to not let him steal my café."

"Dad, what happened between you and Ron Nelson, anyway?" Wes asked, and this time I didn't mind him butting in, because I was curious, too.

Our dad and Ron were best friends growing up, but the two hadn't spoken since Ron left Golden Falls, as far as we knew.

My dad picked up his cloth napkin, wiping his mouth and meeting my mom's eyes across the table. "Well," he said slowly, "Ron always wanted to get out of Golden Falls and head to the city. Any city, really. Nothing wrong with that. We kept in touch here and there while we went to different colleges, and when I got back to Golden Falls and started to think about what I wanted to do, he was the first person I called when the idea of Lake Ridge came to mind. We were going to be business partners, but I pulled back my offer when I started to realize he didn't have the town's best interests in mind. I could tell even from the beginning that it was going to be tricky to work with him, and I never had dreams to sell Lake Ridge to make it big. My focus was always to do this for the town—and for myself. Not for the money. Fortunately, it worked out because"—he looked over at Mom, creases forming at the corners of his mouth from his smile—"not long after that did I convince your mom to take a job with me. Turns out, she was the perfect partner—in more ways than one."

The conversation quickly shifted after that when my mom started to ask Cooper, who was a park ranger, what the winter season looked like for him this year.

My brows knitted together as I thought about what my dad had said. I tapped my fingers against my thigh under the table.

Ron had intentions on setting up business in Golden Falls. Had Gabriel come to town to finish the job?

From: Lily Richards <lily@purrfectblend.com>
To: Gabriel Nelson <gabriel@nelsongroup.com>
Date: Sunday, December 5, 8:22 p.m.
Subject: Tomorrow's plan

Hi Gabriel,

I wanted to get this to you sooner, but the day got away from me. For tomorrow, could you meet me at the café at seven in the morning? I can show you around and what I might need help with—that is, if you still intended on showing up? I would totally understand if you decided not to return to Golden Falls and stayed in Milwaukee.

That would be such a shame. But I bet I would find a way to survive.

- Lily

From: Gabriel Nelson <gabriel@nelsongroup.com>
To: Lily Richards <lily@purrfectblend.com>
Date: Sunday, December 5, 8:47 p.m.
Subject: Re: Tomorrow's plan

Lily,

I appreciate your concern, but luckily for you, I'm already back in town. It's nice knowing you missed me, though.

I intend on helping you and have no plans on backing out. I'll be sure to mention if anything changes during one of the many times we'll be seeing each other over the next few weeks.

- Gabe

From: Lily Richards <lily@purrfectblend.com>
To: Gabriel Nelson <gabriel@nelsongroup.com>
Date: Sunday, December 5, 9:03 p.m.
Subject: Re: Tomorrow's plan

It wasn't concern, and I didn't miss you.

And please don't remind me how many times we'll be seeing each other. I'd rather not think about you any more than I already am.

From: Gabriel Nelson <gabriel@nelsongroup.com>
To: Lily Richards <lily@purrfectblend.com>
Date: Sunday, December 5, 9:21 p.m.
Subject: Re: Tomorrow's plan

So, now you're thinking about me? At this hour? Interesting.

11

LILY

Monday

"You're early." I tried (and failed) to hide my surprise when I saw Gabriel leaning against the café's brick exterior.

He looked up, pocketing his cell phone in his coat and standing straight. "So are you."

"Well, yeah, but..." I trailed off. Of course, I was early. I *always* was.

"But you expected me to be late?" he asked, tilting his head to the side. There was a hint of something in his voice. Amusement? Frustration?

I rolled my lips, carefully thinking over my words, because I couldn't tell him the truth. That *yes*, I had expected him to be late, because neither of us wanted to be here. I thought he would push his arrival to the very last minute—not show up early. And it was *early*. I'd asked him to be here at seven, and it was six thirty. We had an hour and a half until the café opened.

"I didn't expect you to be *so* early." I settled, grabbing the keys out of my bag and unlocking the door. "How did you know I'd be early? If I wasn't here, you'd be standing for another thirty minutes, and it's chilly." I knew the winter temperatures were only going to drop, especially in January, which was typically the coldest and snowiest month in Golden Falls. By then, today's temperature in the low thirties would seem warm.

"Careful or I'll start to think you're concerned about me being out in the cold." This time I very clearly heard the amusement in his voice. I bit down on the inside of my cheek to keep from smiling.

I turned around to face him, nearly smacking him in the chest with the end of my French braid. When Gabriel realized how close we were, he took a few steps back, creating distance and tucking his hands into his pockets.

I didn't know Gabriel, nor did I like him, but I didn't feel uncomfortable being alone with him in my café. For one reason or another, Hal trusted him, and that meant something. Still, I appreciated Gabriel's awareness, because he was nearly a foot taller than me. I'd normally find his height attractive, but in this case, I didn't. For obvious reasons. At least his height was practical. He'd be able to help me get various ingredients and supplies that I typically needed a step stool or ladder for. That's the only reason I noticed.

"I'm not concerned about you," I emphasized. "I wouldn't want you to turn into a block of ice outside my café. It'd be bad for business."

"Right." He huffed a laugh.

I flicked on the lights and tied back the deep-blue curtains. I led us over to the coat rack behind the front counter. I hung my bag, and once I slipped my coat off, I hung that, too. I brushed a few loose strands of hair away from my face and adjusted the red ribbon bow at the end of my braid so the loops were even.

When I looked back at Gabriel, he was hanging his coat up, too. I hated—*absolutely hated*—how his biceps and forearms flexed in his light-blue dress shirt from the simple motion. He dropped his arms back to his sides, and I noticed his sleeves were rolled up to his elbows. His shirt was tucked into a pair of dark pants with a belt.

"So, where should we start?" he asked, snapping me out of my daze. "How's this all going to work between working at the café and completing your list?"

"I've been thinking about it, and while it's unfortunate we're stuck in this *arrangement*, I have some ideas that will hopefully make this as painless as possible." I gestured for him to follow me to the cat room. "I start off the mornings by checking on the cats. Refilling water bowls, feeding them, scooping the litter boxes, swapping out their toys." I flicked on the overhead lights, as well as the string lights along the side wall. "And petting them, *obviously*. Three of the current cats are pretty social, and then two are shy and usually find a sneaky hiding spot."

I crouched as Sugar Plum, a one-year-old gray cat who still very much looked like a kitten, spotted us and blinked slowly while walking over. Gabriel kneeled next to me, and what looked like a genuine smile came over his face.

"I thought this could be something you could help me with since you're familiar with cats," I explained. "Everything you need is in that supply closet, but if you can't find something, let me know."

Sugar Plum (how cute was that name?) went to Gabriel first, sniffing his hand and ultimately deciding he was worthy enough to pet her. She leaned her head into his touch.

"How do you know I'm familiar with cats?" he asked, raising a brow.

Shit. I kept my gaze down, trying to hide the flush creeping up my cheeks. "Oh, uh, Hal mentioned that you have a cat." He already knew I looked him up. I wasn't about to admit that I had severely creeped on his social media.

"Right," he said, drawing out the word. "Figured that was it."

I felt Gabriel's eyes on me, but I refused to look at him. We were too close in this position, anyway. If I turned my head to the side, we'd be face-to-face. *Too close.*

I stood, brushing my palms on my jeans. "As for the list, I think hiring help at the café and decorating the cat room will be the easiest to complete first. I finally looked through applications this past weekend and will try to get someone hired this week or early next. We can decorate the cat room this week, too. Then, once someone is hired, we can think through how to tackle the rest of the list. Does that work?" I asked.

"Works for me," Gabriel said—*agreeing* with me—and I heard the smile in his voice. I allowed myself to finally look at him. Instead of kneeling, he was sitting on the floor now. Sugar Plum had flopped and was rolling around on her back, showing off her fluffy belly.

"I take it she's one of the social ones?" he asked.

"No, actually." I let out a sigh. "Sugar Plum is usually more reserved."

Gabriel might've quickly gotten on Sugar Plum's good side, but it wouldn't be that easy to win me over. Impossible, even. I was stronger than that.

Having Gabriel help me with the cats allowed me to start on my café prep work earlier than usual.

I turned on the espresso machine, set up the first pot of coffee, and prepped my drink ingredients for the day before heading back to the kitchen.

I was happy with the work I'd done yesterday and how it set me up for the week. Sunday mornings were my big prep days for the week and different from a typical day at the café. Only tea and coffee were available—no specialty drinks or pastries—and it was self-serve. Jodi and Henry, two volunteers from the animal shelter, came in to help take care of the animals and brought in people who had shown interest in adopting the cats. Usually, it was people from Golden Falls or one of the surrounding small towns, but sometimes, people from all over the state saw the shelter's social media posts and fell in love with a cat.

I used the time they were here to prepare for the week ahead. I checked inventory, placed orders for supplies and ingredients, and set my baked goods menu for the week. I made dough or batter for the week in advance and kept it refrigerated. This allowed me to simply stick the batter in the oven each morning for fresh pastries.

Last week's menu of baked goods—spiced gingerbread loaf and cranberry orange scones—was a hit and quickly sold out. Like I'd told Marnie, I decided to keep it the same this week. I put two gingerbread loaves in one oven and two trays of scones in the other. Then I set two timers.

I let out a sigh, finally having a moment to breathe. I had my day-to-day routine, but it still felt overwhelming and like I didn't know what I was doing. But I'd gotten this far.

I was also trying to focus on the positives—I finally had some help. It wasn't the help I *wanted*, but it was better than having to do everything on my own.

I moved from the kitchen back to the main room of the café, the golden sun streaming through the front windows. It was easy to forget the cold weather when the sun shone brightly without a cloud in sight.

"Smells good in here already," Gabriel said as he walked in through the door between the cat room and the café.

I nodded in agreement. An awkward silence filled the air between us before I finally spoke up. "I assume you got things figured out at work for the time you'll be in Golden Falls?" I asked, leaning my hip against the counter.

"Yeah, I'll be working remotely. My boss isn't thrilled about it, but...it'll work out fine. I'll have meetings, answer emails, and keep my projects moving, but I'll be able to do that on my own schedule for the most part. I'll work evenings and such if I have to."

There were a couple of things that caught my attention. One, if he planned on being with me in the café during the day and working extra hours in the evenings, that would mean he'd literally be working the whole day. And two, boss? "You mean your dad? Don't you work with him?"

"*For* him," Gabriel muttered. "But yes, my father."

I hummed, curious about his word choice, but didn't press. His relationship with his dad—*father*—wasn't any of my business, even if I was nosy.

"Okay, well," I started. "It'd be nice to have you help with prep in the mornings and possibly taking orders during the morning rush, especially as I'm training the new employee. The rest of the day, you're welcome to do what you need for work."

"I'll be around for that, and if I need to respond to emails or calls, I'll do so from the café. So, caring for the cats, taking orders..." he listed. "I can also help you clean up."

"Yeah, that'd be great. Are you sure, though? I don't want you to spend your whole time in Golden Falls working."

He shrugged with a humorless laugh. "It's not much different than my life back in the city. Plus, it'll allow me to get to know people in town and what they're looking for in terms of new storefronts or properties."

"You seem to be confident people in town are going to be willing to talk to you."

"Over time, hopefully." He turned toward me. "I'll be here as long as it takes, Lily."

Warmth curled in my stomach at my name leaving his mouth. I stood up straight and locked my eyes with his. "You say that now, but I have a feeling you're going to leave as soon as things get tough, as soon as you realize the people in this town don't want whatever luxury high-rise or chain restaurant you want to bring in."

Gabriel scoffed. "You think that's my plan?"

"I don't care what your plan is," I said, even though I actually did care and wanted to know. "Because it doesn't matter. This building is going to be mine, and you're going to forget about Golden Falls once you leave. Don't pretend like you want to be here. You wanted this to be over in a weekend." I crossed my arms over my chest.

His jaw clenched, but his gaze didn't waver. "Don't act like you didn't want this to be over just as quickly. You don't know a damn thing about me, Lily. Don't pretend like you do."

"And you don't know a thing about me."

Our stare off was interrupted by the door opening, and the first customers of the day walked in. A shiver ran up my spine from the chill that came through the door—and from how quickly our exchange had turned ice cold.

"Let's get today over with," we both muttered.

Today and every day after that.

Tuesday

"This isn't working." Gabriel gestured toward the tablet,

although his words could've easily referred to our new partnership.

Once the café opened yesterday, we didn't talk much. Gabriel helped me with the cats, spent time working on his laptop, and then helped me clean up for the day. All with minimal conversation. Which was fine. Preferred, even.

With how things wrapped up yesterday, I wasn't sure what today would bring. When I had arrived at the café, Gabriel was leaning outside the door, waiting. *Of course*, he was early again. Show-off.

Even though it'd only been a day, Gabriel quickly picked up the routine I'd suggested. He tended to the cats, and I prepared the baked goods, as well as got the various coffee machines ready. I also spent time looking through the applications yesterday afternoon and lined up interviews for later in the week.

We had about half an hour until the café opened, and I had finished explaining to Gabriel how to use the tablet for taking orders and finding the various items on the menu. So far, things were civil.

I looked at him over my shoulder. "That's because you're not doing it how I showed you."

"I am," he argued, tapping the screen. "I'm doing exactly what you showed me." As soon as he touched it, the screen flickered black before turning on again. It was a problem I was aware of, and I knew how finicky the tablet could be. Which was why I'd perfected the pressure of how to tap the various buttons.

"Here, let me show you again," I said as he stepped to the side.

He crossed his muscular arms across his chest, watching me expectantly. I was surprised his shirt didn't rip with how it strained against his biceps. (See, show-off.)

I waited for the tablet to turn back on. "Look, you have to do it like this." I waved for him to step closer. He moved forward and uncrossed his arms.

I reached for his hand and took his pointer finger, placing it on the screen and tapping the screen with the *perfect* amount of pressure. "Tap it gently, or else it gets mad." Warmth from his touch simmered through me, which made me realize I was still holding his finger.

I immediately dropped his hand, and we both stepped back, our shoes squeaking with how quickly we moved. There was plenty of distance between us now.

Gabriel broke the silence first, clearing his throat and saying, "Lily, you need a new tablet. Say what you want, but this one is on its last leg."

I inhaled deeply, my patience suddenly thin. I didn't mind sharing about my café and how things worked, but what I did mind was him telling me what I did and didn't need, especially when he was indirectly the reason why I hadn't splurged on a new tablet yet.

"Gabriel, I very well know I need a new tablet. And I'd get one if I wasn't saving every spare dollar to buy the building that *you're* trying to take from me."

He scoffed. "Considering we're both being offered the opportunity to buy, I'm hardly taking anything from you. If you don't like the competition, you can back out. It's not too late."

I took a few steps toward him, standing in front of him with our shoes toe-to-toe. I wasn't intimidated by his presence, but I was definitely overwhelmed by it...just not in the way I expected. He towered over me, and his clean, fresh scent took over. I steeled my spine and tipped my head back to look at him. "I've said it once, and I'll say it again—I'm not backing out. I don't know why you want this building, but you don't care about Golden Falls. I'm not letting you ruin this town."

His gaze hardened. "And you think you'll be able to run this café and the building? What if Hal sells to you and it's too much?"

My jaw clenched, and I narrowed my eyes at him. He had some nerve saying these things to me. Things that I'd thought about over and over, things I was insecure about.

"You're acting awfully entitled to something that's not yours, Sunshine," he added another blow, disdain dripping from the nickname.

Sunshine. He said it like it was a bad thing. Like it left a sour taste in his mouth.

I'd show him the opposite of sunshine. I lifted my chin and squared my shoulders. "I could strangle you right now," I gritted through my teeth. Childish? Maybe. But it was the only comeback I could think of through the frustration roaring in my mind.

Unfazed, he dipped his head, his hot breath against my ear, "Too bad you can't reach."

Oh, now I really *could* strangle—

"Am I interrupting?" Louise asked, and I stepped back, setting my hand on my chest.

"Louise, when did you walk in?"

"About twenty seconds ago. Haven't been here long. I could come back, though, and stop in on my lunch break, if my grumpy boss lets me," she teased, affectionately referring to my older brother.

"No problem. No need to come back. Gabriel here can take your order. Since he's so good at using the tablet." I looked up at him with a mock-smile. "I need to get a couple of ingredients from the kitchen, so I'll be a minute."

"Wait, Lily—" he started.

"You're on your own!" I called over my shoulder.

I didn't plan on leaving him out there alone for long...but if he wanted to play, so could I.

12

GABRIEL

Wednesday

LIAM

How's it going over there?

ME

Fine.

LIAM

That was convincing.

ME

Counting down the days until I can leave.

LIAM

Because you're having such a great time but
miss me and Beans soooo much?

ME

Something like that…

Wednesdays were another of Lily's prep days, and she opened the café later than normal to allow her time to get dough and other ingredients ready for the second half of the week.

It was impressive how efficiently and strategically she ran the café. And she did it all with a smile. She found time to chat with every customer, asking about their day or what they'd been up to, as well as offering suggestions on what to order. If someone ordered a drink that was from one of her past menus, she made it for them as long as she had the ingredients. She wasn't only attentive with the customers—she was like that with the cats, too.

When she wasn't talking to someone, she was humming along to the goddamn Christmas music playing through the speakers and swaying her hips to the rhythm.

Her energy and optimism both confused and intrigued me.

Lily's personality was as sunshine as it got. Well, to everyone but me. It meant she had an edge, and I liked that. I got more amusement than I wanted to from her witty comebacks and sharp tongue.

Admittedly, we had a rough start, and I knew some of my comments weren't helping, but I couldn't help it. Something about getting under Lily's skin made me feel alive, exhilarated... and I hadn't felt that in a long time. Especially during this time of year.

For most people, the Christmas explosion inside the café likely brightened their mood. For me? I couldn't stand it.

I'd never been a big fan of Christmas. It was hard to enjoy the holidays growing up, because my parents were either arguing or ignoring the holidays all together. It wasn't uncommon for my mother to jet off on a vacation with her friends or for my father to be working. When most of my friends were surrounded by their families, I was alone, and I felt like I couldn't tell anyone about it, because how pathetic would that sound? The time or two I did bring it up with my parents it went about how you'd expect. My mother ignored me and found her phone to be more interesting, and my father rolled his eyes, muttering something about how I had to *grow up* and that *work didn't stop for fucking Christmas.*

Growing up, the few good memories I had during this time of year were waiting for the annual card from Hal and Vera. I remember being so excited to tear the envelope open. That was a memory I hadn't thought about much until getting into town. It was hard not to think about how different my life could have been if I was able to spend more time with Hal and Vera. If maybe I'd come to Golden Falls sooner.

The last couple of years, Liam invited me to spend Christmas with his family, but I always felt like I'd be intruding, even if he insisted I wouldn't be. I never felt like I fit in around this time of year. Being in Golden Falls—in this café— constantly reminded me of that.

But I meant what I said about seeing this through. I was serious about staying.

That wasn't to say I didn't feel on edge being in town. I did. There had been a lot of curious glances and whispering during my time in Golden Falls so far. At least they were no longer glaring, or taking photos...as far as I could see.

Those who had spoken to me had been polite but wary. The small talk had been limited to how long I'd be in Golden Falls, what I thought about the town, and how wonderful Lily was. They didn't *ask* if I thought Lily was wonderful—they told me. If it were up to this town, I know without a doubt they would choose for her to own the building, which made me wonder even more why Hal brought me into this.

There had been a couple of residents, like Louise, who had been more welcoming and receptive to conversation. I hoped to keep building on those connections, and ultimately, talking more openly about the building and what residents envisioned for the space.

Yes, I had my ideas and a few proposals in mind, but none of that mattered if it didn't match up with what the residents wanted. I needed to build up the rapport and then see if they'd be willing to hear out my ideas.

I finished refilling the cats' bowls with dry food and started to pet Sugar Plum. The gray cat from my first day was quickly wiggling her way into my heart. I wasn't sure how Lily worked here and didn't adopt every cat.

After giving Sugar Plum and the other cats lots of head scratches, I stood. I wanted to check in with Lily before I pulled out my computer for the day. Earlier, she'd said she wouldn't need much help since it was a prep day and customers weren't coming in until later.

The café was quiet, which meant the Christmas music cut through the silence like nails on a chalkboard. When I stepped into the café area, I saw Lily cleaning the various machines. As expected, she was rocking her hips side to side in rhythm, her blonde hair—which was pulled into a ponytail—swaying with her.

I approached the counter slowly, her presence annoyingly hypnotizing, and cleared my throat before saying, "Cats are all taken care of. Do you want me to help with that so you can start on prep?" I asked, tipping my chin toward the espresso maker she was cleaning.

"Oh, uh, yeah, that'd be great." Her voice was hesitant, like she wasn't sure if she could believe me—or trust me.

She shouldn't.

"Would you be able to wipe the counters down, too, when you're done? And then after that, I think you can head out for the day."

I took the dish towel from her and nodded. "Yeah, I can do that, but I don't mind sticking around for the afternoon. I might need to make a couple of calls, but I'll step outside for those."

"Okay, thanks." She chewed on her bottom lip, rocking on the heels of her feet. "If you need a quieter place, you can head up to my apartment. It's on the second floor of this building. Let me know, and I can grab you the key if you have calls or meetings when it's too loud in here."

I stilled, surprised by her offer. I found myself wondering what her apartment looked like. Would it be as festive as the café? Did she have photos of her friends and family? Was it neat and tidy? Messy? My apartment in Milwaukee was practical, but I had to believe Lily's had warmth and felt like a home.

I quickly shook my head. "There's no need for that." I didn't want to know Lily or where she lived. That wasn't why I was here.

I removed a few items from the espresso machine, bringing them over to the sink and rinsing them with warm water. I'd watched Lily do it on Monday and felt like I had the hang of it. I thought she'd gone back to the kitchen already, so her voice took me by surprise. And so did her question.

"Do you prefer to go by Gabe or Gabriel?" she asked, breaking the silence between us.

My brows furrowed. Oddly enough, no one had asked me that, besides Liam. They just assumed, which I'd never minded, but it felt...nice to have someone ask.

I held back the comment that, in a way, my parents had ruined my name for me. But hearing my name come from Lily's lips? That was a whole other story. Probably better if she refrained from using my name altogether.

"Uh, I guess I don't mind too much either way, but Gabe is typically what I prefer with people I know. It's a little less formal." I glanced over my shoulder and saw her nod.

"Okay, yeah, I'll call you Gabe, then. Sorry I've been calling you Gabriel."

I shrugged, dismissing her apology. "Nothing to be sorry about. It's still my name."

"Gabe," she said my name carefully, like she was testing it out. An unfamiliar rush coursed through my body, sending a jolt of electricity throughout my veins. What was that feeling? "I guess we do *sort of* know each other. Not very well, though."

"No, not very well at all," I agreed with a sigh. It was better if we didn't know each other and kept this distance between us.

Lily leaned her hip against the counter, tilting her head to the side as she watched me. I tried to ignore her, focusing on my hands, on the warm water, on literally anything but her.

"Do you enjoy working with your dad? Hal mentioned you want to be working on other projects."

My spine stiffened at the unexpected question and the fact that she'd caught that during our meeting. In the few days we'd known each other, we hadn't broached *real* topics. This wasn't what we talked about. We talked about the building and how neither of us wanted to be in this situation—safe conversations.

I wiped my hands on the dish towel before turning toward her. There was something in her blue eyes that made me want to trust her, to tell her everything. But I couldn't.

This was business. Just business. It had to stay that way. We shouldn't get to know each other.

"What are you doing?" I asked, my voice coming out more frustrated than I would've liked.

"I was—" she started, and I quickly shook my head.

"Let's not pretend we want to get to know each other. You don't care about the answer, and we don't need to waste time making conversation."

As soon as the words left my mouth, I regretted them immediately. Because the hurt that flashed over her expression looked genuine—and I hated that I sounded exactly like my bastard father.

"Lily, I didn't—" I tried to pivot from what happened, but it was too late.

Now, it was her turn to cut me off. "No, you're right." She pushed off the counter, any emotion on her face gone. "Let's not pretend." With that, Lily turned and walked away.

I stared at the space she'd been standing long after she'd left, replaying the conversation in my head and how it would've been better if I said *literally* anything else.

I could've stopped her. Insisted that I didn't mean it. That maybe we *could* get to know each other, especially with all the time we'd be spending together.

But I didn't do any of that. Even though I didn't know her well, I was smart enough to know that getting close to Lily Richards was dangerous.

13

LILY

Thursday

THE CONSTANT CHATTER, LAUGHTER, AND WHIR OF THE COFFEE machine was music to my ears. It meant people were happy in my café, enjoying each other's company, in addition to their drinks or pastries. Jules had stopped by earlier today to conduct a client meeting for her interior design firm Campbell Creations. It had been nice to see her during a busy week at work.

After interviewing a few candidates, I decided to hire Tiffany, who moved to Golden Falls about a year ago with her husband and five-year-old twins.

I'd gotten to know Tiffany and her family well over the last few months, and we got along well. She often popped into Purrfect Blend with her kids in the afternoons.

Tiffany had owned her own café before having kids but had sold it when life got busy. Now that her son and daughter were a little older, and her husband wasn't traveling as much for work, she wanted to get back to her career. She wasn't interested in opening her own business but wanted to find a job in the service industry, and when she saw that I was looking for help at Purrfect Blend, she thought it would be a great fit.

I agreed.

I couldn't wait for her to get started. I was going to take time this weekend to finalize onboarding materials and how to ease her into the routine here, which was honestly easier after going through a similar process with Gabe. Tiffany would mostly be helping me make and serve drinks, but she had a background in baking, too. I couldn't wait to learn from her and have the help.

It would be one thing checked off the list—and one step closer to Gabe leaving Golden Falls.

I was busy making a toasted marshmallow chai for Layla, who owned Golden Finds Thrift Store and was one of my regulars, when I heard the door to Purrfect Blend open louder than usual.

Marnie sure knew how to make an entrance. Not only that, but her hands were filled with bags of groceries. Why would she get groceries and *then* come here?

I was about to walk around the counter to help her when a mischievous smile crossed her lips. I stayed right where I was, confused.

But then, when I saw Gabe walking over from the table he was sitting at and asking Marnie if she needed help, I had a feeling about what she was doing. I rolled my eyes with a shake of my head.

"Oh, why thank you for your help. Gabriel, right?" Marnie asked as Gabe took the groceries from her hands. I'd seen Marnie carry twice as many grocery bags without any problems—even refusing help, for that matter.

"Of course. And just Gabe is fine. Did you want to sit at one of the tables or up by the coffee bar?"

Marnie locked eyes with me, sending me a wink. "Let's go up to the coffee bar. I need to say hi to my dear Lily."

Layla glanced over her shoulder then leaned in to whisper, "That's Gabe Nelson?"

"Sure is." I sighed. "I'm sure you've heard about the whole building thing." I waved my hand. "He's helping me out at the café for the time being while Hal figures out what's next."

She hummed in thought. "Okay, but not a bad deal..." She trailed off, biting down on her bottom lip before looking at me. "He's *really* handsome. No wonder Louise and her friends are fawning over him."

While residents overall were still wary of Gabe, the older ladies in town were definitely the most intrigued. Turned out, Gabe made a better impression on Louise than I realized. And now with people seeing how helpful he was being to Marnie, that was only going to get him more points. What was his game here?

"He's average looking," I lied to Layla.

She raised her brows without a second thought, calling my bluff immediately, but I didn't budge.

"Did you see the latest article? Nelson Group is proposing another high-rise in Milwaukee. I don't want them anywhere near this building." I finished making Layla's drink and snapped the lid on the cup before handing it to her.

An article in the *Milwaukee Times* popped up on my phone this morning about the first round of proposals that were submitted to the city for redeveloping a vacant warehouse. There was still time to submit additional proposals, especially because the council member quoted made it sound like the common council wasn't all that intrigued by the ideas. It was more of the same, including a mixed-use development with luxury apartments from Nelson Group.

She took the cup from me, giving me a *duh* look. "Obviously, I want you to own the building. You'd be amazing at it, and you know this town better than anyone. Just saying your competition isn't too bad to look at." Layla brought the cup to her lips. She hummed in delight. I also prided myself on making drinks that were the right temperature to take a sip of right away. "Delicious as always. Thanks, Lily. I'll see ya next week, if not sooner."

On her way out, Layla greeted Marnie and introduced herself to Gabe. He gave her a polite smile before nodding for Marnie to follow him over to the counter.

"Why don't I put these back in the kitchen for you?" Gabe offered. "It'll be better than setting the bags on the floor."

"Why thank you, Gabe. I'd really appreciate that. Once you're done, make sure to come right back. I'd like to get to know you better." Marnie pulled out a stool and made herself comfortable.

"You got it. I'll be right back."

Once Gabe was gone and out of earshot, I crossed my arms over my chest and gave Marnie a pointed look. "Marnie, you know I love you, but what do you think you're doing?"

"What do you mean?" she asked innocently, taking off her coat and setting it over her lap. While her tweed coat was a dark gray, the clothes Marnie wore underneath were loud and bright. She had on a flowery blouse with embroidered jeans and a pair of suede winter boots. Her nails were painted blue with tiny snowflakes to match her earrings of the day—also snowflakes.

"You're fraternizing with the enemy!" I whispered with wide eyes. "That whole grocery bags thing was a test."

"It sure was," she confirmed matter-of-factly, her attention quickly going to the pink bakery box with her name on it that I'd set aside. "And he passed."

I picked up the box and handed it to her, along with a small plate. "What do you mean?"

"As soon as he saw me, he got up. No hesitation."

I twisted my lips to the side as I realized Marnie was right. I turned around to fill a mug with hot water and grabbed three different types of tea for her to choose from. "Okay, yeah," I said, confused, "but that doesn't mean anything. Anyone would have helped you."

Marnie reached over for the mug and tea, thanking me. Her ring-clad fingers picked up the peppermint tea bag and tore the wrapping. "Because they know me. He doesn't, and he helped without expecting anything in return. That doesn't come out of nowhere. Your enemy might not be as bad as you think."

My stomach flipped, that same inkling of guilt I felt when I was talking to my mom gnawing at me. Was I being unfair to Gabe? I was trying to be confident and stand my ground—this was my café—especially after our brief interaction yesterday. He didn't want to be friendly. That much was obvious.

When it came to Gabe, I was in an impossible position. My first instinct was to be nice. To avoid conflict. To be agreeable.

But I didn't want to do any of that, and it was clear he didn't want that from me either.

I had worked my ass off to prove to Hal that I could handle owning the building. So, the fact that Gabe was here for the first time in his life as a contender for the building frustrated me. But it also felt wrong not to hear him out and to automatically have all these assumptions about him.

My grumpy older brother had acted similarly when Jules first came to town over the summer, and I'd scolded him for it.

Marnie dipped the tea bag into the hot water, a patient smile on her face as she waited for me to come out of my thoughts. "I know it's an unfair situation you're in, but maybe some good will come out of it."

I looked toward the kitchen as Gabe came back into the main room and started striking up a conversation with Marnie.

I wanted to believe Marnie. I trusted her.

But I didn't trust Gabe, and I didn't think I ever would.

Sunday

After the third heavy exhale from the other room, I peeked my head around the corner to see if the person was okay. When I saw Gabe pinching the bridge of his nose, my pulse picked up and my chest tightened. My first thought was that something was wrong, either with him or Hal.

"What's wrong?" The question came out quickly, and his shoulders jumped from surprise.

He looked at me, puzzled. "Should something be wrong?"

I exhaled in half-relief. If something *was* wrong, then that wouldn't have been his response. But the response he gave me didn't give me insight into what was going through his mind.

Reluctantly, I approached the table he was at, pulling out a chair and sitting. "I don't know," I said with a gentle laugh. "You tell me. You're the one sitting here sighing every couple seconds."

We didn't do this—we didn't talk or ask how the other was doing. We said our *good mornings*, our *see you tomorrows*, and the usual comments about the weather. *Oh, it wouldn't be so bad out there if it wasn't for the wind.*

But since I'd asked him if he liked working with his dad, we hadn't talked about anything real.

He let out a chuckle, resting his forearms on the table and looking up at me. "I honestly didn't realize I was doing that. I guess..." he started but stopped. He drummed his fingers on the table.

While he contemplated if he wanted to tell me, I stayed quiet, wanting to give him the space to decide.

"It's nothing," he said ultimately. "It's stupid. I'm over-thinking it and being too sensitive."

Initially, I wasn't going to push him, but I didn't like the way he dismissed his own feelings. "It's not stupid. Something's clearly on your mind. I mean, you don't have to tell me, obviously, but don't dismiss it."

Something I couldn't pinpoint flashed in his eyes, like he'd heard those words for the first time in this very moment. Gabe was right when he'd said we didn't know each other. Did I have him all wrong?

His throat bobbed as he swallowed. "Sugar Plum was adopted."

Understanding dawned on me. While I didn't want to admit it, seeing Gabe interacting with the cats every morning and afternoon was among the highlights of my day. He was so gentle and patient with them, and I knew from the first day that he and Sugar Plum had formed a quick bond.

"I didn't realize that. Jodi usually gives me an update, but I haven't seen her yet."

"See, I told you it was stupid. I've known that cat for...what? Less than a week? I shouldn't get so attached."

"It's tricky," I admitted. "It took me a while to find a balance of bonding with the cats but also being excited when they find a home, and even then, it's not foolproof. She was really social around you, and maybe that's why she got adopted today," I offered. I hadn't been exaggerating when I told Gabe earlier this week that Sugar Plum was one of the shy cats. She normally hid under the couch or behind one of the bookshelves until it was just me in the cat room. This week, she'd been roaming around, especially when Gabe entered.

"Here," I said, getting up, "let me take a look at the paperwork and see who adopted her." I walked to the counter, flipping through the stack of papers until I saw Sugar Plum's application. "Tom and Susan adopted her. They're two regulars. I'll introduce you next time they stop in." I set down the paper and walked back to the table Gabe was sitting at. "Their youngest daughter recently went off to college, and it's the two of them now. They have two cats—well, three now, I guess—and a dog. I think Sugar Plum will like it there, especially since she's good with other animals, even if it might take her a little bit to warm up to them. And Tom and Susan are *so* nice. If you asked to stop by to say hi, they would one hundred percent let you." The corner of my lips tipped up in a smile. "Something tells me you like cats more than people, huh?"

A laugh escaped him, a smile staying on his face as he looked up at me. Light returned to his honey-brown eyes, a sparkle I hadn't noticed before. "I guess I do sometimes. It's easier to interact with them than some of the people in town. The cats don't have preconceived notions of me. They just see me as the person who brings them food."

I twisted my lips to the side as his words set in. Everyone in town had their thoughts about Gabe, including me, but we didn't really know him. That couldn't have been an easy situation to walk into. I wanted to bring that up, but I also didn't want to ruin this moment. We were finally having what felt like a real conversation. I settled on a light-hearted response. "And if you don't bring their food, they'll scream at you to make it clear that's what they want."

"Exactly." Gabe chuckled. He ran his fingers through his hair and rubbed the back of his neck. "Thanks, Lily. I really appreciate you taking the time to see if I was okay. I...didn't realize it until now, but I needed that."

I nodded. "Of course. I'm glad I could help." I rolled my lips.

"I'm going to see if Jodi needs anything before I close up. Feel free to head out whenever."

I started to make my way toward the cat room, my hand pressed against the door. In a split-second decision, I turned around. There was something I wanted to tell him before I second-guessed it. "What you felt and the reason for it wasn't stupid. It means you care."

I pushed the door open, quickly walking away before he could reply.

I had a feeling Gabe cared a lot more than he let on. I wasn't sure why he hid it. Or why I wanted to find out.

14

GABRIEL

After finishing at Purrfect Blend, I returned to Hal's. He'd given me my own key, so coming in and out of the house was easy. Or, rather, sneaking in and out of the house, because I was doing my best to avoid him and the small talk.

I was grateful he was letting me stay with him, but what were we going to do? Catch up on however many years in the span of a month? I had no interest in doing that. Me being here was for business, and this visit was already taking up way more of my time than I anticipated.

We had a few interactions throughout the week, mostly in the evenings when Hal was back from the store, but our conversation was often cut short by a work call I needed to take.

I wasn't sure what Hal typically did on Sundays, but I doubted he'd be home. I easily turned the key in the lock and pushed the door open. I slipped off my shoes and unzipped my coat, my mind wandering to my conversation with Lily right before I left. How she validated what I was feeling when she didn't need to. She didn't need to check on me, but she did. It made me feel even more shitty for what I'd said to her earlier in the week.

What you felt and the reason for it wasn't stupid. It means you care.

Her words were so simple but impacted me so deeply—especially when my whole life I'd been told the opposite. That I wasn't supposed to care. That what I was feeling didn't matter. That I should suck it up and move on.

I let out a heavy sigh, rubbing my eyes as I walked to the kitchen. It wasn't until I heard Hal's voice that I realized he was home, sitting at the table.

"I thought I heard the door open," he said, setting down his pen. He'd been working on a crossword puzzle. "Why don't you come over and have a seat. I made a fresh pot of coffee."

I swallowed the lump in my throat, trying to quickly come up with an excuse as to why I couldn't.

"Come on," he encouraged. "For a few minutes. It's Sunday. No work calls should be popping up today, and if they do, they can wait until tomorrow."

I hesitated but ultimately agreed. "Sure, just a few minutes." I glanced over and didn't see a mug on the table yet, so I grabbed two from the cabinet. I never thought it was too late for coffee, and it seemed like Hal agreed. After filling each mug, I set them on the kitchen table and pulled out the chair to sit across from Hal. "I guess I'm not sure how you take your coffee," I admitted. "Should I grab some cream or sugar?"

Hal waved his hand. "No need. This is great. Thanks, Gabe."

Since we were both here, maybe this would be a decent time to bring up the building. Try to see if I could gain some insight into his plans to sell. "I was wondering about the building—"

Hal shook his head and cleared his throat. "Let's avoid talking about the building. You're in town, and I'd like to hear more about what you've been up to."

Avoid talking about the building? But...that was the whole

reason I was here. "Avoid talking about the building *today*? Or..." I trailed off.

Hal tilted his head, thinking, before answering, "How about until the end of the month. I'd like to use this time to get to know my grandson and the man you've become. I won't have any updates for you until you and Lily get through the list, anyway. Tell me more about living in Milwaukee, your friends, what you enjoy doing when you're not working." He brought the mug up to his lips, taking a sip and watching me expectantly.

So much for only being here a few minutes. It seemed like we'd be here a while, so I got comfortable in the chair and wrapped my hand around the mug, using the warmth to center me. "Well," I started, "I have an apartment in the city and live with my cat Beans. My good friend Liam is watching him while I'm here, actually. Liam was never much of a cat person, but the two of them are bonding with the time they've spent together." I pulled my phone out of my pocket and pulled up a photo of Beans. It wasn't hard to find one, considering that was practically my whole camera roll.

Hal leaned over, sliding his glasses on his nose. A smile quickly appeared on his face. "He's adorable. I never had house cats growing up, but we had plenty of barn cats. Smart creatures. And when you're not working? What do you like doing?"

"It's—well, I don't have much free time with work, but Liam and I usually go out to dinner once a week for burgers. Our favorite spot has these retro pinball machines that we'll sometimes play, even if we're not very good. I'll throw on a movie sometimes or go for a walk along the water." I scrolled through my photos. "This is the view from my apartment, and there's a nice trail nearby that takes you along the shoreline of Lake Michigan."

"That's a great view." Hal nodded in agreement, scooting his chair closer to me.

I swiped to another photo. This time it was an event I went to with Liam. "Liam's company does a fundraiser every year, and he saved me a seat at his table. Dinner was a whole multi-course thing, and I had to get some photos. The food was incredibly good—the best meal I've had."

"No kidding. Looks amazing. Then again, anything from a restaurant or event does, especially since I'm not much of a cook."

"What are your favorite restaurants in town? Any place I need to check out?" I asked.

"Oh, most definitely." Hal grinned and reached over for a scrap of paper. "Here. I'll write down a few for you to check out and my favorite thing to order, so you have an idea."

I watched as Hal started to make a short list, and I found that I was looking forward to trying his favorite spots.

I wasn't sure how long we sat at the kitchen table going through photos and sharing stories, but I enjoyed myself more than I thought I would.

15

GABRIEL

Monday

I hadn't been able to stop thinking about my conversation with Lily or my whole last week with her. We would take one step forward but then two or three steps back. Part of it was that I didn't want to get close to her. We also didn't trust each other.

And yet, here I was at the café, ready for another week. I'd developed somewhat of a routine in the short time I'd been in Golden Falls. I helped Lily get the café ready, helped with the initial rush, got my own work done and answered any calls or meetings, and then helped her clean up for the day. I was ready to do it all again as she brought on her new hire Tiffany, whose first day was today. She should be arriving any minute.

I'd already taken care of the cats for the morning and was standing at the counter, trying to power on the goddamn tablet. I was getting more used to the very delicate pressure I had to use to tap the various buttons to take people's orders. Soon, my time in Golden Falls would mainly be used to help complete Lily's list, so I wanted to use this next week at the café to build upon the handful of relationships with residents I was forming and to strike up more conversations with people, if they were willing.

Lily came out of the kitchen, bringing out a tray of chocolate crinkle cookies and a warm, sweet scent with her. I couldn't tell if it was the cookies or *her*. I didn't have much of a sweet tooth, but...I was starting to second-guess it.

Lily organized the cookies on a glass platter, right next to the slices of chocolate peppermint loaf. Her menu this week, including the specialty drinks, was all about chocolate.

She carefully placed and adjusted each item, leaning back slightly to take a look from farther away. She tilted her head to the side, biting down on her lip as she focused.

I swallowed and turned back to the tablet, shaking my head slightly to get any thoughts of Lily out of my mind. But that was tough to do when her sweet scent was fucking *everywhere*.

"Gabe?"

"Yeah?" I asked, keeping my gaze focused on the tablet. When she didn't respond right away, I looked over at her. She was facing me and looking down, fiddling with the hem of her apron.

"I, uh, I wanted to talk to you about something," she stammered, trying to find the words. "I haven't been able to stop thinking about it, and I wanted to clear things up."

I stilled. "Is everything okay?" My brows drew together. I wanted to take a step toward her—but I used every ounce of restraint to stay right where I was.

"I just...I've been thinking about what you said. About how I've been acting entitled, and I wanted to apologize that it came off that way."

Guilt twisted in my stomach. I remembered that conversation clearly. How our bickering about the building turned into me saying something I didn't truly believe and regretted immediately.

"You don't have to apologize," I assured her.

"I want to. And I hope it helps you understand where I'm coming from." Lily rocked on the balls of her feet, her fingers now wrapped around the dainty charm on her necklace as she pulled it side to side. "I don't think I'm entitled to the building. I know that it's Hal's choice, and I'm grateful he's even considering selling to me. I just saw this all going differently. I've talked about the building to him, and I thought he was going to sell to me. I love Golden Falls, but I often feel underestimated in one way or another, whether it's people in town still seeing me as a kid or me comparing my success to my siblings'. I've always felt like I have something to prove, regardless of if that's actually the case."

Lily's words cut deep in my chest, and while our experiences were different, I understood having something to prove better than she likely realized.

"And I *know* we agreed not to get to know each other, but I needed to get that off my chest. I needed you to know that my issue is with the situation, not necessarily with you." Lily's gaze moved from the floor up to me, and her mouth tipped up. "Although, I'm not crazy about you being here, the extra set of hands has been nice. So, thank you. It means a lot that you're showing up."

I swallowed the lump in my throat. "Thanks for sharing that with me. I shouldn't have said that to you, and that's not how I see you." I leaned against the counter, my hands gripping the edge to keep myself propped up—and again to prevent myself from taking a step toward her. "You've built something for yourself here, Lily. Something that you're proud of and that adds value to the community—not everyone can say that. Try to remember that perspective next time you doubt yourself or feel like you have something to prove."

I let out a heavy sigh, running a hand over my face. I knew I didn't need to, but I wanted to share something in return. I shifted my gaze from her to the floor, knowing if I kept my eyes on her, I'd hold back. "Last week you asked me if I enjoyed working with my father," I said. "I don't. Not even a little bit. My relationship with him is the most strained it's ever been, and the more I think about it, I don't think it ever was a *normal* relationship. I've spent my whole life trying to prove myself to him, and it's never enough. I don't think it will ever be enough."

Lily took a few steps forward, leaning her hip against the counter next to me. She was closer, but there was still distance between us.

I turned to the side to face her. "I'm not trying to take away what you're going through, but I want you to know that I get it, in a way. That I understand what it's like to have to prove yourself. But I also want you to understand how much you've accomplished. I mean, look at this place." I gestured at our surroundings. "Look at what you've created."

Lily followed my movement, her eyes slowly taking it all in. But when she turned back to me to speak, it wasn't about the café. "People in your life shouldn't be making you feel that way. I know that makes it sound like it's simple—and I understand it's not—but people in your life should be supporting you, not tearing you down."

"And I have those people, too." My best friend Liam came to mind immediately. And...Hal. I wasn't necessarily close with him, but I couldn't deny that he'd supported me, even if I hadn't realized until now how much.

But I knew what Lily was getting at. That it shouldn't be my family—*my parents*—making me feel this way.

"What Hal said during our meeting, about your passions for sustainability and community development. That's what you want to be working on?"

I nodded. "That's what I thought I'd be working on when my

father hired me. I've pitched countless ideas to him, but it's never the right time or the right idea. Really, what he means is there's not enough money involved. That's what it's always been about for him."

It was the most open Lily and I had been with each other. The most open I'd been with someone new in a long time.

"He hired you knowing what you wanted to work on and hasn't been letting you move forward with your ideas?" Lily asked, her brows knitting together. When I nodded, she said, "That's...that's so frustrating."

I appreciated that she didn't apologize for my situation, and that she acknowledged it for what it was. Although, hearing her say it out loud made me realize how fucking miserable it sounded.

"And you can't leave?"

I ran a hand through my hair, tugging on the strands. "It's complicated," I settled on, not ready to get into specifics. But even without the details, Lily picked up on at least part of what I was grappling with.

"Yeah, I can see how. You'd have to step away from working with your dad and start over, I'm assuming. You shouldn't have to be in a position where you have to do that if you don't want to."

It was on the tip of my tongue to tell her how this building could turn my career around—or at least, how I thought it could —but I held back. Maybe I'd tell her another time when it felt right, but I didn't want it to seem like I had opened up to her to get her on my side on why I should own the building. I opened up to her because I wanted to. Because it felt right.

We were still on opposing sides and wanted the same thing, but maybe spending time with each other would be smoother if we actually knew more about the other.

"I'm sorry, too," I offered. "For calling you entitled. I regretted it as soon as I said it. And I'm also sorry that we didn't have the best first impression."

"It sure was something, wasn't it?" The corner of her lips twitched. "Well, it's behind us now. We're starting fresh...as two people who have to get through a winter wish list?" She tilted her head, her voice rising an octave with her words coming out more like a question. "Whatever our situation is, it's strange, but we're making it work."

"Yeah, we are," I agreed.

"Hey, I accidentally made an extra of these."

I stopped typing at the sound of Lily's voice and tore my attention away from my laptop screen as she set the mug in front of me. The café was quiet, with most customers having left for the day since Lily was about half an hour from closing.

"Would you like it? It's a peppermint mocha, also known as a Peppermint Paws. Otherwise, I'll likely have to dump it since we're about to close for the day and I've already had enough caffeine."

I lowered my laptop screen and eyed the drink. The mug was white and had a drawing of a cat surrounded by holiday lights with *Merry Catmas* in cursive writing. I couldn't quite see the drink with the mountain of whipped cream.

"Peppermint Paws," I said slowly, the corner of my lips twitching up, fighting a smile. "Did you poison it?"

She twisted her lips to the side to hide her smile. "I didn't, but I'll keep that in mind for next time. I can even take a sip of it to prove it to you."

My lips quirked, and I gestured toward the cup. "Please. It'll give me peace of mind."

She rolled her eyes with a laugh, picking up the mug carefully so the liquid wouldn't spill over the sides. Lily brought the mug to her lips for a careful sip. She set the mug back on the plate and pushed it toward me. "See, delicious. Plus, poisoning you with coffee would be too obvious, since I'd be the first suspect."

I huffed. "You're right. I'd be disappointed, too. I'd expect something more creative from you. Oh, you have"—I gestured toward her mouth and reached over to grab a napkin—"whipped cream on your lip."

Her tongue darted out to catch it, and I stifled a laugh as she failed.

"Hold still," I murmured as I stood from my seat. With one hand holding the napkin, I wiped the bit of whipped cream off her lip. My other hand likely should've stayed at my side, but...I cupped the side of her face, my fingers ever so slightly in her hair.

We were close, *too close.*

I wanted to search her face, get lost in her bright-blue eyes, stare at her strawberry lips, or the delicate slope of her nose. But I couldn't. Because if I looked...I didn't think I'd be able to look *away.*

"Thanks," she said breathlessly.

I cleared my throat and stepped back, knocking into the table and nearly spilling the drink over. I reached out to still the wobbling surface. "Yeah, no problem."

"I'll go ahead and toss this for you." She grabbed the napkin from my hand, her fingertips gently grazing mine. "I'll, uh, likely stay behind a little longer to clean up, so feel free to leave once you're done. I'll see you tomorrow?"

I nodded. "Yeah, see you tomorrow."

I sat back at the table, wanting to finish up the email I'd been writing, but I couldn't tear my eyes away from her as she moved around the café. It was only when she'd made her way to the kitchen that I looked back at my screen.

I wasn't much of a sweets guy, especially when it came to drinks, but how could I say no? Plus, it was one drink. I picked up the mug, inhaling the smell of chocolate and peppermint. I took a sip from the spot where her lips had been and hummed in approval.

Delicious, warm, and sweet. The perfect temperature, too.

As I sipped on the drink and the sweetness hit my tongue, the only thing I could think of was the bright-eyed blonde in the other room who likely tasted sweeter than anything in this café.

16

LILY

Tuesday

"Need help?" Gabe asked.

The only way I knew it was him was by his voice, because my vision was obstructed by the two plastic bins of Christmas decorations I was carrying. Yes, even after I decorated my apartment, I still had two bins of unused decor... Don't judge me.

Gabe and I were checking off the second thing on my winter wish list by decorating the cat room while my new employee Tiffany closed up. Today had only been Tiffany's second day, but she was catching on quickly given her experience. I appreciated hearing her suggestions and things she'd done with her own café as ideas on how to streamline work at Purrfect Blend.

"No, I got it. I can carry these on my own," I responded, about to take another step forward toward the cat room.

"I know you can carry them on your own, but I'm offering to help anyway. To let you know that you don't *have* to do it on your own." Not giving me a chance to respond, Gabe lifted the top bin, which immediately lightened my load. "Lead the way." He tipped his chin toward the door to the cat room.

I did my best not to read too much into his words and actions, or what they stirred within me. I wasn't great at asking for help, but I was trying to be better about it, especially since Tiffany and Gabe were both helping in their own ways.

I didn't argue with him and instead pushed open the door to the cat room with my shoulder and set the plastic bin in the middle of the room. Gabe did the same. A few of the cats walked over to greet us and investigate what was in the boxes. I walked over to the supply closet and pulled out three cardboard gingerbread houses for the cats that needed to be assembled. The houses would be a spot for the cats to sleep but also act as scratching pads.

Once I was back by Gabe, who ensured each of the cats got a proper greeting from him, I set my hands on my hips and surveyed the task ahead, one I was really excited about. I regularly decorated the main café space depending on the season, but this was the first year I had time to do the same to the cat room.

"Okay, so, I was thinking we keep the decorations simple and out of reach of the cats." I knew if we tried to set up a plastic tree, even if it was small, the cats would be chewing on the branches, trying to knock off the ornaments, or trying to climb it. Possibly even all of the above. "There's three gingerbread cat houses to assemble, some decorations to place, and lights to hang up. I think for the decorations we can set them up on the shelves so they're out of reach. What do you think about that?"

"Sounds fine to me," Gabe said while petting Blaze, one of the orange tabby cats. He had more enthusiasm about saying hi to the cats than decorating for the holidays. "Tell me what you need me to do so we can get this over with." He sighed.

"We're supposed to be having *fun* while completing the list," I reminded him, even though I didn't disagree with his desire to get this over with as quickly as possible. I unlatched the lid and opened the bin, revealing the string lights, decorations, and tiny paper Santa hats I'd made.

"I'm not big into decorating for the holidays." Gabe reached for the Santa hats—which were red construction paper with white cotton balls as pom-poms—and held them up. The corner of his mouth twitched, as if he was fighting a smile. "What are these?"

"Those"—I tried to snatch the hats out of his grasp, but he lifted his arm so I couldn't reach—"are Santa hats to put on the pictures of the cats." On the wall near the door, I had photos of each of the cats who were in the room and ready for adoption, along with their names.

"When in the world did you have time to make these?" Gabe asked, brows shooting up to his forehead. I couldn't tell if he was impressed or dismissive. I settled on the latter, because there was *no way* Gabe thought I was impressive, and certainly not for making Santa hats.

"I made time, because if we're going to decorate this room, it's going to be perfect," I replied, letting out another huff. "Now, will you give them back to me?"

Gabe took another look at the hats and handed me the stack. He shifted his attention to the string lights. "I'll start untangling these." As soon as Gabe picked up the tangled lights, the cats ran over, pawing and jumping at the strand dangling from his hands. Maybe Gabe wasn't a fan of decorating for the holidays, but it was clear that being around the cats calmed him for one reason or another, because the smile that came across his face was...devastating.

"I must be dreaming, because I didn't realize you knew how to smile," I commented, a light-hearted teasing in my tone. When he let out a low chuckle, I added, "Or laugh."

"What? So now you've been dreaming about me, Sunshine?"

My cheeks heated, and I quickly shook my head with a scoff,

turning my back to him to gather my composure. I hadn't been dreaming about Gabe—I really hadn't!—but it was the way he'd said it. His voice low, suggestive, whether he meant to say it that way or not. "No, of course not. If you were in my dream—which for the record, you're not—it would be more of a nightmare."

When I looked at Gabe over my shoulder, his smile had widened to a grin. I ignored the way my knees buckled and how I liked the sight more than I wanted to admit.

It didn't take us long to get the cat room festive for the holidays. I hung the Santa hats and placed the decorations. Gabe untangled the lights and assembled the cardboard gingerbread houses.

The most tedious part was hanging the lights, but even that didn't take us long once we found what worked for us. I was on the step ladder securing the lights with push pins while Gabe helped hold them in place. Two of the cats remained close, circling his feet and giving him tail hugs while we worked.

Our conversation was minimal, but I didn't mind the silence. It was comfortable, and I was surprised by how well we worked together.

"Hey, you two," Tiffany said as she entered. "My husband stopped by with the kids to pick me up, and Maddie is asking if she could pop in to say hi to the cats. Is that okay?" she asked hesitantly. "I don't want her to be a bother if you're still working in here."

"It's not a problem at all!" I assured as I secured the end of the Christmas lights and carefully climbed down the step ladder. I swore I saw Gabe's hand move, as if he was going to help me down...but I had to have been imagining things. I wanted Tiffany to be comfortable at work, and I wanted her to feel okay bringing her kids around, because I knew how important family was to her. I also loved seeing her adorable kids. "We just finished up."

"Oh, that's great! Okay, I'll let her know. The kids dropped off their letters to Santa in the mailbox." Within moments, Tiffany returned with her daughter, who burst into the room, and her son, who was more timid and stayed behind his mom.

"Lily, look!" Maddie said as she spun around, showing off her brown hair that was pulled into a French braid. "Mommy made my hair like yours."

"I love it! You look absolutely fabulous."

Her eyes widened at my compliment, and her smile turned bashful. "Thanks," she said sweetly. Maddie then turned toward her mom to ask, "Can I go say hi to the cats now?"

Tiffany laughed gently. "Go ahead, Maddie. Remember to be gentle and that we're leaving in fifteen minutes."

"Hi, Jack." I greeted Tiffany's son gently, knowing he was much more shy than his twin sister but just as sweet. "Your mom said you dropped off your list, huh? What did you ask Santa for?"

Jack nodded with a smile, staying close to Tiffany but stepping so he was next to her rather behind her. It didn't take him long after that to start to tell me about the various books and games he wished for.

After about five minutes, Maddie ran up to us with a pout. "The kitties keep running away from me! I just want to give them love!"

Gabe chimed in this time. "Here, why don't you try using this toy to get their attention." He reached down to pull a wand toy with a feather and a bell out of the basket and looked at Tiffany first. When she smiled with a nod, Gabe handed the toy over to

Maddie. "It also helps if you sit down on the ground and let them come to you. Want to sit over here on the rug?"

Maddie listened intently and ultimately agreed, following Gabe. "I'm Maddie. Who are you? You know Lily and my mom?" Maddie got comfortable next to him and paid close attention as Gabe introduced himself and helped her move the wand toy to entice the cats. Sure enough, within moments, two cats trotted over.

I continued my conversation with Tiffany and Jack, but I couldn't help but glance at Gabe and Maddie. Gabe explained to her how to greet the cats before petting them and then how to pet them so they wouldn't get startled.

"It worked!" Maddie exclaimed, looking at us over her shoulder. "Mommy, look!" Two of the cats were eagerly watching the toy while another came over to Maddie and brushed up against her side. Now that the cats were out, Jack seemed intrigued, too. He walked over to Maddie and Gabe before sitting down. Gabe gave Jack the same advice he'd given Maddie moments earlier, being patient with the kids and not bothered by having to repeat himself or overexplain things.

"Gabe's the best!" Maddie exclaimed then looked toward me. "Don't you think, Lily?" she asked sweetly, her eyes wide and bright.

I had to agree with Maddie—I *had* to. If I said anything else, I'd be breaking her heart, and potentially, upsetting my new employee and her daughter. I didn't have a choice and was backed into a corner. Gabe likely knew it, too, because he had a smug, amused look on his face.

I mustered as much enthusiasm as I could before responding to Maddie. "He sure is, Maddie. I'm glad the cats came over to say hi."

"Me, too! I can't wait to come back." Maddie turned back to Gabe. "Will you be here next time I come by?"

I didn't hear Gabe's response, because Tiffany spoke up, her voice low so only I could hear. "You two seem to be getting along. It's so festive in here! How'd decorating go?" When I had met with Tiffany, I'd filled her in on the situation with Gabe, the building, and Hal's conditions on making a choice.

I let out a sigh, twisting my lips in thought. "It went...better than I anticipated. It was nice to have his help," I admitted, looking in Gabe's direction again. "I'm still not sure about how this is all going to work out, though."

But there was one thing I *was* more sure about. There was a lot more to Gabe than he let on.

17

LILY

Wednesday

FROM THE STICKY CONSISTENCY OF THE DOUGH, I QUICKLY realized I needed more flour. My gaze flicked from my dough-covered hands up to the bag of flour on the shelf above me. Unless I washed my hands, there was no way I'd be getting that down without a mess.

I was about to make my way to the sink, but Gabe's voice stopped me. "You forgot your apron."

I looked down and realized he was right. In my excitement to get the dough prepped, I must've completely forgotten.

We were checking another item off the list today: making a holiday recipe for fun. When I found out Gabe had never made or frosted Christmas sugar cookies, the decision was made for us. The dough needed to chill for a few hours before we could use our festive cookie cutters.

I looked at my dough-covered hands again. "Would you be able to help me get my apron on?" I asked, looking at him over my shoulder. "And grab the bag of flour while you're at it? I'd get it myself, but—"

"Yeah, no problem," Gabe answered before I finished explaining myself.

He came up behind me, his body warm and his clean, fresh scent overpowering my senses. It didn't matter that I had a chocolate peppermint loaf baking in the oven. The cocoa and peppermint had nothing on Gabe.

He stepped behind me, lifting my hair off my neck and placing the neck loop of the apron over my head. It wasn't until right now that I realized how intimate my request was—and how *close* Gabe was to me. I couldn't see him, since my back was toward him, but I could feel his touch. On my hair. Gently grazing my neck as he fixed the loop. And, now, on my waist as he wrapped the too-long string around me.

"How do you like it?" he asked, his voice a low rumble.

I gulped. "Wh-what?"

"How do you like your apron tied?"

"Oh," I said on an exhale, not wanting to admit where my mind had gone. "I wrap it around twice and then tie it off in the back."

He hummed in response and followed my instructions, silence filling the space between us again. But it wasn't *just* silence that was consuming me. All I could focus on was his low, steady breathing. The hot air fanned my neck, and I felt my cheeks getting hot. Thank goodness he couldn't see my face.

"All set," Gabe finally said. His voice was steady and calming, which was such a contrast to the emotions whirling through my mind. Emotions I needed to get a grip on. "Is this the bag of flour?"

I nodded with a hum of confirmation, worried if I spoke he would hear the shakiness in my voice.

I expected Gabe to reach for the flour while standing *next* to me, not while standing *behind* me. I gulped as he reached forward. My body and mind weren't on the same page, because my body was weak.

My body wanted to lean into his strong chest, press myself against him to see how we'd fit. Like a puzzle? Or like two people who had no business being together?

My mind, on the other hand, wanted to create as much distance between us as possible—and ultimately, my mind won out. I leaned forward against the counter, trying to create separation between us.

"Sorry," he muttered against my ear as he reached forward and wrapped his large hand around the bag. The veins in his forearm flexed, and I nearly passed out right then and there. *Here lies Lily. Death by hand and forearm flexing while grabbing flour.* Was that a good way to go or pathetic?

"It's fine," I assured, although my voice came out more like a squeak, several octaves too high.

Gabe set the bag on the counter and stepped to the side. I was finally able to let out a heavy exhale.

"Would you be able to open the bag and pour a decent amount on the dough?"

He drummed his fingers on the counter. "Should I get a measuring cup or something?"

When I looked over at him, I saw how deeply he was contemplating, and I couldn't help but roll my lips to hide my smile. "It's not rocket science," I assured him. "You can eyeball it. I promise it'll be fine."

He narrowed his eyes at me, but the corner of his mouth tipped up. "Alright...if you say so."

There was a soft rustling as Gabe uncurled the top of the bag. And then a cough.

I stepped back as a soft cloud of white dust billowed, settling around him like a snowstorm.

"Oh my gosh." I stifled a laugh. This time, I stepped over to the sink, quickly washing and drying my hands so I could help him clean up. "It's everywhere. I've...never seen that happen before."

When he turned toward me—the flour covering parts of his face in a fine powder and the top of his dress shirt—I couldn't hold my laugh in.

Gabe reached up, trying to dust the flour off his shirt...which didn't quite work. He spread the flour over the fabric, making it worse.

"Here, let me—" I stopped him. First, I handed him a clean towel so he could wipe his face. Then, I grabbed another clean dish towel and wet it with cold water. I gently pinched the fabric, trying to shake off any loose flour, before blotting where it had stuck most.

"You promised it would be fine," he grumbled, wiping the powder off his face. There was amusement in his tone. He didn't seem angry or frustrated.

"I thought it would!" I let out a giggle. I lifted my head, peering up at him, which was a mistake given how close we were. How easily I could see the golden flecks in his eyes, the light stubble grazing his jaw. "I told you, this has never happened to me."

"Hm...never?" he hummed.

I looked down and moved to another spot on his shirt. I shook my head to answer.

"It would be a shame if it happened right now, huh?"

I furrowed my brows, not following. "I mean, I guess. But the bag is already open."

When I looked back up at Gabe, the flicker of amusement on his face gave his plans away immediately.

"You wouldn't..." My eyes widened as I prepared to take a step back.

Gabe was faster.

I hadn't realized it, but his ammunition was already loaded. He tossed a small handful of flour in my direction, creating a cloud between us.

I waved my hand in front of my face but didn't want to waste more time. Instead, I lunged toward the bag, wanting to get my own fistful of flour to toss at him. I succeeded, but so did he, both of us lobbying a throw.

Flour was flying everywhere, the white dust creating a thin layer on the floor and counters. I wasn't thinking about the mess or how we'd have to clean it up. I was simply letting myself enjoy the moment with him. I used the back of my forearm to wipe my forehead, eyes flicking between the bag and Gabe. If I could get one more throw...

"You've started a war, you know," I informed him, my cheeks hurting from my wide smile.

His lips spread into a smile that matched mine. "Oh, I know. Knew you were a fighter from the moment I met you."

I quickly reached to grab more flour and tossed it at Gabe, but it came at a cost. As I prepared to run to the other side of the kitchen, Gabe's arm wrapped firmly around my waist— like when we'd first met. He hauled me against his chest to keep me in place.

My breath hitched at how his broad chest pressed against my back. How the heat radiated from his body. While my mind might have won earlier, my body won this time. My feet stayed firmly planted. I glanced at him over my shoulder.

"Should we call a truce?"

His grip on my waist lessened—and I knew I shouldn't have been disappointed, but a small, *small* part of me was— enough for me to turn around to face him. My lower back pressed up against the edge of the counter, my hands wrapping around it. He moved his arm from around my waist, setting both of his hands on the counter to box me in. Our hands weren't touching, but if I moved my fingers an inch, I'd feel his skin on mine. If I leaned forward, my chest would be pressed against him.

The smell of his cologne—warm, fresh, and masculine—once again invaded my senses. There was some sweetness beneath the heat, too. I wouldn't admit it out loud, but I didn't think I'd be able to forget his scent even if I tried.

I swallowed, finally looking up at him. His eyes were already on me, watching closely and intently.

"What do you say?" His voice was low, as if he was inviting me to lean forward. Tempting me.

I was in a trance. I had to be, right?

"About what?" I asked, my throat dry.

"About the truce."

"But," I started, my eyes looking over to the bag of flour then back to him, "you have me right where you want me."

He hummed. "Not quite where I want you."

I parted my lips, about to ask him where it was that he wanted me *exactly* when a sharp, harsh burnt smell filled the air, breaking me out of whatever haze I was in. "The chocolate peppermint loaf!" I exclaimed, slipping past him and quickly moving toward the oven.

I grabbed an oven mitt and pulled the door open, a plume of smoke exiting. The heat fanned my face as I pulled out the loaf. The top of it was burnt to a crisp. I set it on top of the stove, turned off the oven, and let out a sigh. Luckily, the fire alarm hadn't gone off.

But what was I doing? That was the closest I'd gotten to Gabe, and I nearly burned the kitchen to the ground. Dramatic, maybe, but also true. It was a chocolate loaf this time, but what about next time I got caught up in the moment with him?

He likely had the same thought, because he was cleaning the flour off the counter.

"I'm going to get a broom," I said and didn't wait for his response before I darted to the supply closet.

I found the broom within seconds, but I took another minute to myself, letting out a heavy exhale.

What just happened? And why did I want it to happen again but without the interruption?

18

GABRIEL

Friday

I'D GOTTEN USED TO HELPING LILY AND SPENDING TIME AT Purrfect Blend. As much as I enjoyed my office in Milwaukee with big windows, double monitors, and a large desk, I was more at ease sitting at the café.

In the office, I was usually glued to my desk, only taking a break for lunch. Here, I took a few short walks throughout the day while on the phone with current and prospective clients.

I glanced down at my phone when it started vibrating on the table. *Ron Nelson* appeared on my screen, and I let out a heavy sigh. This was definitely a phone call I was going to step outside for.

I closed my laptop, picked up my phone, and threw on my coat. Lily was nice enough to keep an eye on my things whenever I stepped outside, so I didn't have to pack everything up. I felt her gaze on me as I closed the distance to the door in a few quick strides.

"Hey, Dad," I answered once I was outside.

"Where are you?" My father's tone was always annoyed to some degree. Today, I could tell he was already fucking irritated.

"I'm in Golden Falls. Is everything—"

"Still?"

I inhaled deeply through my nose, keeping my composure as I started to walk down the block. "Yeah, still. It's been about two weeks. I imagine I'll be here for a few more. I'm still taking calls and meetings and getting everything I need done. Did you need something?"

"I thought you'd be back by now. You haven't purchased the building yet?"

"Not yet. That's what I'm trying to do."

"Make him an offer he can't refuse. There has to be a dollar amount. Find out what it is."

I didn't want to admit to my father that I already tried throwing money at the problem. It had been my first instinct during the meeting with Hal and Lily, and I still felt ashamed about it.

"It's not about the money. I don't think there *is* a dollar amount. It's about more than that, which is why I'm taking my time here. I mean, you're the one who said to not come back until I had things figured out."

"Yeah, because I thought it would take you a week—two at most. You're not wasting your time there, are you? That place is too small for you. There's nothing there."

Irritation bubbled inside me, and my grip on the phone tightened. Securing this building meant more to my father than Hal. Accumulating money meant more to him than taking time to ensure a project was done properly with input from the community. I wasn't surprised, because he'd always been like this, but lately, it had been striking more and more of a nerve. I couldn't turn out like my father—I refused to. I didn't want to be that cold and unfeeling, whether that was now or in twenty years.

"I'm not wasting my time here. I'm making progress," I said to him, my voice firm. "If Hal sells the building to me, I'll handle it at Nelson Group. This is my opportunity to put a proposal forward. I don't want to move forward with an idea that's not right for the town or the building."

Silence filled the other end of the line before Ron let out a deep exhale. "Yes, Gabriel. It'll be your proposal. You're getting worked up over nothing."

I held back my laugh. Yup, I was paranoid about my father screwing me over for no reason. Even hearing him say it would be my proposal had me skeptical.

I didn't believe him. But what choice did I have?

"Has your mother called you recently?"

"No, not recently." I realized the last time I'd talked to her was before I left for Golden Falls.

"I reinstated her credit cards. Well, *my* credit cards that she uses. So, next time she calls you to complain about what a selfish bastard I am, go ahead and tell her the good news."

I had no idea what to say in response to that. "Uh, okay? Listen, Dad, I have to—"

"I need to go to my next meeting. Close the deal in the next few weeks and be back in the office. I bet you're eager to get the fuck out of there. Bye, Gabriel."

Not waiting for my response, he hung up. I ran a hand through my hair, gripping at the strands.

Closing the deal over the next few weeks was still the plan, and while I was looking forward to being back in Milwaukee, I disagreed with him. I wasn't eager to get out of here. I was starting to like this town more than I wanted to admit.

I liked certain people in town more than I wanted to admit.

I was eager to get past the holiday season, though, and to

have all these damn decorations taken down. I turned around and made my way back to the café, feeling the same sense of defeat I always did after a call with my father.

Once I was back, I made my way over to the table. I initially planned on finishing my day from here, but now I wanted to be alone.

"Hey, Gabe?"

"Yeah?" I asked, my tone coming out sharper than I intended because of the weight of the conversation with my father. I closed my eyes, pausing what I was doing and letting out a deep exhale to center myself. I turned toward Lily and said, "I'm sorry for how that came out. What's up?" I then continued sliding my laptop and various papers into my backpack, trying not to think about the concern written all over her expression. I didn't deserve her concern—I didn't deserve to take up any ounce of her mind.

"What's wrong?" she asked gently.

"Everything's fine," I answered with a sigh, my tone gentler than earlier. "Just work stress." With the way her blue eyes softened, I knew how easy it would be to tell her what was on my mind, but that wasn't the dynamic we had. "What did you want to ask me?"

She chewed on her bottom lip, ultimately nodding and dropping her question. "Oh, um, would you be willing to drop off a drink and treat for Hal? He called in an order, and normally, I'd deliver it to him, but a few customers walked in, and I want to help Tiffany. But if you're busy, I can take care of it in a little bit."

I glanced toward the line that was forming at the counter and then turned to face Lily. "It's not a problem. I'd be happy to help. I was going to head out of here anyway, so I'll stop by his store before heading back to the house."

With my work materials all packed up, I slung my backpack

over my shoulder and followed Lily. She had a pink bakery box prepared, as well as a to-go iced coffee.

"These are the chocolate crinkle cookies and then the drink is the s'mores latte. But *please* tell him that this is the last time I'm making this drink for him. When I run out of ingredients, I'm not ordering them again—and I'm serious this time," Lily said with a laugh, a gentle smile on her face.

The tension in my shoulders lessened a fraction from her smile.

"Take care of yourself, okay?" Lily said. "Don't feel like you need to come in this weekend. I have it handled."

I knew she could handle this all herself, and now, she had Tiffany's help, but a part of me liked helping her. I saw firsthand how hard she worked. How she put every ounce of herself into her business. For some unknown reason, I didn't want her to have to handle it on her own. I wanted to be there for her, even if it was only for a few weeks until we finished her wish list. It also took my mind off the whole situation with my dad and Nelson Group.

"I won't be in on Saturday, but I'll stop by Sunday. That work?"

"Yeah, of course. The fact that you're helping me in the first place means a lot." She handed me the bakery box and drink. "I should get back to taking orders. See you on Sunday." It didn't take long for her to eagerly start chatting with the customers in line.

With the bakery box in one hand and the drink in the other, I left the café and made my way to Hal's Hardware.

"To what do I owe this surprise?" Hal greeted, a grin on his face as I walked in. He folded his newspaper and set it on the counter.

I lifted the bakery box and drink. "I've come with treats and a message that this is the last time Lily is making this drink for you. She said she's serious this time."

Hal chuckled, amusement twinkling in his eyes. "I suppose that's fair. Although, she did say the exact same thing last time. You two getting along okay?"

I made my way inside and set the bakery box on the counter along with Hal's drink. "Yeah, I think we're getting along fine. It's strange at times, but we're making it work."

"I can understand why it's been strange," Hal acknowledged. "I appreciate you two being patient and entertaining my conditions. I think it'll all work out in the end. Just a little bit more time. Why don't you take off your coat and stay awhile." He tipped his chin to the other chair.

I hesitated.

"I know we haven't seen much of each other. I wanted to give you time to settle in and not feel like I was in your space constantly," Hal continued. "Well, I think you've settled in now, and I'd like to spend some time with my grandson while he's in town."

Fuck. How could I say no to that?

"Yeah." I cleared the lump in my throat. "Yeah, I'd like that, too." The admission left my mouth easily, but I was still surprised by it. I pulled the chair over and sat after taking off my coat and backpack.

"And look at that. Lily packed four cookies when I only asked for two."

"Is she usually one step ahead?" I asked with a chuckle.

"More often than not," Hal said fondly. "She's the youngest

out of the Richards kids and was always up to something growing up."

"I take it you're close with Lily's family?"

Hal nodded. "Your dad and Lily's dad Mark were best friends growing up. When Mark's parents moved away, I figured the least I could do was help Mark and Laura when their kids were growing up."

My brows furrowed. I hadn't realized that. "Dad has never mentioned Mark."

"That...doesn't surprise me. The two of them didn't exactly end on the best of terms, as far as I know. After your dad left Golden Falls, he kept in touch with Mark. The two of them were going to start Lake Ridge together but had differences on how to move forward. Mark ended up continuing without him, which was good. It was the right thing to do. Wes, Lily's older brother, owns Lake Ridge now."

I nodded slowly, putting the pieces together. I couldn't wrap my head around what Lake Ridge would have turned into had my father been involved. Surely, not the spot it was today. "Lake Ridge was one of the first places I stopped by here. I didn't meet Wes, but I did meet Louise. She's..." I trailed off.

"A character?" Hal finished for me with a grin. "She's a good person to know. She's fond of you already." He grabbed one of the cookies and then passed the box over to me.

I took a cookie and leaned back in the chair. "Dad said he tried to buy the building from you?"

Hal huffed a laugh. "Something like that. I think *tried to buy* is putting it mildly. He tried to make me an offer I couldn't refuse, but it's not about the money for me."

My mind went back to the meeting with Hal, again thinking about how I did the same thing.

"Do you think I'm like him or turning into him? Is that why

you invited me to town?" I asked bluntly, not wanting to skirt around it anymore. He wouldn't be the first person to think so.

Hal reached over, grabbing a napkin and setting the other half of his cookie on it. He leaned forward, elbows resting on his knees. "Listen here, Gabe. You are your own person, and you have the potential to be whoever you want to be. Yeah, maybe you do have parts of your father in you. But you also have pieces of me, of your grandmother, of everyone in your life who has made an impact on you. The relationship I have with your father is...a complicated one. I didn't ask you to come to Golden Falls because I thought you're turning into him. You're not him and you never will be. A part of me did wonder, though, if you were forgetting who you are."

You're not him. Those three words were simple, and yet they were exactly the reminder I needed. I was my own person with my own career and my own goals. It sounded so obvious, but somewhere along the way, I'd forgotten.

"My career isn't anywhere close to where I wanted it to be at this point. I feel like I've wasted time working for him, but I don't exactly have a choice."

"That's where you're wrong, Gabe. You always have a choice. Sometimes you might have to get creative, but you *always* have a choice."

19

LILY

While Hal was never in a bad mood, I knew he tended to be in a better mood *before* poker night at Lake Ridge than after, especially if Cooper was playing. At one point or another when we were growing up, Hal had taught my siblings and I, as well as Cooper and Eliza, how to play. We used chocolate instead of money, which growing up was a more valuable currency, anyway.

The game never stuck with me, but I remember Wes, Jade, and Cooper playing often. Sometimes Eliza joined, too.

These days, Cooper played poker with Hal the most often, and I knew he was going to be at the table tonight, which meant I needed to talk to Hal before the game started.

I pushed open the door to Lake Ridge, seeing a line of people sitting at the bar and various tables filled already. I was so proud of what my brother had done with the bar. He turned it into more than a place to grab a drink. It was a spot to socialize, catch up, and see people you normally didn't throughout the week.

My brother would be the first to say that it wasn't just him. That he had help from our dad, Cooper, and his staff in revamping Lake Ridge, which was true, but it wouldn't have been possible without his vision and dedication.

Summers tended to be more lively with more nights dedicated to music, dancing, and sitting around the fire pits, but Lake Ridge was truly a year-round stop. Tonight, people were playing pool, darts, grabbing a drink, or stopping by to chat.

Wes had even decorated for the holidays, although that was likely more Jules's doing. The decorations were simple. Red tinsel garland wrapped around the edge of the bar with candy canes hanging off it. Each chair by the bar had a giant Santa hat on the back of the it, and there were Christmas lights wrapped around the various pillars.

Eliza, who started bartending here over the summer, moved effortlessly as she prepared drinks. When she spotted me, she grinned, waving me over. "Why are you just standing there?"

I smiled back at her, walking up to one of the few open spots at the bar. "Zoned out," I admitted with a laugh. "I was thinking about how much work has gone into this place. How Wes has really changed it to be a top spot in the state." My recluse brother, who disliked when new people came to town, created something that drew in people from all across Wisconsin—and the Midwest. He'd been more open since meeting Jules, although the first impression he made on her wasn't great. Yet, they still found their way to each other.

Eliza nodded fondly. "Yeah, he's really built on what your dad started. I've enjoyed working for him. I can give him shit *and* get paid for it."

I laughed at the mischievous smile on Eliza's face. "The dream, honestly. Has Wes said anything more about hiring a chef?"

My brother wanted to hire a chef to join Lake Ridge and bring a vision for a potential menu. Wes wanted to work with local farmers to source ingredients, minimize food waste, and use other sustainable practices. He wanted to hire someone who believed in this vision and his goals.

"A little bit. He still has to solidify the timeline, but I think he's trying to start the search in the first couple months of the new year. He wants them to start in the spring, so they have time to get things figured out before things pick up in the summer."

"I can't wait." I beamed. "I'll be stopping by every day for a late lunch after closing up the café."

"Speaking of the café..." Eliza trailed off, raising a brow.

"What about it?" I tried—and failed—to play it off.

She rolled her eyes. "You know what—or rather, you know *who*—I'm asking about."

I blew out a breath. "Things are fine. Better than last week, that's for sure. But still ...confusing. We're getting along better, so that's good. But we still don't know much about each other, so it's hard to trust him. Plus, we're on opposing sides. I don't think we'll ever *fully* get along. I don't really understand how him being around is supposed to help me. That's part of the reason why I stopped in. I was hoping to catch Hal before poker to see if he's thought about the building at all."

"At least things are better, though?" Eliza offered.

"Yeah, they are," I agreed. "I mean, we haven't killed each other yet, so there's that." I grinned, trying to play off any indication that there might be something else going on between us.

To be clear, there wasn't. But my mind did wander to our moment a couple of days ago in the kitchen. And to the other moments throughout the week when it felt like things *could* be different, like we might actually get along.

I normally told Eliza everything, but I held back these tiny details, because saying them out loud would imply it meant more and that I hadn't been able to stop thinking about him.

It would mean admitting I was wrong about Gabe, and I wasn't sure if I fully trusted my judgment yet.

I was grateful he opened up to me, and I meant what I told him. But he still worked for Nelson Group, and that was the part I didn't understand. He clearly wanted to be doing different work...so what was keeping him working for his father? Was it naive of me to think he could leave?

"Let's keep it that way," Eliza said. "I'd rather not bail you out of jail—although you know I would in a heartbeat."

"And I'd do the same for you."

Out of the corner of my eye, I saw Hal coming out of the back hallway with Wes. It took everything in me not to run over to them, but I remained calm.

"Wish me luck," I said under my breath to my best friend, and she gave me a sympathetic smile before saying, "You got this. I'll see you later tonight for our movie night with Jules."

I pushed off the bar and made my way over to Hal as Wes was wrapping up his conversation with him. "Give 'em hell, Hal." Wes jutted his chin toward the table in the back of the bar set up for the poker game. When I looked over, I saw Gabe sitting at the table with Cooper. He was sitting slightly off to the side, as if he was there to hang out but not play. That was...interesting. I didn't expect him to be here. I would've thought he had no interest in stopping by Lake Ridge or spending time with people in town.

On one hand, I was glad Gabe was spending time with Hal and giving Golden Falls a chance. He deserved to get to know Hal, to have a relationship with him. On the other, my insecurities about the two of them getting closer and Hal potentially giving the building to Gabe because he was his grandson floated to the surface.

Even though Gabe was in a conversation with Cooper, it was like his attention was solely on me when our eyes locked. I watched Gabe bring his beer up to his lips, eyeing how his hand flexed around the bottle and how his throat bobbed as he swallowed. I wondered what was going through his mind. Was he as confused as I was?

Hal's voice broke me out of my thoughts. "You know I will, but something tells me Cooper has us all beat."

Cooper lifted his head at the sound of his name and waved over to us, a grin on his face. "Damn straight!" He then turned his attention toward Gabe, and the two resumed their conversation.

The corner of Wes's mouth tipped up, and he shook his head with an amused chuckle before turning to me. He searched my face, narrowing his eyes as he observed me. "What's on your mind? You look stressed."

"Everything's great!" I replied, hoping my cheery voice wasn't too over the top. Things were fine, but I knew if I used that word, Wes would start asking a million questions. He'd learned well over the years growing up with two sisters and now being with Jules.

Fine did not mean fine.

"Okay," he said slowly. He wasn't pushing it, but I could tell he didn't quite believe me either. "I'll leave you two to it." Wes nodded before walking over to Cooper and Gabe.

I turned to Hal, suddenly feeling nervous, which I never felt around him. "Think we can chat for a moment?"

Hal's eyes softened. "Of course, Lily. However long you need. Here, let's sit down." He gestured for me to follow him toward one of the booths, giving us a quieter place to sit and talk compared to the front of the bar. I appreciated the privacy, especially since you never knew who was listening in our small town. Gossip spread faster than one of my cats zooming around at midnight. Luckily, it wasn't only bad news that moved quickly. Good gossip spread just as easily.

"What did you want to talk about?" Hal asked once we sat across from each other.

"Well"—I let out a heavy sigh—"I wanted to see what you were thinking about the building. It's been about two weeks now... Do you think you're closer to making a decision?"

I held my voice steady and calm, although the nerves were buzzing inside me. My fingers fiddled with the threads of my distressed jeans under the table.

I hoped he was closer to figuring this out. I hoped it was now obvious that I was capable of handling this. While I imagined that Gabe had good ideas, I still didn't think he was right to own the building.

An amused smile came across Hal's face. That wasn't a good sign.

"Let me ask you this, Lily." Hal's voice was gentle but firm—also not a good sign. "Have you and Gabe finished your list yet?"

I opened and closed my mouth. "Well, no. Not yet. But we've made good progress. We decorated the cat room and made Christmas cookies. It's been nice to have Gabe's help." That much was true, but I also wondered if it would help butter Hal up. It was his idea to have Gabe help *and* he was his grandson. "Plus, I hired Tiffany."

"I'm glad he's been helpful, but I think you answered your own question. You need more time. You still have seven items to complete, right?"

"Right," I muttered.

"Which is good, because I'm not ready to make a decision yet. And I said this to Gabe, too, but I'm putting a pause on talking about the building until the end of the month."

That was the exact thing I didn't want to hear. I didn't want more time—I wanted to know who Hal was going to sell the building to. And this conversation added additional worry I didn't expect. I was still in the running to own the building, but my chances didn't seem as good as I initially thought. What should have been a no brainer was something Hal was actively considering.

"Lily," Hal said gently. "Trust me on this. When have I ever steered you wrong?"

He must've read the disappointment on my face. I never was very good at keeping my feelings hidden. I let out a sigh, lifting my gaze to meet his. I honestly couldn't think of a single moment. I'm sure there were little things here and there—Hal was human, after all—but nothing that came to mind immediately. "Never," I muttered.

"I always have your best interests in mind. I promise. I think you'll see that if you let yourself enjoy the journey."

"How's your winter wish list coming along, Lily?" Jules asked, shaking red pepper flakes onto her pizza slice. Eliza, Jules, and I tried to get together at least once a week to watch a movie and catch up, even when our schedules were hectic. Tonight, we were watching *The Holiday*, which was one of my and Jules's favorites. Eliza had *never* seen it. Thankfully, that was changing.

I let out a sigh, setting the slice on my plate and picking up my glass of wine.

Eliza and Jules both laughed.

"Well, I think I got my answer," Jules said, shaking her head.

I swallowed my gulp of wine and wiped the corner of my mouth. "Maybe that was a little dramatic. It's..." I paused, thinking through what I wanted to say. "It's going okay. Honestly, I've enjoyed getting to know Gabe more, when he lets me in. He seems..." I twisted my lips to the side. "Very guarded, and I think it has to do with his dad or work. Both, maybe. When we've let our guards down, things have been good. We actually work pretty well together. But I don't think we trust each other, and how can we? We're on opposing sides."

I got up from the couch and walked over to where my purse was, shuffling through the bag to pull out my list. I plopped back down on the couch and handed the list to Jules and Eliza to look. "We've done three things, but that leaves seven."

"Well," Jules started, "what if the next thing you did was get dinner together at Pasta Fresca? That might be a good opportunity for you to get to know each other and come up with a game plan to tackle the rest of the list."

Eliza nodded in agreement. "Plus, you deserve to treat yourself. You hired help for the café—something you've been talking about for months. That's such a big accomplishment, Lil, and worth celebrating."

I looked at both of my friends and couldn't believe how lucky I'd gotten to have two incredible women supporting me, cheering me on, and helping me celebrate my wins. "You two are the best. I appreciate the reminder to celebrate. It's so easy for me to skip ahead to the next thing that needs to be done."

Although I wished I could celebrate at my favorite restaurant with my best friends, I started to get excited about the idea of getting dinner with Gabe as friendly rivals. There was one item on the list that was causing me more anxiety than the rest. My eyes zeroed in on number six: *romantic kiss under the mistletoe that takes my breath away.* We didn't have to do that one, right? I took another sip of wine to calm my nerves.

"Now, *that's* a good kiss," Eliza said before taking a bite of pizza. On the screen, the iconic kiss between Cameron Diaz and Jude Law's characters played out.

"So good, but not as good as my kisses with Wes," Jules said in a daze.

I rolled my eyes, although I couldn't help the smile on my

face. Wes and Jules were so in love and perfect for each other. I was obsessed with them together, especially because I'd never seen my brother this happy before. His face lit up and his eyes always followed her when she walked into a room. It was like no one else existed.

"You two are so in love it's sickening." Eliza shook her head, but I could see the tiny smile on her lips. "Although, he's been way more chill at work ever since the two of you got together, so no arguments here. I'm happy for you both, really. It's just the whole being in love thing...well, I don't think it's for me."

Eliza might have claimed to not care about falling in love—and to not be looking for it—but she had a soft side. She was like a mini cactus: prickly but adorable. She'd hate being called adorable, but...I was her best friend, which gave me immunity.

"That all might change when you meet the right person." Jules used her elbow to nudge Eliza's side. "Your soulmate is out there. I know it. For both of you." Jules looked between us.

"Considering the last few guys I dated wouldn't be able to find my clit if it slapped them in the face...my hopes are not high." Leave it to Eliza to put it bluntly.

I snorted, and Jules let out a laugh.

I wanted to believe Jules, but I had my doubts that kind of love was out there for me. And it wasn't like I had time to find him, which was part of the reason I was in this situation with Gabe. I had my café, I had my cats, I had my family. That was enough for now. Love would come later.

I did wonder what it felt like, though. To fall in love. To *be* in love. While I'd dated here and there, none of it was that all-consuming, life-altering feeling. I wasn't sure if it was even out there for me. Maybe some people got it and others didn't. Jules and Wes got it. My parents got it. As long as those around me got it, that would be okay. At least I'd know it was real, even if it wasn't in the cards for me.

"Oh my god," Eliza blurted, "I almost forgot." She reached over for the remote to pause the movie.

"What?" Jules and I both responded, eyes wide.

"I think Cooper was talking to Jade on the phone today. In between the poker games, he went to the back hallway, and I had to walk past him to grab more limes and lemons from the fridge. I couldn't make out much of the conversation, but he *definitely* said her name and something about how they can't keep avoiding each other."

Jade and I were close growing up, but she spent a lot of her time with Cooper and Wes, who were two years older than her. Them being closer in age—whereas I was six years younger than Jade—meant they spent a lot of time together. Jade and Cooper always seemed close, up until she left after college and moved to California. Everything changed after that, but she never said anything to me, regardless of how many times I tried to subtly ask. Whatever happened, they'd kept it so close to their chests that there was no gossip around town that I was aware of.

"So there *is* something going on between them?" Jules asked. "I could've sworn I picked up on it over the summer when you FaceTimed Jade during the first family dinner I was at."

I nodded at the memory. "Yeah, that was super awkward. But I have no clue if there's *still* something going on. I mean, there *was* at some point, right?"

"There had to have been," Eliza agreed. "Is Jade coming home for Christmas?"

"No, my mom said she has to work, and it's not like she's been picking up my calls," I grumbled. "Do you think that's what they were talking about?"

Eliza shrugged. "It's possible. Either way, she has to visit at some point, right? I mean, it's been a few years since she's been in town."

I was painfully aware of how long it'd been since Jade had

been in Golden Falls. My sister and I kept in touch here and there over text and FaceTime, but I still missed her.

I was proud of her and knew how much she'd dreamed of getting out of town to travel and pursue her career. I never wanted her to worry about us or visit because she thought *we* needed it. I wanted her to visit because she wanted to.

As proud of her as I was, I felt like she had forgotten about us or thought less of Wes and me for not getting out of Golden Falls. She'd never said anything to make me feel that way, but I wondered.

Once the comfortable silence fell over us, Eliza reached for the remote again, resuming the movie. "How is this going to work out between them? I mean, their homes are on opposite sides of the world."

Jules and I shared a knowing look with a smile, watching as Eliza, who started out the least invested, was glued to the screen.

"Guess you'll have to keep watching," I taunted playfully at the same time Jules said, "Because love always finds a way."

From: Lily Richards <lily@purrfectblend.com>
To: Gabriel Nelson <gabriel@nelsongroup.com>
Date: Saturday, December 18, 1:27 p.m.
Subject: Dinner at Pasta Fresca

Hi Gabe!

Hope you're having a good Saturday. Would you want to get dinner with me at Pasta Fresca tomorrow evening? We can check off another thing on the list and make a plan for the rest.

Let me know what you think.

- Lily

From: Gabriel Nelson <gabriel@nelsongroup.com>
To: Lily Richards <lily@purrfectblend.com>
Date: Saturday, December 18, 1:39 p.m.
Subject: Re: Dinner at Pasta Fresca

Lily,

I'd like that. It's a date. Let me know what time I should pick you up.

Hope you're having a nice Saturday, too.

- Gabe

From: Gabriel Nelson <gabriel@nelsongroup.com>
To: Lily Richards <lily@purrfectblend.com>
Date: Saturday, December 18, 1:41 p.m.
Subject: Re: Dinner at Pasta Fresca

And by date I meant our plans are set. Not like a romantic date. I'm sure a date with you would be pleasant, but that's not what we're doing.

From: Lily Richards <lily@purrfectblend.com>
To: Gabriel Nelson <gabriel@nelsongroup.com>
Date: Saturday, December 18, 1:50 p.m.
Subject: Dinner at Pasta Fresca

Right! I knew what you meant. It's plans between two friendly rivals! Totally normal!! Nothing to be anxious about!

And you don't have to pick me up. Let's meet at the restaurant!

From: Gabriel Nelson <gabriel@nelsongroup.com>
To: Lily Richards <lily@purrfectblend.com>
Date: Saturday, December 18, 1:55 p.m.
Subject: Re: Dinner at Pasta Fresca

You might've exceeded the amount of exclamation marks allowed in one email.

From: Lily Richards <lily@purrfectblend.com>
To: Gabriel Nelson <gabriel@nelsongroup.com>
Date: Saturday, December 18, 2:00 p.m.
Subject: Dinner at Pasta Fresca

No, I didn't!!! There's no such thing as too many!!!!

Wouldn't kill you to use one once in a while.

From: Gabriel Nelson <gabriel@nelsongroup.com>
To: Lily Richards <lily@purrfectblend.com>
Date: Saturday, December 18, 2:03 p.m.
Subject: Re: Dinner at Pasta Fresca

It might.

From: Lily Richards <lily@purrfectblend.com>
To: Gabriel Nelson <gabriel@nelsongroup.com>
Date: Saturday, December 18, 2:05 p.m.
Subject: Dinner at Pasta Fresca

!!!!!!!!!!

20

LILY

I took a final look in the mirror, turning my head to the side to see what my half up, half down hairstyle looked like and if I needed to fix anything. What my hair looked like from the back usually wasn't any of my business, but we were going to my favorite restaurant, so I wanted to look good. That was the only reason.

I smoothed my hair, happy with the outcome. I slipped on my pair of dark boots that paired nicely with my soft brown sweater and flared medium-wash jeans. I finished the outfit with my coat, opting to skip my scarf, hat, and gloves today, since the walk to the restaurant was short.

Pasta Fresca had delicious, mouth-watering pasta, pizza, and other Italian delights. I typically ordered takeout from there, and it'd been months since I'd gone for a sit-down dinner. Even longer since I'd been there for a date—not that *this* was a date.

I slipped my phone into my small black shoulder bag and pulled open the door. Right as Gabe raised his fist to knock.

"Oh, hi!" I blinked, not expecting him. "I thought we were going to meet at the restaurant?"

Gabe's gaze slowly took me in, and under his careful watch,

it took me twice as long to button my coat with my fumbling fingers.

"Did you really think I would let you walk to dinner alone?" His voice was low, sending vibrations throughout my body. "I agreed earlier only because I knew arguing about it would get us nowhere, but I always planned on picking you up from your apartment."

That was...considerate of him. Although him picking me up from my apartment made this feel *slightly* more like a date, even if we both knew it wasn't.

"Maybe you just couldn't wait to see me tonight," I teased.

Gabe tipped his head back, looking at the ceiling, likely begging for patience. I used the moment to take *him* in. He had on a black knit winter hat, dark jeans, and a dark-gray coat. If I had to guess, he likely had one of his signature dress shirts underneath.

He exhaled and met my gaze. "Exactly, I just couldn't wait to see you."

The way his words came out caught me off guard, because while his tone was teasing, it also sounded...genuine? But there was no way.

I stepped out of my apartment and locked the door, clearing my throat. "Are you okay with walking there? It's not too far. Only a few blocks."

"Fine by me."

We walked down the stairs of my apartment building, and once we reached the bottom, Gabe pushed the door open and stepped out, holding it open for me.

The gust of wind hit my face immediately, the evening chill making my eyes water. We still didn't have any snow in Golden Falls, but the temperatures continued to drop.

I regretted not bringing my hat and gloves as soon as we stepped outside.

"Which way?" Gabe asked once I stepped outside, and I tipped my chin to the left. I was about to start walking but was stopped when Gabe's hand gently wrapped around my wrist. "You're shivering." He frowned, dropping my wrist and reaching into his pocket. "Here." He passed me a pair of gloves.

"Oh, no, Gabe, I'm fine, really," I assured. "Let's start walking. The faster we go, the sooner we'll be there."

A low growl escaped his throat. "Take the gloves, and then we can take our time getting there. You can show me your favorite decorations on the way."

Tempting. Very tempting.

"Okay." I nodded, taking the gloves from him. As I was putting them on, I felt his hands on the side of my head slipping on a hat. When I looked up at him, I realized he was no longer wearing his winter hat. "Gabe—" I started in protest.

"Much better. Now I don't have to worry about you getting hypothermia before dinner. I'd be an immediate suspect."

The corner of my mouth twitched in a smile, and I thanked him, immediately feeling more comfortable for our walk. Although I wasn't sure what made me more comfortable—my new hat and gloves or the feeling of Gabe's hand on my lower back as we started our walk. Even through my various layers, his touch caused a flutter in my stomach I couldn't ignore.

We took the long way to the restaurant, and as promised, I pointed out my favorite decorations and the light displays I helped set up.

And Gabe was taking it in and listening the whole time.

"Okay, this isn't quite going how I anticipated," I whispered to Gabe.

"You think?" He let out a gentle chuckle before reassuring me. "We'll get a new table, and it'll be fine. I'm sure people will forget all about it."

We followed Teresa, co-manager of Pasta Fresca. She owned the place with her sister Maria. The two women were in their early sixties and moved to Golden Falls with their husbands about a decade ago as they were both getting close to retiring. Turned out, retiring from their corporate jobs meant opening a small town restaurant that pulled in their Italian roots.

Their goal had been to create authentic Italian food in a romantic atmosphere with dim-lighting, candles, and intimate seating. The tables were spread out to give each couple or group their own space and privacy. Pasta Fresca was a hidden gem in the Midwest, but more people were finding out about it as they traveled to Golden Falls for vacation.

"I hope this table will be better for you two," Teresa said, gesturing to a small table. She'd taken us to the back of the restaurant. "Try not to burn the place down...again." She gave me a pointed look before her expression softened and she squeezed my arm.

I draped my coat across the back of my chair and sat across from Gabe with a heavy sigh.

To say the start of our dinner was a disaster would be an understatement. Our walk to the restaurant was fine, but things started to go wrong as soon as we got to our table. Or rather, as soon as *I* got to our table.

I wasn't sure what had come over me, but I suddenly and inexplicably felt anxious. Gabe and I had spent a lot of time together over the last couple of weeks, so it wasn't that I felt uncomfortable around him, because I didn't. But this did feel more...intimate. And it also reminded me—not that I needed the reminder—that I hadn't been on a date with someone in such a long time.

I could get over knocking over my glass and spilling water on the floor, mainly because I caught the glass in time before it shattered. What I didn't think I'd be able to live down was knocking over the two tealight candles and catching the tablecloth on fire. Maria ran over with the fire extinguisher, swearing under her breath as she put out the fire.

It was a *very small* fire, in my defense, but a fire, nonetheless.

"Lily, hey." Gabe's voice pulled me out of my thoughts. He reached across the table, taking my hand in his—and not knocking anything over in the process. "It's okay. It's not like you *literally* burned the place down."

"I just...I hate doing things wrong."

"Well, luckily, I don't think there's a manual on how to have dinner with your friendly rival. That's what you called me, right?"

My shoulders relaxed, and I let out a breathy laugh. "Yeah, I guess you're right." I looked down at his hand over mine, soaking in the gentle feeling of his thumb running over my knuckles. "I know this isn't a date, but I got nervous because it's been so long since I've been on an actual date," I admitted, rolling my lips. "You likely go on dates all the time." He had to, right? I mean, *look* at him. Not only was Gabe handsome, but as I peeled his layers back, I was finding out he was considerate, a good listener, and thoughtful.

He let out an amused snort, and I raised my brows.

"Oh," he said with a chuckle, "you're serious." He shook his head. "I haven't been on a date in a long time. My priority over the last few years has been my career, which leaves little time for dating. I tend to keep things casual because of that."

I nodded in response, not wanting to think too deeply about the twinge of disappointment when I heard he preferred casual.

There was nothing wrong with that, but I knew myself enough to know that I couldn't do casual. I got attached too easily.

"Anyways," Gabe continued. "What'd you have in mind for next steps with your wish list?" He gave my hand a squeeze before pulling away, and I immediately felt the loss of warmth.

I reached for the menu to keep me from reaching for him. "So, there's a Christmas festival downtown on Christmas Eve." Christmas Eve was only five days away, and I couldn't believe how quickly the holidays were sneaking up. "That will give us a good opportunity to knock out sledding and building a gingerbread house. It's overall a really fun evening, and everyone in town shows up."

Gabe's face pinched whenever Christmas was mentioned, and right now was no different. But, ultimately, he relaxed and said, "That sounds fine. We'll do that next."

I shifted my attention back to the menu. "Do you want to get an appetizer to start?" I asked. "The burrata is really good here and so are the meatballs. Oh, and the focaccia is to die for." My stomach growled on cue as I listed off food—and thought about the pizza and pasta options.

"Are you two ready to put an order in?" Teresa asked. "I'll take care of you two lovebirds tonight, since you scared my other servers away."

"Oh, no, we're not—" I said at the same time Gabe said, "This isn't—" We looked at each other and both let out a laugh.

Teresa, who looked between us, had a grin that was far too amused. "First date?" she asked.

I shook my head, my cheeks getting hot. "It's dinner with a... friend," I said, looking from Teresa to Gabe and giving him a hesitant smile. "Does one of those I mentioned sound good to you?"

Gabe looked up from the menu, first at me and then at Teresa. "Yeah, why don't we start with an order of the burrata, meatballs, and the focaccia. And a bottle of your nicest red, please."

Teresa's brows raised. "You got it," she said while writing down on her notepad. "I'll get that right out to you."

"Gabe," I whispered once Teresa was gone. "What are you doing?"

"I ordered us appetizers," he said simply, casually. Like we did this regularly.

"But the wine—" I started.

"I saw you looking at the list when we were at our other table. Plus, isn't this dinner on your list to treat yourself? We might as well go all out. You deserve it."

He remembered that? My expression softened, and a grateful smile crossed my lips. "I appreciate that. Thank you. I'm glad we're able to do this together," I admitted.

Gabe looked at me, adding, "And if we're celebrating on our *first date*, I want to make sure my girl gets what she wants."

Heat unexpectedly flared in my stomach. *My girl.* Those two words shouldn't have had the impact on me they did. I wasn't his girl—not even close—and he was just playing off of Teresa's joke, but then why did those words coming out of his mouth sound so good?

21

GABRIEL

EVERY INCH OF OUR SMALL TABLE WAS COVERED BY PLATES OF FOOD once our appetizers and wine arrived. Warm smells of basil, marinara, and freshly-baked bread wafted into the air.

Lily's eyes brightened at our spread as Teresa poured us each a glass of wine before setting the bottle off to the side—in the last remaining free spot on the table.

"Enjoy, and let me know if you need anything," she said before walking away.

Lily reached over to grab a piece of focaccia to dip in the fresh burrata, urging me to do the same. I followed suit, about to take a bite when a satisfied moan escaped her. Her eyes were closed, and she was blissfully unaware of what that noise had done to me. Of the shot of desire going straight to my cock. No... no way. Lily was beautiful, but I wasn't attracted to her in this way. She was the one person I couldn't be attracted to. The one person standing in my way.

"Oh my god," she said, taking another bite. She opened her eyes slowly. "Better than sex." She grinned, and I nearly choked.

While Lily might've started out nervous during our dinner, she appeared to be more relaxed at our new table and after she shared what had been on her mind. I was surprised that it had been a while since Lily had been on a date, because she was so welcoming to be around, so easy to talk to, and so thoughtful. For a moment, I found myself thinking about what it would be like if this *was* a date. How easy it would be to let her in.

Concern flashed over her features as I coughed. "Are you okay?" she asked, looking around for help.

I waved my hand to dismiss her concerns. "I'm fine," I choked out, grabbing my glass of wine to wash the food down. "I'm fine, see." I repeated more convincingly this time, trying to calm her worried and skeptical expression. At my second *I'm fine*, Lily relaxed into her seat. "Nice to know you're concerned about me, though. Couple weeks ago I would've thought you'd be the one to poison me."

"You were thinking that *last* week," she pointed out, raising her brows.

"See, look how far we've come."

Lily rolled her eyes, and I saw her trying to fight her smile. Eventually, it won out. She dipped her bread again, but this time —thankfully—there were no moans involved.

"So, you live in Milwaukee, right? What's that like? I haven't been."

"It's great," I answered honestly. "I love living in the city. How close everything is, all the opportunities and people. Meeting and talking with people in the line for lunch or at the grocery store who I might not get to interact with otherwise. I like hearing what people are working on, what they're passionate about. My apartment and the building I work in are right next to Lake Michigan, which makes for a great view. Lots of sporting events and concerts. There's always something to do." I picked up my wine glass to take another sip, but not before saying, "We'll have to visit, since it's on your list, and I'll show you my favorite spots."

Lily's eyes sparkled at my offer, and I wished I could capture the excitement in her eyes. "I'd really like that. I'd love to see where you go and how you spend your free time."

I set my wine glass down, cocking my brow. "Really?"

She shrugged one shoulder, her voice teasing as she said, "I guess it wouldn't be the *worst* thing in the world. Plus, then you'd show me all the best spots and the best food. Consider it a favor for bringing you to the best restaurant in Golden Falls."

"Ah, yes, such a favor to be brought to a restaurant by someone who tried to burn the place down." My voice was light-hearted, and I was glad Lily picked up on it, because she tipped her head back with a laugh.

"Oh, stop it!" She gently bumped my leg with her foot underneath the table. "We both know it was an accident. If I'm going down, so are you as my accomplice."

I narrowed my eyes. "That's how it's going to be?"

"Maybe. We'll see if it gets to that point." She innocently took a sip of wine, fluttering her black lashes at me. Once she set the glass down, Lily's tongue darted out to catch a drop of wine from her bottom lip. If she noticed me staring, she didn't say anything. "I'd also like to visit a few cafés in the city. See how other people run their businesses and chat with them about how they've expanded and all that. When Eliza was down in Madison for college, I had a chance to do that before I even started and found it to be helpful. I'd...well, I'd like to open a second location of Purrfect Blend one day." Lily's gaze dropped down, and I hated how soft and small her voice got. "It's silly."

My brows furrowed, and I quickly shook my head. "No, it's not silly. Tell me more about it. What are you thinking?"

From working with Lily, I'd picked up on her passion for her business and entrepreneurship right away. She was good at it, too—she had a balance of trusting her instincts but also doing research and being prepared for that next step. She also seemed scared and nervous, though, which was understandable. But she already took the biggest step there was—opening her business. Most people didn't even get to that point and let their dreams exist solely in their minds.

Lily rolled her lips and sat up straighter. "Well," she started, looking back up at me, "it's more in my long-term plan. I need to get things under control in Golden Falls first, like prioritizing baking classes, since I'd love to learn more and get better and more creative at baking. Once that's in place, in the next few years, opening a second location feels like a good next step, but I'd need to find people I trust to run it, since I can't be in two places at once. I'd love to follow the same model of having the cat café partner with the local animal shelter. What do you think about all that?"

I was initially surprised that she was asking for my thoughts—it sounded like she had it all figured out—but I liked that she was seeking my opinion. It felt nice to be wanted in that way. "I think it sounds great," I answered. "I think it's good you're thinking long term. Gives you more time to experiment, hire, and focus on this location. And once that feels good, inquiring about storefronts. Doing research in the meantime is great, too. It'll give you ideas of what to do and what not to do."

As Lily listened, she had her elbow up on the table, resting the side of her face in her palm. I took the moment to admire her features. How her blue eyes sparkled underneath the dim lighting, the flush in her cheeks from the wine, and the way her berry-colored lips spread into an appreciative smile.

"Thanks, Gabe," Lily said, her voice soft but in a different way than earlier. She didn't sound small—she sounded hopeful. And if my words played a small part in that? That was something I was holding on to. She dropped her arm and reached over for the plate of meatballs. "You being nice to me *and* agreeing with something I said? Who would have thought?" Her tone was teasing, and her smile turned cheeky.

"Ha ha, very funny," I deadpanned, this time giving her leg a gentle nudge with mine.

She grinned in return and passed the dish over to me once she'd put a couple of meatballs onto her plate. "I'm messing with you. I'm glad we're getting to know each other. *Really* getting to know each other." She looked up at me, her voice gentle. "You're different than I thought you'd be. During our first meeting, I thought you were arrogant and stand-offish, but you're..." She paused, shaking her head. "You're not that at all. You're thoughtful and attentive. You notice the little things. You're open to ideas and a good listener. I like that. I know this is a strange situation, but I'm glad you're letting me in."

My grip on the plate tightened, as did my other hand that was holding the serving spoon. I was also glad that we were getting to know each other, but I hadn't expected Lily's vulnerability, which was another aspect that I admired about her. I found it difficult to accept that she thought those things about me, but...I'd try. I cleared my throat, meeting her eyes for a moment before looking down. "Thank you, Lily. That, uh, that means a lot," I said genuinely. I wished I said more, gave her more about how much her words meant to me. For the first time in a long time, I felt seen and understood, and there weren't enough words to convey to her how much that meant.

I was grateful when Lily switched the conversation, telling me more about the town and its various businesses, as well as about her friends and family.

This dinner, like my trip to Golden Falls, was just business. I had to remember that.

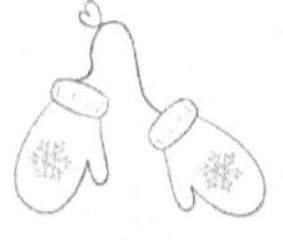

"Can I ask you something?" Lily asked as we walked out of Pasta Fresca after dinner.

"Yeah, of course," I responded genuinely. The words slipped out before I even had a chance to give it a second thought.

But as I waited for her question, I realized she really could ask me anything—and I'd answer. I didn't know when it happened, but I realized I could be myself in Golden Falls—that I could be myself around Lily.

"You're not a huge fan of Christmas," she said slowly, running her tongue along her bottom lip as she pulled on the gloves I'd given her to wear. She also had my hat on, which looked way better on her than me. "How come?"

I handed her the paper bag with our leftovers. It was safe to say we'd ordered too much food, but now she had dinner for tomorrow and the day after that and wouldn't have to worry about cooking.

Even though she'd insisted on paying, or at least splitting, I ended up paying for the dinner. It had been my idea to order the wine and all the food—it was the least I could do. Plus, I learned a lot from Lily tonight about the town and its residents, including more about her brother and best friends.

"Is it that obvious?" I asked with a dry laugh.

"Yeah, kind of," she replied softly, gently, giving me the space I needed to think through my words.

Lily started to walk in the direction of her apartment, but I nodded the other way. For us to take the longer way back. She followed without asking another question, still waiting for me to respond to her earlier comment.

"It's not my favorite time of the year." That was putting it lightly.

I wasn't sure how to tell her that for me, this time of year wasn't filled with the aspects she likely thought about—sledding, family, music, decorations. My parents had never prioritized the holidays, especially not after getting divorced. It wasn't until I got to high school that I realized that wasn't normal. That Christmas wasn't just another day for most families.

"Hey, where did you go?" Lily's voice brought me back to the present—as did the gentle squeeze she gave my arm.

I swallowed the lump in my throat. I desperately needed to create distance—physically and emotionally—between us. And yet, I found myself sharing more with her than I anticipated.

"This time of year hasn't ever been all that magical or special to me," I admitted. "It's always just been another day. Another week in the winter. My parents never celebrated or acknowledged it, especially not after they got divorced."

"That sucks, Gabe. I'm so sorry. That's so unfair to you."

"It's the way it is. My friend Liam has offered for me to spend Christmas with him, his brothers, and family, but I usually work on Christmas Eve and Christmas Day. This year will likely be the same." I didn't add that even though I appreciated Liam's offer, I never took him up on it because I didn't want to feel like I was intruding. It was a concern that wasn't valid at all—and probably one that Liam would be frustrated I had in the first place.

Lily stayed quiet, which I found was never a good sign. It typically meant she was coming up with something. "What if we make an addition to my winter wish list?"

I hesitated but figured there wouldn't be harm in entertaining her idea. "What are you thinking?"

"In addition to sledding and building a gingerbread house at the Christmas festival, I'll use it to show you the magic of Christmas. The music, the food, the lights, snow, if we get it by then. Santa will be there."

"Santa is—"

Lily gasped, tugging on my arm. "There are children around!" she scolded in a whisper. "You can't say that so nonchalantly."

"I wasn't going to ruin the secret of Christmas. I was going to say he's creepy. Also"—I looked around, confirming there were no kids around—"I'm pretty sure all the kids are sleeping, and if they aren't, then it's not my fault they found out the truth."

A laugh bubbled out of Lily, and she hooked her free arm around mine. "He is not creepy!"

"He's always watching, he sneaks into your house, he eats your food," I said appalled, mainly playing up the ruse to continue seeing the amused sparkle in her eye.

"Well, when you say it like that..." A smile tugged on her lips. "This time of year is magical, especially in Golden Falls. I'm excited to show the magic to you."

I would at least entertain her suggestion, especially since we were going to the Christmas festival anyway.

"And you'll spend Christmas Day with me and my family."

I didn't respond immediately, thinking through her words. She stepped in front of me and stopped, nearly causing me to run into her. I let out a heavy exhale and looked down at her.

"Come on," she urged. "I think it'll be good—both for your Christmas spirit and our wish list. You shouldn't be working on Christmas Day. Plus, Hal usually spends Christmas with us, so you two can come over together."

I was still hesitant, because I didn't want to intrude, but I liked Lily's idea more than I wanted to admit. I wouldn't be in Golden Falls for long, and I wasn't sure if I'd be back for another Christmas. I wanted to get to know Hal more, spend time with him, and this was a good chance to do that.

"I'll come to dinner," I agreed, and Lily squealed with a grin. She returned to my side, and we resumed our walk, her apartment building now in sight.

"Here, why don't you give me your number. I can text you the details and we can move on from email." She pulled her phone out of her purse and handed it to me.

I took it from her and put my number in. I sent a text from her phone to me so I'd have her number, too. I handed her the phone as we approached her building. We both stopped walking, facing each other.

"This is going to be good. You'll see," she assured confidently, sealing her words with a nod.

Now that we were standing in front of each other, and I wasn't just stealing glances of her from the side, I could see how flushed her cheeks were—likely a combination of the wine and the cold—and also how happy she looked. Her lips pulled into a smile, and my gaze flicked to her mouth.

Lily more often than not had a smile on her face at the café, but she carried a tension in her shoulders and jaw. It made sense, because she was running a whole damn business. But as I looked at her now, I didn't see that. She looked...relaxed. Beautiful. Warm and inviting, like sunshine.

I swallowed the lump in my throat and kept my hands at my sides, fighting the urge to pull Lily closer. To find out if her lips tasted as sweet as I'd imagined.

"Do you—"

"I should get going," I interrupted before Lily could finish her question. Before I could do something that would threaten the *just business* relationship we had. "It's late." My voice was softer this time.

"Right, of course." Lily nodded. Her smile faltered ever so slightly but quickly returned. "Thank you again for dinner. I had a really great time. Goodnight, Gabe."

"Goodnight, Lily." I took a step back before I changed my mind. Once she'd made her way inside, and I saw her walking up the stairs through the window, I turned around and started the short walk back to Hal's house.

All I could think about on the walk back was how our dinner was better than any date I'd ever been on.

22

LILY

ME

> How's planning going for Christmas dinner?
> Anything I can help with?

MOM

> It's going great! I made the grocery list, and your
> dad is getting everything tomorrow. Everyone is
> able to make it this year except for your sister.
> We'll FaceTime her in for a moment!

ME

> Any chance there's room for one more person
> to join us?

IT TOOK MY MOM LESS THAN TEN SECONDS TO CALL ME AFTER I sent my last text. "Hey, Mom," I answered with a laugh.

"You didn't think I would let you off the hook without a call when you ask a question like that, did you?"

"No, I figured I'd have some explaining to do."

My mom's gentle laugh filled the line. "Is it the same person you were out having dinner with yesterday? And who's helping you with your list?"

I hummed in confirmation. "That's the one."

"See, what did I tell you about giving him a chance? Of course, we have room for him to join. You'll pass along the information to him?"

"Yeah, I will. I hope he's looking forward to it." I thought back to what Gabe had shared about his past Christmases and how this wasn't his favorite time of the year. A part of me hoped this would be a holiday he'd want to remember. "Do you think Dad will be okay with it?" I thought back to what my dad had shared at the last family dinner about working with Ron.

"Of course, your dad will be okay with it. He might not be in touch with Ron anymore, but he's been looking forward to connecting with Gabe while he's in town."

I smiled at my mom's words, forever grateful that I would always have her in my corner. "I appreciate that, Mom. Thanks."

"Any time, my dear. I'm excited to get to know Gabe more, and I'm glad you two are getting along. He's *very* easy on the eyes, too."

"Mom!" I laughed.

"What? Am I wrong?"

"Okay, that's the sign we need to wrap up this conversation. I'll see you later this week for the festival and dinner." I paused, smiling again. "Goodnight, Mom. I love you."

"Love you, too, sweetie. Can't wait to see you soon."

Once I hung up the call, a part of me felt relieved. This was good—Gabe was going to join us for Christmas dinner.

But then there was the part that made me realize I was possibly in over my head. I'd been so anxious at the start of our dinner, and while I'd been able to relax and have fun the rest of the night, this was going to be more time together. Plus, there was an item on the list that I couldn't stop staring at. Literally. I had my winter wish list on the counter, and I was staring at *romantic kiss under the mistletoe that takes my breath away.* Why did I put this on my list?! I hadn't kissed anyone in well over a year, and the kisses I had weren't anything to write home about. Was it because I was a bad kisser?

And now I was looking for a kiss that would take my breath away! What was I thinking?! Gabe was likely a *great* kisser. What if he kissed me, and it was the worst kiss of his life?

I knew I shouldn't care, but I did. I hated being bad at something—and in this case, I had no idea if I was good or bad.

Oh, no. This was not good. With each passing second, I started to spiral further and further into my worries.

This called for emergency baking.

I walked over to the kitchen and opened the cabinet, my eyes scanning the ingredients to figure out what I could make. I was craving something extra sweet...and luckily, I had everything to make white chocolate peppermint brownies. I'd been wanting to offer this on the Purrfect Blend menu but had been meaning to test the recipe. Now was as good of a time as ever.

As I gathered the ingredients and started making the batter, my mind was still racing. Naturally, I texted the one person who would understand the situation I was in.

23

GABRIEL

I WAS SITTING AT THE DESK IN MY ROOM WORKING WHEN MY PHONE lit up with a text from Lily.

LILY

Can you come by my apartment? I need you.

My heart skipped a beat, and my mouth felt dry. It was just after nine at night. Was she okay? What was wrong? I quickly typed out my reply.

ME

I'll be there in less than ten.

Without giving it a second thought, I slipped on a pair of shoes, grabbed my coat, and left a note for Hal, who had gone to bed already.

As promised, I got to Lily's in under ten minutes. I parked my car in front of her building and took the steps up to her apartment two at a time.

I knocked on the door. Not getting an immediate response, I knocked again, calling Lily's name.

The door swung open as Lily pulled one of her headphones

out of her ear. She held a mixing bowl under her arm. "You're here! That was fast. Come on in." She stepped to the side, giving me a clear entrance to her apartment.

Lily's blonde hair was pulled into a messy bun. She was wearing a pair of black yoga pants that hugged her body perfectly and a light-blue tank top. She had a dusting of flour on her cheek and nose. Her blue eyes were bright, watching me curiously as I scanned her apartment for any signs of issues.

Everything looked fine—except for, maybe, the mess in her kitchen from whatever she was baking.

I stepped into her apartment, closing the door behind me. "I got here as quickly as I could. Is everything okay? What's wrong?"

Lily blinked. "Oh! Oh my gosh, I'm so sorry. I see how that sounded. Nothing is terribly wrong, but we might have a slight problem."

"Lily," I rasped, my voice a strained, low growl. "Explain."

Her breath hitched, lips parting ever so slightly, and her cheeks flushed. Something flashed across her face—something that looked awfully close to desire, but there was no way that was what it was. Luckily, Lily spoke up before I could overthink it.

"Gabe, wait!" She set the bowl on the entry table. She slid between me and the door—the very small space between me and the door. She smelled sweet. Sweeter than I wanted to admit. "It's about an item on my wish list. I started to overthink it and got freaked out. It's about the romantic kiss under the mistletoe."

A smart man would've paused this conversation for another time and left the apartment. But, clearly, I wasn't a smart man, and the first giveaway that this was a bad idea should have been the shot of arousal that went straight to my cock at the mere thought of kissing Lily. Of feeling her soft, pink lips on mine, or hearing the sounds she would make when my tongue slid against hers. The second giveaway should have been that this wasn't the first time I was having any of these thoughts, especially given that I nearly kissed her after our dinner.

"Lily, I really thought something was wrong," I admitted.

Her brows furrowed ever so slightly as she watched me, likely confused why I had been so worried. Join the club. I was confused, too. Lily was my competition—not someone I should be worried about.

"I'm sorry for worrying you." The tone in her voice was genuine. Everything about Lily was genuine. Another reminder that Lily Richards was way too good for me. "You're all dressed up. Did I interrupt something? We can talk about this tomorrow."

I looked down at my slacks and dress shirt, shaking my head. "I was at Hal's getting some work done."

"You were lounging at home in that? In dress pants and a dress shirt? That's...that should be illegal! You don't change into comfy clothes after getting home from work?" Her eyes were wide.

I shrugged. "Sometimes, but not always."

Lily shuddered, which caused me to huff a laugh.

"Is flour part of your comfy outfit?" I asked, reaching up to gently brush away the flour from her cheek and nose with my thumb. When she didn't pull away, my touch lingered on her skin for a beat longer.

A blush came over Lily's cheeks. I didn't have a chance to ask what had been on her mind, because there was an eager chatter followed by tiny paws resting against my leg.

Lily cleared her throat, and I dropped my hand, stepping away and instead crouching to say hi to Lily's cats.

I sighed, looking up at her. "Tell me more about this romantic kiss under the mistletoe and why you're worried."

24

LILY

Giving Gabe additional context over text likely would have been helpful. In my defense, I had a whole paragraph typed out but then the oven beeped, signaling it was ready for me to put the brownies in. So, I got distracted.

And now I was distracted again. This time, by Gabe Nelson, who had the sleeves of his dress shirt rolled up to his elbows. This man loved showing off his forearms. It was tragic for me. Great for everyone else.

Why didn't I step away from him earlier? What would have happened had my cats not interrupted us? I didn't want to let my mind go there, but it was impossible not to. Would he have kissed me?

I had one more batch of brownies, and without asking, he'd stepped in and helped me stir the batter while I started cleaning up ingredients I no longer needed.

"So, I mentioned during our dinner that I hadn't been on a date in a while, which was why I was nervous. Then tonight I was looking at my list, and I got nervous again. I mean, a romantic kiss under the mistletoe that takes my breath away? How are we going to accomplish that?" My voice got way too high at my last words. There was no denying that Gabe was handsome. There were likely plenty of women in Milwaukee who were interested in him. Women who were prettier, smarter, and better than me.

"With it getting so close to Christmas," I continued, "there's going to be mistletoe everywhere. People might force us under it."

"People are going to force us to stand underneath mistletoe?" he asked, like the concept was hard to believe. Which, in his defense, did sound ridiculous. But I knew this town, and forcing us to stand under mistletoe (or chasing us with it) was not off the table.

"It's very likely. Weirder things have happened in Golden Falls."

He ran a hand through his hair, and I noticed that his normally perfectly styled hair was messy tonight, as if he'd been running his fingers through it on the whole way over to my apartment. "What if we practiced?"

There was no hesitation in his voice, but I still thought I heard him wrong. "Practiced?" I asked. "Practiced what?" There was no way he meant—

"Practiced our kiss," he said simply, setting down the mixing spoon and pouring the batter into the brownie tin. He was calm, cool, and collected—like he didn't just suggest that we *practice* kissing.

My jaw dropped, and I blinked. "Um, I mean, sure. Yeah, I guess we could practice," I stammered, my cheeks heating up. *Smooth. Real smooth, Lily. Did you forget every word in the English language all of a sudden?* I chewed on my bottom lip, one thought in particular plaguing my mind. One that caused all the nerves in the first place. "But what if I'm bad at it?"

Gabe stopped what he was doing, set the bowl down, and gave me his full attention. "Did someone say that you were a bad kisser?" he asked roughly, but the rasp in his voice wasn't directed at me. He seemed...frustrated, angry even, at the idea that someone would say that to me.

"No," I clarified quickly, but then added, "but I haven't exactly been told I'm a *great* kisser. Plus, it's been a while. What if I was okay at it then but now I'm bad?"

Gabe rubbed his forehead and shook his head. "Lily, there's no way you're bad at it. You're likely a fucking fantastic kisser. What morons have you been kissing who have made you think otherwise?"

I rolled my lips to hide the smile pulling at them and started to move past him to put more of the ingredients away. "So, what you're saying is I should be kissing more—"

"No." Gabe's hand gently wrapped around my wrist, and he pulled me to his chest. Again, we were in nearly the same position as when we first met. Although, this time, I saw warmth in his brown eyes instead of a cold gaze. He likely had warmth all along...I just hadn't noticed it at first. "What I'm saying is that we should practice. Right now, if that works for you."

"Right now," I repeated quietly, breathlessly. "Yes, that, uh, that works for me."

He let go of my wrist, but I didn't move. I *couldn't* move. I was drawn to him like a magnet. Gabe's eyes darkened as his gaze moved to my lips. I inhaled a sharp breath, suddenly getting nervous for a whole different reason.

Gabe's presence was overwhelming every single one of my senses. He was *everywhere*. He crowded more into my space, pushing my back against the edge of the kitchen counter.

"So," I said, wetting my lips, "how does this work? Should you...pretend I'm your girlfriend or something?" I tore my gaze from his mouth but not before seeing a smirk form on his lips.

"Sure, we can do that for our practice." He hummed low in his chest, and because we were so close, I felt the vibration.

Slowly, he trailed his gaze from my eyes to my mouth to the slope of my neck.

"If I was your girlfriend," I started, my breath hitching, "what would you do?"

"If you were my girlfriend, I'd first tell you that I haven't been able to stop thinking about you—about what it would be like to kiss you—since our dinner."

This wasn't real—this was practice. And yet, my heart lurched in my chest and heat coursed through my body. I'd been thinking about our dinner, too. How easy the conversation had been. How I didn't want the night to end. How I wanted him to come upstairs so we could keep talking and getting to know each other. How desperately I wanted him to kiss me.

"Can I touch you?" he asked, and when I nodded, he took a step closer, closing the remaining distance between us. My hands rested on the edge of the counter, propping me up in case my legs gave out.

Gabe gradually moved his hand up, his large palm cradling the side of my face. His thumb brushed along my cheek once gently and then again while his gaze was focused on me the whole time.

He ran his tongue along his bottom lip, his fingers ever so slightly digging into my hair, pulling me closer.

My heart was pounding in my ears from anticipation, and it took everything in me not to wrap my fingers around his shirt and pull his mouth to mine. As if he'd read my mind, Gabe's mouth lifted into his signature crooked half-smile.

"If you were my girlfriend," he whispered, mouth inches from mine, "I'd find any and every opportunity to kiss you."

His other hand went to the small of my back, large fingers splaying and anchoring me to him. The tension was so thick I could barely breathe.

After what felt like *years* of waiting, Gabe captured my lips. I melted into him immediately, like we'd done this a million times before. One of my hands rested on his chest while the other moved higher, my fingers curling around the hair at the nape of his neck.

His tongue explored my mouth, tasting and teasing with every sweep.

A low growl sounded in the back of his throat, the rumble sending vibrations throughout my body.

I'd never been kissed like this. Granted, I didn't have a ton of kissing experience, but it was never like *this*. I understood now what it meant when people said time stopped. Like nothing else in the world mattered or even existed. All I was focused on right now was Gabe's mouth and how perfect it felt against mine. How the heat of his palm seared against my lower back.

He started to pull away, but I didn't want this to end...not yet, at least. I leaned up on my toes, my hand on the back of his neck pulling him closer, which elicited another growl from him. But it was deeper this time, lower. More desperate.

I needed to catch my breath—I needed air—but I needed him more.

As our mouths moved, Gabe's other hand trailed from the curve of my waist up to the side of my breast, his thumb inching dangerously close. I couldn't help the moan that escaped me.

I wanted to feel his hands everywhere on my body. I wanted—

"We should stop," Gabe panted against my mouth, his voice strained in a way I'd never heard from someone before. Ever. He let out an exhale, his grip on my side tightening for a second before his hand dropped. He rested his forehead against mine, and it would've been *so easy* to capture his mouth in another kiss...but I held back.

Because he was right.

"We...yeah, we should." I could barely get the words out, and savory." But I'd seen him eating pastries at the café...and I also saw him drinking the peppermint mocha.

"But..." I started, and he must've followed my line of thinking, because he added, "You're hard to say no to, and maybe I like sweets more than I thought."

"I don't want you eating the pastries because you feel like you have to."

"Trust me, Lily, I haven't done anything I didn't want to." Gabe's voice was low, and I swore his gaze dropped to my mouth.

Before I could respond, Gabe stood from the couch, reaching for my empty plate and walking the few steps over to the kitchen to set the plates in the sink.

When he sat back down, I curled my legs underneath me and turned to face him, my arm resting against the back of the couch.

"Can I ask you something?"

Gabe raised his brows, and I swore the expression on his face read *Really? I think considering I had my tongue down your throat, you can ask me anything.* "I meant what I said when I told you that you can ask me whatever you want."

I played with a frayed thread on the couch, tugging it and trying to buy myself some time. "It's...more personal than some of the other things we've talked about."

He shrugged. "Ask anyway. If it's something I don't want to share, I won't." He reached over, setting his large hand over mine and calming my fidgeting fingers. "You can ask me anything, Lily."

My heart lurched in my chest at his openness, but I was worried he wouldn't think that after my question. "I was wondering," I said, thinking over my words carefully, "why you weren't at Vera's funeral. I don't think you were there. Or maybe I didn't see you?"

Had this been a few weeks ago, I wouldn't have offered him

once they were out, I wasn't sure how convincing they
"That was...good practice."

"It was." He closed his eyes, his nostrils flaring as h
clenched and the muscle in his cheek fluttered. As if he
using all of his restraint.

I slowly, reluctantly, moved my hands to my sides, using
counter to steady myself. Yes, that was practice, but it...it fe
real. Did it feel real for him, too?

After a beat, Gabe opened his eyes and stepped ba
running a hand through his messy hair and tugging on
strands. "You're"—he cleared his throat—"you're a very go
kisser, Lily. You have nothing to worry about."

Gabe's gaze went to the clock on the oven, and I had a feelin
of what he was going to say. Before he had the chance to,
blurted, "Will you stay for a while longer? I'm making brownies
and I need to make sure they're good. I could use a second
opinion."

His lips twitched.

"Yeah, Sunshine, I'll stay a while longer."

The nickname sounded different this time. Warmer. I wasn't
sure what made me happier—the nickname leaving his mouth
or that he was staying.

"What do you mean you don't have much of a sweet tooth?" I
asked, appalled, my eyes bouncing between him and his plate—
which was empty, by the way. For someone who claimed he
didn't have a sweet tooth, he ate his white chocolate peppermint
brownie *very* quickly.

"I just don't," he said with a laugh. "I've always preferred an out. I also didn't think I would've asked him—I would've instead told him I thought he was an asshole for not showing up. But that wasn't fair, and that wasn't who I was. I usually gave people the benefit of the doubt—and I wanted to do the same for Gabe.

His whole body stiffened, but he kept his hand on mine. His throat bobbed as he swallowed, and he looked around the room. Anywhere but me.

"No," he ultimately said, the one word packing an emotional punch. "I wasn't there."

I stayed quiet, giving him the space and time to share more if he wanted to.

"I didn't know about it. Not until a few weeks later." His voice brought my full attention back to him. "And it was too late by then. My father knew, and you'd think he would've told me but... I was out of town for a business meeting, closing a deal for him. He said later he didn't tell me because he didn't want to distract me. But...in reality, I think he didn't tell me because he knew I'd leave the meeting for the funeral without any hesitation. He put his business—money—above family yet again, and it's—" Gabe shook his head. "It shouldn't surprise me by now, but it still does. Because I don't *get it*. I don't get how he knew about it and didn't show up, how he kept it from me and told me in passing once I got back. Like he just fucking forgot. I should've gotten the chance to make that decision, but I didn't, and now I have to live with it."

There was a tightness in my chest, my heart in my throat as I listened to him, the pain dripping from his words. My stomach twisted in guilt over how I thought the worst of him when he first got to town, how I held this against him without knowing the truth.

My heart shattered for him now that I knew.

"Gabe, that's so unfair to you," I said softly. I slid my hand from under his, resting it on top and gripping his fingers tightly. "I'm so sorry that you couldn't make the decision for yourself and that he kept this from you. And I'm sorry for what you've had to deal with since getting into town, me included, when no one's known the truth."

Gabe turned his head, finally looking at me. His expression softened. "Thank you," he responded, as if no one had acknowledged what he'd gone through. "Vera and I weren't all that close as I got older, but..."

"It still hurts," I finished.

"Yeah," he said quietly with a nod. "It still hurts." Gabe inhaled deeply, held his breath for a few counts, and slowly exhaled. "He always"—Gabe let out a dry, humorless laugh— "tells me I care too much. I'm too sensitive. Maybe he's right." He looked over at me, pain swirling in his golden-brown eyes. "Maybe it's true. Maybe I do care too much and I shouldn't."

The way he rasped the words caused my heart to crack—not only for the man next to me but for the boy who likely grew up hearing this over and over.

Tears welled in my eyes as I vehemently shook my head. "There's nothing wrong with that. It's not a bad thing. It's a *good* thing. People should care more about others."

There was so much emotion swirling around in his eyes that I couldn't believe I ever thought Gabe was cold. That he didn't feel.

He felt *so much*. He felt everything around him.

And I saw now that he carried that with him, whether he wanted to or not. Maybe it weighed him down at times, but it never stopped him. He was here, after all.

I swallowed the lump in my throat and blinked my tears away. "I like that you care so much. That you feel so deeply—it's a strength. You're willing to help people you don't know, like Marnie, or come visit a town where you're walking into the unknown and are still making an effort to get to know people. You care deeply, and I think that's one of my favorite things about you."

His brow quirked, and he tilted his head to the side. "One of?"

Of course, that's what he picked up on. I let out a laugh. "Yes, one of. Turns out, you're not so bad, and there's a few things I like about you." I stopped there, but he looked at me expectantly.

"C'mon, what's another?"

Twisting my lips to the side, I hummed as if I needed more time. "Even though it's a bit of a pain for me, I like how determined and dedicated you are. I like how good you are with the cats. And...I like that when I said I needed you, you got over here as fast as you could." I gave his hand a squeeze. "You have a big" —Gabe looked over at me, the corner of his mouth tipping up— "heart," I finished.

"Right." He huffed a laugh.

I swatted at his arm, picking up on where his mind initially went. He likely had that, too...but I wouldn't be finding that out.

My expression softened. "I mean it, Gabe."

"I know you do." His eyes met mine. "That's...quite possibly the nicest thing anyone has ever said to me. Thank you."

"You don't need to thank me for that. Also, when you're ready, you should ask Hal to tell you more about Vera. He loves talking about her, and I'm sure he would be happy to share some of his favorite moments. They both talked about you a lot—Hal still does."

Gabe kept a tight grip on my hand and nodded. "Okay, yeah, I think I will," he said eventually.

I wasn't sure how long we stayed like that, but it felt like our walls were coming down. Maybe at the end of this, regardless of how the building sale turned out, I'd have a new friend in Gabe.

Because I liked him more than I wanted to admit.

The conversation turned lighthearted after that. And he did have another brownie after all.

He left just before midnight, and as he drove back to Hal's, all I could think about was that I wanted more time.

More time to get to know him. More time to have these conversations. More time to tell him what I liked about him.

More time with Gabe in Golden Falls.

25

LILY

There's been an interesting development with my winter wish list.

Did you lose it again???

What happened?!

Maybe it would've been better had I lost it.

Gabe and I kissed.

YOU WHAT?

Kissed???

Omg the romantic kiss under the mistletoe!!!
Was that why?!

ME

Sort of…

I told him I was nervous about the romantic kiss under the mistletoe, and he suggested we practice.

ELIZA

He suggested you practice?! He was totally looking for an excuse to kiss you.

ME

He wanted to take the pressure off our actual kiss! It wasn't anything more than that!

JULES

Oh, it was definitely more than that.

How was the kiss?!

ME

It was fine. Nothing special.

Average.

Just okay.

ELIZA

LOL even over text you're a horrible liar. I don't believe any of that.

JULES

What you meant to say was it was an amazing kiss and you haven't been able to stop thinking about it, right?

ME

Gah! No comment.

JULES

Also, did you nearly start a fire at Pasta Fresca?

ME

No comment!!!!

I SLIPPED MY PHONE INTO MY APRON'S FRONT POCKET, KNOWING very well Eliza and Jules would have a list of questions next time I saw them. I didn't blame them, because I would want to know everything, too.

When Jules told us over the summer she was going on a first date with Wes, Eliza and I wanted all the details on how their relationship had evolved to that point. Well, *nearly* all the details. He was my brother, after all.

I thought about how much things had changed for the better since that moment. How Wes and Jules fell deeply in love. How strong my friendship with Jules had gotten in the months since she'd been in Golden Falls. And how lucky I was that my friendship with Eliza was stronger than ever after so many years.

It was more fun asking the questions than being on the other side of things, though, especially since I had no clue how I felt about the kiss. It was practice, and we were going through a list...but it also felt so *real*.

One thing was for sure—I couldn't stop thinking about it. Or Gabe's warm body pressed against mine. His large hand on my lower back. How effortlessly his lips moved against mine. How I never wanted to stop.

I didn't think I'd be able to survive another kiss from Gabe with how all-consuming this one was.

With Christmas quickly coming up—three more days!—I didn't have time to focus on anything else, and my holiday orders showed that. I had a handful of customers who placed their orders for the holidays at the start of December, but most stopped by the café or ordered over the phone this week. Everyone would pick up their orders the morning of Christmas Eve, and I closed the café on Christmas Day and the following week. Jodi and Henry at the animal shelter, along with other volunteers, helped foster the cats during this time.

I pulled myself out of my thoughts when the door opened,

and Wes walked in. Once my brother was within earshot, I turned to Tiffany with a teasing smile. "I'll take Wes's order and spare you having to deal with his grumpiness."

"I'm not that grumpy," Wes grunted in his typical fashion, but the corner of his mouth twitched as he fought a smile.

Tiffany let out an amused laugh, already used to our antics. "Sounds like a plan." She turned to Wes and gave him a small wave. "Good to see you, Wes."

Wes nodded in return, and Tiffany turned to the next customer.

Wes stepped to the side to look at the day's pastries. My brother drank his coffee black, so most of the time when he was here, it was for a treat, either for himself, Jules, or his staff. He hummed as he looked at the trays behind the glass. This week's menu was festive frosted sugar cookies and thumbprint cookies.

"Do you want some of each?" I asked as I grabbed and assembled a medium-sized pink bakery box.

"Yeah, that'd be great. Let's do four of each."

"You got it." With a pair of tongs, I carefully placed each treat into the box. "Are you excited for Christmas Eve and Christmas? It's the first year Jules is celebrating with us."

"I'm really excited," he said, and I swore there was a twinkle in his eye. My brother was a big softie, especially for Jules. "I enjoy this time of year, but it's different with her. There's more magic year-round."

I raised my brow, and he waved his hand.

"Yeah, yeah, you don't need to give me shit about how fucking cheesy that was. I know."

I tipped my head back with a laugh. "Hey, you said it, but I love that. You two are perfect together, and I'm so happy you found each other. She's the best."

"Really is, isn't she?" A rare grin formed on his face. "I'm glad you two are such good friends. I'm excited for Jade to meet her eventually."

I held my tongue, not saying that for our sister to meet Jules that would require her wanting to visit Golden Falls.

"Feels like Juliette's been part of the family for longer. Her parents are flying in from Florida in a couple of weeks, which she's excited about."

"That's great! You get to celebrate with us and with them." I closed the box and set it on the counter. Once Tiffany finished up at the tablet, I stepped over to ring up Wes's order.

His brows shot up to his forehead. I should've known with how observant he was that he'd notice right away I had a new tablet. Like, very new. Earlier this morning new.

"You finally got a new one of those, huh? When did that happen?" He tipped his chin with an amused chuckle.

"Uh, yeah, I did." I cleared my throat. "This morning, actually. Go ahead and tap your card when you're ready."

Wes reached for his wallet but paused. "Wait. You've been adamant about how you didn't need a new one and it's not worth replacing it yet. What changed?"

What changed was that Gabe walked in this morning, set the tablet on the counter, and sat at what had turned into his usual table in the back right corner. A table that had a view of the front counter but also was next to the window looking into the cat room. When I insisted he return it, he gave me every excuse in the book: he couldn't return it, he lost the receipt, it was past the return date.

Eventually, I gave up, thanked him, and started my day. Turned out, I wasn't as persuasive as he claimed.

You're hard to say no to, and maybe I like sweets more than I thought, Gabe's low voice rumbled in my mind.

"Nothing changed," I said, trying to sound casual as Wes

tapped his card. "Gabe got it for me. He brought it this morning."

My gaze drifted to Gabe. He was working at his laptop, his brows furrowed as he looked at his screen. His light blue-dress shirt was pulled taut across his chest. As if he knew I was looking at him, Gabe slowly lifted his head and met my eyes. He watched me for a moment, his expression not giving away anything that was on his mind. But I didn't miss the way the corner of his mouth lifted and his eyes softened.

I rolled my lips to hide my smile, feeling a blush form on my cheeks. I turned my attention back to Wes, who was carefully watching me.

He raised his brows, sliding his wallet into his back pocket. "The same Gabe you're competing with for the building? What's his motive by getting you the tablet?"

A part of me understood where Wes was coming from, because a couple weeks ago, I would've also thought Gabe had an ulterior motive. Maybe about how he was trying to get on my good side or improve his appearances around town. But...it was just the two of us when he stopped by—not even Tiffany was around yet. I also knew him well enough now, and he wasn't that type of person. He was...thoughtful, considerate, and told me how he didn't want me to worry about the tablet. How I had enough things on my mind.

"There's no motive," I defended, my voice firmer than usual. "He knew I needed a new one and picked one up when he was at the store."

"He just so happened to pick one up?" My brother repeated. I knew the words were ridiculous as soon as they left my mouth, but hearing Wes say them back to me? A tablet wasn't like orange juice or eggs—you didn't just pick one up when you were at the store. This required thoughtful planning, which was something I didn't want to admit out loud. "Mom said he's going to spend Christmas with us."

"He is," I confirmed. "And I don't want you to give him a hard time. He's...different than I thought. He's not this ruthless, cold guy." *That I made him out to be.*

Wes's expression softened. "I'm not going to give him a hard time." He tilted his head to the side, amending, "Well, I'm not going to give him a hard time for no reason. I don't want to see you get hurt, but you know him better than I do. You two have spent a lot of time together these past few weeks."

We had, which made me feel like I'd known Gabe longer than I had. We also opened up to each other more than I'd expected us to.

"I have your back, Lily, but I know you can hold your own."

My heart warmed at my brother's words, and I gave him a grateful smile. "Thanks, Wes. That means a lot. I'm excited for you to get to know him a little better."

"Honestly, me too. Cooper and I enjoyed hanging out with him during poker night." And by the small smile on my brother's face, I knew he meant it. Wes grabbed the bakery box and held it under his arm. "We'll have to keep you away from the fireplace and any candles on Christmas. I don't think Mom would be very happy if you tried to burn down her house." Wes's genuine smile spread into a shit-eating grin.

My nostrils flared, but I couldn't hold back my laugh. "It was two tealight candles! I wasn't trying to start a fire!" I defended, raising my arms and letting them fall at my sides. "I don't appreciate all the gossip!"

"What did you tell me over the summer?" he asked over his shoulder while making his way toward the door. "Oh yeah—people are always going to be gossiping about some small town drama. It's Golden Falls."

I crossed my arms over my chest, letting out a sigh. My words kept coming back to bite me. "You're a pain in my ass, Wesley Richards!"

"I love you too, sis. See you around."

I scanned the ingredients in the kitchen, jotting down in my notepad that I needed to buy more flour, sprinkles, cocoa powder, and chocolate chips for the upcoming Christmas orders.

I was in the middle of writing when the music in the café cut out. It happened every so often and usually meant I needed to reconnect my phone. I set my notepad on the counter and walked closer to the doorway to the main area of the café. I leaned against the doorway as I pulled my phone out. Luckily, the conversation and chatter continued, and the lack of music, albeit temporary, hadn't impacted anyone.

My eyes found Gabe, but this time, he wasn't looking at me. He was wrapped up in a conversation with Louise, and I found myself curious about what they were talking about. Were they talking about the building? Was Louise telling him more about town?

My conversation with Wes earlier today came back to my mind. As close as Gabe and I were getting, there was still a building on the line. I couldn't lose sight of that.

I took my time trying to fix the music, giving myself the opportunity to eavesdrop. My spot in the doorway was perfect—I could hear them fairly clearly but was largely out of sight.

"I told you from the start not to underestimate her, didn't I?" Louise asked.

Gabe let out a chuckle. "You sure did, and I appreciated the heads up. She's...something else."

"You better mean that in a good way," Louise said with a laugh, and Gabe quickly added, "Of course, I mean it in a good way. I could tell when I first met her how important she is to this town. How Golden Falls wouldn't be the same without her or this café."

My brows furrowed. They had to be talking about me, right? But...why?

Louise hummed in thought. "I heard you two had quite the first meeting. What was your first impression of her?"

"Well," Gabe said slowly, "at first, she was simply the woman who had bumped into me in front of Hal's store. But when I turned around and saw her. I...I thought she was the most beautiful woman I'd ever seen. Looking into her eyes calmed me in a way I'd never experienced. My worries, concerns, all of that disappeared. Time stopped. Her hair was wild, her cheeks pink, and she had this crease between her eyebrows. My first impression of her was that she had the power to bring any man to his knees."

The corner of Gabe's mouth tipped up in a lopsided smile. A smile that had no business being so charming. I braced my palm on the doorframe to keep myself steady, unable to hear Louise's response because my heart was jackhammering in my ears.

Did he really mean that? Or was he saying that to Louise to win her over even more? Did he know people were listening?

His voice sounded so raw and real, and everything he said actually happened.

I had no reason to doubt Gabe—earlier today, I was defending him to my brother—but I couldn't help the nagging feeling that I needed to protect myself and my heart. That, maybe, this was too good to be true.

Our priority was still getting the list done and figuring out next steps about the building, but as much as I wanted to tell myself that nothing had changed since the moment we met, I knew that'd be a lie.

Everything had changed.

26

LILY

"Tiffany, I don't want you to worry about me and the café. Focus on Jack." I held up my phone with my shoulder as I cleaned the espresso machine later that same day.

Tiffany had to rush out after getting a call from Jack and Maddie's school that her son had a fever and wasn't feeling well. She left to go pick him up and called me with an update as soon as she got home.

Purrfect Blend was closed for the day, but with Tiffany leaving quickly, Gabe stuck around to help. It was only us in the café.

"You should also take tomorrow off to be with him," I added. Tomorrow was the last day of school before the kids' winter break, and I didn't want Tiffany to worry about scheduling child care to come into the store.

"But I know how busy this time of year is, and you *just* hired me."

I stopped what I was doing as soon as I heard the stress in her voice. I leaned my hip against the counter and repositioned my phone so I was holding it. "Things happen, and your family comes first. Always. Whether I've recently hired you or we've been working together for years, I never want you to feel like you have to choose between this job or being there for your kids. Yes, it's a busy time, but I'll figure it out. Please don't worry about it, and take the time you need. Besides," I said as I walked over to the tablet to check the number of orders, "I've handled the holidays on my own before. It'll be a breeze."

My eyes scanned the tablet screen, and as soon as I saw the number of orders placed for the holidays, my mouth went dry. This number was double what I typically took, which made sense given that I had planned on Tiffany's help. Still, I didn't want to worry her. I meant what I said earlier—I didn't want her to feel guilty for prioritizing her family.

"You're the best, Lily. I really appreciate it. I'll keep you posted on how he's feeling and if my husband might be able to stay with him."

"That sounds great. Talk to you soon, Tiffany."

I ended the call and set my phone on the counter. I looked at the tablet again, trying to convince myself that I'd seen the wrong number or I imagined something.

"Forty orders..." I said under my breath. I typically kept holiday pre-orders between fifteen to twenty customers, since people often ordered more than one item. I had a limited holiday menu that they were able to choose from, but still...

Forty was double the amount of customers I typically took on.

I felt my chest closing in on me, spots dancing in my vision. My palms got sweaty, and it suddenly started to feel like a million degrees in the café.

"Lily?" I could see Gabe out of the corner of my eye, but his voice felt far away.

"That's...I can't..." I shook my head, my vision getting blurry.

This was exactly why Hal didn't want to sell the building to me. Because I could barely take care of the responsibilities I had, and I was so focused on growing the café that I didn't have a backup plan if things went wrong.

"I'm right here, Sunshine. I got you." His voice was slow and steady. It didn't matter how many times I blinked—he wouldn't come into focus.

Gabe untied my apron, lifting it over my head and setting it on the counter. The simple action made me feel slightly less claustrophobic in my own body.

He gently set his hands on my arms, guiding me around the counter to sit at one of the tables. Instead of pulling out the chair next to me, he kneeled in front of me. He reached over for my hand, taking it in his and holding on tightly, grounding me.

"I'm right here," he repeated. "We're in the café, and you're safe. What can I do to help?"

I parted my lips, but no words came out.

"Take your time," Gabe assured. His other hand wrapped around mine, and he squeezed gently. "Breathe with me."

I nodded and took a deep inhale, slowly letting it go. I repeated the action and used the time to gather my thoughts and slow my heart rate down.

"I...I saw the number of Christmas orders and got really freaked out, because I don't know if I can fulfill them all," I admitted, my voice not sounding like my own. "And I don't want to stress Tiffany out when Jack isn't feeling well."

"Let's see what we can do and figure it out together. What's stressing you out the most?"

"I shouldn't have doubled the number of orders during the first season I had help. That was so irresponsible of me not to have a backup plan. I also didn't expect that we actually *would* double the orders. Why would so many people want to order from me?"

"Lily," he said with a laugh. "You're the most talented baker in the area—I'd even go so far to say the state."

I rolled my eyes, but he continued.

"Of course, people want to order from you. People are willing to drive to Golden Falls for your baking."

"No way." I was a no-name baker in a small town with limited training. There were *so* many other bakers who were more skilled than me.

As if he heard my inner thoughts, Gabe gave me a pointed look. "Yes, really. Stop doubting yourself. You're talented and skilled at what you do. Don't diminish that."

I was speechless again, but this time it wasn't from my stress or panic. It was from Gabe's compliment.

My lips rolled together, and I nodded. "Thank you." My voice was quiet.

I realized he'd let go of my hands. Instead, his large palms were splayed on the sides of my thighs. Now, my throat was dry for a *whole other reason* as I thought about him moving his hands up to my hips to grip them tightly. If I moved my hands—which were tightly gripping the side of the chair—to his broad shoulders. Or maybe to tangle in his hair.

I gripped the chair even tighter, my knuckles turning white. I needed *something* to keep me from reaching out.

"Okay, so, double orders." Gabe got back to the task at hand. "Usually, you're handling them on your own, right? Depending on if Jack feels better, maybe Tiffany will be able to help. If not, you have me to help. I can't say baking is my specialty, but I'm sure there's other things I can help with to make things go smoothly. We can also recruit your mom to help with baking? I'm sure Eliza and Jules would be willing to help. Your brother and dad, too. Hell, I think if I went outside and asked *literally* anyone walking by, they would be willing to help you. You have this whole town on your side."

"I just...I don't really like asking my friends and family for help when it comes to the café," I admitted. It was my first time saying this out loud. "Having my mom come in when it was busy already felt like a big ask to me. I don't want them to think I can't do this on my own. To think I made a mistake or that I can't handle it."

I did my best to focus on the conversation, but it was challenging when his thumb ran small circles over my jeans.

"I haven't been here all that long, but I can safely say no one thinks that."

"But what about Hal? Isn't that the reason we're in this mess?" I raised my hand to gesture to the café.

"I don't know what he's thinking—I don't think anyone does—but I think part of it is he wants you to realize you *can* ask for help...and that you should when you need it. Hiring Tiffany was a big step. Look at how much more you've been able to get done over the last few weeks with her help."

I tilted my head. Gabe made a good point—and it was a good reminder, too. Asking for help didn't make me weak, and it didn't show that I couldn't run my café. It made me more responsible. It showed how many people I had in my corner. How many people wanted to see me succeed—and help me get there.

"How do you know just the right thing to say?"

A low, derisive laugh escaped him. He averted his gaze before speaking, his eyes focused on the café wall. "I don't think anyone's ever said that to me before."

"I'm glad I could be the first."

His eyes met mine again, and I could have sworn he leaned forward the smallest amount. I nearly closed the distance, unable to handle the tension in the air.

Then his phone rang.

Gabe moved his hands from my thighs and reached into his pocket to pull his phone out. He tilted the phone away from me, but not before I saw the name *Ron Nelson* flash on the screen.

"I should, uh"—he cleared his throat—"I should take this." He stood, about to walk away, but paused. "Are you okay? Feeling better?"

A part of me wanted to lie, to keep him in this moment with me a little longer. But I didn't. I smiled softly up at him, nodding. "I'm feeling better, yeah. Thanks again for what you said."

"I meant every word."

With how his feet were glued to the floor, I thought maybe he'd stay. But when his phone rang again, Gabe grabbed his backpack and answered it without hesitation this time. I tried not to think about how my heart dropped at the sight of him leaving the café with his shoulders slumped and head hanging low.

When I got back to my apartment that evening, I was doing my best to focus on Gabe's assurance. I'd already texted my mom, Jules, and Eliza. And I knew I had other people in my corner, too, if need be. I texted Tiffany to reassure her that everything would be fine.

It was all going to be okay. Which was exactly why I was trying to relax tonight by watching *Home Alone*. I was lying on the couch, with one leg hanging off and my head turned sideways toward the television. Bandit was curled up on my chest, purring, while Sylvie roamed by the food bowls, acting like she hadn't been fed in *days*. When, in reality, she ate half an hour ago.

Sylvie lifted her head when a very particular pattern was knocked on the door, letting me know Eliza was on the other side.

"I'm sorry, but I need to get up." I scooped Bandit and set him on a blanket on the other end of the couch, where he promptly curled up and resumed his nap. I paused the movie and walked to the door, grinning when I saw Eliza on the other side. "What's up?"

"Wanted to make sure you were okay. Your text sounded... panicked." She narrowed her eyes at me, as if trying to get a sense of how I was feeling. Whatever she saw in my expression caused her shoulders to visibly relax, and the worry eased from her face. "You're feeling better about it all?"

I nodded to confirm. "I am. Gabe reassured me and reminded me that I don't have to do it all alone, which sounds obvious, but..."

"But you need that reminder pretty often," Eliza said with a laugh.

Once she walked in, I closed the door and followed her to the kitchen, where she opened the fridge and grabbed a sparkling water. I took a seat on the stool next to the island. Memories of Gabe being in my apartment flooded my brain, especially our practice kiss.

"How are things going with Gabe and your list?"

"Huh?" I returned my attention to Eliza, who was standing on the other side of the island, sipping her sparkling water and staring at me. "The kiss?"

Eliza grinned. "I asked how things are going with Gabe and your *list*, but I see where your mind is at."

I rolled my eyes but didn't bother arguing with her since she was right. "Things are going well, and I'm realizing that I really like spending time with him," I admitted on a sigh.

"You like him," Eliza said matter-of-factly.

I rolled my lips, not ready to say those words out loud yet. Instead, I settled on, "It doesn't matter if I do or not. There's so many reasons why this would never work, starting with the building. I might've been wrong about him at the start, but that doesn't change that we both want the same thing and only one of us is going to get it."

Eliza listened carefully, nodding. She let out a sigh. "Well, the sooner you get done with the list, the sooner he's out of town. Then you don't have to worry about how you feel about him."

If it wasn't for the pit in my stomach, I likely would've laughed, because that was such an Eliza answer. Except all I could focus on was that I *was* worried about how I felt about him. My feelings for him were completely different than when he first got to town, and I couldn't wrap my head around how much had changed in such a short amount of time.

Eliza watched me, and I could tell she was ready to say more, but she decided to drop it. She exhaled and offered me a smile instead. "Be careful, okay?"

"I will," I promised her. "It'll all work out."

I wasn't sure if I was convincing her or myself. Either way, I hoped I was right.

27

GABRIEL

Hal wasn't the best at texting, but he was great at emailing. Go figure. I emailed him earlier today to let him know I was going to pick up ingredients for dinner after wrapping up at the café.

When I got to the house, I didn't see Hal yet. I wasn't sure if he had poker night tonight, but I figured I would cook the turkey chili anyway, even if he was busy and we couldn't eat together.

I'd finished tossing in the ground turkey, beans, onions, peppers, crushed tomatoes, and various spices when the door opened.

"Smells incredible, Gabe." Hal pulled off his coat and toed off his boots. He was wearing his typical outfit: a warm flannel, white undershirt, and a pair of worn jeans. "Thanks for the meal. I've been looking forward to it all day."

I gave the food another stir before setting the lid on top and turning the heat to medium-low to simmer. "Yeah, I'm happy to," I told him, walking around the counter and pulling out one of the stools to sit as Hal sat at the table right in front of me. "I wasn't sure if you had poker tonight or not."

"I don't, but even if I did, I wouldn't miss this for the world. Not every day my grandson cooks for me."

I knew Hal didn't mean it that way, but it made me think of all the meals we'd missed. How maybe I should've been making the drive over to cook dinner for him once in a while. But...I was here now. That was what I was trying to focus on. "I'm happy to do it. There's also going to be plenty of leftovers, and I can make us something new next week. My cooking abilities are...limited," I admitted with a laugh. "But chili, pasta, and burgers are my specialties."

"Those happen to be my favorite foods," Hal said.

When I eyed him skeptically, he simply grinned. I let out a low chuckle and moved from the stool over to one of the chairs at the table. "Food should be ready in about thirty minutes or so. Want to play a game of cards?" I offered.

He nodded. "I'd love to. What'd you have in mind?"

"What do you think about teaching me how to play poker?" When I'd attended poker night with Hal at Lake Ridge, it was just to watch, and I'd been meaning to ask him about the rules.

Hal's eyes glistened as he looked over at me. "I'd like that very much. Let me go grab the cards. Why don't you go and grab some chocolate from the cabinet. I should have a bag of Hershey's Kisses in there."

"Chocolate?" I asked as Hal went down the hallway toward the living room.

"You're a beginner! I'm not going to swindle you out of money. Not yet, at least. I'll teach you how to play first."

I grinned to myself as I shook my head. Fair enough.

"I'm bound to win *at least* once, right?" I asked as Hal shuffled. We'd been playing poker for the last couple of hours, only taking a break to eat dinner once it was ready.

Hal dealt us another hand. "Maybe. I do have decades, upon decades, of experience. Does feel good to win, though. Lately, over at Lake Ridge, Cooper has been cleaning me out."

A comfortable silence fell over us. I thought back to my conversation with Lily a few days ago, about how she encouraged me to talk to Hal about Vera. The thought made me anxious, but there never would be a *right time.* I peeked at my cards before setting my hand on them, tapping my fingers against the wooden table.

"I wish I would've been here for Vera's funeral. I'm sorry that I wasn't." I stumbled over my words, breaking the silence between us. I regretted it for a split second, but when Hal set his cards down on the table and looked over at me with a gentle, understanding smile, I had no regrets.

"I know, Gabe. I never doubted it for a second that you would've been here. I thought the message would get to you, but clearly, I shouldn't have made that assumption."

"He told me a few weeks after the fact. I should've reached out then, but...it felt like it was too late. I was, I don't know, embarrassed? That I didn't know. That I didn't reach out sooner. In hindsight, I should've called you as soon as I found out."

Hal slowly nodded as he said, "A call from you would've been nice, but I don't hold any of that against you, Gabriel. Life is too short to live with regrets. What matters to me—what's important to me—is that if you have regrets, you take that feeling and do something positive with it."

I mulled over his words, truly letting them sink in. *If you have regrets, you take that feeling and do something positive with it.* "I'm trying to do that in Golden Falls." Because I did have regrets. I regretted aspects of my career and my lack of a relationship with Hal. But being here allowed me to do *something* about both of those things.

"I was hoping that'd be the case." Hal grabbed three pieces of chocolate and put them in the center of the table. I did the same with my last three chocolates. "I think spending time here has been good for you, including the time you've spent with Lily." Hal raised his brows, a knowing look on his face. There was no way he knew about our kiss. But then, what was up with that look? "Sounds like you two had a nice dinner."

No, of course, he didn't know. He was commenting about the dinner and that we *had* to be spending time together because of the list.

"I've liked spending time with her," I admitted. "I didn't anticipate enjoying it so much, but..." I paused, carefully thinking through my words. "But I've liked getting to know her and learning about the town from her. She's incredibly talented and kind, and I've never met anyone like her. She lights up whatever room she's in, brightens the mood immediately. She's...sunshine. I don't think she even realizes the positive impact she has on others."

"I thought the same thing when I first met your grandmother," Hal admitted, a nostalgic smile on his face as his eyes twinkled. "She was one of a kind. Always put others first but also didn't hesitate to speak her mind if she didn't like how something was being done. When you find a woman like that and you're lucky enough to get an ounce of her attention, you don't let go."

I focused on what Hal was saying about Vera, because if I thought too deeply, I would start to wonder if my time with Lily could turn into something more—and it couldn't.

But I wondered what about us together made Hal say that. Was it our dinner? The time spent together at the café? Something else he saw?

I flicked my thumb along the edge of the cards, fairly confident I was going to lose this round, too. "Will you tell me more about Vera?"

"Be careful what you ask, son. How much time do you have?" Hal glanced over at the clock.

"I have all the time in the world." I let out a low chuckle, shrugging. "And nowhere else I'd rather be."

And I truly meant it.

The rest of the week went by quickly, and before I knew it, it was Christmas Eve, which meant the town's Christmas festival and an opportunity to check off a few things on Lily's wish list.

The two of us spent the morning together at the café as customers came in to pick up their orders. It all went well. Tiffany's husband was able to stay back with the kids, so she was able to come in and help Lily. In fact, Lily had a whole team today with the help of her mom, friends, Tiffany, and me. All the orders were made on time, and pickup was a breeze. She handled everything with confidence and excitement—while wearing a Santa hat. She looked fucking adorable.

Once all the orders were picked up, Lily closed the café early for the day, and as if right on cue, the first snowfall of the winter started and hadn't stopped. Thick, heavy flakes had been falling for the last six hours, at least. I lost count of how many times I went outside to shovel Hal's driveway and sidewalk.

Most people, including Lily, were thrilled about the timing of the snow. *A Christmas miracle*, she'd said.

My Christmas miracle would be once all the lights and decorations got taken down.

I'd gone back inside from the latest round of shoveling snow and was prepared to start getting ready for tonight when my phone rang. "Hey, Liam. What's up?" I answered, holding the phone up with my shoulder while pulling off my gloves and hat.

"Merry Christmas Eve, man!" I could tell Liam was grinning without seeing him, the joy radiating over the call. "I know you'll likely turn me down, but you know I have to remind you anyway. There's a spot with your name on it if you want to join my family for the holidays, either today, tomorrow, or both."

Even though I'd never taken Liam up on it, he always called and offered. No matter what. "Thanks, man, but I actually have plans of my own this year. I'm not working for once and...I'm spending both days in Golden Falls."

"No shit." Liam chuckled. "That's great. What're you up to?"

Liam and I had texted here and there over the weeks, so I'd been able to fill him in on how things had been going at the café, getting through Lily's list, and reconnecting with Hal. What I hadn't told him about was the kiss.

"Things have gotten...interesting around here," I said slowly. "I'm going to the Christmas festival tonight with Lily."

"Lily," he said, not missing a beat. "The *blue-eyed blonde* you haven't been able to stop talking about?"

"I don't remember not being able to stop talking about her," I argued, although there was hesitation in my voice. Had I been talking that much about her? "And I'm only talking about her because we have to complete this list together."

"Uh huh." Liam sounded unconvinced. "Are you two going to this Christmas festival together as a date?"

"No," I said quickly. A little too quickly, apparently, because Liam barked a laugh. "Not a date at all. There's a couple things on her list that we'll be able to check off tonight. I'm also spending Christmas with her, her family, and Hal tomorrow."

"Sounds festive," Liam said, and I could imagine his grin. "And romantic."

I rolled my eyes.

"You do know how this goes, right?" Liam asked, as if it was obvious. When I didn't say anything, he continued. "First, you're going to start to love Christmas because it'll remind you of her... and then you're going to fall in love with Lily. Haven't you seen a romantic comedy?"

"Uh, no, I haven't, actually."

"We'll change that as soon as you're back. But, anyways, did you not hear what you said? You have actual plans for the holidays and aren't working. I've been trying to get you to come over for dinner for years, but because *Lily* asked..." He trailed off, amusement lacing his voice.

"It's not like that. I'm...I'm trying to spend more time with Hal. I'm trying to show him that I'm committed to the town." I wasn't sure if I was trying to convince Liam or myself.

"Don't get me wrong—I think this is great. You're not working over Christmas, you're spending time with people in town, and you sound less stressed. But face it. You like her."

I stayed quiet for a moment, thinking over Liam's words. Did I sound less stressed? Was that because of Lily or something else? With Liam's reaction, I knew I couldn't tell him about the kiss. The *practice* kiss that I hadn't been able to stop thinking about. That would give him more evidence. "I've enjoyed getting to know her," I said. "But that's all this is. I don't want it to turn into anything more." *Because Lily deserves something*—someone—*better*.

Liam's voice turned more serious, which was unusual for him. "Keep an open mind, alright? You never know what might happen."

I grunted noncommittally, which seemed to be enough for him.

"And, hey, if you need advice or tips, I'm your guy," Liam added.

I held back a laugh, shaking my head. "You haven't had the best track record with women. I don't know if I trust your tips. Why don't you tell me about what you're up to on Christmas instead?"

Liam and I continued chatting as I finished getting ready.

Tonight, I opted for a long-sleeve, dark-green Henley shirt and pair of dark-wash jeans instead of my typical dress shirt and pants. I had on my usual coat, along with an extra hat and pair of gloves in case Lily forgot hers.

And then I left to meet Lily to check a couple more things off her list.

28

LILY

GABE ENDED UP BEING RIGHT. EVERYTHING WENT SMOOTHLY regarding the holiday orders, and I knew part of that was because he instilled the confidence in me that I could do it and that help wasn't a bad thing.

Even though I hadn't asked her, Tiffany stopped by, too. She said she couldn't leave me hanging, and her husband insisted on staying with the kids so Tiffany could focus on helping. Luckily, Jack was feeling better. He'd miss the Christmas festival tonight, but Tiffany told me she'd bring Maddie.

My mom, Tiffany, and I took the lead on baking while Eliza and Jules packaged orders. Gabe had the order sheet and was double-checking everything, and he also helped me this morning when customers stopped by to pick up their orders.

I couldn't believe it was already Christmas Eve. The month was flying by.

When Gabe had told me that people from across the state had placed orders, I didn't believe it until I saw for myself.

I had orders from Golden Falls, of course, but there were also people coming in from surrounding towns. Sometimes even upwards of an hour away. I couldn't describe how amazing it felt that word was getting out about Purrfect Blend, and it made me more excited to try to find time to pursue the baking classes I'd been eyeing.

For the next week or so, however, I was taking a break. After all the orders were picked up this morning and volunteers from the animal shelter came by to pick up the cats, I closed Purrfect Blend for the week. I'd reopen after the new year.

At first, when I decided to take time off, a part of me realized it would be strange not seeing Gabe every day. Then I remembered I'd see him both tonight and tomorrow, and the ache in my chest lessened.

My eyes searched for him as I stood outside my apartment building. The cheers, laughter, and conversation from the Christmas festival echoed in the air, the event already in full swing. And the snow was coming down hard.

Since we'd gotten a decent snowfall, the festival included sledding, a gingerbread house building contest, and snow tubing, in addition to food, holiday music, and spots to sit around fire pits. The lake had frozen over and was safe to walk and ice skate on.

As I stood outside the building, I had to blink away the snowflakes that were floating down. Paired with the decorations, lights, and smell of hot chocolate, the ambiance was magical.

Once I saw Gabe, I straightened, a grin appearing on my face. It didn't take him long to spot me, and his own smile spread across his lips. His gaze zeroed in on me, and I lifted both my hands to show off the two cups of peppermint hot chocolate. The one for me had a mountain of whipped cream, and the one for Gabe was more tame.

"You made it!" I exclaimed, rocking back and forth on my feet.

"And you're prepared." His smile stayed on his face as he nodded toward the drinks.

"They might not be as hot anymore, since it's been a little bit, but the line gets crazy long. I didn't want our first stop to be waiting. That's not a good start to our night." I handed him his hot chocolate. "This one should be less sweet, although I'm happy to share the whipped cream if you want. Or you could even have this one if you prefer."

"The one you got me is perfect," Gabe assured, his eyes softening. "Don't worry so much, Sunshine. I'm fairly easy to please."

That might have been true, but I wanted to give him what he wanted. I didn't know *why* I wanted to do that, but I did.

He didn't take the hot chocolate right away, though. He eyed me, his eyes narrowing in on the top of my head, which by the feeling of it, likely had *lots* of snowflakes on it. "You have snow everywhere," he said with a chuckle. "Did you forget your hat again?"

"I did," I admitted sheepishly. "I considered running back upstairs, but then I had the hot chocolates and only two hands to hold everything...which meant having to figure out how to get the door. It didn't seem possible."

"I brought a spare for you." Gabe reached into his pocket, pulling out a spare winter beanie. He carefully slipped the hat onto my head, moving a few strands of hair away from my face. "Can't have you freezing before Christmas." He then took one of the drinks from me.

My lips parted at his gesture, at how he was thinking about me. I swallowed the lump in my throat. I often felt like I had something to prove or that I wasn't successful if I had help along the way, but Gabe was dispelling those myths day by day. I liked having him care for me. I liked having him thinking about me.

"That's really sweet," I said softly. "Thank you."

"Of course," Gabe said, reaching into his pocket with his free hand. "I brought these for you, too." He handed me a pair of gloves, which I'd also forgotten upstairs.

I took them from him and slid them into my own pocket for now, giving him an appreciative smile. "You're one step ahead of me, aren't you?"

Gabe grinned, shaking his head. "Barely. I'm just trying to keep up."

I let out a laugh, unable to help the smile on my face. The snow crunched beneath our boots as we started walking.

Gabe reached for my hand, murmuring, "Wouldn't want you to slip."

I rolled my lips, nodding in agreement. "Good thinking." I intertwined my fingers with his and gave his hand a squeeze. Even though it was frosty outside, Gabe's palm—his presence, really—was warm and inviting.

"When I asked Hal earlier today if he'd be here, he gave me a weird and mysterious response. Do you know why that might've been?" Gabe asked. We started to walk toward the heart of downtown where all the attractions, food, and shopping were set up.

I hid my smile by taking a sip of hot chocolate. "I do," I said slowly. "It's because Hal isn't...himself tonight."

Gabe raised his brow. I tipped my chin toward what was coming into view: a large red sleigh set up next to one of the tallest Christmas trees I'd ever seen.

"No way," Gabe said under his breath with an amused laugh. "You're telling me out of *all* the places in the world, Santa decided to come to Golden Falls." I liked the light-hearted teasing in his tone and how playful our interactions had gotten.

"He's going to travel to other places, too, but this is his first stop."

Gabe chuckled, shaking his head and pulling me in toward

his side as I was taking a sip of hot chocolate, a trace of whipped cream clinging to my nose and upper lip.

"Hey!" I laughed, bringing my cup up to shield my face and glancing around to see if there was a napkin I could grab from one of the nearby stands.

Gabe was quicker, though. He gently tugged my hand for us to stop walking and turned so he was facing me. When I lowered my cup, he brought his hand closer, using the pad of his thumb to wipe the cream that was on my nose. I watched carefully as he brought his thumb up to his lips, sucking the whipped cream with a hum.

My lips parted slightly as my gaze dropped and stayed on his full lips. I felt his hot touch on my upper lip, and he swiped more of the sweetness off. Before he could pull away, I captured his thumb between my lips. His warm, brown eyes turned dark, and his jaw clenched. His throat bobbed while his eyes stayed firmly glued to me.

I would say this moment reminded me of my kiss with Gabe, but that'd be a lie.

Because I hadn't been able to stop thinking about our kiss. It was all I'd been thinking about and if we'd get a chance to do it again. Maybe tonight, even. There had to be mistletoe around here somewhere.

I pulled away after a moment, acting unfazed and taking another sip of my hot chocolate, more carefully this time. "What'd you think of the whipped cream? Too sweet for you?" I asked, hoping that my voice stayed even and didn't give away how wound up I felt, heat coiling deep in my stomach.

"No, not too sweet," he said, voice low. "Just the perfect amount of sweetness." With the way he was looking at me, I started to think maybe he wasn't talking about the whipped cream, but that would be ridiculous.

"Well, don't you two look adorable and cozy!" A voice cut in.

I turned to see Susan approaching us, unsure when she'd gotten close. Her hands, which were covered by knitted mittens, were holding two small mason jar candles. Susan loved making candles, and all of us in town encouraged her to sell them beyond the Christmas festival.

"I wanted to bring you a couple of candles." Susan handed one to me and the other to Gabe.

"You didn't have to do that," I said as I took the candle from her with my free hand. "Thanks so much, Susan. I was going to show Gabe the booths after our next stop." I glanced down at the cranberry peppermint candle. "What did you get?" I asked Gabe, peering over.

"Cinnamon gingerbread," he told me, angling the candle so I could see. "That's so nice of you, Susan. I'd be happy to buy these from you. You don't need to give them to us for free."

"Oh, nonsense!" She waved her hand. "Consider it a small gift for the holidays—and a thank you to you, Gabe."

My brows furrowed in confusion until Susan explained, "I had a grocery run to do before the first snowfall came in, but my car was in the shop. Gabe picked up the groceries for me, which was so helpful."

"It wasn't a problem at all. Plus, I got to see Sugar Plum, so I'm happy to help."

Susan smiled warmly. "You're always welcome to come over. Well, I won't keep you two kids much longer. Enjoy the rest of your night, and stay warm!" She gave us both a wave before walking to where she had her booth set up, joining her husband and continuing to talk to the line of customers.

I looked over at Gabe, my eyes searching his face. I kept learning more about him, and the more I learned, the more I realized I had been completely wrong about him.

"Ready for our next stop?" I asked as we put the candles in my purse for safe keeping.

"Lead the way, Sunshine. Let's see what you have planned next."

29

GABRIEL

The crisp wind bit at my face, making my eyes water and my smile freeze to my face. I hadn't been sledding in *years*. Who knew it was even more fun as an adult?

"How were you going so fast?" I huffed, out of breath as I came down from the adrenaline.

"Lots of practice," Lily said with a grin. "As the youngest of my siblings, I didn't usually win much, except for when we'd race down the hill." She'd been laughing the whole way down, the melodic sound one that I never wanted to forget. I'd recognize it anywhere, even after I left Golden Falls.

We'd gone down the hill at least three times now, and each time, she came down faster than me. We only needed to go down once to cross it off Lily's list, but I couldn't remember the last time I had this much fun over the holidays, if ever.

"Should we go down one more time?" I nodded toward the sled that was for two people, as two kids came up to us to ask if we were done using the single sleds.

"Yeah, one more time." Lily's smile widened...and I saw a mischievous twinkle in her eye. "Race you up the hill!"

Without giving it a second thought, I reached for the sled and ran after her.

I caught up to Lily eventually, but it came at a cost. I was panting once we reached the top.

Once I set down the sled, Lily held it in place so I could get in first. Then, I held it steady for her to sit between my legs, her back facing me. As Lily settled and got comfortable, I could smell her fruity shampoo and her floral perfume—her sweetness and proximity overwhelming my senses.

"Ready?" She looked over her shoulder at me, berry-colored lips spread into a smile. She looked both angelic and mischievous.

"Ready," I confirmed, wrapping an arm around her to keep her close.

We pushed off the ground, and within moments, we were flying down the hill, my heart pumping wildly inside my chest. Our speed picked up, causing the wooden sled to sway side to side.

We went down a different section of the hill than our other runs, and a ridge of packed snow snuck up on us, causing the sled to buck sideways.

"Oh, shit!" Lily called out, followed by a shriek.

In trying to prevent the sled from turning, we overcorrected—and flipped over. I landed on the fluffy, powdery snow with an *oomph*. I wrapped my arms tightly around Lily, hoping that landing on me would break her fall.

Luckily, we were already toward the bottom of the hill, so our tumble wasn't much, but it was still enough to knock the wind out of us.

"You okay?" I asked, out of breath.

"Yeah," Lily exhaled. "Are you?"

I was distracted by the way her eyes moved from my gaze to

my mouth, reminding me how close we were. She was lying on top of me, strands of blonde hair framing her face.

Somehow, even through all of our winter layers, I could feel her heart beating rapidly. Or was that mine?

"I'm fine," I assured her. "What were you saying earlier about *lots of practice*?"

She smiled and rolled her eyes at my teasing. As Lily parted her lips to respond, a man's voice interrupted us. "You two know this is a kids event, right?"

I looked up, recognizing the man as Wesley, Lily's older brother.

Lily didn't even need to look up to know who it was. She let out an annoyed huff. "We're fine. Thanks for asking. And was it still a kids event when you were making out with Jules earlier?"

"In our defense, there was a mistletoe!" A brunette woman with rosy cheeks walked up next to Wesley. Jules, who I'd met earlier today at Purrfect Blend while helping Lily with the holiday orders, was holding two hot chocolates.

Wes extended his hand, first helping Lily up and then extending his hand to me, too. Once Lily and I were both standing, I tried to push how close we'd been out of my mind. "Nice to see you both," I said to Wes and Jules.

"Good to see you, too, Gabe!" Jules grinned. "Hopefully you've been enjoying your time in town and at the festival. Hard not to when you have the best tour guide." She nodded to Lily.

"I couldn't agree more. Lily has made my time in Golden Falls really welcoming...and eventful," I said with a chuckle. "There's never a dull moment with her."

The corner of Wes's mouth twitched. "That's one way of putting it." Wes took one of the hot chocolates from Jules and then used his other hand to pull her into his side.

"Where are you two heading next?" Jules asked.

"We're going to enter the gingerbread house competition," Lily said with a grin. "What about you two?"

"We're getting ready to wrap up for the night. The hot chocolate was our last stop. It's my prize for beating Wes in a snowball fight," Jules said proudly. "Okay, I know he let me win, but still."

I hadn't been around much genuine love in my life, but even I could tell that the connection between Wes and Jules was as real as it got.

"We'll see you two tomorrow for Christmas, right?" I asked.

Jules nodded eagerly. "Yes! It's my first Christmas in Golden Falls, and I suppose it's your first one here, too. It's going to be a great time. We'll see you both then. Enjoy the rest of your night, and good luck with the competition!"

Wes gave us each a nod before the two of them turned and walked away from the festival.

"Sounds like we have a competition to enter," I said, amused.

Lily beamed. "Not just enter—win."

30

GABRIEL

"Sunshine, I think winning this competition is going to be harder than we thought."

Lily paused icing one of the sides of the gingerbread house and looked up at me, brows furrowing. "Why?"

I blinked and then gestured around the room filled with screaming children. Happy screams, but screams, nonetheless. "Uh, because we're competing against a bunch of kids who are building skyscrapers, dragons, and god knows what else with their gingerbread."

The gingerbread house making competition was in a small assembly room within the town hall, which was one of the buildings off Main Street. There were three plastic tables covered with red tablecloths set up for the competition. On the tables was everything we needed: gingerbread, icing packets, and plenty of edible candy decorations. At least I assumed the candy was edible...I had no idea how long it'd been packaged or if someone would break their tooth on one of the gumdrops.

Lily raised her brows, an amused smirk forming on her lips. "Sounds like we need to get more creative. Channel some of your Grinch energy into inspiration."

I huffed a laugh and shook my head, picking up a ginger-bread piece with one hand and the bag of icing in the other. "Funny," I deadpanned. "What do I do next? You seem to like bossing me around."

"I do. It's becoming one of my favorite activities," Lily chirped, attaching the final piece to finish off the base of our house. She then turned her attention toward me. "You'll want to put icing on the two shorter sides, attach it to the base, and then do the same with another piece to make the roof."

On our walk over, I'd shared with Lily that I'd never made a gingerbread house. When she heard that, Lily was determined to make sure I had the best and *most festive* experience. So far, it hadn't been too bad. Dare I say I was enjoying myself...but that was likely more due to the company than what we were doing.

Once we had the house built, it was time for decorating. A few moments into adding various chocolates onto our house, we heard our names called out.

"Lily! Gabe!" Tiffany's daughter Maddie came running over, waving wildly, with Tiffany trying to keep up with her. "I was hoping I'd see you! Oooh, a gingerbread house. Can I help?" she asked sweetly, looking between us and her mom.

"Honey, remember we were going to grab two of the kits to go so we could make them with your brother at home," Tiffany said to her daughter before looking over at us with a warm smile. "Good to see you both. Merry Christmas."

"Please, Mommy?"

Tiffany tried to hide her smile, and she looked over at us, trying to gauge if we didn't mind Maddie joining.

"We *do* need some help decorating," I offered with a shrug.

Tiffany rolled her lips and nodded, a gentle laugh leaving her. Meanwhile, Maddie looked up at her mom with the biggest puppy dog eyes possible.

"Okay, ten minutes, and then we're heading home. Do we have a deal?" Tiffany said to her daughter.

"Yes!" Maddie jumped, clapping her hands. She then turned her attention toward our house. "Can we add a unicorn? Oooh, what if we made the house into a unicorn!" she exclaimed with wide eyes.

Lily and I looked at each other with a grin. "That's a wonderful idea, Maddie," Lily said. "Where should we begin?"

I wasn't sure how we were going to turn a gingerbread house into a unicorn, but luckily, Maddie had a vision. As a team, we frosted the sides of the house and added eyes to the front and a horn to the top that was decorated solely with pink M&Ms. Maddie's hands got messy with frosting pretty quickly...which she then got on her face and hair, but hey, that didn't stop her from directing us on what to do next.

"It looks soooo pretty!" Maddie beamed.

"You're a good project manager, Maddie," I complimented. "We couldn't have done this without you."

Maddie tilted her head to the side. "What's a project..." She trailed off, twisting her lips as her brain worked on how to pronounce the word.

"A project manager is someone who plans and organizes how to do something. They assign tasks to other people on their team and make sure the project is done on time."

Maddie nodded slowly, taking in the words but not quite understanding.

I tried again. "Like how you told me to work on the front of the house while you and Lily decorated the unicorn horn. Then we all worked on the roof together."

Understanding dawned on Maddie's face, and she nodded. "I liked how we all worked together! This is the most fun I've ever had building a gingerbread house." Maddie looked between us. "Did you have fun, Gabe?"

"The most fun," I responded without giving it a second thought, and it was true. There was something about the complete and utter joy on Maddie's face as we brought her vision to life that warmed my heart. Not only that, but the screams and squeals from the surrounding kids warmed my heart, too. It was clear how much fun they were having.

I looked first at Maddie and then shifted my gaze to Lily, locking eyes with her, trying to convey without words that I had fun because of *her*. As if she read my mind, Lily's expression softened.

"What about you, Lily?" Maddie turned and gently tugged on Lily's coat to get her attention.

Lily looked down at the little girl. "I had the most fun, too. I'm so glad you were able to help us. We wouldn't have been able to do it without you, Maddie."

"I heard there's some gingerbread houses for me to take a look at," a low, booming voice sounded from the entry way.

A chorus of "Santa!" and squeals rung through the room, bouncing off the walls.

In came Hal dressed in a classic crimson Santa suit with a hat, black boots, and beard.

I shook my head with an amused laugh, bringing my hand up to cover the shit-eating smile I had on my face. "Does he do this every year?" I asked Lily, keeping my voice low so none of the kids would hear.

"Duh, it's Santa. That's kind of his thing," she teased with a twinkle in her eye but then shook her head. "Only for the last couple of years. He tries to keep busy during the holidays." What Lily didn't say but that was implied was that this had been since Vera's passing. "Because he's Hal, one of his favorite ways to stay busy is bringing a smile to people's faces."

I looked around, and that's the only expression I saw. Kids, parents, and community members were grinning at the sight of not only Hal but how excited and happy the kids were, including Maddie, who had run up to Hal with her mom following behind.

When Hal looked out into the crowd and spotted me and Lily, his beard-covered smile only widened, followed by a wink.

"It means a lot to him that you're here," Lily said softly, and I nodded.

"It means a lot to me, too. It's been"—I looked over at Lily, the corner of my mouth tipping up as I tried to diffuse some of the emotional tension that was building in my chest—"the most wonderful time of the year."

She gasped, her eyes wide as she leaned over to grab my arm. "Did...did Mr. Grinch himself quote a classic Christmas song?"

"Maybe I did. What're you gonna do about it?"

Lily didn't need any time for her witty response. "Tease you incessantly."

I playfully narrowed my eyes at her. "You were going to do that anyway."

She innocently shrugged before turning her attention back to Hal and the kids. I did the same but not before setting my hand over hers and giving it a squeeze.

Not long after that did Hal—*ahem*, Santa—judge the various gingerbread houses. We didn't place in the top three, but we won "best teamwork."

Turned out, Lily and I worked better together than I realized. I wasn't sure if that was a good thing or if it meant I was completely and utterly fucked.

31

LILY

On our walk back to my apartment from the Christmas festival, Gabe told me more about his best friend Liam and showed me a handful of photos that Liam had sent over the last few weeks. Most of them were selfies of Liam and Beans, Gabe's cat.

It was nice to get a small glimpse into Gabe's life in Milwaukee, even if there was a pinch in my chest at the thought of him leaving. That had always been the plan, and yet, I wanted to slow down time. We were more than halfway done with my list and had four things left to cross off: signing up for baking classes, romantic kiss under the mistletoe, visiting Milwaukee, and seeing a shooting star.

We'd taken the long way back to my apartment, but the building was coming into view.

I searched for a conversation—anything to keep us walking longer—but Gabe beat me to it. He asked, "Have you ever been in love?"

The question wasn't what I expected, but I didn't mind. I shook my head. "I haven't. What about you?"

"Me neither," he answered. "What do you think it feels like?"

I kept my gaze on the snow-covered ground, but I could imagine the slight crease forming between his brows, like it typically did when he was deep in thought. "This is going to sound so painfully cheesy, but...like every day is Christmas."

He barked out a laugh. "That's about as cheesy as it gets."

I turned my head to look at him, my smile widening. I swore his face brightened in return.

"What specifically about Christmas would it feel like?"

"That excitement and giddiness of waking up on Christmas Day. I think you would feel a version of that every day. That happiness to wake up and see your person. To hear about their day. To do literally anything with them because it's *them*. My parents could be doing the most mundane tasks together and yet they're having fun. Wes—who hates shopping with every fiber of his being—lights up when Jules asks if they could go to the store. When she told me about how he sits in the fitting room waiting for her to show him every single outfit, I was convinced we were talking about two different people. But he's happy to do that because he loves her so deeply. And, actually, it was my brother who earlier this month talked about how because of Jules the year overall feels more magical."

Gabe stayed quiet.

"What about you?" I asked. "What do you think it feels like?"

He set his hand over where his heart was, rubbing at the spot.

"I think if you had asked me at the start of the month, I would've told you I don't know. I never saw my parents in love. It always felt like it was a business transaction for them. And I grew up thinking that's how it was for everyone. That, yeah, if you were one of the select few, love could be more. But for most people, it was transactional. I'll do this if you do that.

"But now..." He let out a sigh. "I think it feels...like your heart is living outside your body, which is both terrifying and special."

"I think that's beautiful, don't you? That we can love someone so much that they feel like a piece of us. That we can be so connected to someone."

"I do think it's beautiful," he agreed. "But..."

"Doesn't mean it isn't scary," I filled in.

"Exactly."

"I bet it's less scary with the right person." It had to be. Life was scary and intense—but it could also be so beautiful. Love helped take away some of that pressure.

"Yeah," he said quietly. "I sure hope so."

Disappointment consumed me as we approached my apartment building. I turned toward Gabe, searching his face. I knew what he was going to say before the words came out.

"I shouldn't," he said quietly, voice strained.

"No, I get it." I did my best to hide any emotion, plastering what I hoped looked like a cheery smile. The corner of my mouth wobbled, and I quickly turned around, grabbing my keys and pushing the door open. "Thanks for a fun night. I'll see you tomorrow, Gabe. Merry Christmas Eve."

I didn't give him a chance to respond. Instead, I walked up the stairs two at a time and quickly made my way into my apartment.

This was the right decision.

Once I closed the door, I leaned my back against it and let out a heavy sigh.

If it was so *right*, then why did I feel like this? Like there was a weight crushing my chest from disappointment.

I closed my eyes, trying to compose myself, when there was a knock.

I pulled open the door, seeing Gabe on the other side, out of breath and hair messy. Like he'd sprinted up the stairs. How did

—he must've gotten into the building before the door closed. My eyes flicked to the mistletoe attached to the top of my doorframe, and butterflies swarmed my stomach. When did that get there?

"Did you forget something?" I asked.

"Yeah," he breathed, "this."

In one long step, Gabe closed the distance between us. He cupped my face in his hands and pulled my mouth to his in a romantic kiss that took my breath away.

32

GABRIEL

I was addicted to how sweet Lily's lips tasted. So addicted that I knew I wouldn't be able to stop kissing her once I started.

It was part of the reason why I didn't think coming up to her apartment was a good idea. Because I didn't want to stop. Neither of us did.

Kissing her was more than a want—it was a need.

I'd purchased the bundle of mistletoe earlier tonight from one of the booths, wanting to give Lily the breathtaking kiss she deserved, but no moment had felt right. It all felt too public. Even though this was on her list, I wanted this moment to be for us.

For someone who hadn't been in love before, Lily spoke about it like she longed for it but had realized it was just out of reach. She seemed to know *exactly* what it felt like yet had given up on it before experiencing it for herself. I wondered why that was. Why she recognized all this love around her but didn't think it was within her grasp.

It almost sounded like she'd given up, and while I hadn't known Lily for long, I knew her well enough to knew she was a fighter and went after what she wanted.

So, why wasn't she fighting to find love?

She parted her lips eagerly, a soft whimper escaping as my tongue tangled with hers. I guided us further into her apartment, the door slamming behind us.

I carefully maneuvered us to the couch without breaking the kiss. The world would have to be on fire before I pulled my lips away from hers.

Lily's hands moved quickly, undoing my coat and pushing it off my shoulders. I did the same with her hers, letting it fall to the floor.

She ran her hands along my shirt, a hum escaping as she felt the fabric. "You're not wearing a dress shirt."

"Wanted to look my best for you tonight," I mumbled against her lips.

I could feel Lily smile. "You always look your best. Actually, I'm convinced it's impossible for you to look bad."

Once we were close enough, I sat on the couch, my hands firmly finding Lily's hips and bringing her with me. She straddled me with ease, grinding her hips into mine and causing a rush of arousal that went straight to my cock. "Fuck, Lily," I grunted, digging my fingers into her hips and pushing her harder onto my growing erection.

Despite the layers of clothing between us, the friction felt fucking incredible. Lily must've agreed, because she let out a breathy moan, her fingers moving into my hair and tugging hard. "More," she breathed, tilting her hips toward me. "I need... more, Gabe. I—I need *you*," Lily stammered, and the words kicked my pulse into overdrive.

If she needed something—anything—I was going to give it to her. No questions asked. I wanted to be the person who gave her *everything*.

But...I was also going to make her tell me exactly what she needed and wanted. I wanted to hear her say it.

I pulled away from her mouth, finally breaking the kiss. My hot breath hit her ear as I asked, "What do you need, Sunshine? Use your words and tell me." I pressed my lips to the side of her neck, getting a shaky shudder from her. She pressed her hips harder into mine.

"I—I want," Lily panted. "I know I shouldn't, but I want you to touch me."

I hummed. "And why shouldn't you?"

"Because...we shouldn't. This isn't...part of the list," Lily stammered.

A growl formed low in my throat at the mention of the list, and a muscle in my cheek fluttered. "But you want this? You want me to touch you?"

I wanted to confirm this was what Lily really wanted. I pulled away, leaning back against the couch to get a look at her flushed cheeks and kiss-swollen lips. Her eyes, usually a bright blue, were dark like the ocean.

The pause allowed us both to catch our breath, and I watched as Lily's tongue ran along her bottom lip while her gaze took me in. Her hands rested on my chest, and she leaned forward, forehead pressed against mine. "I want you to touch me. If you want to—"

"Oh, Sunshine, I fucking want to," I said with a low chuckle. I reached into my pocket, pulling out Lily's wish list and grabbing a pen that was lying on her side table. I flipped the paper over, and in my messy scrawl wrote *Make Lily come.*

"There. Now, I have a list, too, with one fucking priority," I said, tossing the paper and pen off to the side. I had a beautiful woman on my lap who needed a release and wanted me to give it to her.

Lily's lips parted, and she let out a small laugh of disbelief. "Gabe," she breathed.

I cut off the rest of her words with a hungry kiss, teeth

nipping at her bottom lip. My hand snaked down her side, relishing the curve of her waist and digging my fingers into her hip. I anchored her down and guided her over my jeans. "Where do you want my touch?"

Lily's lips parted, another moan escaping her as she rolled her hips. "I want your touch everywhere," she breathed. "But I—I'm not really sure what I like. I mean, I know what I like when it's just *me*, but with someone else...it's—well, it's been a while," she admitted, vulnerable eyes locked on me.

"Let's figure out what you like, then."

I didn't like the idea of Lily with someone else. And while she *technically* wasn't mine, at this moment, she was. And I was going to show her exactly what it felt like to be my girl.

33

LILY

Heat and tension coiled in my lower belly as I rocked against Gabe's cock over the barrier of our clothes. I couldn't get enough of him or the hunger in his eyes. His erection pressed against me, and how hard he was turned me on even more, because I had the power to do this to him.

This tension had been simmering between us all night—for the last few weeks, really—and was finally about to snap.

Let's figure out what you like, then.

I liked the sound of that.

I was trying not to think too hard about what this meant and the possible consequences. My café, the building, Gabe leaving. Those were all important pieces...just not important at this moment.

What was important *right now* was how we both wanted this.

"Show me what you would do if I was yours," I said breathlessly. For one night, we could pretend.

Gabe's expression was hard to read at first. I couldn't tell if he was challenged by my words or if they reminded him that whatever was between us was temporary.

Either way, he quickly gathered his composure and let his

gaze slowly move down my body, his eyes searing every inch of my skin. I still had all my clothes on, but with the way he looked at me, I might as well have been naked. He took in every dip and curve with such awe.

"If you were mine, I would do everything in my power to make you feel good. To make you feel beautiful. I would learn your body and what you enjoy like the back of my fucking hand."

My breath hitched as he slipped his hand underneath my sweater, which was suddenly too hot and suffocating. I grabbed the hem and pulled it over my head, carelessly letting it drop to the floor, my attention fully on Gabe.

The thick column of his throat bobbed, his eyes taking in my sheer, light-blue bralette.

"Fuck, Lily," he rasped. "You're the most beautiful woman I've ever seen. So fucking perfect."

I'd been called pretty before, but never beautiful. Not only that, but Gabe didn't just say those words to me. I felt them. I'd never had someone look at me the way he was right now. Like he wanted to make me his.

Gabe pressed his mouth to my neck, peppering slow, hot kisses to my skin. I tipped my head back, giving him more space to explore. It didn't take him long to find a spot—right where my neck met my shoulder—that drove me wild. A soft noise escaped me as he pressed another kiss, and I moaned even louder when he sucked at my skin. I continued to grind against him, reveling in the pressure between my legs and his hot mouth on my skin.

"Gabe." My hand found the back of his neck, fingers tangling in his brown hair that was getting messier by the minute.

"You like being kissed here," he murmured. "You like being kissed all over your neck but especially here." He continued his painfully slow exploration with his mouth, moving his lips to the tops of my breasts.

"Do you want my mouth here?" he asked, his golden-brown eyes looking up at me.

I licked my lips and nodded. "I do."

I knew I wanted his mouth there, but I wasn't sure how it would compare to the feeling I got when he kissed my neck. I wasn't kidding when I said it had been a while since I'd been intimate with a man, and even the times I had been, I didn't have a lot of confidence. But I felt safe with Gabe. I felt safe to tell him what I did and didn't like—which, so far, I liked everything. I also felt safe to be vulnerable with him.

He pulled down my bralette and exposed my breasts.

"Do you like this?" he hummed, palming one of my breasts while using his mouth on the other. Gabe's tongue flicked and teased my nipple, which elicited another moan from me. He chuckled, as if that was enough of a response.

He then shifted his attention to the other, repeating the careful, calculated motions with his tongue and getting another reaction out of me—faster this time. I moved harder over his length and dug my fingers into his shoulders. I was *so* close.

I gasped as Gabe pinched my nipple with his thumb and forefinger, reeling in my attention. I eagerly nodded for him to continue. "Don't stop," I breathed. "That feels so good. It all feels *so* good."

He pinched my nipple harder, eliciting another moan from me as my orgasm started to build. The rhythm of my hips faltered, and Gabe took over. One of his hands played with my nipple while he used the other to rock me over his length faster than before. "That's it, baby. Come for me."

"I'm—I'm so close. Oh my god, Gabe."

I was desperate for him, and I wasn't even ashamed of it,

because I could see how much he enjoyed it. His mouth found that same spot at the curve of my neck and he sucked—hard.

The sensations of his mouth, touch, and the friction at my center tipped me over the edge.

"Gabe!" I cried out, letting my head fall back and eyes close. I dug my fingers into his back, holding on for stability as heat coursed through my body. Within moments, my pulse started to thrum wildly, and my orgasm took over—overwhelming my senses and leaving me moaning, breathless, and aching for more.

34

GABRIEL

She was absolutely mesmerizing.

Her blonde hair was messy and wild. Her cheeks were flushed. Her chest was rising and falling rapidly with each breath, and her lips spread into a lazy smile that took my breath away.

She opened her eyes, and there was a hunger, a desire, in her gaze that let me know she wanted more—and I'd happily give that to her.

My hand squeezed her hip as I searched her face. I wanted to give her a chance to catch her breath. "Are you good?" I asked.

She nodded, fire quickly building in her eyes. "I'm great." She gently pulled me closer, pressing kisses along my jaw. "I want you to touch me. I *need* you to touch me." Her hand inched down, fingers trailing over the fabric of my shirt. She pulled it over my head with ease and tossed it on the floor.

I adjusted us so we were lying on the couch. While Lily pressed soft kisses to my jaw, I made quick work of unbuttoning and unzipping her jeans.

I slipped my hand underneath her panties, running my

finger over her slit and getting a gasp out of her. "So fucking wet. Is this all for me? Does my girl need to be taken care of again?"

Lily nodded in response, her breathing growing more rapid.

I spread her wetness along her entrance and slowly pushed two fingers inside.

Her back immediately arched off the couch, a moan escaping her. "Gabe," she whined. "Y-yes, please. Feels *so* good." Her hand found my bicep, and she held on tightly.

The pace of my fingers sped up, and I watched her face for any tells of what she preferred, what she enjoyed, what she *needed*. As my fingers moved faster, Lily's body started to tremble.

When I pressed my thumb against her clit, her hips bucked in response.

"God, Lily, you look so beautiful, and you're doing so fucking good. Are you going to be a good girl and come on my fingers?"

When I praised her, Lily nearly unraveled right then and there. Her eyes started to flutter closed, and while I allowed that during her first orgasm, I wasn't going to this time.

"Eyes on me," I rasped. I wanted her to see that it was me making her come—that it was me who would do anything to send her over the edge.

She easily obeyed, her eyes staying open and locking on mine. "I'm...I'm close," she warned, licking her lips.

I slowed my fingers down ever so slightly before building up speed again. "That's it, baby. Come for me again."

Lily's legs started to shake as another orgasm consumed her body, and she moaned my name again. My full name this time, and I'd never heard a sweeter sound.

"Gabriel," she cried out, making good on her order not to close her eyes. She rocked her hips against my hand as she chased her orgasm, her cheeks and chest flushed from the heat coursing through her body. Her hands dug into my biceps as she finished on my fingers with another moan.

I could have come from this alone, and it took every ounce of restraint to keep myself from doing so. I wanted this to be all about her.

"That's my good girl," I murmured, leaning in to press a gentle kiss to her lips. I was about to pull away when Lily's hand found the side of my face, and she pulled me closer, her lips moving as her tongue lazily stroked mine. *Fuck.*

She began to reach for my belt, and I set my hand over hers. "This was all about you, Sunshine."

She huffed but ultimately conceded. "Fine, but next time, I want it to be about you, too."

Oh how I fucking wanted there to be a next time.

I told Lily this was what I would do if she were mine. We both knew this was pretend.

But the way I felt right now, looking at her, nothing in my life had ever felt more real. Truthfully, nothing in my life felt like it mattered in this moment *besides* trying to figure out how I could make this real.

I pushed those thoughts away, instead focusing on the current moment between us.

When Lily pulled away from the kiss, she kept her face close, nudging my nose with hers and gently running her fingers through my hair. "Will you stay a little longer?" she asked, voice soft.

"Of course," I answered. I lifted my head, glancing over at the clock in the kitchen. It was just past midnight, which meant it was officially Christmas Day.

"Merry Christmas, Lily."

Her face brightened, and she pulled me in for another kiss. "Merry Christmas, Gabe."

We stayed on the couch for another couple of hours, curled

up under a mountain of blankets and talking about anything and everything. About Lily's dreams for her café. My vision for my career. Where we wanted to travel to. What kind of music we listened to. Our favorite movies. There was so much I had yet to learn about her, and I wanted to know everything.

I hadn't wanted to leave her, but I needed to get back to Hal's and get some sleep. The one thing that kept me going was knowing I'd see her for Christmas dinner in about fifteen hours.

It was the first time I found myself counting down the hours —the minutes—until Christmas. I couldn't wait to see Lily and spend the holiday with her. A holiday that I was starting to enjoy all because of her.

I was starting to feel that magic from this time of year, but I didn't think it had anything to do with Christmas. Lily was the magic.

35

GABRIEL

I wasn't sure what to expect when Hal and I arrived at the Richards's family home for Christmas dinner, but I hadn't expected immediate warmth.

Literal warmth radiated from the fireplace in the living room, but it was more than that.

The Richards's home was warm and inviting. Christmas music played low in the background coupled with the hum of multiple conversations. Every inch of the house, from what I could see, was decorated in one way or another, but it wasn't overwhelming. It was well-thought out and strategically placed. I quickly realized where Lily got her love of Christmas.

Admittedly, Christmas was growing on me. Hal and I enjoyed the day together before coming over for dinner. We ate breakfast, drank our coffee, and exchanged gifts. I asked Hal all about his favorite Christmas memories, which included memories with me I hadn't remembered. He even pulled out the photo album to show me.

But the best part about Christmas? The warmth from Lily's smile as soon as she saw us.

"Merry Christmas!" she exclaimed.

That alone eased my nerves of spending the day with her family. I wanted to make a good impression, but I also recognized they likely had already formed their opinions about me. But maybe I could change them. Show them that I wasn't my father and that I cared about this town more than I wanted to admit. That I was starting to care deeply about Lily and wanted her to succeed.

I couldn't tear my eyes away from how Lily's hips swayed as she walked over. The long-sleeved maroon sweater dress she was wearing hugged her body, and her long blonde hair was down, wavy strands bouncing with each step.

She hugged Hal first, her arms wrapping tightly around him. When she made her way over to me, there was a small, knowing smile on her face before she pulled me into a hug, too. "Merry Christmas, Gabe. Again," she whispered.

"We're so happy to have you here with us, Gabe. I'm Laura, Lily's mom." She didn't give me time to wonder if I should shake her hand or give her a hug, because she pulled me into an embrace. "Merry Christmas."

"Merry Christmas," I repeated. "Thank you for having me. I hope it's not too much trouble that I'm here."

Laura pulled away and gently squeezed my arm. "What in the world are you talking about? Of course, it's not too much trouble!" She stepped out of the way to make room for who I assumed was Lily's dad, Mark.

I'd been most nervous to meet him, because he had a history with my father. I wasn't sure how that would translate to his thoughts about me. Or if he wanted me here.

But those thoughts seemed foolish as soon as I saw the smile on Mark's face. "Great to have you, Gabe. I'm echoing what Laura said—it's not too much trouble, and you're always welcome." He extended his hand, and I took it. I couldn't help but compare it to the times I'd shaken my father's hand, how he would always use it as a battle for dominance.

Mark seemed nothing like that. I wondered if my father had been like this once. Warm, inviting, caring. He had to have been, right? How could you not be after growing up in Golden Falls with Hal and Vera?

"I really appreciate that," I told him, giving his hand a shake. "I'm excited to be here with everyone."

"I love to hear that," Mark said, clapping a hand on my shoulder. "Let me show you around and get you introduced to everyone."

"I can show—" Lily cut in.

"It'll be fine, Lily bear. Don't worry about us. Go ahead and take a seat and relax."

As the two of us walked away, I glanced at Lily over my shoulder. *Lily bear?* I mouthed, my lips pulling into a grin.

Lily tipped her head back with a laugh.

The dinner table was full with tonight's group: Mark and Laura, Wes and Jules, Lily, Cooper, Eliza, Marnie, Hal, and me. I'd been most nervous to be around Lily's parents, but it turned out maybe I should've been more nervous to be around Eliza. She was kind and welcoming but eyed me cautiously, like she was watching my every move.

We'd all filed into the dining room, where a large decorated rectangular table for ten greeted us. I could barely see the festive green table cloth with all the food that was waiting for us. Sliced ham, mashed potatoes, and green bean casserole caught my eye immediately, but there was also roasted carrots, green beans, mashed sweet potatoes, and pickles. I was eager to dig in, and by the looks on everyone's faces, I wasn't the only one. At each seat, there was a carefully curated place setting: silverware, plate, cloth napkin, and drinkware all part of the same red-and-gold dinnerware set.

As Lily grabbed the two seats next to Hal, I was initially going to sit next to Hal with Lily on my other side, but then I heard Marnie's voice come up behind me.

"Look at that. I get to sit next to Gabe. Lucky me." She patted my arm with a smile.

"I think I'm the lucky one," I played along. "You look beautiful, Marnie. Merry Christmas." I pulled her chair out.

Marnie grinned and looked over at Lily. "Keep this one," she mock-whispered.

Once Marnie's chair was pulled out, I did the same for Lily. Lily tore her gaze away from Marnie and looked up at me with a smile. "I might have to."

Lily's tone was teasing, but I found myself thinking about a life in Golden Falls, which was something I hadn't thought about before. From the beginning, my plan had been to get to town, get the building, and leave. I no longer felt that urgency, and that...was perhaps the scariest thing of all.

As much as I loved Milwaukee, there was something about Golden Falls I hadn't experienced before—being part of something. I thought I would feel like an outsider tonight, but everyone had welcomed me and made me feel like I belonged. I knew it likely would've been the same had I joined Liam for dinner with his family, but this felt...different. Like this could be my family, too.

Was that more important to me than the building? I wasn't sure if I was ready to admit the answer.

With Laura and Mark at the heads of the table, it was

Marnie, me, Lily, and Hal on one side with Wes, Jules, Eliza, and Cooper on the other.

Mark cleared his throat once we were all seated. "I'm going to keep this short, because I know the food is why we're all here, but I want to say how grateful I am that we're all able to get together. That you decided to spend your Christmas with us, and that our table continues to get bigger. Jules and Gabe, we're so glad to have a spot for you this year and for the years to come. This is one of my favorite days of the year, and it's truly because of the people, so thank you."

"I couldn't have said it better, dear," Laura echoed. "Now, let's dig in before everything gets cold. There's more of everything in the kitchen, too. And help yourself to whatever drink you want. Make yourselves at home."

"Don't mind if I do." With a grin, Cooper reached for the mashed potatoes, setting off the rotation of food with nearly everyone grabbing a dish to start and passing it around.

I'd texted my parents Merry Christmas today, and last I checked, I hadn't gotten a response. But...that was okay. In the past, it would've bothered me. I would've spent the whole day working, keeping busy because I didn't want to sit with the fact that I would never get *this* type of feeling over the holidays.

Turned out, this feeling was waiting for me in Golden Falls thanks to my grandfather, Lily, and a group of people that made me feel like a part of something.

That was what Christmas was truly about.

36

LILY

The conversation and wine flowed easily over dinner, which I was grateful for. People included Gabe in conversations and asked him questions, but it was never awkward. None of the *off-limits* topics were brought up, which mainly included his father. Not that I thought anyone would say something, but I'd made it clear before Hal and Gabe got to the house that if anyone brought up something off-limits, there would be consequences. Said consequences were no more baked goods from me. That seemed to be threatening enough.

Gabe heard lots of stories from when I was growing up, mainly about all the trouble I'd get into for being too curious, having a wild imagination, and always thinking about the next idea or plan—some things never changed.

What I enjoyed most was that now Gabe was part of the years of history that were captured at this table.

We also briefly FaceTimed my older sister Jade to hear about how she was celebrating in Hawaii. I could tell by the tone in her voice and the look on her face that she wished she could be here with us, and I hoped one year, she could be. But I was glad she had friends in Hawaii who were keeping her busy with their own celebration.

Eliza and I gave each other a look, both noticing that Cooper's excusing himself to grab a second beer and help Wes clear off the table for dessert was *very* conveniently timed. He nearly missed the whole conversation.

We were starting to dig into the apple pie my mom had made when she asked, "What's everyone doing for New Year's Eve this year?"

While Eliza and I hadn't talked yet—or filled Jules in—every year we typically spent New Year's Eve at Lake Ridge. Eliza looked at me and shrugged.

"If Wes is doing something at Lake Ridge, probably head there like we do every year?" Eliza offered. "Which, by the way" —she leaned forward, and Jules leaned back to give Eliza sight to Wes—"could the best boss in the world give me New Year's Eve off so I could spend it with my best friends?"

"Pretty please?" Jules joined in, leaning into Wes.

"Yeah, come on, Wes. Please?" I chimed in.

Everyone at the table was trying to hold their laughter in.

Wes, with a *really?* expression, looked between us. He ultimately cracked a small smile and nodded. "Of course, you can. I had already planned for it, anyway."

I knew Wes wasn't going to say no, but having Jules on our side certainly helped. I was pretty sure it was physically impossible for him to say no to her. She had my brother wrapped around her finger, and I loved every second of it.

Cooper coughed into his elbow, but his cough sounded a whole lot like *sucker*. Wes leaned and flicked the back of Cooper's head.

I shook my head with an amused smile. The two of them were in their thirties, and these moments brought me back to when we were all growing up.

Gabe leaned over to me, and I heard the amusement in his voice. "Is it always like this?"

I laughed, nodding. "Pretty much." I turned to look at him. "Hopefully it hasn't been too much for you."

I loved my family with everything I had in me, but I also recognized that being thrown into this—on Christmas of all days—could be a lot.

To my relief, Gabe answered, "It's been perfect. I'm glad to be a part of it."

I liked how easily he fit into the environment today. By the tension in his shoulders when he first walked in, I could tell he was nervous, but it seemed like he felt more at ease as the night went on. I especially appreciated how welcoming my parents had been.

What I appreciated a little less were the looks and eyebrow wiggles Eliza and Jules would give me.

I reached over to give Gabe's hand a quick squeeze, loving how his warm touch felt in mine. "I'm glad you're part of it."

Eliza caught sight of it, which earned me another eyebrow wiggle, but her amused expression was short-lived, because Marnie asked, "Will Colin be in town for New Year's Eve?"

"Colin?" I asked, not expecting to hear the name of Eliza's ex-boyfriend. "Have you been talking to him again?"

"She answered a call from him the other day when she was at my house," Marnie responded nonchalantly, taking another sip of wine.

"A wonderful conversation to bring up at the dinner table, Gran," Eliza said with a sigh.

We all looked at Eliza expectantly.

"We're friends!" Eliza finally said. "We talk from time to time, but I don't want to get back together with him or anything. He was thinking about stopping by for New Year's Eve but is going to see his brother instead."

Eliza and Colin met when she was doing her undergrad at the University of Wisconsin-Madison. Colin was from Maple Bluffs, a town about an hour south of Golden Falls known for its pure maple syrup, nature, and historic downtown. While Golden Falls was the town to visit over the summer, Maple Bluffs was the place to be during fall.

Colin was part of the group of men who, as Eliza so expertly put it, wouldn't know where a woman's clit was if it slapped them in the face, which was why I was wondering why she was talking to him again. Unless they truly were *just friends.*

"His brother is older, right? Isn't he out in Portland?" Marnie asked. "What's he been up to?"

Eliza rarely, if ever, blushed, but color crept up her tan cheeks. She cleared her throat. "Uh, yeah, he does have a brother. Leo. I'm not sure what he's up to. Last I heard he was trying to become head chef at some fancy restaurant."

Wes, who was largely checked out for most of this conversation, looked at Eliza. "You know a chef? Tell him to apply to the Lake Ridge role. I'm getting it posted in a couple weeks."

Eliza scoffed. "Okay, first, I don't know him very well at all. And two, do you really think he's going to want to leave his cushy city life to move to Golden Falls?"

Wes shrugged at the same time Jules said, "You'd be surprised."

"Could you at least tell him about it? Or ask Caleb to," Wes added.

"It's Colin," Eliza and I both said, to which Wes waved his hand and muttered, "Same difference."

"But, sure, I'll at least mention it." Eliza rubbed the back of her neck. I furrowed my brows, watching my best friend. She looked...nervous. Eliza didn't get nervous. She was fearless, not scared of anything.

What wasn't she telling me? And why had she never mentioned Colin had an older brother?

37

LILY

"I have something for you," Gabe whispered as we sat on the living room couch. I had been listening to Marnie tell a story about a fortune teller she'd visited last month, and as interesting as that was, Gabe had my full attention now.

I angled my body toward him, taking in the faint scent of his cologne. "I have something for you, too," I admitted, and surprise flickered across his face. Did he *really* think he'd spend a Christmas with me and not get a present?

His expression softened, and he reached for my hand. I'd grown to love the way he ran his thumb over my knuckles. It had a way of calming and grounding me to the present moment.

"And don't say that I didn't have to get you anything," I said before he could get a word in. "I wanted to."

Gabe let out a low chuckle, shaking his head. "I know better than to stand in the way of you and something you want."

"Smart man," I teased. I thought about where we could go to exchange our gifts. This moment was for us. "C'mon, I know just the spot. It might be a little chilly, but it'll be worth it."

I loved the view from my parents' backyard in the winter. The rest of my family preferred being out here during the other seasons, especially summer, but there was something breathtaking about seeing the line of snow-covered trees and frozen Lake Golden with a backdrop of stars sparkling in the night sky.

Even after years of living here—and countless winters—it was mesmerizing.

While Gabe was still inside, I turned the knob on the outdoor gas fire table. My parents had both the gas fire table, which my dad prepared so we could still use it in the winter, and a traditional wood-burning fire pit.

Within moments of the soft *click* and pressing the igniter, the flames came to life, casting a golden light. The warmth reached me instantly.

I pulled off the covering that protected the couch from the snow and sat on the cushion, pulling the blanket over me as I waited.

"You look cozy already," a low, familiar voice sounded behind me.

I turned toward him with a smile. "Doesn't take me long once I find a comfy spot."

His full, gorgeous lips spread into a smile—one that I was seeing more often. Gabe finished walking down the wooden steps and unbuttoned his coat before sitting on the couch next to me. I moved some of the blanket over his lap and scooted closer.

The warmth from the fire was comforting, but the fire *and* Gabe's presence? That was something else.

"Is this the house you grew up in?"

I nodded. "It is. When my parents first got married they lived in the house Wes and Jules are currently in. Once they decided to start a family, they moved in here and haven't left."

"I don't blame them. I'd likely spend all day out here with this view, especially if this fire is involved."

"I feel the same way. I love it. I enjoy living downtown, and it works perfectly to be above the café, but I'd love to get a house that's a little more tucked away one day and have a view of my own."

When the conversation stilled, we sat in the comfortable silence, listening to the deep, echoing calls from an owl and the soft rustling of the tree branches.

Gabe peeled back one side of his coat, reaching into a pocket and pulling out a red envelope with *Lily* written on it. "Merry Christmas, Lily. Thank you for making this a day I'll never forget."

My chest squeezed from his simple words, and a quiet pride stirred inside me, because that was exactly what I'd set out to do. I took the envelope from him and opened it, pulling a card out. It was a watercolor drawing of three cats sitting on the snow, and above them in cursive it read *Have a Meowvelous Christmas*. I let out a laugh, holding the card up to him. "This is absolutely adorable."

"I had a feeling you'd like it."

As amusing as the outside of the card was, the message written inside was what captured my attention.

Lily,

As I've mentioned to you, the holidays haven't been anything special to me. I expected this year to be the same.

I should've known from the moment I saw the fire in your eyes that I'd be wrong. You are constantly putting those around you first, and I'm grateful for all you've done for me during my time in Golden Falls.

But it's time you do something for yourself.

Merry Christmas, Sunshine.

- Gabe

There was a folded up piece of paper in the card, but I couldn't look at it yet. There was one part of his message that I was stuck on: *during my time in Golden Falls.* It sounded like he was leaving. Which, yes, I knew he would eventually, but was he leaving soon? We hadn't heard the fate of the building or completed the list...he couldn't leave yet.

I looked up at him, swallowing the lump in my throat. "Are—are you leaving? The list...we haven't..." I stopped myself, not wanting him to hear the ache in my voice.

Gabe watched me carefully. He took a moment to respond, but when he did, he said, "Eventually, I am. But we haven't finished our list yet, and we still need to hear Hal's decision. That's...that was the plan all along, right?"

I nodded slowly. I knew Gabe was right. We had both agreed

to try to complete the list as quickly as possible. But...so much had changed since then. We'd opened up to each other. We'd formed a genuine connection, one I hadn't ever felt before with someone.

"But not, like, soon, right?" I at least had to clarify that.

"No, I don't have a date in mind. I haven't heard anything from Hal, either. I bet eventually he'll want his house back to himself." He tipped his chin toward the folded paper in the card. "Go ahead and open it. I expected you to be more curious."

I let out a shaky laugh, trying to hold in the emotion that was clawing at my throat and behind my eyes. I didn't expect to get so choked up, and I still wasn't quite sure *why* seeing those words written out had such an impact on me.

I set the card on my lap and unfolded the paper, a gasp leaving me. "Gabe." I looked at him with wide eyes. "I can't accept this."

"And why not?"

"Because...because," I stammered, looking down at the paper again. It was a gift certificate for a full year of the virtual baking classes I'd been eying, with the opportunity to drive down and participate in the classes in-person, too. Once I signed up for these classes, it would be another item checked off my list, leaving the visit to Milwaukee and seeing a shooting star left.

"Because?" Gabe asked. He reached over, gently tipping my chin up to meet his eyes. "You deserve this, Lily. You've been wanting to do this, and I know you would've gotten around to it on your own, but this way, you can jump in without having to worry when to start."

My chest squeezed again at how much care and thought he'd put into this. And money. Because I knew how much these classes cost, and when I'd been considering signing up, I was only going to do a month or two. Gabe had purchased me a *whole year*.

Yes, this was an item on my list, but it was so much more than that coming from Gabe.

While I'd been shocked initially, excitement started to course through me at the possibilities—what I'd learn to make, the feedback I'd get, how this would improve Purrfect Blend's offerings. How this could potentially lead to me opening another location. All of this seemed much more within reach—thanks to Gabe's support.

"I can't thank you enough, Gabe. This...this means the world to me." Tears stung my eyes, and I knew they'd fall if I looked at him too long, so I leaned over, wrapping my arms around him in an embrace and nuzzling my face into his neck. "Thank you."

He wrapped his arms around me in return and pressed a kiss to the top of my head. "It's my pleasure, Sunshine."

I would've stayed in his arms longer, but I had to give him his gift. As excited as I was, I was also incredibly nervous. So nervous that as I pulled away from the embrace and reached for the gift bag, I couldn't meet his eyes. Was the gift too much? Was it not enough? What if he hated it? What if it brought about emotions that he didn't want to be feeling?

Gabe took the bag from me and carefully reached in. He pulled out the rectangular shape and began unwrapping it. His hand stilled once he'd pulled away enough wrapping paper to put the pieces together of what this might be—a photo scrapbook.

"When in the world did you have time to make this?" he asked, awe in his voice as he flipped through the first few pages.

"Well, I've had a few days off," I said with a laugh.

It was hard for me to sit still, even on days when I knew I needed the rest. Taking the time off was a big step for me, but I had to keep busy *somehow*.

"Lily, this is…" He trailed off, shaking his head.

While Gabe might not have been around in Golden Falls growing up, I wanted him to have a piece of town and his family when he left. I also wanted to show him how much Vera and Hal adored him and kept up with his accomplishments throughout the years. I'd conspired with Hal this past week after telling him my idea. Hal was good about displaying photos in his home and at the hardware store, but there were still hundreds of photos in storage. This was a perfect way to put them to good use.

There were photos of Hal and Vera together, the two of them with a young Gabe, and pictures of Gabe throughout the years that Hal kept. I'd also added a few more recent photos, including some from the Christmas festival and our time at the café.

But my favorite photo—well, apart from the adorable photos of Gabe when he was younger—was a selfie we took last night with the festival in the backdrop. I ended up taking the photo too early, catching Gabe mid-laugh. I couldn't remember what I'd said to him, only that it was something I said that had made him laugh like that. I had to add the photo into the scrapbook.

"This is the most thoughtful gift I've ever gotten," Gabe admitted, closing the book. "Thank you for making this for me. I love seeing the photos of Hal and Vera. Looking at the photos brings back memories of the two of them visiting Milwaukee that I had forgotten about. I wish"—he cleared his throat—"I wish that things could have been different. That I could have been here when Vera—"

Realizing he was talking about Vera's funeral, I reached over for his hand.

"I know I have to live with the fact that I wasn't here, but if there's any good that can come out of missing Vera's funeral, it's that I don't want to miss out on moments with people I care about. I don't want to miss out on forming those connections. And I also don't want to waste another moment working for my father when I *know* I can be doing work that is valuable and brings people together."

"It says a lot that you're taking that moment and what you were feeling and learning from it. That's not easy. I also know now that it couldn't have been easy for you to come to Golden Falls in the first place. But I'm glad you did."

His throat bobbed as he swallowed. "Yeah, I'm glad, too. For so many reasons."

The more I got to know Gabe and understand his relationship with his father, the more I realized how miserable he was working at Nelson Group. And yet, he was still there. There had to be more to it.

"There's a reason you haven't been able to quit."

He sighed heavily, nodding. "There is. I didn't realize it when I joined Nelson Group, because I didn't review the contract carefully. I was excited to work for my father and thought this would help our relationship. I couldn't have been more wrong."

I scooted closer to Gabe, and he wrapped his arm around me.

He continued. "Part of the contract is a five-year non-compete clause. If I leave Nelson Group, I'd have to do something else for five years. I've struggled a lot with that, and I feel like regardless of what I do—stay or leave—my career would be over."

"And you thought Hal's building would be your chance to have a project for yourself, to work on the community-focused projects you've wanted," I finished for him, the pieces coming together.

He looked down at me, smiling sadly. "I did, but a lot's changed since then. Also, I don't trust my father to stay away from this project, especially since he tried to buy the building from Hal years ago."

That caught my attention. "Really? I had no idea."

I nuzzled closer into Gabe's side, finding myself wondering about if the building even mattered. Would I give it up if it meant Gabe would stay in Golden Falls longer? My stomach churned with unease, and my chest pinched. I wasn't sure of my answer.

In a simple world, I would give up the building for Gabe. But...this wasn't a simple world. I didn't want to give up my dreams for someone, even a man I was falling for. And if Gabe knew me, which I believed he did, he wouldn't want me giving up, either. He would want me to fight like hell for this building and prove that I'm the right person for it.

But if I got the building, then that meant Gabe didn't. I didn't want him to have to put his dreams on hold again and to continue to feel stuck. I knew how much this building meant to him and *what* it meant—an opportunity to finally work on community projects he'd been envisioning for years. I wanted to see his ideas come to life, and this felt like the only way now that I knew the truth about why he couldn't leave.

Regardless of how this turned out, one of us wouldn't be able to fulfill a dream we'd worked so hard for. A heaviness settled over me, and what seemed so simple at the start of the month suddenly wasn't.

We stayed outside longer, thankfully changing the subject to lighter topics, until Wes called from the back door, asking if we were still alive. My brother liked to tease our parents for worrying, but he had a soft side, too.

As Gabe and I walked up the steps back to the house, I thought about how in trying to create a Christmas for Gabe that he wouldn't forget, I did the same for myself.

There was no way I'd ever forget celebrating with Gabe or the rush of being around him. How much I enjoyed bringing a smile to his face but also pushing his buttons.

I couldn't tell if that made me happy or if it devastated me.

Years from now, would I be sitting in my living room thinking about *this* day? Thinking about Gabe and wondering what he was doing? Who he was with?

Would he be thinking about me, too? Or would he meet someone in Milwaukee and forget about me? The latter was probably the right thing for us both, but...I knew I'd never forget Gabe.

My mom had always told us *the only constant thing in life is change.* But it wasn't until this moment that I realized just *how* quickly things could change.

One moment Gabe and I were rivals, and the next there was an ache in my chest at the thought of him leaving.

At the thought of him falling in love with someone else.

At the thought of us being on this world at the same time but not together.

38

LILY

The days between Christmas and New Year's Eve were a blur of watching movies on the couch, kissing and touching Gabe, snuggling with my cats, eating leftovers, and snacking on all the chocolate, cookies, and candy canes I could muster. By the time New Year's Eve rolled around, I had no clue where the days had gone. What I did know, though, was I loved a night out with my girls.

Jules, Eliza, and I were getting ready for the night. Jules was curling her hair in the bathroom, which was right across the hall from my bedroom, while I was flipping through the clothes in my closet.

Eliza was lying on her stomach on my bed, scrolling through her phone. Her dark hair was down, and she'd opted for a pair of black jeans with an olive-green satin camisole. She paired her outfit with a black belt, rings on her fingers, an array of earrings along both ears, and her signature nose ring hoop. I always loved when she wore tank tops or T-shirts, because it showed off the small to medium-sized tattoos she had along her arms. The lily flower tattooed on the back of her right arm was, unsurprisingly, my favorite.

"You're *so* going to have a romantic midnight kiss with Gabe!" Jules exclaimed, and even though I kept my gaze focused on my closet, I could imagine the bright smile on her face.

I'd finished telling Jules and Eliza about my night with Gabe after the Christmas festival, which included his addition to the back of my winter wish list. I also told them about the sweet and thoughtful Christmas gift he'd given me after dinner, but I kept the rest of our conversation and what Gabe had shared to me about his father and job to myself.

"It's...possible." I tried to keep my voice calm, but it rose an octave.

That got Eliza's attention. She locked her phone and set it to the side. Jules set the curling iron on the bathroom counter and came into my bedroom.

"What's going on, Lil?" Eliza asked.

I let out a heavy sigh, turning toward both my friends. "I don't know," I admitted. "I feel...really confused about all this. About how I've been thinking about Gabe more and the building less. How I enjoy spending time with him. How he's so thoughtful, caring, and sweet. How..." I trailed off, swallowing the lump in my throat before continuing. "How I think I might be falling for someone who isn't looking for love. Someone who I won't be able to forget even after he leaves." I rolled my lips, pressing them together in an effort to compose myself and stop the tears welling in my eyes.

At the start of the month, I was okay if love wasn't in the cards for me. I was surrounded by different types of love in my life. Now? Something flipped, and I wanted that for myself. I wanted something all-consuming and real. And it didn't get more all-consuming than Gabe and how he made me feel.

I crossed the distance to my bed, sitting on the edge while Eliza readjusted to do the same. Jules joined us, too, which put me in the middle.

Jules spoke first. "Your relationship and thoughts about Gabe have shifted so much since he got into town. But...I think Gabe might be more open to love than you realize."

My brows furrowed as I tilted my head to the side. "What do you mean?"

When I looked between Jules and Eliza, they shared a knowing smile.

"Lil," Eliza started with a gentle laugh, "that man is gone for you. Did you see how he was looking at you during Christmas dinner? Yes, he was talking and getting to know all of us, but his eyes always went back to you. He's in complete awe of you—and probably thinking of more ideas to add to your naughty wish list." Eliza wiggled her brows. "See, I knew I was onto something when I was making my list."

My cheeks flushed, and this time, I was trying to hide my smile for a whole other reason. "You really think so?"

Eliza and Jules both nodded confidently.

"There's something magical between you two," Jules said gently. "It might be confusing and scary with all of these unknowns, but that doesn't mean it isn't real or that it couldn't work. When Wes and I were trying to figure out what to do, I realized we're better together, and it's easier to come to a decision as a team. I think it'll be easier for you and Gabe to figure it out if you're honest with yourself and with each other about what you want and what's important to you."

I let Jules's words sink in, realizing that the first step was figuring out what I truly wanted. And then not being afraid to say it out loud, even if there was a possibility of rejection.

I had some decisions and priorities to think through, all the while Hal's decision on the building continued to loom over us. Luckily, I didn't have to decide anything tonight. Tonight was all about celebrating the new year.

Wanting to change the subject, I turned to Eliza. "Anyways,

tell us more about reconnecting with Colin." Now it was my turn to give her a sneaky smile. "You haven't said anything, and we have to find out from Marnie?"

Eliza tipped her head back with a groan. "There's nothing to tell! And I feel like *reconnecting* is too intense of a word. We dated in college. It was fine. Nothing special, but I liked the guy. Turns out, we're way better as friends. Yes, *friends*. Actual friends." She gave Jules and me a pointed look. "We've kept in touch over the last couple of years, and I saw him when I was in Madison for the yoga conference over the summer. He texted me asking about New Year's Eve, and I knew we'd be here so..." She shrugged. "Figured an invite wouldn't hurt. But he's going to see his brother instead."

"His older brother Leo," I said in a sing-song tone. "You haven't told us anything about him. Did you meet him when you dated Colin?"

"Yeah, I did. A few times before he left for Portland," Eliza said casually. A little too casually, if you asked me. She got off the bed and strolled out of the room before I had the chance to continue pressing her. "I'm going to prepare three tequila shots while you two finish getting ready," she said over her shoulder.

With a groan, I lay down on the bed. "I have nothing to wear. Jules, will you pick out my outfit?" She was the fashionista of the group and *always* had on a killer outfit. Tonight, she was wearing a glittery silver skirt with a long-sleeved black mesh top over a lacy bralette. Her outfit was paired with her signature strappy heels.

"Gladly!" Within seconds, Jules was at my closet, her wavy brunette curls bouncing as she flipped through my clothes. "I'm thinking...sexy chic. We want Gabe to drop dead when he sees you."

I leaned up on my elbows, eyes wide. "Don't kill the guy!"

She grinned at me over her shoulder. "No promises."

It didn't take long for Jules to work her magic. Within five minutes, she had a full outfit prepared for me—which included items I didn't even realize I owned.

I was wearing a pair of medium-wash jeans that hugged my body paired with a black long-sleeve top that had an open back. Jules also picked out gold hoops and a small gold purse for me. My hair was pulled in a loose, low bun with pieces framing my face. My makeup was done already—mascara, liner, concealer, blush, and a glossy pink lip.

I took in my completed outfit in the full-body mirror in my room, a smile spreading on my lips.

Jules came up behind me, hugging my shoulders. "You look perfect!"

I felt beautiful and confident—and I couldn't wait for tonight.

My stomach started doing somersaults as soon as we got to Lake Ridge.

Well, that was a lie. It started doing somersaults as soon as I got a text from Gabe saying he was at Lake Ridge and had found Cooper and Wes. It warmed my heart that they had another opportunity to hang out, even if it was because they were waiting for us.

We walked from my apartment to Lake Ridge, our boots immediately sticking *ever so slightly* to the bar floor. "Wow," I said in awe. While Lake Ridge was typically the spot to be on New Year's Eve, Wes didn't care much for decorations. This year was different. "How much of this is your doing?" I asked Jules with a grin.

She laughed. "Most of it, but I had help from Wes, Louise, and Eliza to make it all come together. Thought it would be fun to make things feel a little different as we ring in a new year. Only thing Wes said was no glitter, which is fair."

Jules had an eye for design, and the decorations were no exception. She kept the traditional feel of Lake Ridge that Wes and others loved but elevated it for the occasion. There were clusters of gold, white, and black balloons stuck to the walls, as well as streamers and signs ringing in the new year. There was also an area in the corner to take photos, in addition to the typical dance floor and bar.

I couldn't wait to get out on the dance floor with my girls.

We shrugged our coats off, and Eliza took them to the back to safely stash them. It was the best of both worlds—we didn't have to be cold on the walk over and were able to show off our outfits.

"I found the guys!" Jules waved.

My brother was already looking at her, as if he'd spotted her the second she walked in and was waiting for her to notice. The corner of his lips tipped up in a smile.

I scanned the group and spotted Gabe, and...he was already looking at me.

But that wasn't the same as Wes and Jules. Right? I pushed those thoughts away for now as Jules and I approached the guys. She went straight to Wes, and I greeted Cooper before turning my attention to Gabe. "Hey," I said with a smile.

"Hi." His greeting was simple, but the way his eyes bore into me was anything but. Heat coursed through my body at the way his golden-brown eyes darkened. He took in every inch of me, and somehow, I felt more vulnerable in this moment than I did a few days ago when he gave me two orgasms on my couch.

Even though I liked my outfit and felt pretty in it, I wanted

Gabe to think the same. I didn't need his approval or praise—I knew that—but that didn't mean I didn't *want* it.

"Lily, you look…" He swallowed. "Absolutely perfect." He took a step closer, setting a hand on the curve of my waist right above the top of my jeans. His fingertips grazed my bare skin, which was how he found out the top I was wearing dipped low and showed off my back. His hand moved, splaying along my lower back, his hot touch searing into my skin. "I don't know how I'm going to keep my hands off of you tonight, Sunshine," he rasped, voice low, only for me to hear.

Feeling bold, I responded, "Luckily, you don't have to."

The corner of Gabe's lips tipped up into a smirk.

"Alright, alright," Cooper interrupted. "I know I'm fifth-wheeling, but you all will have plenty of time for your couple shit later. For now, let's get the night started."

"What'd I miss?" Eliza asked as she approached.

"Coop groaning about how he's a fifth-wheel," Wes said with a smirk. "As if one of the many single women throwing them-selves at him from town—or surrounding towns, for that matter—weren't good enough. Do you know how many inquirers I had to fend off this week—in person and over the phone—about where you'd be on New Year's Eve and if you had a date? I lost count after twenty."

"Shit," Cooper said with a chuckle as he ran a hand through his messy, dark-blond hair. "Didn't realize I was such a wanted man." A boyish grin was plastered on his face.

Wes, Eliza, Jules, and I collectively rolled our eyes.

"What can I say? I wanted to hang out with my favorite people tonight and not worry about a date. Now, let's get a game of pool going. Teams? And warning that Wes has been rusty lately."

"No, I haven't," Wes argued, taking the bait. He pressed a kiss to Jules's temple before grabbing a cue. "Who else is in?"

"I'll play," Eliza chimed in, and Gabe nodded, too.

Wes nodded at Gabe before grunting, "You're with me," which left Eliza and Cooper on a team.

"You better not cost us the game with your big mouth," Eliza said to Cooper, elbowing his side.

Jules and I looked at each other and immediately grinned. "Dance floor?" she asked.

I quickly nodded in agreement. We linked arms and started to make our way toward the bar and then the dance floor.

"I'll meet you two out there soon!" Eliza called after us.

Luckily, there was no rush. We had all night.

3 9

GABRIEL

I didn't think losing the pool game got me any points with Wes, but at least it was fun and a chance to get to spend more time with Lily's brother and the people in her inner circle.

Wes and Cooper were competitive, but it was good-natured. It was amusing, especially because growing up, my father's competitiveness was nothing like this. He always wanted to win —no matter the cost. For a while, I had that same mentality. I wanted to be the best at anything and everything. If I wasn't, then I needed to spend time getting better.

But that quickly took the fun out of things.

Tonight, it felt good to be bad at pool. It felt good to let go and get to know Wes, Eliza, and Cooper better. I'd had a chance to talk with them during Christmas dinner, but this felt more casual. It was also amusing to witness the banter between the three of them.

Once we finished playing best two out of three—which Wes and I did win one of the games—I looked around for Lily, who was no longer on the dance floor. She'd been there a minute ago. My eyes scanned the crowd until they landed on her, and my shoulders relaxed a fraction. She was standing by the bar...but who was standing next to her?

Trying to be casual, I asked Eliza, "Who's Lily talking to?"

Eliza glanced over. "Oh, that's Reid. He must be back home visiting his parents. He's had a crush on Lily for years."

Nope. Didn't like that. A pain radiated throughout my jaw, making me realize how clenched my teeth were.

An amused snort left Eliza. "Huh, the vein in your forehead is throbbing. Does that happen often?"

"What?" I brought my hand up to my forehead and quickly shook my head. "No, it's not." At least, I didn't think it was. That'd never happened before.

She grinned at me, and I couldn't tell if she was messing with me or not. "Interesting," she commented slyly, tipping back her drink and finishing it.

"I'm not jealous or anything."

Eliza shrugged. "Didn't say you were, but if you *were* looking for an excuse to go talk to Lily, one of the dart boards opened up. She loves to play." With that, Eliza walked away, getting caught up in another conversation as someone stopped her.

Not wanting to waste more time, I started to close the distance to the bar. My first instinct was to say *Sorry for the interruption*, but I held back.

Because I wasn't sorry. Not one bit. He'd already taken up too much of her time. I tried to relax my face as I approached the two of them. "Hey, mind if I steal Lily for a game of darts?" I asked, wrapping an arm around her waist and pulling her in toward my chest. I normally wasn't so possessive, but...I didn't hate the idea of letting everyone think Lily was mine.

"Oh, uh, we were just—" Reid rubbed the back of his neck as he shifted his weight from one foot to the other.

"I'd love to play!" Lily chimed in, and my grip on her waist tightened. "I'll catch up with you later, Reid. It was great to see you."

Over my dead body was she catching up with him later.

"Y-yeah, of course." Reid nodded, and I realized the poor bastard was tongue-tied around her. Didn't blame him.

I gave him a tight-lipped smile and guided us toward the still-open dart board. It was against the wall on the far left, which gave us more privacy. With how much the place had filled up, it was lucky we were still able to snag it.

"What was that all about?" Lily asked as I pulled out my wallet to grab a dollar bill for the machine. "Gabe." Lily drew out my name, raising her brows with an amused smile, like she knew something I didn't. "I was in the middle of a conversation, and you swooped in. Not that I minded, but..."

I shrugged, trying to downplay it. "I...didn't like how close he was standing to you."

Lily let out a giggle. "Because it was hard to hear over the music," she explained, although I didn't believe those were his only intentions.

"Eliza said he's had a crush on you for years."

"Oh, really?" Lily asked, amused. "And that bothered you?"

I bit the inside of my cheek to keep from saying something I'd regret and instead focused on pressing the display to set up our game.

"What?" Lily asked gently, stepping in front of me. "There's more you don't want to say. You can tell me anything."

That was the problem. I felt like I could tell her things I hadn't told anyone else. That was how comfortable I was around her.

"I don't know if I can tell you this," I said slowly.

"Try me."

"I hated seeing him that close to you. He doesn't deserve to be in the same room as you, let alone talking to you. No man does."

"What about you?" She tilted her head to the side. "Do you deserve to be in the same room as me?"

"No," I said on a self-deprecating laugh. Maybe I was least deserving of all. "I really don't."

"Well, you're wrong." Lily pulled the darts out of the board. She kept three for herself and handed me the others. "You do, and you know what? Tonight, I realized you're the first person I look for when I enter a room. That's going to be a hard habit to break once you leave."

Those words knocked the air out of me, leaving me winded. Because she was the first person I looked for, too. I'd been watching the front door to Lake Ridge like a fucking hawk waiting for her to enter tonight.

"Now, let's play. I'm excited to win." She skipped over to the white line on the floor, and once I was out of the way, threw her first set of darts. "Well, look at that." She grinned over at me. "A bullseye on my first turn."

40

LILY

I started playing darts younger than any kid should, but luckily, it had served me well, especially tonight. I didn't think there was a way Gabe could catch up, but I didn't want to get *too* confident.

"So," I said as I turned toward him, "if I win, will you admit you were jealous?" I smiled sweetly and batted my lashes at him.

Gabe rolled his eyes. "You mean *when* you win?"

I took my turn and stepped out of the way. "I suppose that would be more accurate."

He shook his head with a laugh and threw his first dart, hitting a triple twenty, which shaved off quite a bit of his score. "What about if I win? What do I get then?"

"What do you want?"

"A kiss from you. At midnight."

My heart skipped, because all night I'd been thinking about kissing Gabe. Wanting to find any excuse to kiss him—or to give him an excuse to kiss me. Now, I wanted him to win. His prize seemed way better than mine.

"That would work, especially since you had a good turn." He could likely win on his next one.

Since we were playing 301, I needed to hit exactly the number I had left or less, but I couldn't go over. I needed to hit the seventeen, but if I veered left, and just so happened to hit the nineteen...

"Shoot. I busted."

Gabe blinked, looking between me and the board. "Hmm," he hummed, amused, taking his turn and hitting exactly thirty-four between his three darts.

"Oh, bummer. Guess you win after all," I said with a grin, and he narrowed his eyes at me.

"Don't think I didn't know what you were doing. You want to kiss me that badly, huh?"

I bit down on my bottom lip, sucking in a breath. My eyes met his, and a shiver ran up my spine at how his gaze darkened and focused on my lips. "Maybe I do. Is that okay?"

"More than okay," he murmured. "Because I want to kiss you that badly, too. More, even. You have consumed my mind, Lily Richards."

"And you've consumed mine," I admitted, looking up at him.

He took a step toward me, closing the distance. He took the darts from my hand, setting them on the cocktail table near us and leading us toward the corner of the bar.

My bare back hit the cool, wooden wall. Gabe leaned in, and I smelled the whiskey and mint on his breath. Our mouths were painfully close, and my body ached for there to be nothing between us.

No man had ever made me feel this way. I wanted to tell Gabe that he had nothing to be jealous of with Reid, or any man for that matter. No one compared to him.

And what was that look in his eyes right now? Did he want this as much as I did?

"Earlier you said I'm the first person you look for when you enter a room," Gabe said. "It's impossible for me to keep my eyes off of you. Do you know why I sit at the same table at the café every day? Why that's my favorite spot?"

My brows furrowed, and I shook my head. I figured it was because the spot was a little more tucked away and allowed him to focus when he was working.

"Because regardless of where you are—behind the counter, in the kitchen, or the cat room—I get to see you in your element. You're a force to be reckoned with, Lily, and the fact that I even get to be in your presence is a gift."

"Gabe," I said softly. I had no clue how to respond, because my brain short-circuited. That was quite possibly the most beautiful thing anyone had ever said to me. Gabe's compliments always stirred something in my heart, but him appreciating how I looked when I was doing something I was passionate about meant more to me than I could say.

He tucked a loose strand of hair behind my ear, his touch lingering as he grazed my cheek with his thumb. Slowly, he moved his hand to the back of my neck, and the anticipation was killing me. I could barely hear the countdown to midnight, because all of my focus was on him.

Gabe's mouth tipped up in a breathtaking smile, as if he sensed my impatience. Right as the clock struck midnight, he pulled me closer and captured my lips in a searing kiss. The lights dimmed, and a chorus of cheers and confetti erupted around us.

Every part of my body melted into Gabe, and his tight grip on my waist pulled me against his body, away from the wall. Had it not been for his support, I was convinced my legs would've given out.

I didn't think I would ever get used to being kissed by Gabe. He put his whole body into it, his whole heart. Gabe kissed me like his life depended on it.

And I figured he always kissed this way. But in this

moment...I wanted to believe he had only ever kissed *me* like this.

His mouth was hot on mine, searing my lips and claiming me. My hands found his arms, then his shoulders, as I clung to him like *everything* depended on it. On him.

Gabe pulled away, but only to press kisses to my cheek, jaw, and neck, his fingers digging into my lower back. I'd have to wear this shirt again if only to feel his touch.

I leaned my head against the back wall, my lips parting. This kiss felt different than the others. More raw. "So, this...this thing between us is—it's real for you?" I panted. "Because after the Christmas festival, I asked you to show me what you would do *if* I was yours."

"And what did I tell you?" he gritted against my skin. I almost didn't hear him over my pulse thrumming in my ears.

"You...you said you would do everything in your power to make me feel good and beautiful. That you would learn my body like the back of your hand."

"And?" Gabe asked, dipping his head and sucking at my skin at the exact spot that drove me wild.

I sucked in a breath, my grip on him tightening as I struggled to keep quiet. Between the way my body reacted to him and the way his erection pressed against me, it was hard to focus.

"I asked you a question, Sunshine." His voice was rougher this time, more demanding. And I couldn't get enough of it.

"And I would say you know my body pretty well," I managed to get out.

"Look at you being a good girl and using your words," he praised, and my whole body lit up.

Gabe leaned back, his expression growing more serious. His fingers gently grasped my chin, tilting my head up so our gazes locked. "Lily, this is real. Every second of us has been real. You make me feel alive in a way I didn't think was possible. I have never felt this way about someone—and I never will. No one compares to you and the magic you bring to every room you walk into."

My chest tightened, and I let out a shaky exhale. The words were everything I'd longed to hear but didn't think I'd ever get. But here was Gabe showing me his heart.

"It's real for you," I said quietly, more to myself than to him. A fragile truth I hadn't dared to say out loud. His hand moved from my chin to cradle my cheek, thumb brushing gently across my skin.

"It's real for me," he said, steady and sure. "All of it. I've been chasing something for so long—trying to build a life that made sense on paper. But none of it meant anything until you. I don't want anything if you're not in it."

He paused, eyes searching mine. "I want all your midnights, Lily. Not just tonight. Not just Christmas Eve. I want them all."

And there it was. The dam inside me broke.

Tears welled, not from sadness, but from the weight of being seen, chosen, and wanted.

"I want all your midnights, too, Gabe," I said without an ounce of hesitation. I looked over his shoulder, noticing that everyone was wrapped up in their own celebrations. "What do you say we get out of here?"

"I'd say that's one of your best ideas yet."

ME

Happy New Year!!! Gabe and I are going to head out for the night.

ELIZA

Figured that was the case with you two making out in the corner. :)

JULES

Been there, done that lol.

Is Lake Ridge two for two for couples falling in love?

ELIZA

Huh, yeah, I guess it is.

ME

Okay, extreme. It was one kiss!

But he did say some swoony things…I'll fill you both in later.

Wait, does that mean Eliza's next?!

JULES

Oooh I think it does!!!

ELIZA

I'm turning my phone off now. Talk to you in the new year.

ME

It's already the new year!

ELIZA

The next one.

41

GABRIEL

After successfully slipping out of Lake Ridge, Lily and I made the short walk from the bar to her apartment. She texted her friends that we were leaving, and once she was done, she slid her phone into her purse. "Okay, it's just you and me for the rest of the night." She grinned and pulled her jacket tighter.

"I like the sound of that." I looked down at her, relishing the way her eyes sparkled at my words.

"Me, too."

Lily pulled her key out of her bag and quickly opened the door to the building, offering us a reprieve from the blistering cold. We still had a flight of stairs to go up before we were at her apartment, but I didn't care. I couldn't wait any longer.

I wrapped an arm around her waist, pulling her toward me and crashing my lips against hers.

"Gabe," she breathed against my mouth, her voice soft and needy. The keys jangled as she nearly dropped them, and I took them from her hand.

I'd spent way too long without Lily's lips—and I sure as hell wasn't going to stop now.

We stumbled up the stairs, too wrapped up with each

other to care that what should've taken less than a minute took us double, if not triple. To me, it meant more time kissing her.

Once we reached her floor, Lily pulled her mouth away from mine, instead peppering kisses along my jaw and gently nipping at the skin.

I tipped my head back with a low groan that vibrated throughout my whole body. "Fuck, Lily."

"I like the way you say my name," she panted, unzipping my coat and starting to push it off my shoulders. We walked into her apartment, and the door slammed behind us. I felt around the wall for the light switch.

It was then I realized how flushed from arousal Lily was, the color spreading from her cheeks down to her neck.

"How do I say your name?" I asked.

"Like I'm yours." She pushed my coat all the way down and started to work on the buttons of my dress shirt, her fingers moving quickly.

"That's because"—I dipped my head down, resting my forehead against hers—"you *are* mine."

"I'm yours," Lily repeated, her words sounding more like a moan.

While she worked on getting my shirt off, I peeled off her black long-sleeved top to reveal that she hadn't been wearing a bra. *Fuck.* "You're stunning," I rasped at the sight of her. "So perfect."

"You're not too bad yourself," she teased, pushing my shirt off and leading us to her bedroom. "I got a taste of being yours... but what would it be like"—Lily's eyes trailed along my body, up my legs, abdomen, chest, all the way up to my eyes—"to be fucked by you?" Her voice had a slight rasp to it. She sat on the edge of the bed and leaned back on her palms.

My eyes trailed along her body, taking in every curve and dip of her body. This was a sight I wanted engraved in my brain forever.

I'd always kept my emotions and actions under control, but Lily had the power to unravel me. She was the only one who could make me lose control, and I didn't want to fight it. I wanted to give in, to give her everything, *especially* when she looked at me with those hooded eyes and bit down on her plump bottom lip.

"Well, baby," I said as I undid my belt, pulling it through the loops and letting it drop to the floor, "you're about to find out. Do I need—"

"No," she breathed. "Well, unless you want to. I have condoms."

My jaw clenched immediately. I was glad she was being safe, but...*fuck*, I didn't want to think about her with someone else.

She must have sensed the tension on my face, because she smiled before adding, "I got them *recently* just in case...but I don't want to use them tonight. I'm on the pill, and I don't want anything between us."

I nearly came right then and there. I swallowed, nodding slowly. "I'd love nothing more, Lily. It's been at least a year for me, and I got tested after my last partner."

"Same here," she breathed, leaning back on the bed and propping herself up with her elbows.

"And you're feeling okay? Didn't have too much to drink?"

She shook her head to my second question. "I had two drinks early in the night and then switched to water. I feel great. Impatient, but great."

I let out a low chuckle, my own patience barely hanging on by a thread. I'd also switched to water after my first couple of drinks. I kneeled at the foot of the bed, reaching to undo her jeans and sliding them off her hips and lean legs. I then moved onto the bed, hovering over her.

I dipped my head down, my mouth finding the spot where her neck met her shoulder—the very spot that drove her wild last time. I sucked at her skin—hard—while my hand snaked down her smooth skin and the dip of her waist, all the way to between her legs. I pressed my thumb against her clit through her panties, getting a moan out of her. Her legs spread instinctively.

I hummed, sucking at her skin again and then pressing a soothing kiss as a red spot formed. I slipped my hand underneath her panties, running two fingers over her wetness. "So fucking wet for me. Have you been this wet the whole night?"

Lily nodded, a crease forming between her brows as she struggled to get the words out while my fingers slowly circled her clit. I paused only to get rid of the lacy fabric between us. "Y-yes. All night."

I gradually picked up my pace, which caused her back to arch and her hands to find my shoulders, her fingers digging in as she tried to hold steady. "Much better," I praised, moving my mouth down to the tops of her breasts, pressing a series of kisses along her smooth skin. "Last time you said you didn't know what you liked. Has that changed?"

Lily licked her lips. "I...I liked everything you did. I liked when you touched my clit, just how you are right now." Her head tipped back, the column of her throat bobbing as she took another breath. "I'm so close. Just from that—I'm so close."

I added extra pressure and kept the speed of my fingers steady. Within moments, Lily was detonating under my touch, her moans filling the room and her hips rocking against my touch. "Gabe!" she cried out.

"That's my good girl. Just like that."

She unraveled right in front of me—the flush on her cheeks deepened and her breathing increased as she fell apart. I moved my middle finger lower, teasing her entrance and feeling her wetness. As I pulled my hand away, she let out a small whimper but watched with hooded eyes. I brought my middle finger up to my lips and sucked it clean.

"So fucking sweet," I rasped. "Are you ready for me, baby?"

Lily bit down on her bottom lip, nodding lazily. "Yes, *please*," she begged, reaching to undo my pants. "I'm ready, and I want to feel all of you."

42

LILY

not if it meant getting another orgasm. I loved how attentive he was to what I enjoyed and how he knew exactly what I needed before I even did.

He took off his pants and tossed them on the floor.

I knew the year had only started, but could I claim today as the best day of the year? Because I wasn't sure how the rest of the days were going to top this.

Gabe's body was cut from stone. The dips and curves of his muscles. The slope of his nose. The sharp edge of his jaw.

My gaze dipped, seeing his thick cock hard and erect for me. My muscles tensed, and my stomach clenched with pure desire. He was going to make me come instantly again, wasn't he?

"My eyes are up here, Sunshine." I heard the smile in his voice.

"I know," I teased, biting down on my bottom lip. I reached for him, wrapping my hand around his cock and stroking it with pressure.

He let out a low groan, biceps flexing as he propped himself up above me. I parted my legs, giving him enough space to settle between them.

He replaced my hand with his own, stroking himself before lining up against my entrance. Just feeling his tip pressing against me was enough to arch my back, wanting more of him. But he was so *big*.

"Relax," he said gently, guiding his cock inside while he used his thumb on his other hand to rub soothing circles along my hip bone. My body softened immediately from his words, my legs around his hips relaxing. "That's my girl. Just like that. I'll start slow."

I nodded, knowing I'd need a few moments to adjust, but after that...I didn't want him to go slow. I wanted his restraint to snap, like it did when he kissed me at the bar earlier tonight.

He pushed deeper and effortlessly moved his hips. I tipped my head back and nearly saw stars. I wasn't sure what was hotter —how good he felt or the groan that left him as he gradually picked up the pace.

"Feels so, *so* good," I panted between breaths. I reached up to cup the back of his neck, pulling him lower and crashing my lips against his. It seemed like that was his undoing, because his hips moved faster. His tongue battled with mine, and I felt his grip on my hip tighten.

"You"—*thrust*—"Are"—*thrust*—"Mine." Gabe groaned against my mouth, breath hot. "No one else gets to see you like this or hear those pretty moans. Say it, Lily."

"I'm yours," I moaned. Tension coiled in my stomach—ready to snap—and I was aching for another release. I was nearly right there—

"Not yet, baby. You'll come when I let you."

Fuck. I didn't think Gabe could get any hotter—but, clearly, he could. I held off on my release, my thighs and legs trembling. What I realized added to my attraction to Gabe was the emotional connection we'd built over the last month. I trusted him with my body and my heart. A part of me couldn't believe that we were here together in *this* moment and how far we'd come. These days, I couldn't imagine my life without Gabe.

"That's my good girl," he praised. My eyes flicked up, and I saw the affection and desire in his gaze. "You're taking my cock so fucking well and look so beautiful doing it. You feel like a goddamn dream."

His hand on my hip snaked up along my side, until he cupped the side of my face and ran his thumb along my bottom lip. With my eyes on him, I wrapped my lips around his thumb, sucking with a hum.

"*Fuck*, Lily." His voice was strained, a muscle in his jaw fluttering. I could tell he was close, and I wanted him right there with me. I sucked harder and wrapped my legs tighter around his waist to pull him closer, deeper.

"Are you ready to come for me again?"

I nodded and brought my hand over to add extra pressure to my clit.

"Eyes on me."

Of course, I was going to listen to him. Plus, I wanted to see him fall apart, too.

"Fuck," he hissed. Gabe pulled his thumb out from between my lips and grabbed the headboard instead.

"Gabe!" I cried out, arching my back off the mattress. A rush of electricity coursed through my body as my release neared.

Gabe's jaw clenched, and he didn't tear his eyes away from mine. The look of pure desire in his eyes and the low growl that escaped him was my undoing. As I reached my peak, Gabe was right there with me.

I let out another gasp as I felt him finish, my eyes never leaving his.

He lowered his body, resting his forehead against mine and

pressing a gentle kiss to my lips. "You're unbelievable," he murmured, pulling out and lying on his side.

I scooted closer, laying my head on his chest and letting out a deep exhale. "So are you." I tipped my head back to look up at him, taking in his flushed face and messy hair. Normally, Gabe looked put together. His brown, wavy hair styled, clothes pressed, and expression composed. Right now? I'd never seen a more perfect sight. His hair was messy, clothes tossed aside, a smile on his face, and his honey-brown eyes on me.

"You're doing great on your one-item list," I teased him with a laugh.

Gabe grinned in return. "I told you. It's my one and only priority."

He leaned over, grabbing his jeans from the floor and pulling out his wallet. He flipped it open and pulled out a pink piece of paper. The list. "You really should be more careful with leaving this around."

Gabe lay back down, and I readjusted so I was lying on his chest again. He wrapped an arm around me and held out the paper so we could both take a look.

"We've done nearly everything on it. Just two more things to check off. It's been"—Gabe lowered the paper and looked at me —"an absolute honor to be able to do these things with you, Lily. I'm never going to forget this."

My stomach flipped and my mouth got dry at the mention of the list nearly being done. At the thought of him leaving. How neither of us would forget the past month.

I swallowed the lump in my throat and tried to calm my rapid heartbeat. That pounding in my head...was that my heart or his? "I'm never going to forget either," I admitted quietly before trying to sound light-hearted. "Well," I said with what I hoped was a convincing laugh, "looks like we have a trip to Milwaukee to plan."

Gabe stayed quiet and set the paper on my nightstand. "Yeah." He cleared his throat. "I guess we do."

I'd gotten to know Gabe well, but in this moment, I wasn't sure how he felt. Was he ready to go back to the city and his old life? Or had Golden Falls changed what he wanted? He said he wanted all my midnights...but did that mean *forever* or until he left town?

I thought back to our walk to my apartment after the Christmas festival and our conversation about how neither of us had been in love. How we didn't know what it felt like.

If he asked me again, I'd answer differently. Love felt like lying in Gabe's warm embrace. It was the feeling of staying up talking about anything and everything. Spending the whole day together and not getting enough. Spending a whole *lifetime* and it still not being enough.

Love sounded a lot like Gabe's heartbeat.

But had his views on love changed? He shared with me the relationship his parents had and how the divorce changed his family. He told me he saw love as transactional.

The goal at the start of December seemed so clear: fly through the list with Gabe and get Hal's decision. I still wanted the building, but I also wanted to stop time.

I wanted all the time in the world with Gabe without either of us putting our dreams on hold.

I sucked in a breath as I thought through my words. I wasn't ready to tell him how I was feeling or to face the sting of possible rejection, but I hoped he would give me a glimpse of how he was feeling.

"So," I started, "about the whole falling in love thing. Are you —are you more open to love these days?"

He stayed quiet for a beat. "Yeah," he said on a heavy exhale that rocked the room. "I'm more open to love these days, Sunshine."

I wasn't brave enough to ask if that meant he was more open to love *with me*. But even if he wasn't...if what was going on between us made him more open to love with *someone else*, I wanted him to be happy.

Either way, I had him for now, and I was going to enjoy every moment.

I sat up in bed, pulling the sheet over my waist. When I looked at Gabe, his expression was strained, as if his thoughts were as complicated as mine. Or maybe the issue wasn't that my thoughts were complicated—I was just making them that way.

I rolled my lips. "Will you stay the night? Maybe we throw a frozen pizza in the oven?"

He rolled onto his side, reaching over and splaying his large palm on my thigh. His thumb stroked gently. "I'd love nothing more. C'mon, let's clean up first. I'm not done with you yet," he murmured, leaning over to press a hungry kiss to my hip, right where his touch had been.

Gabe, pizza, and sex. I didn't need anything else.

I tried to quiet my racing thoughts and instead enjoy what had turned into one of the best nights of my life.

43

GABRIEL

ME

Happy New Year, man! Sorry, I didn't respond last night.

LIAM

No worries. Hope you had fun. You did have fun, right? You weren't sitting in your room… alone…working…

Because that would've been depressing.

ME

You make me sound so lame.

LIAM

Am I wrong?

ME

Usually not…

But this time, yes. I celebrated New Year's Eve with Lily and her friends.

LIAM

Oh…you were with Lily…

That's what you should've led with!

ME

Don't worry, I'll call you later and fill you in.

LIAM

You better. Beans and I are waiting.

Attachment: Selfie of Liam and Beans on the couch

ME

You do know once I'm back, you'll have to return my cat?

Right???

LIAM

We'll see. We've bonded in the last month.

THERE TRULY WASN'T A FEELING LIKE BEING TWENTY-EIGHT AND sneaking into your grandfather's home in the late morning. I was an adult, and I hadn't done anything wrong, and yet...I didn't want to have a run-in with Hal.

Not right away, at least. I needed to first find a way to wipe this stupid grin off my face that hadn't left since last night. Honestly, it was hard not to smile when I was around Lily.

After staying up for pizza, we fell asleep in her bed, and I had the best night's sleep I'd had in a long time. Possibly ever. This morning, we woke up, and I had my way with her again in the kitchen before breakfast.

It was like weight had been lifted off my shoulders now that I knew that our connection was real and that she felt it, too.

But...as quickly as one weight was removed, another was thrown down. I was falling in love with Lily Richards.

And I couldn't do anything about it. I couldn't stop it—not that I wanted to—but I also couldn't do anything if I was lucky enough for her to feel the same way. I couldn't stand in the way of her dreams with the café or with the building. I couldn't ask her to move with me to Milwaukee.

I slid the key into the lock and turned the doorknob, trying to quietly push the front door open. The hinges squeaked and cut through the living room, and I swore under my breath.

I closed the door behind me and started to unzip my coat, again trying to be quiet.

When I looked up and saw the light on in the kitchen and heard Hal flipping through the newspaper, I quickly realized there was no point. Hal was home.

I hung my coat, toed off my shoes, and made my way into the other room. As predicted, Hal was sitting at the kitchen table, his glasses low on his nose as he read today's edition of the *Golden Falls Gazette*.

"There you are," he said with a knowing smile, taking off his glasses and folding the newspaper on the table. "Your sneaking in could use some work."

I let out a laugh as he broke the tension. "I wasn't sure if you'd be home or not."

"Had to make sure you'd get back okay." Hal gestured to the seat across from him. "Well, grab a cup of coffee and take a seat."

I did as Hal said and sat across from him. I expected Hal to say the first word, but he didn't, just sipped on his coffee. His expression was warm, inviting.

"I like her," I admitted eventually, sighing. "A lot."

Hal nodded, like he already knew that, like he saw it coming from a mile away. "I know it's early, but I think you two bring out the best in each other. Make each other realize that what seems out of reach really isn't and help each other see the small everyday joys."

That was exactly how Lily made me feel. I came to Golden Falls because I wanted to buy the building to prove myself to my father, to salvage my career. But being here made me realize that life was so much better when you had people in your corner who supported and uplifted you. I had that with my friendship with Liam, but I'd never felt that with my parents.

And in my month in Golden Falls, I'd felt that from Hal, from Lily, and from people I'd barely gotten to know. People who I wanted to get to know more.

Lily meant more to me than the building, than my career, frankly. With her, it felt like anything was possible. Even leaving Nelson Group and figuring out what to do until my non-compete was up and I could go back to doing the work I set out to do.

"She's changed my perspective on a lot of things, and you have, too." I lifted my eyes to look at him. "Things feel less scary knowing I have people on my side."

Hal's expression softened. "You've always had me on your side, Gabe, and you always will."

"I know that. Now, at least. Maybe I didn't before—not because you didn't make it clear, but because..." I paused, my gaze flicking down to my clasped hands on the wooden table. "Because I wasn't sure if you'd forgive me for not being here for you when Vera died."

The silence hung in the air for a moment, and I felt another weight lift off my shoulders. I'd been holding those words in since I entered Golden Falls—and even before that, if I was being honest. It wasn't easy to say them out loud, to be vulnerable with the guilt and regret, but it felt better.

"Oh, Gabe," Hal said quietly. "There wasn't anything to forgive."

I looked up at him. Seeing the way his tears glazed over his eyes had me feeling equally as emotional.

"Of course, I would've wanted you here," he continued. "But I was never mad at you, and I knew you were beating yourself up enough about it." He let out a heavy sigh. "What I was frustrated about was how your father handled it all by not telling you, by putting business first and not letting you make a choice. Your father and I...we don't see eye to eye on a lot of things. I don't like the way he treats people or the way he runs his business—and I've made that known over the years. He's tried to cut me out of his life, and that's his choice, but the main reason I haven't let him do that is because of you. Because I never wanted you to feel alone. Maybe I could've done a better job at that."

I wasn't sure why my father was the way he was, and maybe I would never know. I'd spent years trying to please him—to live up to his expectations—but I was realizing I never had a chance. Because I wasn't like him. I thought back to my earlier conversation with Hal, when he reminded me that I was my own person. It was time to start acting like it, time to start doing things for me. I'd finally gotten a chance to do that in Golden Falls and it had been great. Who knew a work-life balance would do wonders for my mental health?

"I think you did a great job," I assured Hal. "I don't think I was ready for it yet, but I am now. Being here in Golden Falls has reminded me that I'm not alone. That if I distance myself from him and set boundaries, that I'm not on an island. Honestly, some boundaries would probably do me good. With both him and my mom."

"I'm proud of you, Gabe. I really am."

"That—" I cleared my throat. "That means a lot."

"Anytime you need a reminder, you know where to find me."

I let out a laugh, reaching for my coffee. "You have a nice group of people here supporting you, Hal."

"They're your people now, too."

44

LILY

As much as I loved my job, going back to work after a week off took some getting used to. But it was time to open the café, get back to baking, and do something productive with my days that wasn't only spending time with Gabe...even if that had become one of my favorite pastimes.

Tiffany and I spent the first couple of days getting back into our routine and brainstorming new ideas that we wanted to try this year, and it was another reminder that I didn't have to do any of this alone. Now, the fourth day back, I felt a rush of excitement about all the new drinks and treats we'd be able to try out, as well as the baking classes I'd signed up to start in the coming months.

A month ago, expanding Purrfect Blend and opening a second location felt like a pipe dream. Now? It all felt within reach, although I wasn't going to rush it. I wanted to take my time getting there, building my team, and expanding on my skills. I had loyal customers in Golden Falls who I was confident were going to support me each step of the way.

And I had Gabe.

I loved telling him about my ideas and getting his input. He was always supportive but sometimes mentioned aspects I hadn't even thought of, which helped me think more strategically and be more confident in my ideas. We were a good team.

Unfortunately, I hadn't had much time with Gabe this week. While he still stopped by in the mornings, he was swamped with work at Nelson Group, more so than usual. I wasn't sure if it was because he was catching up after the holidays or if his dad was giving him more work on purpose. Maybe both.

My eyes flicked to the table he normally sat at when he was here, which was empty again. My heart clenched. I couldn't be thinking about that as Gabe's table. What about in a year from now—in two years from now—would I still look at that goddamn table and think about him?

I let out a heavy sigh and returned to rearranging today's pastries for the fifth time.

An embarrassing boost of serotonin coursed through my body when my phone vibrated in my apron pocket. I pulled it out, hoping for a text from Gabe but instead seeing it was from Grant, Jules's older brother.

GRANT

Hey, Lily. Sorry I missed your call earlier. I'm in meetings with clients all day today, but I can give you a call tomorrow morning, if that works? Happy to answer whatever questions you have as best I can.

I typed out a reply.

ME

Tomorrow morning works for me! Before 9 a.m. would be great, but if there's a time that will work better for you, let me know. Looking forward to it! Thanks again for making the time to talk with me.

GRANT

I'll call you at 8 a.m. And it's no problem at all.
Talk to you soon.

Grant was one of the top lawyers in Chicago and specialized in labor and employment law. I'd asked Jules for his number, saying I had a couple of questions after hiring Tiffany and potentially bringing on another employee in the coming months. That was true...to an extent. It was more that I had some questions about non-compete agreements.

Being on my feet normally didn't take such a toll on me. But being on my feet after a week of time off?

It was Friday afternoon, and I was both beat and energized. All I could think about was lying down on my couch, and I was nearly there. Tiffany was going to close up the café and take care of the cats, allowing me to head home earlier.

I climbed the stairs to my apartment and pushed the door open. Gabe had come by the café about half an hour ago, asking if he could get my key to wait for me at the apartment. He had one more call to do and then said he'd be mine for the rest of the day. I couldn't wait.

Sylvie and Bandit came running toward me, and I crouched down. "Hi, my lovelies," I cooed, petting them both and relishing the immediate purrs I got. My cats had gotten used to having me around this past week and were as eager to have me home.

"Gabe?" I called out, standing. I toed off my shoes and slipped off my coat, hanging it by the door.

"In here!" he called out.

Confused, I walked over, the cats following me.

The bathroom door was half open, allowing me to peek inside before I opened it fully. The blinds were drawn and the lights were off, but the room was illuminated by candles lining the edge of the tub. There was a tray resting across the tub with a plate of charcuterie, a glass of wine, and a new book.

The aroma of eucalyptus from the bubble bath immediately calmed me.

Gabe had transformed my bathroom into a relaxing oasis.

"How did you..." I trailed off, closing the distance and wrapping my arms around him.

He pulled me flush against him, his palm on my lower back. "I wanted to do something for you. Something to help you relax now that you're back at work and on your feet all day."

My eyes got watery over the gesture, over how thoughtful he was, over how he knew—even before I did—how much I needed this. "Gabe, this is so sweet. Thank you."

He cupped the side of my face, resting his forehead against mine. "My pleasure," he murmured, running his thumb over my cheek. "Enjoy, and try to relax."

By his words, it sounded like he was going to leave. Like he'd done this *just* for me...but he could use the relaxation, too.

"I want you to enjoy this with me. Don't you think you need some help relaxing?"

He hummed, his nostrils flaring as heat blazed in his eyes. "I have been pretty tense lately." He licked his lips, a smirk forming. He kept his arm wrapped around my waist and reached with his other hand to start to close the door. The cats scurried out before he shut it.

"I have two ideas to help you relax." I eagerly started to unbutton his dress shirt and pushed it off his broad shoulders. I then moved my attention to undoing his belt.

"The bath, and..." Gabe trailed off, his hands starting to make quick work of ridding me of my sweater and jeans.

I decided to show him instead of telling. I dropped to my knees, pulling down his slacks and boxers so his length could spring free. I wrapped a hand around it and stroked.

"Fuck," he hissed. He leaned against the bathroom counter, gripping the edge of it. His cock twitched, and I couldn't wait to wrap my lips around him. Make him feel as good as he'd made me feel.

I ran my tongue along the side of his length eagerly before guiding him into my mouth with a hum.

"Lily. Holy shit..." His head tipped back, mouth ajar. His grip on the counter tightened, making the veins in his forearms even more prominent.

I worked my tongue along him, exploring and tasting as I bobbed my head up and down.

"Just like that, baby," he rasped. "You look so fucking beautiful taking my cock."

When his cock twitched, I took him deeper, using my hand to pleasure the base of him.

He sucked his bottom lip into his mouth, another groan escaping him. "That's my girl."

He brought one of his hands to the back of my head, wrapping my braid around his fist and pulling my mouth away.

"But—" I protested. I wasn't done—not even close.

"I want to feel you," he growled, his voice urgent, restraint snapping. His grip on my hair loosened. He guided me to standing, turning me around so I was flush against the edge of the counter and he was standing behind me, his breath hot on my neck. "You're all I've been thinking about this week." Our eyes locked in the mirror. "Can I have you? Can I fuck your pretty pussy?"

My knees buckled, goosebumps forming on my skin from his breath, from the hungry look in his eyes, and from the way his cock pressed against me.

I let out an airy laugh as my stomach clenched with want. With so much desire I could barely stand.

Was that even a question?

"Yes," I breathed, wanting to tell him *always*.

I stood naked in front of the counter, facing the mirror. And any insecurities I normally had when I looked in the mirror—whether they were big or small—disappeared. Because it was hard to feel insecure when Gabe looked at me like *that*. Like he wanted to devour every inch of me. Like he thought I was the most beautiful woman in the world.

Maybe, to him, I was.

"Oh, fuck," I gasped as he slid inside me from behind. I leaned against the counter, my palms splayed against the cold surface. "Gabe!" I cried out, immediately clenching around him as he moved his hips. He brought a hand to cup my breast, the pad of his thumb teasing my hardened nipple.

"Fucking dream come true," he groaned. "Everything about you." He set his hand over mine, our fingers intertwining.

"Gabe, please don't stop. Feels so good."

Gabe grinned against my neck, pressing another series of kisses to the curve of my neck. I tipped my head back toward him, my eyes about to flutter closed when I heard Gabe's voice.

"Keep those pretty eyes open," he murmured. "I want you to see for yourself how beautiful you look when you come all over my cock."

Our eyes locked in the mirror. Another kiss. Another thrust. Another feeling of his rough touch on my breasts. And I was gone.

My vision blurred, and I came undone for him. Within

moments, I felt him finish, a low groan vibrating throughout his chest as he rasped my name, our gazes staying locked.

I was a mess—strands of hair escaping my braid, my cheeks flushed, a layer of sweat coating my skin—but I wouldn't have it any other way.

Gabe pulled out but stayed behind me, tucking a strand of blonde hair behind my ear and pressing a kiss to my temple. I turned around in his arms, the cool marble pressed against my lower back. His hands cradled my face. His expression was soft, *so* soft. I wondered what was going through his mind, but I didn't get a chance to ask, because he lowered his mouth to mine and kissed me.

And there was no way I was stopping that.

I leaned against Gabe's firm chest, letting my eyes fall closed as I settled into the warm water and his even warmer embrace. He needed to refill the tub since the water had cooled, but now we were both able to sink in and relax, taking in the dim lighting and aroma of eucalyptus.

"How do you manage to do this?" he asked, giving the end of my braid a tug. I had my hair in a French braid today, which was how I typically wore it to work. I loved to have my hair down, but braiding it kept it out of my face as I moved around the café. He slid off the black ponytail holder and put it on his wrist, running his fingers through my hair to undo the braid.

I let out a content hum. "That feels so good." I relished the way his hands gently massaged my scalp and ran through my hair. "And to answer your question, years of practice. My mom used to braid my hair when I was little and taught me once I got older. I've gotten pretty quick with it."

"Oh, I bet." He pressed a kiss to the side of my head and moved my hair to one side, pulling my back flush against his chest.

"Can I ask you something?"

"Anything."

I mulled over my words. There'd been something on my mind ever since Gabe had said it. "A couple of weeks ago at the café, I overheard your conversation with Louise." I bit down on my bottom lip. "She asked about your first impression of me."

"Yeah, I remember."

"You said some...things. Did you mean them?"

I thought she was the most beautiful woman I'd ever seen.

Looking into her blue eyes calmed me in a way I'd never experienced.

My first impression of her was that she had the power to bring any man to his knees.

"I meant every word, Lily."

My stomach pinched, and my brows furrowed. I liked that answer. I just...wasn't expecting it.

"But we were enemies." I glanced at him over my shoulder and saw the corner of his mouth tip up.

"I think it was more so that *you* thought we were enemies," he clarified, which was fair. "And while our first meeting was interesting, that was truly my first impression of you. And I was only more impressed with you the more time we spent together. I was—*I am*—impressed by your kindness, how caring you are, passionate, motivated, determined. All of that only makes you more beautiful."

I swallowed the lump in my throat, hoping that if I took a moment to respond, he wouldn't hear the emotion in my tone. It didn't do any good. "That's the sweetest thing anyone has ever said to me," I croaked.

I loved the way Gabe saw me, and it reminded me to be less critical of myself.

I wondered what this all meant for the building. I still wanted it...but I wanted him, too. It made me uneasy, because I didn't want it to come between us, but I also didn't want to step back. He likely felt similarly, but I didn't want to ask. Not yet, at least. Maybe Hal would put us out of our misery and make a decision soon. He *did* say he'd know by the start of the new year, although Hal had a tendency to be cryptic for a reason.

"What do you say about getting away this weekend?" Gabe murmured, snapping me out of my thoughts.

I raised my brows, curious what he was thinking. "What'd you have in mind?"

"I was thinking"—he ran his knuckles along my arm—"that we spend the day in Milwaukee visiting a bunch of different cafés."

My lips parted, and I nodded eagerly. "Y-yeah, I would love that," I stammered through my excitement. Not only would it check another item off our list, but he remembered what I'd said during our dinner at Pasta Fresca about wanting to visit other cafés to get ideas for my own. "I'm so excited. Can I see your apartment, too? And meet your cat?"

He chuckled. "You can definitely see my apartment. As far as meeting Beans, my friend Liam has been watching him. He started by stopping by my apartment, but since I've been here longer than anticipated, Liam brought Beans over to his condo. He bought him a whole new setup, and I'm worried my cat won't want to come home once I'm back in town."

"I'm sure you could win him back with lots of treats."

Gabe leaned over the side of the tub, grabbing his slacks and pulling his phone out of his pocket. He brought up a text thread with Liam and showed me a series of photos of a sleeping Beans on a new cat tree, him playing with new toys, and the two of them snuggling on the couch.

"Ah." I nodded understandingly. "I stand corrected. You have your work cut out for you."

"The two of them didn't even like each other before I left."

"A lot can change in a month," I pointed out.

Gabe nodded. "A lot can change in a month," he repeated.

45

GABRIEL

Thankfully, the winter weather cooperated with us this weekend, so Lily and I could go to Milwaukee as planned. We left early Saturday morning to ensure we had plenty of time during the day to visit various cafés. I'd planned out our route but encouraged Lily to see if there were other places she wanted to stop.

By early afternoon, we'd visited three cafés, and Lily had a number of conversations with employees and managers. I loved seeing her in her element. The way her eyes brightened when someone happily agreed to talk with her. How she bit down on her lip as she was taking notes on her phone. And how she beamed walking over to me to tell me everything.

If I could, I'd make her this happy every day. But we both knew my time in Golden Falls was wrapping up soon.

The past week had been brutal at work, to say the least. My father was giving me extra work and incessantly texting and emailing me that I needed to be back in the office. I responded to his business questions but ignored the personal ones.

On New Year's Day, I felt optimistic that I could leave Nelson Group, and while that would be ideal, it was starting to feel less and less possible. What was I going to do for *five years* as I waited for my non-compete to expire? I needed to work, and I wanted to have my career in development—just not the work I was doing for Nelson Group.

Maybe I could figure out a plan, but I needed to be back in the city, back in my routine. I loved being in Golden Falls and spending time with Lily, but it was prolonging the inevitable. I was leaving, and I needed to figure out what to do about my career. I also couldn't keep avoiding my father, especially since he was still my boss.

As excited as I was about my ideas for the building, I was increasingly skeptical that it would change anything with my father. His behavior made it clear he simply wanted the building for himself. He didn't care about my plans for it.

I wouldn't be able to forgive myself if Hal decided to sell the building to me and, somehow, my father got his hands on it. That building belonged to Lily. Plain and simple.

"Hey, isn't this the restaurant?" Lily called out, and I realized I'd walked right past it while in my daze. I brought Lily to Half Day Pub, one of my favorite places in the city and where I always stopped by with Liam.

"Yeah, that's it. Sorry, I was on autopilot."

"No worries." Lily smiled, opening the door for us. "This has been such a great day. Thank you for bringing me to the city and for showing me around. I've learned so much already, and I can't wait to get back to Golden Falls." Her smile widened. She then turned to the hostess and asked for a booth for two.

As we were walking, Fiona spotted us and waved. "I didn't realize you were in town," she said with a grin and then turned to Lily. "You must be Lily!"

"I am," Lily said slowly, looking between the two of us.

I stepped in to explain. "Liam and I often come here for dinner and sit in Fiona's section. I assume Liam has been coming by while I've been in Golden Falls and filling Fiona in on what we've been up to."

Fiona pushed her bangs out of her eyes, a warm smile on her face. "I've gotten Gabe and Lily updates *and* Beans updates. I think Liam's been here about every other day. The guy misses you, so hopefully, you'll be back soon."

I didn't miss the way Lily stiffened at the mention of me being back in Milwaukee, and honestly, I felt the same way. I wasn't ready for our time together to end.

"Well, why don't we sit in your section today then, if you have an open table," Lily suggested, any hesitation or concern quickly gone.

The hostess looked at Fiona, who eagerly nodded. "I just had a booth free up. Come this way, and I'll get you some appetizers on the house."

"Perfect, thanks! I love your jewelry, by the way. Did you get it from a shop around here?" Lily gestured to Fiona's rings and necklace, quickly making friends with her.

"You're so sweet. Thank you! I did, just a couple blocks from here."

"Looks like the type of style my best friend Eliza would love." Lily beamed. "I'll have to stop by after we finish lunch."

"You have to. I have a coupon in my bag. I'll grab it for you when I put your orders in."

As Fiona handed us our menus and told Lily about recommendations, the two of them continued chatting, and all I could think about was how easily Lily fit into my life.

"How are you able to become friends with everyone you meet? Well, except me, at first," I teased Lily as we walked into my apartment.

Her and Fiona had exchanged numbers, even making plans to meet up if Lily was in Milwaukee again. Lily also had told Fiona about Purrfect Blend and promised to send photos of her café.

"Hey, we got there eventually," Lily teased back with a grin. She halted when we walked in, and her mouth hung open. "*This* is your apartment? It's, like, the size of a small house."

I rubbed the back of my neck, hitching a shoulder.

"My whole apartment is probably the size of your bedroom!"

"Okay, that's dramatic." I paused. "Maybe two bedrooms."

Lily let out a laugh and walked inside, running her hand along the black marble countertop in the kitchen. She crossed the open living room to the wall of floor-to-ceiling windows that faced a view of Lake Michigan. "Wow, this is stunning." She then turned toward my gray sectional. "And this *couch*"—she plopped down and sank into the cushions—"is as comfortable as it looks." She sighed and unzipped her coat.

After lunch, we stopped by the jewelry store Fiona had told Lily about, as well as two more cafés. Our last stop was a grocery store where we picked up ingredients for dinner. We were going to spend the rest of the evening in and head back to Golden Falls tomorrow morning.

I set the bags of groceries on the kitchen counter and began to put things away. "Make yourself comfortable and at home," I said as Lily got up.

"I'm happy to help, plus then I can do more snooping."

I shook my head with a laugh.

As promised, Lily *did* help, but she also looked in every cabinet, not that I minded. I'd let her do literally anything she wanted.

A knock on the door caught our attention.

"Are you expecting someone?"

I shook my head. Had Liam mentioned he was coming over, and I forgot? I walked over to the door, not bothering to check through the peephole and pulling it open.

In hindsight, I should've checked the damn peephole. But it was too late.

My father stood on the other side of the door, arms crossed and jaw clenched.

I had no clue how he'd found out I was in town, but it didn't matter. Asking would piss him off even more.

"Gabriel," he seethed.

"Ron," I answered with a sigh.

"Why the fuck haven't you been responding to my texts? When are you coming back to the office?"

"I—" I started, trying to keep the door cracked open, but he pushed it open, stalking past me. "Now's not a good time," I told him.

Lily was still in the kitchen, and she stilled at the sight of my father barging in. She set the box of pasta she was holding on the counter and closed the cabinet.

I wasn't sure what to expect. I hadn't wanted Lily to meet my father this soon, if ever. Not because of her or anything she did, but because of *him*. I didn't want her to meet him and see me differently. I also didn't want my father to be aware that Lily and I were together, because I wouldn't put it past him to use it against me, against us.

"Seriously?" he scoffed, looking at me. "Let me guess. You go to Golden Falls and now want to stick around for some piece of ass? You couldn't get that in the city?"

"Hey, don't—" I stepped forward. My voice was louder and my tone firmer than any time I'd spoken to him. Maybe I'd never been able to stand up to my father for myself, but I sure as hell wasn't going to let him talk about Lily that way.

"God, Gabriel. You went there for *business*. Don't be so fucking pathe—"

"No, you don't get to do this." Lily's voice was sharp, stern. I almost didn't recognize it. I'd never heard her like this. She left the kitchen, marching into the hallway so she was closer to me and my father. "You don't get to come to Gabe's apartment and talk to him this way." She was eerily calm and composed. Her expression was neutral, but her hands were balled into fists at her sides.

My father reared back, a rare expression of surprise on his face. "Excuse me?"

People didn't stand up to my father, oftentimes because it meant putting their careers on the line. It was certainly why I had held my tongue for so long.

But Lily held her ground, straightening her spine and looking up at him. "You're not going to stand here and talk to Gabe like this."

"This conversation doesn't concern you. I don't think you realize who you're—"

"I know exactly who I'm speaking to. What I don't know is why you're still here when he said this isn't a good time."

My father scoffed, looking between us. "Whatever this is"—he gestured between us—"it's never fucking going to work. You think I'm going to let you live and work from Golden Falls? Your little *vacation* is over, Gabriel. Your job is here."

He didn't have to say it, but I knew what he meant. *I own you.*

"Gabe is exploring his options, actually. He might decide to come back, but he also might decide to pursue a different opportunity." Lily took a step forward. "His non-compete agreement is unenforceable, and we both know that. You'll be hearing from his lawyer."

What did she mean the non-compete was unenforceable? Was she saying that to get my father to leave, or was it actually true? Because if the non-compete wasn't an issue...well, that changed everything.

Countless thoughts and questions swarmed my mind, but the one that rose to the top was how Lily was standing up for me without any hesitation.

A past version of me might've been worried about the repercussions on my career and relationship with my father. But *this* version of me was in awe of Lily. I also finally came to terms that my relationship with my father had been damaged for a long time. Now that I fully allowed myself to appreciate what it meant to have people like Liam, Lily, and Hal on my side, I didn't want to go back to being isolated when it came to my father or only focusing on work.

My father's face turned a shade of red I didn't think was possible. He didn't say another word as he stalked past me and slammed the door shut.

Once he was gone, Lily exhaled deeply and unclenched her fists. Her eyebrows pinched together as she ran a hand through her hair. "I'm so sorry if I overstepped," she said quickly. "I know your relationship with him is strained, and that probably didn't help, but I hated how he was speaking to you, and I couldn't stand by and—"

I crossed the short distance between us and took her face in my hands and kissed her deeply. No one had ever stood up for me like that, and especially not to my father. Hell, I hadn't ever stood up for *myself* like that.

Any tension I was feeling left my body. My chest expanded, a rush of energy and awe surging through me. "Lily, that was," I murmured against her lips, "so fucking badass."

Her shoulders relaxed, and she leaned further into me. Her

fingers wrapped around my shirt to keep me close. "You're not mad?" she whispered.

I pulled away, continuing to gently cradle her face in my hands. "Are you kidding me?" I asked with a gentle laugh. "No, I'm not mad. I'm proud. I'm grateful. I'm in *awe* of you. Just when I thought you couldn't get any more incredible." I shook my head. "I've never had someone stand up for me like that. You don't realize how much that meant to me. You are the bravest woman I know, Lily Richards. In so many ways."

She blinked up at me. "You think I'm brave?"

"Among so many other things," I murmured to her.

She dropped her gaze down, focusing on how her fingers were fiddling with the buttons on my shirt. "Well, since you think that," she said, looking up at me through her lashes, "I think I should be brave in one more way."

My brows furrowed, and I stayed quiet to give her the space to get her words out.

"I love you, Gabriel Nelson. I fell in love with you without expecting it. And I understand if you can't say it back, if you still view it as transactional or if you're not ready. I get it. You said you were more open to love...and it doesn't have to be with me, but I'm willing to put my heart on the line and prove to you that love *isn't* transactional." Lily spoke quickly, barely taking a breath between sentences.

Time stopped. My vision tunneled. My fingers tangled in her hair. I needed her closer.

Lily loved me.

Lily *loved* me.

Lily loved *me*.

She started to worry her bottom lip, likely mistaking my silence for something other than pure awe and adoration of the woman in front of me.

"Lily," I rasped with a laugh. "I am so in love with you. How could I not be? You are the most incredible woman I've ever met. From the moment we met, I was in awe of your strength, your confidence, your determination, your beauty." I cupped her face, running the pad of my thumb over her cheek. "I didn't expect it, but there was no point in fighting it." I exhaled. "God, Lily, I love you so fucking much, and it feels so good to say that out loud." I paused, my lips spreading into a smile. "You want to know what love feels like for me?"

She nodded, eyes dazed as she looked up at me.

"It feels like sunshine. It's the feeling I get when you smile at me, when you laugh at something I say. It's the feeling of falling asleep with you in my arms, knowing that I get to see you first thing when I wake up. It's the feeling of finding you in a room and locking eyes."

"Oh, Gabe," she said softly, resting her hand on the back of my neck. "There are so many things I love about you. I love your heart, how much you care. I love how when you do something you give it your all. I love how you support me, how thoughtful you are. And I love how you've given Golden Falls a chance, how you've reconnected with Hal. You told me once that it's okay to ask for help, how I don't have to do things alone. Well, I want to tell you that I want to be in your corner. I want to be the one to help you when you need it, to support you, because that's what you've done for me. I don't want to go back to life without you. Gabe Nelson, I want all your midnights, too. Every single one."

"They're yours, Lily. Every single one," I repeated, lifting her and sitting her on the kitchen counter. Her legs instinctively spread, and I eagerly stepped between them.

Her hands ran down my chest. "What else is mine?" she asked breathlessly, licking her lips. She looped her fingers in my belt loops and pulled me closer, her legs wrapping around my hips.

I let out a husky laugh, my palms braced on either side of

her on the cool marble counter. "Whatever you want. Name it, and it's yours." Everything was hers, and I would do anything for her.

"I want"—she bit down on her bottom lip to hide her smile —"every inch of you."

I hummed, my cock twitching in my pants at her words. "You sure you can handle every inch?"

"I've done a pretty good job so far, but...why don't we find out?"

46

LILY

WITHIN MOMENTS, GABE LIFTED ME OFF THE COUNTER AND carried me to his bedroom. He tossed me on his bed with ease, and I sank into his soft mattress and covers. I watched with parted lips as he started to undo the buttons on his dress shirt. Getting impatient, he pulled the shirt off, the buttons popping off and skittering on the hardwood floor.

The action only made me crave him more. I was aching for him, how it felt to be underneath his weight as he touched and explored my body. Once Gabe's shirt was off, the rest of our clothes were torn off, too.

He spread my legs, a growl leaving him. He dipped his head, pressing a trail of hungry kisses along my leg, inner thigh, all the way to my center, where he swiped his tongue.

"Gabe!" I cried, my legs already trembling.

"I love how wet you get for me. I love that I'm the only one who's going to touch you from now on. To get to see you like this."

My hands found his hair, and I gripped and tugged as my back arched off the mattress. Gabe's hand reached up, large palm splaying against my stomach to keep me steady while his mouth sucked, teased, and tasted.

I loved that he was mine, and I would never get tired of saying that. A part of me still found it hard to believe how we'd gotten here, but I wouldn't have changed a thing. Because the way things unfolded brought me to Gabe.

My hands ached with the need to explore his body. I gripped his shoulders and pulled him to me, crashing his lips to mine. I gently stroked my tongue against his before sucking his bottom lip, tasting myself on him.

He groaned, his grip on my hip tightening as he pushed inside me, not wasting any time in moving his hips.

"And I love that I'm the only one who gets to touch you. Who gets to feel you. Fantasize about you." I let out a gasp, my breath hitching low in my throat.

"Only you, Sunshine," he murmured, breath hot against mine. "You'll have to tell me more about these fantasies, though. I'm very curious."

I grinned lazily against him. With my legs wrapped around his hips, I dug my heels into his lower back, wanting more, wanting him deeper. Gabe eagerly complied.

"I'm...I'm close," I warned with another moan among the rhythmic motion of his hips and the headboard knocking against the wall.

"Good girl. Come for me, Lily. Let's hear those pretty moans." Gabe used the pad of his thumb to pull down my bottom lip and tip my head down. "And eyes open. I want you to watch how well you take my cock as you fall apart."

"Oh, fuck!" I did as he said and watched as his hips slammed against mine, our bodies shaking and rattling the bed even further. I gripped the sheets, needing something to anchor me as my vision blurred and pleasure flooded my body as we both finished.

Breathless, I sank further into the bed, letting my head fall back and eyes close.

Gabe lay down next to me murmuring, "C'mere," as he pulled me into his arms, and I nuzzled into his neck. He gently stroked my arm and pressed a kiss to the side of my head as I caught my breath.

I turned my head, pressing my lips to his jaw. "Being in your arms is my favorite place," I whispered.

"Good, because I never plan on letting you go."

I ended up dozing off in Gabe's arms (the best place for a nap) for twenty minutes, and then we cleaned up in the bathroom, which turned into Gabe taking me again in the shower.

Now, I was sitting on a barstool at the kitchen island, swinging my feet as I watched Gabe cook us a lemon garlic sausage pasta for dinner. I was wearing one of his hoodies and a pair of sweatpants—that he rarely wore, which was criminal— and my hair was wet from the shower. "Smells amazing," I sighed as I inhaled again.

"Should be ready in another ten minutes or so." He turned around, and I took in his *casual* look, which was an olive-green T-shirt with jeans. His hair was mussed and slightly damp from our shower. "So, I meant to ask, but what you said about the non-compete agreement. Is that...true?"

Ah, yes. I figured I'd have some explaining to do.

"It is true, actually. I spoke with a lawyer—Jules's brother Grant—about non-competes. I kept things general when speaking with him, because I didn't want to give your information away without you knowing. And Grant said because of that he could only give me general advice, but he's happy to talk with you, if you'd like, or refer you to an attorney in Wisconsin." I fiddled with the drawstring of the hoodie, worried I'd overstepped. He hadn't asked me to do any of this—both with the non-compete and standing up to his father—but I couldn't help myself. I knew how miserable Gabe was at this job and also how exhausted he was, which took away time from looking for other options. If I could do *something* to make it easier, I'd do it.

"You're incredible, you know that? I'm so lucky to have you on my side."

A smile spread across my face. I was relieved that he was appreciative of my help. "But that's it for my meddling! I don't have any other secrets up my sleeve, and in the future, I'll be sure to ask you."

I proceeded to tell Gabe about what Grant had shared with me. To make a long story short, the Federal Trade Commission last year proposed a nationwide ban on non-compete agreements. The rule was being challenged, but non-competes were generally viewed unfavorably under Wisconsin law. They were enforceable, but only if they met specific requirements, including having a reasonable time and not being unnecessarily harsh on the employee. Grant believed the Nelson Group non-competes violated both those clauses. There was likely a bigger issue at hand if other employees had similar non-competes and if company lawyers hadn't notified employees of these changes.

I passed along Grant's number to Gabe, who had a look of hope I hadn't seen before. He was energized and no longer stuck. He could truly turn his career into what he wanted. And I couldn't wait to see what he did.

Gabe nodded slowly as he listened, as if various pieces of what he wanted to do next were clicking in his brain. "I'm going to submit my proposal for the city's old warehouse separately from Nelson Group. I'll talk to Grant, too, about how all this works and see if I can send in my resignation immediately. I had...no idea about any of this. I've talked to the company lawyers about the non-compete, but they always dismissed me, saying there was nothing that could be done. They were likely in my father's pocket. I can't believe it." He rubbed at his brow as he shook his head.

"It also means," I said, "that if Hal were to sell the building to you, you wouldn't have to own it under Nelson Group."

Gabe's eyes shot to me, and he quickly shook his head. "That building is yours, Lily. It should've been yours from the beginning."

I ran my tongue along my bottom lip. "Well, maybe it should be *ours*," I amended. "Plus, you never told me your idea."

Gabe's eyes softened, and he reached over the island to take my hand. "We do make a pretty good team, don't we? Although, last time I tried to tell you about my idea, you said I could shove it—"

"That was *so* long ago!" I defended with a laugh, thinking about our first meeting with Hal. "And I'm ready to hear about it now, and we might need to schedule another meeting with Hal. Hopefully, this one goes better than the first."

Gabe's eyes gleamed. "I bet it will."

47

GABRIEL

From: Gabriel Nelson <gabriel@nelsongroup.com>
To: Hal Nelson <halnelson@email.com>
Cc: Lily Richards <lily@purrfectblend.com>
Subject: Building proposal update

Hey Grandpa,

Lily and I have a proposal for you about the building. We understand that you haven't made your decision yet, but if you're willing to meet with us, we would love to share more about what we're thinking. Your conditions have gotten us thinking about a possible partnership, and we'd like to get your thoughts. Let us know when would be best for us to stop by the store.

Thanks for everything, and see you soon. I'll pick up ingredients for dinner on my way back and cook us something once I'm home.

Gabe

THE PAST WEEK IN GOLDEN FALLS SINCE GETTING BACK FROM Milwaukee had been a whirlwind. One of the first things I did was call Jules's brother Grant to talk about the specifics of my non-compete.

When Nelson Group's lawyers and human resources department got wind of what was happening, they quickly sent out an email to all staff letting them know about the legal changes regarding non-competes. I knew they were saving their own asses, but at least people working for my father now had a choice on if they wanted to stay or work somewhere else. Last I heard, quite a few people had submitted their resignations, myself included.

My focus was now on submitting my proposal to the city for the warehouse building, getting a new job, and...finding a place to live. Because Beans and I were moving to Golden Falls.

I still loved Milwaukee and wanted to do good work there, but I wasn't interested in pursuing long distance with Lily. I wanted to be where she was, and right now, that was Golden Falls. With how much she enjoyed the city, though, I could definitely see us splitting our time between Milwaukee and Golden Falls one day, especially if Lily decided to open another location of Purrfect Blend.

I'd kept Liam updated throughout this whole process, and he had been a huge help during the hunt for a new job. While he didn't work directly in development, he had a lot of connections, particularly with sustainable and community-focused developers—exactly the type of work I wanted to be doing. I already had a few interviews lined up over the next couple of weeks.

Liam was supportive and excited about my potential new job and the move, but he also made it clear he couldn't spend too much time away from me and Beans. We already had his first visit to Golden Falls planned.

I'd reached out to my parents, too, to see if any sense of our personal relationship could be salvaged, but I was met with silence. It didn't surprise me, but it still stung. But maybe that was the final sign I needed. I'd tried everything I could, and if my parents didn't want a relationship with me, I had other people in my life who did, including my grandfather.

I hadn't had a chance to tell Hal that I was staying—or what Lily and I were thinking with the building—yet. That was where the two of us were heading now.

"Do you think he'll like the idea?" Lily asked as we walked up to Hal's Hardware.

I hitched a shoulder. "I think so. I mean, I don't think he'll dislike it, but it's always hard to tell with him about what he's thinking. Maybe he has his own idea in mind or has decided already." I pulled the door open, gesturing for Lily to go in first.

"That's true. I guess we're about to find out."

Hal was sitting behind the counter and looked up at us when the bell over the door jingled. "Is it three o'clock already?" he asked, taking his glasses off his nose. "Time flies, doesn't it? Well, why don't you go ahead and flip the sign from open to closed for now, so we can have our meeting. Let's head back to my office."

Lily and I looked at each other and grinned. "Ready?" she asked.

"With you by my side? Always." I reached over to give her hand a squeeze before we followed Hal through the aisle to his office.

We sat in the same chairs we were in just over a month ago, and Hal looked expectantly at us.

"So, first, we were wondering if you'd made a decision on who you wanted to sell the building to. Or would you prefer we tell you our idea first?" I asked.

Hal got comfortable in his chair, scooting closer to his wooden desk and setting his clasped hands on the surface. "Why don't you tell me your idea and how you came up with it."

Lily started us off. "We propose you sell the building to us both, and we'd split ownership in half. I will manage the day-to-day operations of ensuring rent is paid, seeing if any tenants need anything, and other timely issues that come up. Gabe's priority will be filling the empty storefront, and he has a great idea for it, one that I fully support."

Once Lily finished, I started to explain my idea that I refined with her input and feedback. "With Lily's help and connections to the community, I've been able to refine an idea I had in mind from when I first came to town. For small businesses that want to have a physical location, the cost of brick and mortar can be very prohibitive, especially as rent continues to increase. Even though Golden Falls is small, it's not immune to it. Which is why we want to pitch the empty storefront as an incubator-type space. Instead of it being a storefront for one business, we want to invite two to three small businesses to set up."

Lily picked up the next piece of our pitch. "This would be perfect for residents who might want to test having a physical location, like Susan and her candle business. Or it could be an opportunity for someone in a neighboring town to expand to Golden Falls at less of a risk. Jules's interior design business Campbell Creations will help us design the layout to ensure it's optimal for both businesses and customers. This could also help increase traffic to other businesses downtown, including restaurants, my café, and other spots."

"What do you think?" I asked Hal. I thought we nailed it, and hopefully, he agreed. He'd listened carefully the whole time, nodding along.

He leaned back in his chair, a satisfied smile spread across his face. "I knew you two would come up with something great. I love the idea, and I love that you two are doing it together. Makes it much easier to sell the building to the two of you, which had been my wish all along."

"Wait, what do you mean you *knew* we would come up with something?" I asked, looking over at Lily, who was just as confused.

"And what do you mean you wanted to sell to both of us? That wasn't part of your conditions," she said. "You made it sound like this was, well, a competition."

While we were confused, Hal was clearly amused. He chuckled, and his smile grew. "I had hoped my conditions would lead to you two to working together, to realizing that you had more in common than you realized. I wasn't going to force you to both own the building, I wanted you two to come to a decision together. A decision that was best for both the town and for you both," Hal said, leaning back in his chair and folding his hands over his stomach. "And it was truly delightful to watch you two fall in love."

"How did you—so, this was your plan? The whole time?" Lily asked, eyes wide.

Hal let out a chuckle. "You could say that."

"Even us falling in love?" I asked.

Hal hummed. "That was less of my doing, but I knew you two would bring out the best in each other once you got past your initial impressions. I wasn't sure if that would be as friends or more but...I'm glad it worked out the way it did."

"Me, too." I looked over at Lily. "Everything happened the way it was supposed to." I turned my attention to Hal. "I've also submitted my resignation to Nelson Group and...I'm moving to Golden Falls. You wouldn't mind keeping me and my cat as your roommates until I find a place of my own?"

Hal's eyes lit up, and maybe there *was* something about our plan he hadn't seen coming. "Why, of course, Gabe. However long you need. You're really moving here?" he asked, eyes gleaming.

Seeing my grandfather emotional tugged at my emotions, too. My lips tipped up in a smile. "Yeah, I am. Figured it would be easier this way to continue my relationship with my girl-friend *and* to spend more time with my grandfather. If that works for you?"

Hal's lips spread into his own smile. "I'd like that, Gabe." He cleared his throat. "I'd like that very much."

I stood from my seat, rounding the desk. Once Hal stood, I pulled him into a tight embrace. "Thank you. For everything."

"You have nothing to thank me for, son."

When I pulled away, Lily stepped in to give Hal a hug, too. When she pulled back, she looked between us, saying softly, "You two have the same smile."

As Hal's smile widened, I realized she was right. It was some-thing I suddenly had a new appreciation for.

Lily and I left Hal's store hand in hand, and once we were outside, she threw her arms around me, nuzzling her face in my neck. "You were amazing in there," she murmured. "I love you so much, and I'm so proud of you."

"I love you more, Sunshine." I wrapped my arms around her tightly and pressed a kiss to the top of her head. "I can't wait to work on this together. I wouldn't want to do it with anyone else."

When I first got to Golden Falls, I expected to be in and out of town. I remembered telling myself it was *just business*. I was so glad I didn't listen to myself, that I let myself *feel* while I was here. Because I felt so damn much. I finally felt like I belonged. I felt grateful that I'd reconnected with my grandfather. I felt appreciative of the people in my life who supported me, and I was ready to move on from the relationships that had held me back.

I felt like the luckiest man alive that Lily Richards loved me.

"But wait," Lily said, tilting her head to the side. "There's one more thing on my winter wish list. Seeing a shooting star. Do you think we'll get a chance to see one?"

We started to walk down the street toward her apartment, and a part of me actually missed the lights and decorations that had since been taken down. I didn't think that would *ever* happen.

I swung our clasped hands together, trying to hide my grin. "Something tells me luck is on our side."

48

GABRIEL

OF COURSE, I WASN'T GOING TO LET THE FINAL THING ON LILY'S list go unchecked. Have a little faith in me.

Not long after we got back from Milwaukee, and while we were working on our pitch to Hal, I downloaded an app that tracked meteor activity and turned on notifications for upcoming meteor showers in northern Wisconsin. I also reached out to Cooper and Wes to see what spots they recommended around here for a clear view of the sky. Cooper recommended a farm on the outskirts of town that one of Marnie's friends owned.

Then there was the challenge of figuring out how we were going to comfortably watch the sky without freezing in the chilly January weather. Luckily, I had help figuring that out, too.

"Can I open my eyes *now*?" Lily asked again. Her mitten-covered hands were over her eyes as I carefully drove us to the viewing spot.

"Don't act like you haven't been peeking," I teased, stealing a glance at her and watching her smile widen.

"Okay, but even with my peeking, I haven't been able to figure out where we're going."

Within a few minutes, I pulled into the long driveaway, the snow crunching underneath the tires. I couldn't wait for Lily to see the view in front of us—an open field covered with snow paired with a dark sky and brighter than life stars. I put the car into park and unbuckled my seatbelt.

"Alright, Sunshine. Go ahead and open your eyes."

Lily wasted no time removing her hands from her eyes and blinking into focus. Her lips parted in awe as she looked between me and what I'd set up for us. "Gabe, how did you..." She trailed off with a laugh.

In the middle of the field, there was a clear pop-up bubble tent with blankets, pillows, a thermos of hot chocolate, and snacks for our meteor shower viewing. The exterior of the bubble tent had white string lights clipped to it.

She hopped out of the car, and I followed her, eager for her reaction as more of the setup came into focus. After a few steps, Lily turned around, tears glistening in her eyes. She threw her arms around my shoulders. I wrapped an arm around her waist, pulling her close to me. I never wanted to let her go, and luckily, I didn't have to.

"We're going to see a shooting star tonight?" she whispered. Lily bit down on her bottom lip, but even that couldn't hide her smile. One of my favorite things in life—if not my *very* favorite—was making Lily happy, whether that was reassuring her that she didn't have to do things alone, starting a bubble bath for her after a long day, or anything else that would lessen the stress in her shoulders and bring a smile to her face. She was always thinking about others, and I vowed to be the man who prioritized her each and every day—and reminded her it was more than okay for her to put herself first.

"We're going to see *multiple* shooting stars," I said to her, finding it impossible to hold my own smile back. "A meteor shower is anticipated to start within the next hour or so, and we have a front-row view."

"Wow," Lily sighed. She looked back up at the sky, as if imagining what was to come. She then reached for my hand. "Well, we better get all cozy, right?" She wiggled her brows, and I let out a laugh.

"Right," I agreed.

We climbed inside the warm tent, zipping up the entrance and taking off our coats, hats, and gloves.

"I'm kind of bummed that this is the last thing on the list to complete," Lily admitted once we got comfortable. She pulled out the pink piece of paper from her pocket—the list that started it all. "I know the point was to finish this"—she twisted her lips to the side as she looked at the paper—"but checking these things off the list with you and making these memories was incredible. And now it's over."

I wrapped an arm around her, pulling her into my side and pressing a gentle kiss to her temple. "We might've finished one list..." I started. I had one more surprise for Lily.

I leaned over to the bag with the thermos and snacks and pulled out two pieces of stationary and various pens. Yes, I'd even picked up a pack of glitter pens. I wanted to make sure my girl got everything she wanted in this life.

"But that doesn't mean we can't start another. One that we could make together and keep adding to this year, next year, ten years from now." My tone grew softer, my words holding more weight. "Or seventy years from now." I set the supplies in front of us and turned my attention back to Lily, only to see tears in her eyes again.

"Oh, Sunshine," I murmured. "I hope those are happy tears."

"Very, *very* happy tears. Oh, Gabe. I love you so much. There's so much I want to do with you. I have a feeling we'll need more pieces of paper for our list, because this is just the beginning."

"I love you, too, Lily. So damn much."

It truly was only the beginning. We had so much ahead of us —getting married, watching Lily expand her business, traveling, and starting a family one day. It was all waiting for us.

"Oh, Gabe, look!" Lily gasped, and our attention turned to the sky as a sudden, thin streak of white light moved across. It lasted only a few seconds. Since the meteor shower wasn't anticipated to start for another hour, this was likely a one off, but it meant the final thing on Lily's wish list was checked off.

"That was so magical." Lily's voice was quiet, wistful. "Did you have enough time to make a wish?"

I tipped her chin up, looking down into her blue eyes. "Didn't need to. I have everything I could ever want right here."

Lily grinned and playfully rolled her eyes before pressing a kiss to my lips, murmuring, "I should've known you'd say something sweet like that. You always do."

"What about you? Did you make a wish?" I asked.

"Uh, of course," Lily said playfully. "I've been thinking about it the last few weeks."

I raised my brow. "Oh, yeah? And what was it?"

"I can't tell you! Otherwise the wish won't happen." She gently nudged my side. "And I really, *really* want this one to come true."

I hummed in thought. "Well, luckily, we have forever to make it happen, don't we?"

Lily rolled her lips, a blush forming on her cheeks as she nodded. "Yeah, we sure do. Forever sounds absolutely perfect with you."

I had a feeling—and hoped—her wish had to do with us. About everything that was to come. I couldn't wait to propose to Lily—soon, if I had my way.

When I first got to Golden Falls—and for most of my life, really—I felt like I was on the outside looking in. I didn't think that would ever change. But now?

I finally felt part of something—part of a town, part of a family—and that meant everything to me. Lily meant everything to me.

With her by my side, life was less scary, way less lonely, a whole lot brighter, and so much more magical.

EPILOGUE

LILY

Three months later

April

I rubbed my eyes with a groan as I woke up to three sets of meows—screams, really. My six a.m. alarm hadn't gone off yet, which meant it was even earlier.

Great.

"They won't let us know peace, will they?" I murmured, turning onto my other side and snuggling against Gabe.

"How can creatures so cute and small be so *loud*?" he asked, voice sleepy and raspy. "I can feed them this morning if you want, *but* that means you're staying in bed for a few more minutes."

"Deal," I agreed.

Gabe rolled out of bed in only his boxer briefs, and I propped myself up on my elbows, watching how his legs flexed and muscles rippled with each step. His hair was messy from sleep.

So hot.

I sank back into the pillows with a grin on my face. It had been near impossible to stop smiling around Gabe, and at the life we'd started to build together. Once we pitched our idea to Hal and got his support, the two of us came up with a plan on how to turn it into a reality, which included getting Gabe settled in Golden Falls. I thought he'd get an apartment to start off, but...he ended up buying a house.

But he had a condition of his own. He'd only buy it if I moved in with him. And how could I say no to the *perfect* house —with a perfect man.

It was a three-bedroom, two-story home with white shutters, a yellow front door, and a back porch that had a clear view of Lake Golden. It was tucked away in the trees and a ten-minute drive away from downtown. I hadn't even known this house was on the market. It'd been one I'd seen throughout the years of living in Golden Falls that I imagined would be perfect to live in. Turned out, Gabe was one step ahead without even realizing it.

Gabe moved in about two months ago, and I moved in a couple weeks later. The biggest challenge of the move was introducing our cats to each other, and while that took some time, the three of them got along great (with the occasional hiss here and there). They got along well enough to terrorize us for food each morning, so that said something. Unsurprisingly, Sylvie was the leader of the pack, and Beans and Bandit didn't seem to mind too much.

Gabe hadn't talked to his parents since leaving Nelson Group, but not for lack of trying. After being met with radio silence from both his mother and father, he accepted that he wasn't going to have a relationship with them. I was proud of him first for trying and second for setting boundaries.

And I knew it wasn't the same, but he'd been building a genuine relationship with Hal, as well as with my family.

Unsurprisingly, it didn't take long for Gabe to find a new job, and he started working for a development group, also based out of Milwaukee, that focused and prioritized sustainable development. The company had a goal of minimizing the carbon foot-print of their projects and promoting resident health and well-being. He worked remotely most of the time but traveled into Milwaukee for presentations and select client meetings, including meetings with the city about Gabe's proposal for the old warehouse. Out of dozens of proposals, the common council selected to move forward with his vision.

Luckily for me, this week, he was in Golden Falls the whole time.

Gabe's bare feet padded against the hardwood floor, and once he was back in our bedroom, he closed the door behind him. "Little demons are fed," he grumbled, which caused me to laugh.

He slid back into bed and wrapped an arm around me, pulling me on top of him and slipping his warm hand underneath the hem of my sleep shirt. His touch seared into my skin and heat throbbed between my legs.

"Well, I *am* awake now...and we still have"—I glanced over at the clock—"fifteen minutes until my alarm goes off."

Gabe smirked, raising a brow. "Oh, I can work with that." Not wasting any time, he flipped me onto my back and pressed his mouth against mine.

"You have your meeting this afternoon, right?" Tiffany asked as she stood in the kitchen doorway. "I'm happy to close up for the day if you wanted to head out earlier."

I looked up at her with a grateful smile. "That would be so helpful, thank you. I'm meeting Gabe and Jules to talk through the interior for the empty storefront."

Realization dawned, and her eyes brightened. "Oh, I can't wait to hear about it."

Things had been going so well that I was considering hiring another employee later this year. Not only did it take a weight off my shoulders, but it was exciting to have someone working for me who was as passionate and excited as I was. Plus, Tiffany's iced raspberry latte was to die for. It was one of the first menu items we were testing for spring, and it was already a hit.

She took a step closer, inspecting the dessert I was making—or trying to make. "Lily, these are looking so good!"

I let out a large breath, and a slow smile spread across my face. "You think so?"

"Oh, for sure." She nodded. "And if this isn't the perfect batch, it's looking a lot better than last week."

She wasn't wrong. Last week's batch of macarons was...something else.

For the last couple of weeks, I'd been taking the baking classes that Gabe had gotten me as a gift. As much as I enjoyed the classes and had learned a lot, they'd been testing me. In a good way.

Or at least, it would be a good way once I figured out how to perfect this recipe—and I was finally getting there. I'd tested more than thirty variations and went through many, *many* pounds of almond flour.

I was hoping to offer them occasionally in the café in the spring. I put a few into a pink pastry box to bring to my meeting with Gabe and Jules.

"Try one at your own risk," I teased with a smile as I finished cleaning up and pulled my apron over my head. "I haven't had one yet from this batch."

"I don't know how you have the self-control." She shook her head with a laugh before waving. "Have a good meeting!"

"See you tomorrow!" I waved back.

I said a few quick goodbyes to the customers still sitting in the café as I made my way out the door. It was in the low fifties today, which I hoped meant that spring was around the corner.

I made the short walk to the empty storefront and pushed open the door, seeing Gabe and Jules.

"Hey!" Jules said as she turned to face me. "How'd the batch of macarons turn out?"

I smiled proudly. "Better, I think. I brought some for us to try."

The previous business that had been here had been an active wear clothing store. The owners had left all the interior infrastructure intact, and we'd been in here a few weeks ago to clean the place up. I walked over to the counter and opened the box.

"Oh, these look *so* good! And they're pink!" she exclaimed with a wide smile.

"I had a feeling you'd like that." I grinned. Gabe and I both reached for one, too.

As we were about to take a bite, the door opened, and Eliza walked in. I tilted my head, brows furrowing. I hadn't expected her to show up.

"What's up? Is everything okay?" I asked.

"I don't know," she groaned, tipping her head back. She then amended, "Well, yes, everything is *overall* fine." She walked over to where we crowded around the box of macarons and took one with ease, popping it into her mouth.

"Fuck, Lil. That's amazing." She tipped her chin. "Why haven't you guys tried it yet?"

"Uh, because you barged in and it seemed like something was wrong," I said with a laugh, looking over at Jules, who looked as confused as I was. Gabe was completely clueless.

Eliza finished chewing and pulled out a water bottle from her tote bag. She then took a gulp, swallowed, and finally started talking. "Colin's brother applied for the head chef job...and Wes wants to hire him."

I...wasn't following. "That's great, right? Hasn't he had a successful career in the city?" I remembered Wes telling me after the interview how the interview went well, and that Leo was excited and intrigued about Wes's ideas. My brother wanted to work with local farmers to source ingredients and also minimize food waste while embarking on the journey of adding a food menu to Lake Ridge.

"I mean, yeah, his career is impressive. From what I've heard, at least. It's not like I've spoken to him." Eliza ran a hand through her hair, gently tugging on the strands. I watched as she swayed on her feet and twisted her gold rings on her fingers.

My eyes widened. "You're nervous!"

My best friend looked at me and sputtered, "No fucking way. I'm not nervous."

Jules and I both raised our brows.

"Okay, *fine!*" Eliza finally exclaimed, raising her arms and letting them fall to her sides. "Maybe I'm a little nervous and very unsure. I think he's going to be great for Lake Ridge—that's not the problem. The problem is...we nearly kissed when I last saw him."

"What?" the three of us—Gabe included—exclaimed, our jaws nearly dropping.

"Colin and I had recently broken up, and..." Eliza waved her hand. "It didn't happen, and it doesn't matter. He was going off to Portland and didn't respond to my text, and it's *fine*. It's been a few years. I doubt he even remembers me or knows that I'm in Golden Falls."

A teasing smile came across Jules's face. "Or he knows you're here, and that's why he wanted the job."

Eliza rolled her eyes with a groan. "No damn way. Plus, that would be stalking."

"Well," I said with a smile of my own, "we'll have to ask him when he gets here."

"No!" Eliza exclaimed, pointing at the three of us. "None of you will mention this. You too, Gabe. You're all sworn to secrecy." She reached for another macaron. "I need to get going, but I'll keep you updated...not that there's anything to be updated about." She backed away toward the door. "Everything's going to be fine!"

"You're not off the hook! We have questions, and you can't avoid us forever," I called after her.

Eliza pushed the door open and left—but not before flipping us off.

"She's screwed, isn't she?" Gabe asked.

Jules and I both nodded, saying in unison, "Very much so."

BONUS EPILOGUE
EIGHT YEARS LATER

The Milwaukee Times

New cat café opens in downtown Milwaukee
Owner Lily Nelson-Richards is bringing her passion for baking and love for cats to the city with the second location of Purrfect Blend Cat Café.

Lily Nelson-Richards hoped that a handful of people would stop by the grand opening of Purrfect Blend Cat Café. She never expected there to be a line out the door that wrapped around the side of the building.

"It's been a dream of mine to open a second location, and it's so special to have such a warm reaction from the community," Nelson-Richards said.

Purrfect Blend's original location, which remains in operation, is in Nelson-Richards's hometown of Golden Falls. Nelson-Richards and her husband Gabe Nelson-Richards frequently split their time between Golden Falls and Milwaukee.

Purrfect Blend's Milwaukee location will also partner with a local animal shelter, which means the cats roaming and ruling the place are available for adoption.

Nelson-Richards said the second location has been a long time coming. It was an idea she thought of years ago—and one she hasn't stopped working toward. She first wanted to get the Golden Falls location operating smoothly without her presence, knowing that she'd have to spend more time in Milwaukee to get her dream off the ground.

"None of this would be possible without my staff, because I can't do it all," Nelson-Richards said. "That was a tough but very valuable lesson to learn. Life is so much easier when you let people help, and I'm so grateful for those in my corner, especially my husband."

Over the last handful of years, Nelson-Richards's baking has become well-known in the state—and across the country. She regularly sells out of baked goods during the week, and around the holidays, has a waiting list for those who aren't lucky enough to place an order in case there are extra quantities.

As for a third location? Nelson-Richards hasn't ruled anything out but is staying quiet for now.

"All I can say is that anything is possible," she added.

Continue reading on page 3A

Lily

"Why do I feel so nervous?" I asked Gabe as we pulled into Hal's driveway.

Gabe turned off the ignition and unbuckled his seat belt. He turned to me with a laugh. "Because telling people you're pregnant is pretty much announcing to the world that we've had sex."

I rolled my eyes playfully. "You're being dramatic." Although, I guess he was technically right.

I unbuckled my seatbelt, but before I could even think about opening the car door, Gabe shot out of his seat, closed the door, and rounded the car. He opened my door and extended his hand. "I don't want you to slip, Sunshine."

"Gabe," I said on a breathless laugh, not even wanting to know how much he'd worry once we had a snow fall and there actually was a danger of ice on the ground. Still, I took his outstretched hand and carefully got out of the car. I recently finished my first trimester, so I knew I had at least six more months of this. I might as well get used to it.

Gabe and I weren't sure at first if we wanted kids. After moving in together, we were both focused on our careers. I wanted to grow Purrfect Blend, and Gabe was starting fresh with his new job. He also had his hesitations given how he grew up and his lack of a relationship with his parents. He'd been worried he wouldn't know how to be a good parent.

He'd even considered dropping his last name and taking mine when we got married, but we decided to combine our last names instead, and that was because of Hal. Since moving to Golden Falls, Gabe and Hal quickly reconnected and it was like there had been no time between them. Their relationship was stronger than ever, and we saw Hal nearly every day when we were in Golden Falls.

Gabe locked the car, and we turned our heads when the front door opened. There was Hal, waving for us to come inside. Hal's interior and exterior were decorated and ready for Christmas. Gabe had helped him a few weeks ago when he was in Golden Falls. Somehow, along the way, Gabe developed a love for Christmas that might have been greater than mine.

"Hi, Hal," I greeted, pulling him into a big hug. Gabe did the same.

"I thought I'd see you two at Christmas dinner. What a treat to see you early."

Gabe let out a gentle laugh. "We wanted to stop by and see you before dinner with everyone. We have something to tell you and wanted you to be the first one to know."

The three of us walked over to the couch to sit. Gabe and I were on the love seat, and Hal was on the recliner.

"Well, don't keep me waiting. You have me on the edge of my seat now." Hal's lips spread into a smile. "Is it about the café? Did you have a good opening, my dear?"

I reached into my purse, pulling out an extra copy of this week's paper. I passed it over to Hal. "It was better than I could have imagined. I thought you'd want to read the article and see the photos."

Hal had wanted to come by for opening day, but given his older age, we figured a four-hour car ride wasn't ideal. I promised I'd tell him all about it when we came into town for the holidays.

He eagerly started reading the article, a warm smile on his face.

"We're actually going to be spending more time in Golden Falls," I informed Hal. I reached for Gabe's hand, holding it tightly. Over the last few years, we'd been splitting our time between Milwaukee and Golden Falls because of both of our careers. "With the baby coming, we both want to be surrounded by as much family and friends as possible. And we especially can't wait for the baby to meet their great-grandfather."

Hal looked up from the paper, blinking as his gaze flicked between us. "Baby?"

I nodded, my eyes welling with tears. I blinked through blurry vision, wanting to catch Hal's expression. "I'm due this summer."

"Well, isn't this news the best Christmas gift I've ever gotten." Hal's eyes glistened with unshed tears. "You two are going to be the most wonderful parents."

The three of us stood, and Hal gave me another hug, pressing a gentle kiss to the side of my head. A lifetime of memories with Hal flashed in my mind, and I couldn't wait for more.

Hal pulled Gabe into a tight embrace next, and I could see the emotion on both their faces. It was going to be so special for Hal to witness Gabe becoming a father. "I am so proud of you, Gabe," he whispered. "Always have been and always will be."

When the two of them pulled away, Hal grabbed a handkerchief from his pocket and dabbed at his eyes. "You both have a whole group of people to tell today, huh? I'm honored to be the first."

"We wouldn't have had it any other way. I don't think we would be together right now had it not been for you," Gabe said before looking at me, his expression softening.

"You would've found your way to each other. No doubt in my mind. I just helped speed up the process, I suppose." Hal tucked his handkerchief back into his pocket and composed himself.

We still had a few hours before we had to be at my parents' house, so I offered, "How about a game or two of cards before we head over for dinner?"

"So I can lose for the millionth time to you two?" Gabe asked. He shook his head with a laugh. "You two get comfortable. I'll go grab them."

Hal and I grinned at each other as we walked over to the kitchen table. "Should we let him win at least one game? It is Christmas, after all," I offered.

"I guess that wouldn't hurt." Hal winked.

"I heard that," Gabe called as he took his seat and started shuffling. "And I still think I'm going to lose somehow."

I tipped my head back with a laugh, and Gabe grinned at me. It was hard not to laugh around him, not to smile around him.

Life hadn't been the same since I fell in love with Gabe. It had been so much better, so much more full of life, adventure, and magic. And all the midnight kisses I could have dreamed of.

THANK YOU FOR READING!

If you enjoyed *All Your Midnights*, please consider leaving a review on Amazon, Goodreads, or social media! Reader reviews are so important to indie authors, and it would mean the world to me if you left an honest review.

Let's connect!
Sign up for my newsletter
Social media: @authorizabelakamila
Visit my website: www.authorizabelakamila.com

ACKNOWLEDGMENTS

I can't say I recommend releasing a book while moving, buying a house, and starting a new job...but I also wouldn't have done it any differently. I'm so proud of all I've accomplished in these last few months, including getting this story in your hands.

Admittedly, it was daunting sitting down to write Lily and Gabe's story. I'd written one book, but could I write another? It took me a while to connect with Lily and Gabe, but once I did I couldn't get them out of my head. These two are soft, sweet, bring out the best in each other, and love fiercely.

I'm so proud of the character growth they both go through, especially Gabe. During my many read throughs of this story, I teared up at the scenes between Hal and Gabe every time.

So many people made this book possible, and I can't thank them enough for their constant support and encouragement.

To my husband: You make every day magical. I wouldn't have been able to do this without your love, support, and encouragement. Thank you for making me feel like I can accomplish anything.

To my parents: You've always believed in me and have been my biggest supporters, regardless of what I'm doing. I'm forever grateful for that.

To Alison: I'm so incredibly grateful for your friendship, and I can't thank you enough for creating the book cover of my dreams.

To my friends and family: Thank you for your encouragement, support, and excitement! I can't wait for you to read this story.

To my editor Nicole: This book would not be what it is today if it wasn't for you. Thank you for your feedback, encouragement, and voice memos throughout the editing process. I love working and brainstorming with you, and I can't wait to see what we come up with for book three!

To my editor Andrea: Thank you so much for your help, feedback, and edits. Your attention to detail is unmatched, and having your thoughtful review always makes me more confident in my story!

To my wonderful beta readers Danie, Katie, Heather, Hilary, Lauren, Michaela, Rachel, Rose, Sydney, Vanesa, and Wren: Thank you for helping me make this story the best it could be. Your comments, reactions, and feedback were amazing, and I couldn't have done this without you!

To my ARC readers: Thank you for signing up to read early. I know the TBR is endless, so the fact that you took time out of your day to read my book means everything. Thank you for taking a chance on my story!

To you, the reader: I can't thank you enough for picking up my book. I hope Lily and Gabe's story brought you all the cozy holiday feels while reminding you that surrounding yourself with people who see your light makes the world feel a little less lonely.

And lastly, to me: You now have two books out in the world! Take a moment to let it soak in and be proud of yourself...and then go start the next one!

ABOUT THE AUTHOR

Izabela writes contemporary romance that will have you kicking your feet one moment and blushing the next. Expect swoony heroes, sassy heroines, delicious tension, and witty banter.

She lives in the Midwest with her husband and two cuddly cats. When she's not writing, she's reading romance on her Kindle, watching a romantic comedy or reality TV, enjoying the outdoors, or spending time with her friends and family.

To stay up to date on Izabela's upcoming projects, connect with her on social media @authorizabelakamila or visit her website www.authorizabelakamila.com.

www.ingramcontent.com/pod-product-compliance
Lightning Source LLC
Chambersburg PA
CBHW030344120726
47901CB00007B/1911